The ALTOBELLA AUTOMATON

This is a work of fiction. All of the characters, organizations, and events portrayed in this novel are either products of the author's imagination or are used fictitiously.

ISBN 979-8-9953011-0-3

Design by A. Warren
Cover art by Susan Ryder. Afternoon Sunlight (oil on canvas) Ryder, Susan (b.1944) Credit: Private Collection, Courtesy of Manya Igel Fine Arts, London/© Susan Ryder. All rights reserved. 2026/Bridgeman Images.
Chapter divider by © cutelittlethings, 2026/Adobe Stock.

www.fleuronpress.com

Printed by IngramSpark
First printing June 2026

The ALTOBELLA AUTOMATON

A. N. WARREN

FLEURON PRESS

To my husband

Harmonia per lucem et per umbram

Harmony, by light and by shadow
The motto of Chateau Desrosiers

The layers of a chateau tell a story. One need only to study the walls of Chateau Desrosiers to understand a fraction of its history spelled out like tree rings. The towers and crenelations from its days as a medieval fortress protected its founding family; the decadent neoclassical expansions made it a haven for artists and creatives at the heyday of the French nobility; and the intricate insulation and modern restorations saved the chateau from ruin during the Second World War. Grouted in between each layer are remnants of plagues and revolution and war. One may argue the aroma of history is the musky scent of blood on stone, the residue of work and exertion.

It is easy to get lost in such an expansive place like Desrosiers—but when you help rebuild these ancient walls stone by stone, you may also find new parts of yourself.

— Claudel Morin, host of *Daily Life at Desrosiers*

One

A SUDDEN JOLT OF TURBULENCE makes her heart jump into her throat, and Simonetta Altobella prays to God for the first time in eighteen years.

The last time she made any effort to speak to God was when she was sixteen years old, standing in the magnificent Cattedrale di Santa Maria del Fiore in Florence, Italy, where it was impossible *not* to feel the presence of some unseen force. Moved by the elusive Holy Spirit she had evaded for most of her life, young Simonetta had lit a prayer tea candle in a ruby glass votive and thanked God with her entire soul, whispering under her breath so the secret devotions wouldn't echo under the frescoed dome. She had expressed gratitude for the privilege of traveling and asked for the protection of her *nonni* back home in Berkeley, who had mixed feelings regarding the school visit to her ancestral motherland. She had assumed then that their lack of enthusiasm was about the itinerary, featuring only quick stops in Italy's most famous cities and tourist attractions.

When she returned home, pale skin bronzed by the Mediterranean sun and her heart renewed with fervor for traveling, Nonno had died a week later, and she hasn't prayed since.

Outside of the small plane window, thousands of miles above the Atlantic Ocean, rain lashes and a silver bolt of lightning lances across the sky. The plane lurches again; Simonetta flinches and reaches for the armrest without thinking, earns the ire of the passenger beside her engrossed in the in-flight action film.

She takes a deep breath and releases the accidental prayer, where it hovers around her in the stale airplane cabin like the lingering smoke of a smothered candle. Nonna would have been glad to know that Simonetta still has the capacity to pray, but Nonna is gone now, too, and there is no one left to worry about Simonetta's soul.

At present, her soul is a pillar of anxiety and grief impaling her identity, weighing her down. It manifests as an ever-present pressure on her chest, invisible hands pushing her to the floor. Other times it's a precarious stack of heavy books resting on her solar plexus, ready to tumble any which way. Sometimes the emotions are a precious, delicate egg lodged in her ribcage, and she tries her hardest not to break it—but every now and then it cracks and the yolk dribbles out, tainting her day with small unctuous splatters of unexpected melancholy and waves of regret.

Simonetta folds her hands in her lap and closes her eyes, breathing in and out in the slow, methodical pattern she adopted after Nonna's funeral. After days spent cresting the waves of grief and uncertainty from the loss, a panic attack had left her shattered on the bathroom floor, and Simonetta had hastily Googled tactics for anxiety treatment. It still feels unnatural to relinquish control via forced puffs of oxygen and small white pills. Six months later and Simonetta had just started to sleep for more than three hours at a time again when she finalized plans to uproot her entire life, put her belongings into storage, sold Nonna's house and most of the items within it, and got a visa approved for her four-month work-stay job in France.

Now she's en route to a place she has only seen on a screen and in the few strange, cryptic notes and pictures of southern France discovered amongst her grandparents' belongings. She clings to those as evidence, as signs, as omens, that something waits for her in Sainte-Madeleine and that she alone is responsible for seeking it out. For months she has envisioned a ley line strung like fairy lights between California and France, to the small hamlet near the border of Italy where she will find… something. A new truth. A solution to her turmoil. A remnant of family or identity to which she can tether. She thinks of what Nonna often espoused: "Idle hands lead to a restless mind."

She keeps this invisible string wrapped around her palm, where it joins the branching nodes of her lifeline, tugging on it as if it were a *call for help* alert beside a hospital bed.

The plane rumbles and jerks again; the seatbelt sign above pings on, the glow bright red in the dimmed plane cabin. The passenger beside her squirms in his seat and readjusts, claiming both armrests for himself, and Simonetta wordlessly acquiesces. She tugs her pashmina closer around her and settles into the crook of the small seat.

Still hours away from Europe, Simonetta looks out over the dark, turbulent ocean far below, wonders what the creatures in the dark depths think of the machine in the sky. She envies them and their home beneath the waves. Simonetta sits suspended above them and crosses the ocean alone, adrift, unmoored.

When the plane finally touches down at Nice Côte d'Azur Airport, the sun smiles brightly in the sky and the iridescent puddles on the cobblestone are the only indication that a storm passed in the night. Simonetta is swept into morning on a Mediterranean breeze and the airport is abuzz with travelers on a non-stop carousel of arrivals and departures. Her old violin case balances atop the battered luggage that rolls unevenly behind her as she purchases a cup of strong black coffee and sits down at an empty table. Bringing the violin was impulsive, she acknowledges. It has been years since she's touched it; a gift from Nonno and Nonna when she was younger, it felt like sacrilege to dump into storage with the rest of her belongings. She underestimated the nuisance it would be as an extra item of luggage, hopes she can justify its presence.

She pulls out a map and her itinerary. Back on solid ground with some caffeine in her system, Simonetta is slightly less frazzled than she was in the air. A fissure of excitement ripples up her spine as she peruses the welcome packet from Claudel Morin, chatelaine of Chateau Desrosiers and the host of *Daily Life at Desrosiers*, the YouTube channel that has given the chateau global notoriety.

She pulls up her favorite video on her phone to rewatch again—a vlog of Christmas at Desrosiers the year prior, in which Claudel and her friend Alba sort through the vast collection of holiday ornaments and talk through the history of each one—and reads through the materials for the dozenth time, still adjusting to her new label as a "volunteer," having discarded her longtime career as a conservator when she was deep in the throes of Grief and Life Confusion. "Volunteer" is somewhat of a misnomer, as her new gig in Claudel's seasonal work-stay program to restore the chateau and assist with historical preservation does, in fact, offer a small stipend along with room and board.

She glances at the tarnished silver watch that once graced her grandmother's wrist, but the delicate hands are still on California time. She fiddles with the knob to recalibrate and finds the current time on the flight departure screen. By now, Claudel is en route to pick her up, and Simonetta evaluates her expectations of the woman she has only seen, and met, on a screen. On *Daily Life*, Claudel seems larger-than-life, flitting about the chateau, storing centuries of historical knowledge in her mind, interviewing the work-stay volunteers that filter in and out once a year. Every time she spoke to Claudel via video or phone during the interview process, the chatelaine sported an impeccably applied swipe of red lipstick and perfectly coiffed white hair. Usually bedecked in toile- or floral-patterned clothing, Claudel is the very picture of a modern estate proprietor, but Simonetta is sure this could have been Claudel's true calling in any era.

Simonetta scans her list of projects and responsibilities for the next few months. Although she has studied the welcome packet by heart, it soothes her to revisit familiar details. She was given her choice of projects to assist with, from carpentry to floristry to upholstery to plumbing. Lacking servants and staff from bygone eras, chateaus like Desrosiers have an endless number of tasks required to maintain such old establishments and keep them open for public research and enjoyment. All Simonetta wanted to do was be useful, and on the volunteer project form she had checked every box. At the very least, she'll return to Berkeley at the end of the program with a new set of skills. The skills she's gleaned from a decade as a conservator include ample knowledge of historical document restoration and cataloging, but at thirty-four, Simonetta figures it's time to become more resourceful.

An hour later, after lazily perusing the luxury shops in the airport and purchasing a copy of Elle France, she waits outside in the arrival pickup area, wound up from coffee, lack of sleep, and nerves. She sniffs the perfume samples in the magazine and practices her French, remnants from the minor she acquired in college to the confusion of her Italian grandparents.

Bonjour, je m'appelle Simone, comment ca va? Hello, my name is Simone, how are you? *Le chateau est belle.* The chateau is beautiful. *Je ne sais pas ce que je fais de ma vie.* I don't know what I'm doing with my life. *Je me sens très seule et certains jours je ne veux plus exister.* I feel very alone and some days I don't want to exist anymore. *Ma petite chou.* My little cabbage.

Every French word she's ever learned evaporates immediately from her memory when Claudel Morin pulls up to the curb in a mustard-yellow Renault with a dented passenger door, the tailpipe emitting a tendril of smog. Claudel leaves it running as she gracefully steps out and goes to Simonetta with open arms. Startled and moved by the gesture of affection, Simonetta embraces Claudel, who is every bit as effortlessly glamorous as she appears online, albeit slightly shorter than Simonetta expected. Simonetta always assumes that bold personalities are matched in height, but Claudel, wearing cream-colored stilettos, teeters a couple inches over five feet and meets her evenly in the eyes. She breathes in Claudel's perfume, something distinctly French—floral, musky, earthy. It's a sweet and pleasant scent, and the embrace brings tears to her eyes that she quickly blinks away.

Feeling disheveled and grimy from the flight, she is relieved that Claudel is not yet filming and doesn't want this first interaction documented for posterity. Simonetta accepts that being a volunteer means being an "on camera personality" throughout the summer; the revenue from the YouTube channel is partly what funds the chateau's restoration, and Claudel's style of vlogging captures all of the highs and lows at Chateau Desrosiers. Still, she's grateful for the buffer period.

"Ah, and you brought your violin!" Claudel exclaims as she and Simonetta load her luggage into the small trunk of the car. Simonetta holds onto Nonno's old leather satchel, worn but freshly oiled, housing her passport and toiletries. She thinks of him carrying it every day to work at the car factory.

"I'm overdue for practice," admits Simonetta.

Claudel claps her hands in response. "I'm sure Monsieur Aubert would be delighted to have additional accompaniment at the workshops later this summer. There is quite a rich musical history at Desrosiers."

Claudel speaks crisp, clear English dotted with a French accent that manifests on the hard end of words, turning up consonants' noses and easing their sharp landing on the tongue. Simonetta thinks of the words as being adorned with red lipstick—familiar yet elevated to something effortlessly beautiful and languid.

Simonetta's heart flip-flops as she slips into the Renault's back seat. The strong scent of the leather seats envelops her and already her senses are on overload, Claudel's perfume dueling with the old car's history.

A woman with dusky skin and long, dark hair sits in the passenger seat and turns to face Simone, lifting a hand in greeting. She introduces herself as Aurelia in more crisp and friendly English, but this accent is adorned with blush that deepens the vowels.

Claudel slides into the driver's seat and arranges herself. "Aurelia Rojas is from Chile! Aurelia, this is Simonetta Altobella—from America."

Simonetta opens her mouth to correct her; for years, she has been "Simone," only her grandparents calling her by her full name. She'd considered Simonetta Julia Cavalieri Altobella a mouthful, had always sought to simplify her existence for others.

Hearing a voice other than her nonni speak her full name makes her wistful. *Why shouldn't she use Simonetta?* she muses. It is, after all, her name. And Nonna would be delighted she was embracing it, and that reason alone makes it an easy decision.

But who is Simonetta? She knows the Simone version of herself well, the practical Berkeley-born woman known for her love of books and travel and music. She could be Simonetta now, and perhaps indefinitely—Simonetta who lives in a chateau in France, wears red lipstick like Claudel Morin, handles literal and metaphorical turbulence with grace and ease. Simonetta envisions sloughing off the old Simone skin, the new Simonetta stepping out of it like the nude and sensual Simonetta Vespucci in the Birth of Venus, her namesake.

Simonetta thinks about her newly born naked self, enveloped in the shell, slightly bloodied from rebirth. Does this version of Venus wear red lipstick? It's such a strange and startlingly gruesome vignette that she emits a nervous giggle, masked by Claudel shutting the Renault's door, starting the engine, and departing for Desrosiers.

"You two are the last of the summer group to arrive!" Claudel chatters. "Everyone else is already at the house. My nephew Jeremy is on supper duty tonight, and he's making something sumptuous to alleviate your travel weariness."

Aurelia glances over her shoulder and raises her eyebrows at Claudel's embellished speech; Simonetta grins in response.

En route to Sainte-Madeleine, the ancient commune nestled at the base of the Alps where she will spend her summer, the newly unshelled Simonetta relaxes against the worn leather seat of the car, wired and weary. Aurelia, also suffering from jet lag, naps in the passenger seat and Claudel hums along to the quiet classical music coming through the old radio—Simonetta hears *Serenade for Strings in E Major* by Dvořák, one of her favorite composers, and accepts it as a good omen.

Bustling Nice outskirts give way to tumbling green hills,

acreage of pastoral land covered in sheep and dotted with blue and yellow wildflowers. In the distance, a veil of mist encircles a ring of mountains, and it reminds her of the ever-present Bay Area fog that clusters under the bridges and shrouds the bay in mystery. The mist here seems more delicate, like a lace trim dangling from the pale sheet of the sky. In May, everything here is alight with dew, even in the late morning when the sun is bright in the sky, and it turns the verdant hillsides a sparkling peridot. Towns make their appearances known in fits and bursts, the sudden modern building flanked by crumbling stone walls. Some villages, built centuries ago atop hillsides, are interwoven with narrow streets winding like labyrinths. The further the goldenrod Renault travels away from the glittering Cote d'Azur and deeper into Provence, the older the towns become. Forests and rivers and mountains separate the pockets of civilization of southeastern France.

The scenery lulls Simonetta into a dreamlike state. Whenever she travels, her mind takes a while to catch up with her body, for her brain to understand that she is very far away from home, comfort, stability, familiarity. She's still in a daze even when Claudel stops for petrol about a half hour away in the outskirts of Sainte-Madeleine, in a very tiny hamlet called Riviere-avec-Pierre, which means "River with Stone" in the uncreative way many ancient towns were named, stating the obvious landmark. A river did indeed dissect the hamlet and Sainte-Madeleine, with a tributary that led to the chateau itself and filled the moat that encircled the chateau's grounds.

Aurelia rouses from her nap, and she and Simonetta step outside to stretch. Claudel waves away Simonetta's offer to pump the diesel. Standing uncomfortably idle, Simonetta makes small talk with Aurelia and together they survey the region that will be their home for the next several months.

"What brings you to the chateau?" Aurelia asks.

Simonetta's heart palpitates even though it's a perfectly normal and reasonable inquiry, and she wonders about the same of her fellow volunteers. Aside from brief glimpses in the email chains confirming their employment, the volunteers have yet to meet one another.

"I needed a fresh start," Simonetta says simply. Trite, but not untruthful. "Thought I'd put my French degree to use. And Claudel makes the work look so fulfilling." Simonetta attempts a smile that she hopes is deflective enough to deter future lines of questioning. "What about you?"

Aurelia's eyes sparkle. Simonetta tries to guess the woman's age, a fruitless effort, since Aurelia could be anything from twenty-five to forty-five with her gleaming complexion and the joie de vivre emanating from her. Simonetta decides that age doesn't matter anyway, because Aurelia is a delight to converse with, chatting animatedly as she explains her family's business producing traditional textiles in Chile and her passion for the fiber arts. Like Simonetta, Aurelia learned about Chateau Desrosiers through *Daily Life at Desrosiers*.

When Simonetta told her ex-girlfriend, Alex, about her plans to move to the chateau for six months, Alex remarked that the endeavor sounded like "adult summer camp." Now that Simonetta has arrived in France, she supposes that's pretty accurate. Already she feels the slight pangs of insecurity she had once felt as a young girl going to Girl Scout camp at Tilden Park, mingled with the excitement of being somewhere new, being on her own. Young Simonetta always enjoyed being alone and fully independent, without the shadow of her grandparents or chaperones or anyone who would dictate her life or schedule— but now that was actually her circumstance, with no elders left to look after her, she wonders if this level of independence and solitude isn't all it was cracked up to be.

Simonetta would have typically called Nonna by now to let her know she had arrived safely at her destination. It's still jarring, the absence of her grandmother, an open sore that Simonetta picks at lest it begins to scab and feel less painful. She knows Nonna had traveled a bit as a girl, had lived in France for a bit in her early life—it's where she had met the man who would become her husband and Simonetta's Nonno—but Simonetta can't remember the details and never wrote it down. Simonetta knew a little of what Nonna had done on her travels but had never asked what she had felt. Why had she never asked? So many questions that, in retrospect, seemed obvious. Who had Nonna been at thirty-four? Did Emilia Cavalieri try on new identities like new shades of lipstick? Which color did she prefer to don while she was Simonetta's Nonna?

Her heart twists again, a splinter of grief burrowing deeper inside. Simonetta tries not to let the discomfort show on her face, is relieved when Claudel finishes refilling the car and they set off toward the chateau.

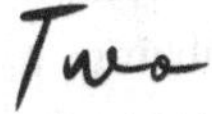

Two

Enfilade:
1. A series of rooms on a single axis; to get to each room, one must pass through another.
2. A volley of gunfire propelled in a line.

CLAUDEL AND AURELIA are considerably chattier as they make the second part of the journey in the winding mountains and Simonetta yanks herself out of her own head to participate. It's easy for her to live in her mind, to get lost in her own thoughts and tune out the world at a moment's notice. It's what she had enjoyed so much about her work in the manuscript restoration lab; she could simply turn off her external senses and focus on the task at hand without interruption.

Claudel refreshes their knowledge of the chateau: Chateau Desrosiers has more than thirty rooms, seven of which include renovated former "servants' rooms" where Simonetta and the other volunteers would be staying—Claudel had assured them during their interviews that there was nothing servant-like about them, and Simonetta had picked out her room based on the photographs online. She saw it had a view of the courtyard and that pleased her.

Fifteen more are earmarked for guests for the bed-and-breakfast component of the chateau, which opens during the summer; some of Simonetta's responsibilities include laundry service and light cleaning for the B&B guests. Two rooms, one of which belonged to Desrosiers' eighteenth-century owner, the marchioness Marguerite de Sainte-Madeleine, are permanently set aside in the medieval tower for Claudel and her nephew, Jeremy, both of whom live at the chateau year-round. Then there are the common areas, including the Grand Salon where extravagant balls were once held; a smaller and cozier Winter Salon for games and socializing; a formal dining space; and an expansive library that Simonetta can't wait to explore. But Claudel explains that the chateau's central kitchen is the most popular of the meeting rooms: "There is almost always someone in there cooking or baking! In my opinion, it's the best room in the house."

Simonetta knows quite a bit about the chateau already based on what Claudel shares on *Daily Life*. She can envision the long wooden table in the kitchen, the pale green wallpaper of the Grand Salon, the whitewashed walls and tall slatted windows in the formal dining room, the winding stone staircase in the medieval tower. The show was how Simonetta had learned about the chateau and its work-stay program, and she's followed it closely for years, enjoying being a part of the chateau's restoration from afar and now near. Nonna had become a devoted fan. In the months leading up to her death, the weeks in and out of the hospital, Simonetta would curl up next to Nonna and they'd watch the show on her iPhone. Nonna didn't speak much by then, but she would sometimes point to things—the garden, the medieval hall, the turret—her eyes wet with an unnamed emotion, followed by a gentle pat on the hand. Simonetta never truly understood what Nonna was trying to tell her, but the smile on her grandmother's face when she would start the show was enough for her. The application to apply for the summer work-stay program had appeared in her inbox just days after Nonna passed. By then, Simonetta was desperate for relief from her grief, and it seemed like the first of many signs to affirm the drastic life change.

Why the Altobellas, herself included, were drawn to the region, Simonetta didn't fully understand; she guessed that it had something to do with the fact that her grandparents had met in France before coming to America. They were both born in

Italy—she knew Nonno's place of birth was in Italy just past the French border, somewhere outside of Turino. Or was it Genoa? The Second World War had scattered both Nonna and Nonno's families across the globe. It was history that Nonno was tight-lipped about—any questions Simonetta had asked about his family were met with a hand wave.

"Non preoccupati," he'd said. *Don't worry about it.*

And now Simonetta is here, too. By the time she started college, she had enough high school credits to score an easy minor in French to complement her history major. She supposes she's following in the family tradition of being adjacently Italian, on the fringes of it, embracing its cultural influence in her life while also not fully immersing herself in it, putting distance between herself and the motherland. She has always only ever referred to herself as Italian-American, never Italian, in the way those of a second-generation diaspora culture do—where does one claim their roots? And now she was on the border of it again, literally, a mountain range between Simonetta and her familial homeland. Would she feel more or less Italian being in such close proximity to it? She peers out the window, seeking for signs of the ley line, long-gone footsteps of those who share her blood.

Goosebumps arise on her arm as the Renault makes its final descent to the chateau and she detects a sense of purpose and clarity she hasn't felt in some years, as if the stars are aligning for her personally. It's not a good feeling, per se; Simonetta feels keenly that the circumstances that led her here are bittersweet. She misses her grandparents fiercely, and leaving California felt like severing a gangrenous limb—necessary but painful to prevent a more serious, incurable infection that would have blighted the rest of her life. With the house sold in Berkeley, Simonetta has no permanent home to return to now. Her time in France will set the stage for the rest of her life, wherever she forges her future journey alone. It's an unknown like Simonetta has never experienced. Even the sudden loss of her mother early in her life pales in comparison to the utter chasm that her grandparents Emilia Cavalieri and Paolo Altobella have left behind.

The yellow car climbs with some effort up the hill about a

mile away from the ornate gates that demarcate the Desrosiers land. As they crest the hill, the valley below comes into view, a sight that gives Simonetta a pleasant pang this time for its sheer beauty.

Surrounded by a dense forest and a low layer of fog, Chateau Desrosiers is a commanding stone fortress standing sentinel among the vibrant foliage. Flanked by tall towers with conical roofs, the chateau is certainly like something from a fairytale, as its booking website boasts—but mysterious and haunted, more Grimm than Disney, with plenty of lessons to tell. This is what Simonetta had always found so appealing about it—its dark history had given it depth and layers. There is certainly a glamour to chateau life, but Desrosiers has witnessed the country's darkest history: plague and famine, the hunting of the Huguenots, the French Revolution, World Wars I and II. The scars of this tumultuous history are evident in every part of the chateau, and Simonetta can't wait to be a part of it.

She summons the vision of New Simonetta, Venus with red lipstick, and considers how to transfer her own pain onto the immovable stone walls of the chateau—it has experienced plenty of its own turmoil and yet still it stands, beautiful and weathered and wise because of it. Perhaps it can withstand her burdens, too.

It's early afternoon when Claudel parks the Renault on the gravel parking lot in the chateau's main courtyard, behind the large eighteenth-century fountain that gurgles pleasantly. A carved nude woman, nymph-like in her pose and long hair, arches toward the chateau; the fountain pumps water through a pipe behind her so it trickles sensually down her body and into the pool below. From the moisture, pockets of moss have sprouted and a faint patina dapples the nymph's skin, making the sculpture alluringly lifelike. Despite the nymph's joyful and dynamic pose, her face is thoughtful and perceptive—Simonetta gives the inanimate woman a nod in greeting, a mutual acknowledgment of respect, a ceding of territory.

Several roaming chickens make no such promise, perched on the nymph's shoulder and head and even one pecking naughtily at a nipple. Rain began about a half hour prior, a warm, lazy drizzle that coats the gravel and the stone and makes everything a few shades richer. The trees in the forest glisten emerald, their pine leaves wet and dripping, and the rose bushes planted around the chateau's perimeter are laden with heavy rosebuds that have yet to bloom. In late spring, Provence is balmy and today it is especially warm—good for roses, less ideal for Simonettas. Her thick hair clings to the back of her neck and sweat begins to pool under her breasts and at her lower back. She craves a shower, bedraggled from travel.

Simonetta remembers Nonna's advice for an on-the-fly spruce-up and pinches her cheeks to bring some color to her face, quickly applies chap stick, and twists her unruly hair into a bun at the nape of her neck. She's all anxious nerve-endings as she retrieves her luggage from the trunk and follows a giddy Aurelia and collected Claudel into the chateau's main entrance. Deep green vines tumble over the façade of the imposing building, framing the huge wooden and iron-wrought door that Claudel pulls open with ease. The sight of vines on stone and wood reminds Simonetta of her home in the Berkeley hills where she lived for most of her life. The tiny brick house had sat for several decades under tall eucalyptus trees, and her grandparents had maintained small, impeccable gardens in both the front and back yards. The Bay Area fog made green abundant, and although the mountainous region of Sainte-Madeleine was far lusher, Simonetta understands and recognizes the conditions that make things blossom.

Now that Simonetta stands before Desrosiers, she's humbled by its size. She has seen the chateau countless times online, viewed its many rooms and outbuildings and land from the many angles in which it has been captured on video, but it is far different being here in person. She delicately touches one of the massive stones as she enters, making her presence known and introducing herself to the place that will be her home for the next few months.

"Bienvenue!" Claudel exclaims. "Don't mind the mess."

Simonetta's eyes water, but not from the sentiment of arriving at the chateau—sawdust is everywhere, filling the air and coating every surface. Drop cloths have been haphazardly laid over the entry tables and chairs, but poorly so, for the dark veneers underneath appear several shades lighter from the small particles of powdered wood that cling to everything exposed. Still, Simonetta can mostly see through the chaos to appreciate the original glamour and awe this entryway once inspired and will again once the work is complete.

The floor underfoot, the ornate wood railing, and the staircase itself have been stripped and sanded down to their original grain. Simonetta assumes by the brushes and tubs that everything is being restored at the same time to ensure congruency. But the grand staircase is the focal point of the hall, leading up to a landing before splitting off into two passageways to the upper right and left wings of the building. Two additional hallways flank the foyer where Simonetta stands, the right one leading to the volunteer rooms and the kitchen, and the left one leading to the formal dining room, salon, and library. A series of paintings hang on the walls above the balustrades, although they too are covered at present. From memory, she recalls that some of the paintings are portraits depicting those who owned and lived at the chateau in centuries past, and she resists the urge to go peek at them under the coverings.

The only natural light in this area of the building comes through a circular stained-glass window embedded in the wall above the entry door. The light trickles in faint and filtered, reaching its colorful fingers out to delicately caress the floor. The decorative iron-wrought chandelier hanging from the high ceiling reads to Simonetta as nineteenth century with its elaborate flourishes. Updated with wiring to illuminate bulbs instead of candles, it is lowly lit, and even in mid-afternoon, the foyer is dim and several degrees cooler than outside.

"Jeremy!" Claudel exclaims as a dark-haired man steps into the foyer from down the left hall, wiping his hands. He, too, is covered in sawdust—evidently the person tasked with this massive project. Simonetta recognizes him from *Daily Life*, although it's a running joke on the show that he prefers to remain off-screen whenever possible, dodging the cameras in humorous ways, preferring to serve as the cameraman instead. A brief glimpse of Jeremy sometimes earned Simonetta a hand-pat from Nonna.

Claudel doesn't flinch from the mess when Jeremy bends to kiss her cheek in greeting.

"Bonjour," he says politely, nodding to Simonetta and Aurelia.

"You may know already that Jeremy is our resident carpenter," Claudel says. "And my nephew. Jeremy, these are the last arrivals for our summer group! Aurelia Rojas—" at her introduction, Aurelia waves and shifts her heavy bags, "—and Simonetta Altobella." Simonetta smiles awkwardly, still adjusting to her new identity, and nods in greeting.

"And where are you two from?" Jeremy asks with an aloof tone, as if he is being polite and doesn't much care. He glances around the room, evaluating his progress and preparing for the next task.

"Chile," says Aurelia, also uninvested in the conversation, her attention captured by the expansive entry hall. After her nap in the car, Aurelia looks bright-eyed and refreshed, her glossy black hair pulled back in a braid and her yellow blouse somehow still crisp. Simonetta tugs at her wrinkled button-down, letting loose a rivulet of sweat that slithers unpleasantly into her jeans.

"I'm from California—America," Simonetta says. Jeremy briefly glances up from the floor and raises his eyebrows.

"Not Italy?" he asks. "Your name?"

She shakes her head. "Born and raised in the States, but my grandparents were both born in Italy."

"I can tell by your nose," he replies casually, and Simonetta's hand instinctively flies to her face to hide the feature he so bluntly addressed. It's not the first time someone has remarked on her curved Mediterranean nose as an indicator of her Italian heritage. When she was eleven, Nonno was amused when the soft sloping cartilage of Simonetta's adolescent nose finally grew and solidified into the telltale aquiline shape that favored his.

When she studied her new preteen profile in the mirror, holding up her grandmother's powder compact in her hands to capture the right angle, revealing Simonetta's arched nose that tapered into her rosebud mouth like a statesman's silhouette on a Roman coin, Simonetta was mortified by her profile—*that is actually what I look like, what others see?* It was as jarring as hearing her own voice played back in a recording, and she'd never forgotten that strange feeling that as well as she knew her own self, she would never see herself as accurately as others did.

Even after living with her Italian nose for more than twenty years and sometimes even liking it more than she had at eleven, Jeremy's comment makes dormant insecurities rise and bubble and threaten to spill out. She turns her head away so he can no longer perceive her features and make additional comments, pretends to find the chandelier very interesting, and bites back a snarky retort about his mussed hair.

Claudel beckons. "Let me continue your tour and you can join the other volunteers!" She sets off down the right hallway and Aurelia follows, with Simonetta making up the rear, relieved that Jeremy remains in the foyer, returning to his project. The sound of the whirring sander follows them down the hall.

Claudel gives a familiar spiel as they go down the hall, some of the details pulled from the script she shares on *Daily Life*. Simonetta half-listens, instead soaks up the reality of being here. Even though this part of the chateau was once relegated to servants, which meant it was sparse and functional in its decor and architecture, it's now quite charming and hospitable. Stone walls ebb into more modern drywall, wallpapered with a forest motif that feels both quaint and wild, depicting trees and flowers alongside rabbits and boar and deer and wolves, creatures native to the area.

The bottom floor of the chateau is essentially one long tunnel, built in the enfilade style; to get to each of the main rooms, one had to pass through another. Such is the case in the right wing, which includes the kitchen, and beyond that, the cluster of volunteers' quarters. They make a brief stop at the small bathroom, to Simonetta's relief, but splashing her face with water does little to improve her appearance. Simonetta wishes Claudel would take them to their rooms first so she can freshen up, but instead she leads them to the kitchen where the other volunteers are already congregating.

The kitchen is a feast for the senses. The air is filled with spiced, herbaceous scents—something savory bubbles in a huge pot atop a large, old stove, releasing salty plumes of steam. Fresh herbs bound in twine and clipped to a periwinkle ribbon strung above the arched brick hearth hang upside down, wringing the moisture out to dry the fragrant sprigs of rosemary and thyme and parsley. The walls are whitewashed, with deep green tiling covering a foot of space above the butcher block countertops. Shelves are cluttered with cups and plates, most of which are gifts from *Daily Life*'s passionate viewers who send all sorts of trinkets to Claudel for use at the chateau. The mismatched cups and teapots and plates sport different toile designs, most of them the classic blue-and-white, but a few in green and red.

In the center of the room is the famous communal table, rough-hewn and weathered, large enough to seat a dozen people. Most of the chairs are occupied, and the occupants stand enthusiastically when Claudel brings Simonetta and Aurelia into the room.

Already the other work-stay volunteers are a lively bunch. Simonetta's head swims from sensory overload, but she tries her very best to remember everyone's names and places of origin as Claudel effortlessly introduces each person. Graham Okafor, from Britain, holds up his teacup in greeting and winks at Simonetta, a gesture she finds endearing. There's a married couple from Japan, Hanako and Jason, engineer-artists who specialize in plein air landscapes and want to experience what many of the French masters had once lived among. Alba Balibar, from Spain, is a longtime friend of Claudel's—both around the same age, Alba is as squat as Claudel is willowy, but the two share an undeniable grace. Diego Serrano (Mexico) and Lotte Vanderlinden (Holland) are both fresh out of university and doing a gap year before entering the workforce.

Feeling closest to Aurelia because they arrived together,

Simonetta lingers nearby but grows suddenly shy when Aurelia launches into conversation with the other Spanish speakers in the group, melding easily into the volunteer melting pot.

As everyone makes introductions, Claudel stirs the literal pot above the hearth, filled with something delicious that Jeremy made, releasing its aromas. Although she wants nothing more than to be shown her room so she can get a quick moment of respite to temper the wave of nerves in her stomach—and perhaps a clean change of clothes—Simonetta follows Aurelia's lead and joins the discourse. Graham saves her from some of the awkwardness by approaching her and, like Claudel, giving her a warm embrace that both startles and comforts her.

"How was your trip over?" Graham asks, fishing a blue toile teacup out of the cabinet. Simonetta delights in yet another accent, feeling guilty and grateful for the American privilege that most people speak English abroad. As an Englishman, it's more Graham's language than hers, truthfully, and his deep timbre makes her appreciate it more than she does back home. She often finds spoken English rather dull compared to the fluid and languid French, or the satisfyingly tactile Italian spoken seldomly in private by her grandparents.

"There was a big storm over the Atlantic," Simonetta says. "I don't do well with turbulence. I'm glad to be on solid ground."

Graham smiles and pours steaming water from a kettle into the cup he procured for Simonetta. "I took the Channel over, and then a bus," he says. "I'm not too keen on flying myself."

"Have you been here before?" asks Simonetta. Graham scoops tea leaves into the strainer and lowers it into the boiling cup, turning the water a dark amber, and nods.

"This is my sixth summer here," he says. "It gives me something interesting to do during the holiday and I'm quite fond of Claudel. I started volunteering here before she started *Daily Life* so she reserves a spot for me every cohort. I teach the rest of the year."

Their mutual passion for academia—Graham teaches chemistry to teenagers—gives them something to talk about as Graham fixes Simonetta's cup of tea. Without asking her preference, he pours in a dollop of cream and stirs in just the amount of sugar that coats the back of the spoon. She almost protests when he also drops in a syrupy blob of honey since she typically avoids additional sweetness, but the scent that arises from the cup is so pleasant that she keeps her mouth shut. Gratefully accepting the steaming cup, Simonetta takes a sip and nearly swears in delight.

"Che buono!" she says, like Nonna used to—*How good!* "Graham, this is the best cup of tea I've ever had."

The combination of bitter black tea and fresh cream and sweetness dances over her tongue, alighting her taste buds. Were it not for the hot temperature, she would have gulped it down with abandon. Despite the balminess outside, the tea warms her insides and soothes her quickly beating heart, alerting another organ: her stomach grumbles. Graham laughs and retrieves a matching saucer from the cabinet. He reaches into a bowl on the large rustic table and places several Biscoff onto the saucer.

"Here, have a biscuit," he says, picking one for himself. He snaps the ends off cleanly with his teeth and munches thoughtfully. "I don't think we'll have supper for a few more hours."

One strong cup of tea and several Biscoffs later, Simonetta is slightly more grounded. Hot caffeinated beverages always did the trick, another life lesson she had gleaned from her grandparents. That gem had been imparted to her by Nonno, who started every day with a cup of espresso from his Moka pot.

At long last, Claudel finally leads Aurelia and Simonetta to their rooms past the kitchen. Most of the volunteers have their own rooms, although the Nomuras are staying together, and Alba travels back and forth from Spain in a camper van that she keeps parked near the chateau's stables when she comes to visit. After a day spent around more people than she's surrounded herself with in months, Simonetta is nearly at her limit for socialization and exhales a breath of relief when Claudel gives Simonetta a moment of private reprieve.

What was once a stark, sparse servant's room is now colorful and charming and comfortable. On each side of the tufted upholstered full bed are two wooden nightstands with gold pulls. At the foot of the bed is a dark green army trunk showing some wear, topped with a golden tray bearing a tea set with a red-toile cup and teapot. On the right nightstand is a stack of books, including a French-English language dictionary, and a delicate ceramic lamp sporting painted cherubim. Opposite the door, a small window on the wall to the right of the bed reveals the courtyard through which Simonetta had arrived. Lotte, the chateau's resident florist for the summer, had arrived several days prior and furnished each room with a beautiful bouquet sourced from the garden. Simonetta's is perched on a small table sat under the room's one window, full of twisting green ferns, sprigs of long grass, and peonies the size and color of ripe peaches.

Simonetta peers out through the window. In the golden afternoon, the nymph is limned by a ribbon of light, and the luminous outline gives her a magical aura as the cascading water winks and glints under the sun.

Simonetta sits on the quilted bed and faces the courtyard. Any remaining energy and adrenaline drain out of her and she deflates. Now that she is alone, the anxiety and grief pile up on her again, this time in the form of heavy ancient stones that she can't move on her own. They pin her heart to the ground, push it into the dirt, build a castle atop the ruins. Simonetta lies down and curls on her side, buries her face into the quilt, and weeps.

Three

Oubliette: a dungeon in which the only point of egress is a hole in the ceiling.

SIMONETTA OPENS HER EYES to darkness. A solitary candle on a white ceramic stand, its golden flame low on the wick, illuminates the small table under the window.

Emerging from such a deep sleep, it takes her a moment to process her surroundings: the books, the lamp, the low-burning candle (*did she light that?*), the toile quilt, the courtyard and fountain and navy sky outside. She remembers where she is with a jolt and a strange feeling of dissociation washes over her, as if she is watching her own life from afar, experiencing it through someone else's body. Hard to explain, hard to identify. She is flooded, once again, with the feeling of being adrift.

She riffles through the stack of books on the nightstand, unearths a leather-bound notebook from underneath the French-English dictionary. Simonetta opens the notebook to find it blank and unused, with a small pencil tied to a thread woven into the binding to keep it attached, and she claims it for her own. She thinks the New Simonetta should embrace journaling as a healthy coping habit, and vows to do whatever the New Simonetta, Venus with Red Lipstick, would do. In her mind, that person is someone composed, someone who doesn't unravel but knows how to weave her pain and joy into something whole. Still, Present Simonetta has awoken with her heart in her throat and her mind somewhere hovering above her like a rude poltergeist. She turns to the first page and begins to write.

Adrift. The nymph makes her home in the water. Can I?

Simonetta stares at the rest of the page for several minutes until she remembers with a start that she is supposed to be at dinner. She has no concept of what time it is; the watch on her wrist has once again stopped clicking, and her internal clock tumbled out of her somewhere over the Atlantic Ocean or into the cup of coffee she consumed hours ago at the airport. Suddenly she is wide awake and starving, Biscoffs long digested.

She pulls a clean shirt from her suitcase. A shower will have to wait—she's not sure she remembers where the bathroom is.

The hallway is dark. Sconces emit a faint glow, just enough to illuminate the tiled floor underfoot. The kitchen in the next room over is brighter, though, and Simonetta tentatively pads down the hall, feeling every bit an interloper.

Sitting alone in the kitchen is Claudel's nephew, Jeremy, hair damp from a shower. A half-eaten bowl of food sits in front of him, along with a sketchbook, a protractor, and several pencils. He glances up when she enters.

"Oh, I'm so sorry," Simonetta says, starting to backtrack. "Did I miss dinner? I have no idea what time it is."

Jeremy points to a small cuckoo clock above the hearth, a detail she missed earlier. "Almost midnight."

That means it's nearly nine in the morning back home in Berkeley; no wonder she feels wide awake. As if on cue, her stomach growls, a keening sound that embarrasses her.

"There's still some food left," Jeremy says, gesturing to his bowl. "On the AGA. It's warm. Bowls are in that cabinet." He points across the kitchen to a cream-colored cabinet with glass doors, revealing neatly stacked blue-and-white china within it.

Grateful, Simonetta follows his instructions and ladles the last scoopful of whatever is in the pot—some sort of rustic stew, chicken and herbs and vegetables—into a bowl. It smells good, fresh and herbaceous and savory. She brings her bowl and a spoon to the table and sits adjacent to Jeremy, whom she notices still holds faint traces of sawdust in his hair despite washing. But he stands and steps out from the bench, sends it scraping against the stone floor.

Simonetta, mouth full, ambles out an apology. "I'm sorry if I interrupted your night. Jet lag seems to have taken over my senses."

"It's fine," he says. Simonetta notices that his accent differs from Claudel's despite the familial relation. It's not fully French; there is a lilt and an edge to it she can't quite place yet. "Just wash your bowl when you're done"—he points to the large ceramic farmhouse sink in the alcove—"and turn off the AGA, since we won't need it lit for the rest of the season. Do you know how to do that?"

Through her groggy, hungry state of mind, it takes a moment for Simonetta to remember that the AGA is the wood pellet stove—old and unwieldy but large and gorgeous, it's a staple of Desrosiers' kitchen that adds a certain *je ne sais quoi* to all of their meals (according to Claudel). Simonetta files through her mental archives and recalls (from her favorite *Daily Life* video, most of which takes place in this very kitchen) Claudel's explanation of the AGA and its main functions: turning it off simply entails flipping the oil lever, and the flame would extinguish. How hard could it be? Simonetta nods in agreement and continues to snarf down the dinner she missed in her post-travel slumber as Jeremy leaves the room without further conversation.

She sits alone at the wide table, stares past her bowl and analyzes the grain in the wood, its stark knots, feels like a wilting flower plucked from a garden and shoved into a strange vase, her torn roots seeking purchase.

Incorrectly turning off the AGA is Simonetta's first mistake.

After she finished her dinner post-midnight, the chateau was nearly quiet save for the occasional creaking of walls and floorboards. Without knowing yet where the light switches were, Simonetta worked by the dim light Jeremy had left on, but the brick arch over the AGA kept the hearth in shadow. Simonetta had fiddled with the lever opening the oil vat, then tried her best to snuff out the flame, first by puffing her cheeks out and blowing, until she remembered that oil fires were made more potent with oxygen. Instead, she turned off all the knobs atop the stove and held a rag to the outside of the filter door to prevent any additional oxygen from seeping in. It seemed to work; once the embers had faded, she quickly washed her bowl and padded back down the dark hallway to her room, where she slept fitfully for another few hours in an attempt to reset her Circadian rhythm.

She awakens to a commotion. Simonetta scrambles out of her room, still wearing the clothes from the night before, to find smoke wafting out of the kitchen and into the hallway; she hears voices coming from the same direction and stumbles toward it. Most of the volunteers are awake already, clustered inside the kitchen despite the air quality, making tea and cutting up slices of bread. Jeremy opens windows to clear the remaining plume and glances at Simonetta as she arrives, sleep-disheveled and wild-eyed.

"I thought you knew how to turn off the AGA," he snaps. "You trapped the smoke inside the oil filter and it smoked out the kitchen."

Simonetta's face burns up to her hairline as her international acquaintances turn to look at her.

"Bonjour to you, too," she says, voice on the brink of shrill. "We don't have AGA stoves in America!" *That's probably not true*, she realizes. "I couldn't even find the light switch." She throws her hands up in exasperation. "I don't even remember where the bathroom is! I just got here!"

"This one's on you, Jeremy," Graham says, wordlessly passing Simonetta a cup of tea that she accepts gratefully. For the second time in twelve hours, Graham's miraculously appearing strong and perfect tea soothes Simonetta's nerves. Despite meeting Graham mere hours ago, she feels a kinship already—tea seems to be the great equalizer, and she feels like one person is on her side.

"Good morning, Simonetta," Graham smiles warmly. "I'll show you how the AGA works later so you'll feel comfortable using it. The rest of the hearth works like a traditional stove, and you won't have to deal with the oil filter from now on."

"I don't know how to use it, either," says young Diego, tucking into a massive slice of baguette smothered with butter and marmalade. His bedhead mirrors Simonetta's. His plate is piled with breakfast offerings; Diego clearly feels at home already, and Simonetta admires and envies this. "I don't really know how to cook."

"You'll have to figure it out before you're on dinner duty," Aurelia replies brightly as she rolls her eyes. "How did you get to adulthood not knowing how to cook?" She squeezes Simonetta's shoulder. "Bonjour, my new friend! Are you feeling as jet-lagged as I am?"

Simonetta simply blinks in response, as Aurelia is as fresh as a summer lemon, as impeccably put together today as she had been the day prior.

"Slightly better after sleeping through dinner, but apparently my midnight escapades nearly burned down the chateau," Simonetta responds. She is both mortified and defensive about Jeremy's response, although the support of the other new arrivals bolsters her a bit.

"Nothing bonds people faster than catastrophe," says Graham.

Simonetta ignores this, drains the rest of her tea. To Aurelia, she says, "Can you show me where the shower is so I can get cleaned up?"

Glad to leave the kitchen where the smoke and the tension are finally starting to dissipate, Simonetta follows Aurelia down the hallway. Aurelia points out her room—across the hall from Simonetta's—then brings her into le V-C (the water closet). Like the volunteer rooms, the bathroom is small but thoughtfully furnished, the floor composed of very old stone bricks that wobble slightly. A simple European-style shower stall shares a wall with a claw-foot bathtub with a gold faucet. Paintings hung on the wall depict pastoral life: a cluster of sheep, an ivy-covered fence, a warren of rabbits. A circular window above the bath lets in a beam of bright morning light, and Simonetta sees that the sky is blue and unobstructed by rain clouds.

Aurelia leaves her to it, and Simonetta quickly pops into her room to gather her toiletries, scribbles a quick note in her journal (*Antidote to anxiety: Graham's tea*), and returns to the bathroom. The steamy shower engulfs her as she sloughs off layers of travel, fatigue, and embarrassment. After a whirlwind twelve hours, she finally takes a moment to breathe. Leisurely she applies her makeup—the first tour of New Simonetta's red lipstick—and pins up her damp hair with a gold "French clip" she ordered online. She puts the rest of herself together with jeans and a blue blouse, and practical close-toed shoes for traipsing around the grounds.

New Simonetta, she reminds herself.

Nothing makes her feel human like caffeine and a shower. Something fragile still sits inside of her—today it feels like a heavy, full, bruised apple, its chalky flesh threatening to spill out at the lightest of thumb presses—but for the moment, she packs moss around it and leaves it snuggly in place. She fakes a brightness she doesn't fully believe and gives herself a stern pep talk: She's in a new place and today she'll get her first project at the chateau. She's only seen a handful of rooms within it; there is much to explore, inside and out. Even better, plenty of room to avoid the grumpy Jeremy, who has managed to level more insults her way than passive small talk in the three short conversations they've exchanged. She's about to have plenty to do and that will fend off the worst of the grief.

By the time Simonetta returns to the kitchen, Claudel is there, polishing off a pain au chocolat. Despite her efforts to achieve French-girl chic, Simonetta immediately feels messy in contrast, somehow clumsy and unwieldy in comparison. A glimpse of her reflection in a shiny copper pan reveals several rogue curls escaped from her pin. She resists the urge to wipe off her lipstick with the back of her hand.

"Bonjour, ma cherie!" says Claudel, seated at the table with Lotte and Hanako. "You look refreshed! I hope the accommodation is comfortable for you. Have you eaten?"

Simonetta warms to the question. In Simonetta's family, food was the universal love language, and *Have you eaten?* was synonymous with *I love you.*

"Just tea," says Simonetta. She sits at the long table and takes a plate from the stack, adding to it two hardboiled eggs and a slice of bread. Like Graham's tea, the simple breakfast tastes delectable and fresh; the pale blue eggshells reveal spotless whites and deep orange yolks within, still oozing slightly. The bread is warm, the inside soft and fresh, the crust perfectly crackled. The bright marmalade Diego had been eating with abandon earlier is tart and vibrant. Simonetta wants to eat more with a spoon and then lick it off her fingers.

Claudel stands and wipes her hands to clear the crumbs. Dressed in a pale yellow dress and dark blue Hunter wellies, she looks ready to take on the day and Simonetta wants to channel the woman's verve. "Alright, my darlings—the chalkboard in the hall has the tasks and projects planned out for the week. Simonetta, since you have just arrived, please take the day to explore! Be sure to visit the chapel—it's beautiful in the afternoon."

"Mmmhm," Simonetta says through a full mouth. Her lipstick leaves a smudge on her bread.

"There's plenty to do!" says Claudel. "Find Jeremy if you need a project. We'll gather outside on the terrace for supper tonight at nine." She bids farewell to Lotte and Hanako, then sets off with purpose.

Simonetta finishes her breakfast alongside Lotte and Hanako, conscious of how much she is eating, abstains from enforcing American stereotypes. She focuses instead on socializing. Lotte is doll-like with bright blue eyes and short auburn hair that cups her vulpine face, pleasant enough to converse with but reserved, responding to Simonetta's questions with brief responses. She brightens only when Simonetta thanks her profusely for the beautiful bouquet.

"Your room has a great view of the fountain," Lotte explains. "I thought the foliage would complement the fountain's coloring."

"It's gorgeous," Simonetta insists. She is sure it's her

enthusiasm that earns her an invitation from Lotte to visit the floristry studio in the stables, once it's all set up.

Hanako is far more outgoing, launching into a detailed overview of the chateau's many paintings.

"There's even an original Rossetti here, in the Chambre de Chat," gushes Hanako. "And a Morisot, although that's more Jason's taste than mine."

Simonetta, who likes most art by virtue of it being art and a skill set beyond her own, has little to contribute to Hanako's detailed overview of the Desrosiers gallery. Through additional conversation, Simonetta learns that Hanako and Jason arrived two days prior to Simonetta and Aurelia. When she isn't painting, Hanako's main project is to help catalog the chateau's art to share with the rural art society downtown. She's also helping Claudel restore some of the missing stained-glass panels in the chateau's chapel. Several had been broken during World War Two, explains Hanako, from mortars that exploded on the chateau's grounds. Through historical records, Claudel knows which saints were depicted in the glass, and Hanako and Jason will draw out new versions of the glass that match the remaining depictions and eventually get them manufactured and installed. More than simply decorative, the stained-glass panels will help keep the elements out of the chapel, which has seen better days.

The three of them clean up the last remnants of breakfast and make their way outside through the main entry hall Simonetta arrived at the night prior. In the daytime, the entry hall of the chateau is far brighter, natural light streaming through the colorful window and catching particles of sawdust in the air. Jeremy has finished stripping, staining, and polishing the lower portion of the staircase and railings, leaving the deep oak gleaming. The floor is half-complete, however, and Simonetta steps delicately around the drop-cloths to avoid making another mistake that could evoke ire.

Four

Belfry: A tower, often attached to a building, in which a bell is hung. Contrary to popular belief, the etymology of "belfry" is unrelated to the word "bell"; the word derives from the Old French term "berfrei," a mobile siege tower.

AFTER SEVERAL HOURS OF exploring, Simonetta gains a tenuous grasp on the lay of the land.

The chateau's grounds extend for more than fifty acres, much of it left forested and wild beyond the cultivated garden off the western wing. A stone- and iron-wrought fence surrounds the perimeter, but the outbuildings, including the stables and a small chapel, sit just outside of it. Most chateaus, castles, and grand estates throughout Western Europe have a small chapel built within or near the estates' main buildings—at the time of construction, the presence of the chapel fulfilled the estates' religious requirements.

Each one was typically dedicated to a saint. Desrosiers's patron saint is the village's namesake, Saint Madeleine—a fifth century saint who, during the fall of the Roman empire, was martyred while proselytizing to fleeing legionnaires. According to legend and some questionable records, the teenaged Madeleine attempted to warn the soldiers of rock slides in the mountains, but when they saw her wildly gesticulating, they captured her instead under accusations of witchcraft and eventually put her to death. Later, in appropriate irony, the same legionnaires later died in a landslide. Simonetta compares Saint Madeleine to

Cassandra from Greek myths: many fear truth-telling women, at their own peril. Madeleine's patronages include healing, protecting soldiers, and communion with nature. *Did Nonna venerate Saint Madeleine?* Simonetta wonders.

She feels pent up still, off-kilter—the rotting, fleshy apple in her chest makes its presence known with occasional jolts. Whenever she travels, she needs a day to adjust and hopes the unsettled feeling curdling in her stomach is due to the change in time zone and atmosphere. At the root, she simply feels homesick, a feeling exacerbated by the lack of home to return *to*, and it turns the longing into something liminal, as if Simonetta exists in a pocket of time, somewhere between the before and the next.

And it is more humid here than she was expecting; a denseness permeates everything. She wants to seek out a cool place of respite, but so far the coolest place is the main entry hall, presently occupied by Jeremy.

Talk about a rude welcome. Simonetta bristles at her interactions with him—the comment about her nose, the lackluster way he offered her a missed dinner on her very first night, the harsh and embarrassing callout for the AGA debacle. Somehow, she has gotten off on the wrong foot, but both of her feet are uncertain and wobbly like a lamb, and she doesn't know how to make the next right step.

While exploring the open grassland near the chapel, she runs into fellow wanderer Diego, who already thinks everything at the chateau is "magnifico!" He's filming B-roll on his iPhone but moving so much that Simonetta is sure much of the footage will be unusable. She doesn't have the heart to offer criticism, though; he rambles enthusiastically about his many observations, rejoicing over the abundance of sheep (Diego has only lived in big cities, he explains, so rustic living is a joyful novelty), but complains about the lack of hot water (Simonetta's second mistake of the day, she realizes, having been less-than-mindful about her own usage during her restorative shower). She keeps quiet about this breach in etiquette and follows him to the pasture, where a half dozen sheep lazily roam like puffy white and black clouds floating in a green sky. One especially rotund sheep stands out among the rest, two round horns spiraling away from its face.

"That one's Bartholomew," Diego explains, spreading apart two fingers on his screen to zoom in on his caprine companion. "Claudel says he's mischievous. He likes to run through the chapel and stables."

Bartholomew turns his naughty face toward Simonetta and chews a mouthful of grass.

She leaves Diego and Bartholomew to their bonding and sets off toward the chapel. By now it is early afternoon, and the sun is bright and potent in the sky, but the light ebbs near the forest where the trees encircle the pale gray chapel. Under the canopy of conifers, the weather is significantly cooler. Simonetta is relieved to find another place of retreat.

Built more than two hundred years after the chateau's first wing had been established, the chapel has a steeply pitched roof with black gables. The impeccable symmetry of the facade is enhanced by an ornate circular stained-glass window placed high above a large wooden door. Three triangular alcoves on the facade each house a beautifully sculpted angel, their wings weathered but unmoved after centuries exposed to the elements. The center divine figure, a young woman donning draped robes with her arms outstretched, is Saint Madeleine.

Madeleine's bell tower was built another two centuries later and protrudes from the back right corner of the chapel. From where she stands, Simonetta can just barely glimpse the bell, copper with a slight patina. She has a sudden urge to clamber to the top and ring the bell; what did it sound like? Did it have the same timbre people heard hundreds of years ago? Would it be loud enough to rattle her skull and drown out the thoughts in her head?

As a child, she told Nonno she wanted to one day live somewhere where she would hear the church bells ring every morning.

"Perche, bambina?" Nonno had asked, amused by this declaration—particularly since Simonetta was not terribly keen on waking up early on Sundays to attend church with Nonna.

She shrugged. "It's like God is reminding us, 'Hello! I'm here! Don't forget to think about me when you go grocery shopping.' I like knowing He's thinking about me."

Nonno laughed, and even though Simonetta hadn't understood why he found that funny, she enjoyed making him laugh, the way his mustache—dark brown, like coffee, but streaked with gray, like cream swirling in—would move at the expression.

In adulthood, she still finds solace in the sound although her connection to God right now is tenuous at best. The church bells reminds her that there are still places connected to history and tradition, and something within her craves that stability.

The chapel door is slightly ajar. Simonetta steps quietly inside, careful not to wake the angels.

The chapel is in rough shape, that much Simonetta had expected—but what surprises her is how reverent she feels despite the faded frescoes, the broken windows, the chipped stone walls. She remembers the prayer that escaped her heart unbidden on the plane, pushes away residual Catholic guilt. The empty window frames with the missing stained glass let in the faint sounds of the farm and forest: chirping birds, bleating sheep, rustling pine needles.

There is much beauty to find even during the renovation. The domed ceiling, painted a faded dark green, is dissected by six richly adorned slats covered in brown and gold vines; the effect is that of the forest floor. The motif is carried onto the deep red walls, where the vines tumble down around the golden fleur-de-lis centered in each tiled square, save for a large panel on the left wall—that space is reserved for a vibrant and surprisingly well-maintained fresco of Jesus aiding an ailing man. Christ's face is surrounded by an orange and gold halo, a contrast to the intricately illustrated blue robes that cover the rest of his body.

Plenty of areas show wear. Although the chapel withstood

the worst of the mortar blasts during the war, deep cracks in the walls hint at its former trauma. The chateau had been inhabited sporadically through the 1950s and 60s, when it was abandoned and left to ruin until Claudel purchased it in the 90s and has owned it ever since. Six scuffed wooden pews—recently purchased from the local brocante, Claudel had shared on the drive from the airport, as part of an estate sale from a demolished chateau in western France—are spaced out in two rows of three.

Simonetta sits in the first pew, facing the altar that has a new piece of red velvet draped over the crumbling stone bench. A golden candelabra holds several white candles, recently lit and partially melted, beads of wax stuck to the opulent cloth underneath. The chapel, even in its current state of disrepair, is still used and very much loved.

In the calm, quiet sanctuary, Simonetta tries to imagine what it would have been like to be within the chapel with a war raging outside. She imagines the ground rumbling from the bombs and tanks, the ear-splitting sound of glass shattering. Did the bell in the belfry ring? Was the sound a herald, or a harbinger? Alone in the presence of God, she stretches out on the pew and puts her hands under her head. Simonetta is sure the chapel would have protected her. She would have made armor from the broken glass, wielded a golden fleur-de-lis as a shield.

She remains in the chapel for a long while, lost in thought. The light ebbs slightly as clouds move across the sky, swirling like meringue dollops. Eventually, the clouds spread and take up most of the view from where she lay, gazing through the arched opening where a window once occupied it. The clouds become heavier as she watches, until she can't tell which is which—are the clouds that deep silver color spilling across the sky, or is the sky darkening and the light clouds encroaching?

She eventually stands and stretches, the back of her knees cold from the wood pew. The meditative time soothed her somewhat, although it seems like her subconscious mind is insistent on reminding her every so often that she is in a foreign country, far away, completely alone. The reminder is like a sudden jerking movement upon falling lightly asleep—the body knows one thing, but the mind fears another.

There would be no way out other than through. That's what people have told her over and over again after Nonna's death: "It gets easier with time." Simonetta knows that after all the loss she's experienced, but she fights against it—she feels guilty to move on with her life, to not constantly think about the woman who had raised her and taught her everything she knew, her unwavering rock. Simonetta recognizes the lack of logic in feeling like any waking moment not spent thinking about Nonna is a disservice to her memory, but the feeling persists anyway. Simonetta's body has found a path forward; she no longer gets sick to her stomach when she thinks about holding the box of Nonna's ashes, at the morbid finality of clutching one's entire mortal being in something so small. But her mind is fixated on it, fully in the weeds, purposefully snagging itself on thorny branches and making tiny cuts that sting and bleed, leaving behind congealed balls of anguish. She forces herself to wear a necklace made from the crimson beads. If she doesn't hurt, if she doesn't feel pain, how will she remember? How can she ever pay enough penance? All Simonetta wants is to feel a semblance of lightness again, but the cost seems too high a price.

She leaves the quiet haven. The clouds, dark after all, crack like eggs, releasing a hot, slow sprinkle. Simonetta ventures toward the garden, passing through an iron wrought gate. The garden is a large, impeccably designed plot, with rows of neat planter beds vibrant with late spring produce, arches covered in spiraling beans, tall barrels filled with fragrant herbs. Flowers are everywhere, planted up against the brick wall that encircles the garden. The green bushes are heavy with roses of all colors: pale pink, juicy peach, deep magenta. In between grow equally bright bushels of peonies and dahlias. In the shaded areas under the laden fruit trees—apples and pears and even a few persimmon trees—ferns curl delicately up from the moist soil, and even a few small mushrooms poke up like tiny gnomes.

An old greenhouse with a slanted glass roof leans against the side of the chateau's left tower. The glass panes have been recently replaced, and the slight greenish tint catches the late afternoon light and mirrors the abundance of greenery surrounding it.

Claudel is knee-deep in a bed of soil, aggressively plucking weeds, while Graham leans on a rake and films her. He pauses recording and waves Simonetta over.

"How are you enjoying your first day?" Graham asks, brushing a few thick rain drops from his suede work apron.

"Everything is amazing," Simonetta says earnestly. "There's so much to see!"

"And *do*," laughs Claudel, standing to place the handful of weeds into the bin next to Graham. "You see now why I bribe you unsuspecting volunteers to come help me." She glances up with a cheeky grin and brushes the dirt off her delicate yellow dress. "Graham, this is a great opportunity to introduce Simonetta!"

Simonetta inwardly grimaces, unprepared to be on camera, but knows it's part of the job. And it's part of the appeal of the channel, the style of vlogging that captures those at Desrosiers going about their day. It's what Simonetta likes so much about it, why she's watched religiously for years.

Avoiding looking directly into Graham's camera, Simonetta relays her journey to the stables, to the pasture, to the chapel, omitting her inner turmoil and focusing instead on the details that delight her. She jumps in to help with the garden maintenance, and for the next few hours, the three of them successfully weed almost all the vegetable beds, glean the fallen fruit from the orchard, and thin out the herb barrels. Simonetta clutches a huge, fresh bouquet of thyme, rosemary, chives, sage, and oregano—the scent is earthy and divine.

Simonetta longs to bathe in the trickling creek that pours into the moat, scrub herself clean with the fragrant leaves, twine the sprigs in her hair. The nymph could have the fountain; Simonetta would be the river druid of the forest, bedecked in wild herbs and ferns—Venus in the petrified trunk of the tree.

The garden work makes her sweaty and sore; Simonetta is so satisfied that she can't stop grinning. Proudly, she carries her herbs to the terrace, a tithing for supper—and when her mind tries again to haunt her, as it has all day, she plucks the apple from her heart and sends it down the river.

Five

Machicolation: A hole in the floor of a battlement through which substances like boiling water, sand, or oil could be dropped on attackers.

AFTER TWO WEEKS, Simonetta learns several important things about life at Chateau Desrosiers:

- Claudel Morin's favorite word is "sumptuous." It's the highest compliment she can bestow, the best descriptor of the things she feels strongly about. Which, apparently, is many things. The William Morris wallpaper in the Chamber de Botanique is "sumptuous." The silky Venetian Fortuny robe Claudel inherited from her mother is "sumptuous." These are obvious things to describe as such, but the compliment extends to even the mundane or expected things in day-to-day life. "This tapenade is *sumptuous!*" "Lotte, your braids are *sumptuous.*" "What a *sumptuous* dinner table you've set, Jason!" It has become Simonetta's new goal to earn this compliment from Claudel.

- Many hands make light work. It's an adage with which Simonetta has long been familiar, but witnessing it firsthand in the labor-intensive setting of Desrosiers makes her a true believer. On a bright, warm morning on the cusp of May, Claudel wanted to clear out one of the stables that has become a catch-all storage room and recruited all the volunteers to help. Simonetta had glimpsed the full stable and grimaced: the room was packed floor-to-ceiling with stuff. Half-upholstered chairs; rusted birdcages and lamps; dusty old books; paintings in need of frames. The clutter raised Simonetta's hackles, but she dove in anyway, and after a mere few hours, the contents of the stable had been removed, sorted, and placed in more relevant areas of the estate. Diego had put the camera on a tripod and later made a time-lapse of the effort that Claudel included in that week's video. The sped-up footage made everyone look like toy robots zipping to and fro. Simonetta found it incredibly satisfying to see work in motion; it inspires and motivates her, gives her a sense of purpose to see a project through to fruition.

- Jeremy Duvain does *not* like her.

This realization manifests after several notable events, one of which is the infamous *AGA smoke show*, as Simonetta thinks of it wryly. But that seemed to be just the start of his disapproval.

Simonetta was on her first supper duty rotation with Alba. Intimidated by the woman's curt, if not abrasive, demeanor—Alba could not be more different than Claudel, and yet their friendship had persisted for decades—Simonetta was all too keen to let Alba steer the ship. She happily acquiesced when Alba suggested making *tapas*, for it meant that they could easily divvy up the duties and prepare separate dishes. Simonetta retrieved the gorgeous, juicy, colorful tomatoes from the garden for the tray of pan con tomate she assembled. She sliced several day-old baguettes and placed them side by side in a tray, drizzled all of it with olive oil, then smashed up the fresh tomatoes with herbs in Claudel's heavy marble mortar and pestle. It reminded Simonetta of making bruschetta with her Nonno, plucking cherry tomatoes from the planter bed hanging from the front window. When she was little, Nonno would burrow holes in the cherry tomatoes with a straw and place them on Simonetta's fingers, alternating between tomatoes and olives. She would pop each one into her mouth until all that was left was the savory juice under her fingernails and Nonno's whiskery kiss on her cheek.

The simple tomato sauce was so good that she shared the rest with Alba, whose approval made Simonetta beam. Alba added it to several of the other plates, dotting it on the spiced deviled eggs, making it a bed upon which to rest the garlic asparagus roasted on the outdoor grill. Alba tasked Simonetta with preparing the table on the terrace, a project Simonetta accepted with relish, for it was her first chance to explore the china room—an entire room, past the servant's quarters, filled with shelves laden with the stunning dishes and cutlery Claudel had collected from the local brocantes or received as gifts from *Daily Life* viewers. A few pieces were original to the chateau, and those were reserved for special holidays, but most were available to use, and Claudel encouraged it.

"Even precious things are made to be enjoyed!" Claudel had proclaimed more than once. "It's the memories that are precious, not the things."

The May evening was balmy and Simonetta was doing her best to embrace the warm spring, although her true nature gravitated toward the chilly Bay Area days. She selected a yellow lace tablecloth and complementary dishes: white edged with a dainty gold pattern. She encountered Lotte in the hall and requested a few small bouquets for the dinner table, to which Lotte agreed enthusiastically without hesitation.

Simonetta set the table for eight, feeling so bubbly that she even included grumpy Jeremy, although his presence at dinners past seemed to be a hit-or-miss and she had mostly avoided him since the "smoke show." Still, she had felt generous that evening. Alba brought out the trays they had prepared and Lotte arrived with two bouquets—yellow camellias and red poppies, nestled in fallen pine needles and bits of moss freshly plucked from the forest floor. Simonetta lit the pillar candles in the white ceramic candelabra and stepped back to survey her work. Alba turned on the fairy lights strung into the pergola above the table and Simonetta clapped her hands with pleasure; she couldn't remember the last time she had felt so proud of something. It was a small task, incomparable to her "real" life accomplishments, but the terrace was suddenly magical, warm and inviting, with the backdrop of the garden and the dark forest beyond.

Claudel brought out two bottles of white wine and a tray of glass chalices, and the staff gathered for dinner. Alba winked at Simonetta from across the table when Diego enthusiastically devoured several tapas in quick succession, singing his praises through a full mouth. After two glasses of wine, Simonetta wasn't even that disappointed when Jeremy finally did show up in his perpetually disheveled state.

"Please sit and have some supper," she said, speaking loudly above the active chatter at the table, hoping her words came out as clear as she intended despite the effects of the wine. She pointed to each tapa and explained what it was. "You have to try the tomato sauce, which we put on almost everything. It's all from the garden, and it's to die for!"

Jeremy remained standing, his expression blank. "I'm allergic to tomatoes," he said, before sauntering off back to his workspace.

Simonetta's heart deflated. She poured herself another glass of wine and stared into the candlelight.

A week later, Claudel asked Simonetta, Hanako, and Aurelia to go to the market and pick up incidentals for a few days. Simonetta had yet to explore the nearby town of Sainte-Madeleine and offered to drive Claudel's mustard Renault. It seemed an idyllic premise, driving through the French countryside with one's friends, en route to the market and boulangerie. Simonetta had driven in Europe once before, on a trip to Amsterdam six years prior; at the time, her girlfriend, Alex, had been shocked by the lack of regard European drivers had for many traffic laws and spent most of the drives with her face tucked into Simonetta's shoulder. But oft-cautious Simonetta enjoyed the challenge and the adrenaline rush and the Renault's manual gear box. She was sure that the drive to the market would be far less anxiety-inducing.

They had just piled into the car and were pulling out of the courtyard, rolling slowly through the gate, when Jeremy came running down the gravel path.

"Wait!" he shouted. Simonetta slammed on the breaks and the three of them lurched forward. She rolled down the window, cranking the lever, which squeaked in protest. Jeremy ducked in and bent over her, invading every speck of her personal space, and smacked the gear box. It made a slight click and the high keening noise emanating from the running engine suddenly ceased.

Simonetta glared at him. "I know how to drive manual," she said defensively.

"I could hear the car from the garden," he said simply. "Old French cars are harder to drive than American ones."

He then left as soon as he'd arrived as if nothing had transpired. Simonetta looked at Hanako in the passenger seat and Aurelia in the back—they both shrugged.

Anger and annoyance gathered in Simonetta's chest and she carried it with her through the market. The charming boulangerie, with its classic glass-and-iron window and display cabinets filled with delectable treats, cheered her slightly. The baker, Nicholas, was a wiry, white-haired man whose old fingers remained perpetually bent and twisted from the onset of arthritis and years of kneading dough. She made small talk with Nicholas in stilted French, and he sent her home with an extra baguette.

Her jolly mood curdled slightly when she returned to the chateau, the boot of the Renault filled with treats and supplies. Simonetta was still feeling sour later and, since it was her night to prepare supper again, she was petty enough to make tomato Bolognese.

Simonetta looks up at the gargoyles that remain watchful over the courtyard: what would they say if they could talk? What secrets do they keep? Simonetta detects the ghosts of hundreds of people around her at all times, with a strange sensation that she could be among the ghosts that roam the halls in the future. The feeling is never stronger than when she lingers near Room of Oddities in the left tower, the ancient-most part of the chateau, where the surviving structure has withstood seven hundred years of strife, where the memory of ghosts is most potent.

"That part of the chateau gives me the creeps," Hanako says the night before Simonetta is set to embark on her Big Summer Project. Together they sit at the wooden table in the kitchen.

Eager to get to work and be of use, Simonetta had volunteered to catalogue and clean the "Room of Oddities," as it had come to be called, for it was a catch-all space for the dozens of objects deemed worthy enough to keep, but not interesting enough to investigate and repair: until now. The room is filled with stuff that Claudel has collected over the years and some items that came with the chateau when Claudel acquired it. Simonetta is to keep an eye out for items that could be delegated to different rooms or places in the chateau, what could be repaired and restored, and what could be donated to the brocante.

Simonetta shrugs at Hanako, her open notebook before her displaying her half-written to-do list for the endeavor. "There are probably some fascinating finds up there. Plus, Graham says there's a ton of furniture, and some of the rooms need new items. Seems like a win-win."

Still, Hanako shudders. She's studying high-resolution images of stained glass in another chateau's chapel. "Don't you remember the vlog where the volunteer from four summers ago fell through the floor?"

Simonetta laughs. "They've replaced the subfloor since then. And when it's cleaned out, Claudel can make it even safer. Are you superstitious?"

"I like to think I'm a logical amount of 'stitious,'" Hanako says, grinning.

Setting small goals is a huge motivator for Simonetta. It's how she has always lived her life, and it was easy when she was younger, for she could set goals around school. Simonetta always felt motivated by some elusive factor, both external expectations and a demanding personal psyche, something telling her to *go, try, succeed.* Some of it came from her grandparents, who had urged her to find a path that suited her and encouraged self-discipline and independence, and so she had. But the pressure and the self-criticism seemed to come from a deep well solely her own.

Once she came to this realization after a particularly rough night of anxiety and grief through which she had cried and tossed and turned in her unfamiliar bed, Simonetta knew she would feel more grounded if she had tangible goals for her time at Desrosiers. The practice had always been far less about praise and accomplishment to her, and more about quantifying life into neat pockets of skill and effort and problem-solving. Without the structure, she feels adrift, and her heart wanders untethered into the depths.

She had sat at the small table under the window in the pale morning light and documented some goals in her notebook for accountability.

— *Sew the curtains for the Chambre de Chat*

— *Master the recreation of Graham's tea recipe*

— *Install the sink in the volunteer bathroom*

— *Fill up this journal with musings and notes by the time I leave*

— *Catalog the Room of Oddities and make it spotless by the end of summer*

After she documented her goals, she approached Claudel about the project. Claudel had laughed good-naturedly at Simonetta's enthusiasm.

"If anyone could do it, it would be you," Claudel said before agreeing. Simonetta can't help but read a bit more between the lines and make her own inference: that there is something to find.

In the light of day, Simonetta doesn't feel especially concerned about lingering spirits. The steepled ceiling makes the Room of Oddities feel spacious, but it's only about thirty-square-feet in total. The "room" is technically a turret, Simonetta has learned, a structure that projects out from the left tower. One standing in Desrosiers's courtyard can see the bulbous structure jutting out from the cylindrical tower on the left, flanked by the same-sized tower on the right, built to capture a sense of symmetry. Inside the turret, a small door leads to the outside battlements that encircle the tower, one of few remaining features that allude to the chateau's original purpose as a fortress.

Simonetta walks across the battlements against Claudel's recommendation, for some of the stones have loosened over the years. But Simonetta wants to see for herself what the fortress's soldiers had seen, peering through the crenellations out into the land and forest beyond. She looks out over the ancient land, takes in the dense forest, the looming mountains, the river encircling the estate. From here she has a good view of the gardens, and watches for several minutes as Lotte and Diego make their rounds gleaning the fruit trees.

Far from any of the chateau's bathrooms and mostly unsuitable as a room without extensive renovations, the turret has become an out-of-the-way archive. It is a veritable treasure-trove, Simonetta is sure of it, but the project daunts her even though it was her idea. The root of her concern: that the project won't pay off. Won't be a solution to her panic.

Streams of sunlight peering through the crenellations catch the disturbed particles of dust in the air, releasing with them a musty scent.

But cataloguing is what Simonetta does best, above all things. She is adept at viewing a pile of something, taking it apart, and implementing a system for it. After Nonna died, Simonetta took inventory of everything in the house to prepare for the estate sale. The logistics of it all kept at bay the immense sadness she felt at selling off her grandparents' things they had painstakingly acquired and curated throughout their lives. The more precious items and family heirlooms she kept for her own use, now packed up and stored in Alex's garage back in Berkeley.

The experience of selling off her grandparents' belongings made Simonetta want very little in her life. Whether she would have a spouse, a child, still seemed part of a hazy future—but she has a feeling that something more awaits her on the other side of grief. How would it feel to date again? Would it ease the sting of loneliness to know that she is loved? She wants her life to be simple, clean, organized. Closing Nonna's many accounts, trying to enact her will in which dozens of friends received numerous items—it exhausted Simonetta to close out another person's life. She hopes her own can be tied up in a neat package.

The chateau is the perfect outlet for Simonetta, for she can still engage in the things she loves—history, cataloging, travel— but none of it is hers. This will make it easy, Simonetta thinks, to keep an objective eye on whatever she's about to unearth.

Six

Buttress: A structural support, composed of stone or brick, built against a wall for stability.

ROOM OF ODDITIES – DAY 1

RAIN LASHES AGAINST the tower and leaves small puddles on the wood encircling the room. Although the turret has a door and its windows are filled with thick slatted glass, the walls are slightly rotting from frequent moisture, and the room smells musty and moldering. Simonetta's efforts to clean and organize the room will allow Claudel to have the room inspected and repaired; all that had been done here for nearly a century was the addition of a sturdier subfloor, so that people wouldn't fall through it into the room below like the former volunteer (Claudel assures her that he's fine now).

From the turret, Simonetta watches from above as two groups of guests—a mother and daughter pairing, and a couple with a small child—exit taxis and run across the courtyard and into the chateau, coats held over their heads. In mid-May, the rain spells are brief and hot, and the sun comes out like clockwork every afternoon. The abundance of water makes the grounds green and lush—the roses are overflowing on their bushes, the trunks of the forest trees are thick with moss, the garden irrigation is kept off in favor of the natural source of water and the vegetables are thriving.

Simonetta, too, is bolstered by the rain. Storms outside always quiet her heart, the outward weather removing the burden to feel as deeply as she felt. When the mist falls thickly over the land after the rain ceases, Simonetta revels in being masked, hidden. The work keeps her busy and the downtime permits her plenty of time in her own head, and between the two, she inches toward the tail end of unpacking the worst of the thoughts that have plagued her since her grandmother died. Simonetta hopes that she is, at last, on the road to some semblance of healing, whatever that elusive concept represents.

Another factor in this is the volunteers, who are quickly becoming Simonetta's friends. Each person is so very different, and she enjoys the special dynamic she develops with each one (excluding Jeremy, whom she very much still avoids). With them, she has new routines and traditions: coffee with fellow early birds Alba and Aurelia on the terrace early in the morning; an afternoon run with Hanako, Jason, and Graham; evening card games and puzzles with Lotte and Diego. The group of them find plenty of common ground, despite the differences in age and language and place of origin. Simonetta picks up new vocabulary here and there:

Hanako taught her names of the animals on the farm: hitsuji (*sheep*), kujaku (*peacock*), usagi (*rabbit*).

Lotte relayed the phrase, "Het zit wel snor," which meant something like "Don't worry," but literally translates to *It sits like a mustache*. (Simonetta, eager for context, asked: "What does that mean?" Lotte said: "You know, like how a mustache just sits?" Simonetta, sensing an impasse, just simply nodded.)

Diego delights in teaching Simonetta offensive phrases in Spanish; he calls her *Simona*, exaggerating the long *A* vowel and drawing out the third syllable for drama like she is the heroine of a telenovela, and teases her for being a rule-follower. He found it hysterical when she recited "¡Vete a la chingada!" (*Go to hell!*) ad nauseam the other night to perfect her accent.

She practices her newly acquired languages while meandering slowly around the attic, clipboard in hand. She hasn't moved anything yet, other than the old sheets draped over many of the items. So far, Simonetta has unearthed an abundance of grandfather clocks, most of them large and quite ornate; those would be easy to put in the chateau's many rooms. There is also a lot of furniture, mostly common pieces in need of repair: a vanity with a cracked mirror but an in-tact frame adorned with gold filigree; a pair of wing-back chairs with deep floral-patterned upholstery, each sporting a handful of tears; numerous end tables, all with different marble or stone tops and legs of various designs.

Another area of the room is piled high with musical instruments. She is pleased to spot a violin amongst the selection, leaning against a hurdy-gurdy, both of which are tucked under a piano bench. Less pleasantly, next to the instruments is a disconcerting assortment of taxidermy and trophy heads, along with several old hunting rifles.

Simonetta establishes four quadrants of the room: furniture; instruments; hunting paraphernalia; and clockwork. This plan helps her figure out who she'll need to recruit for each project. It will likely take her the entire summer to fully complete the room—emptying it, for one, could take weeks; assisting Claudel with a review of the room's future repairs; taking items they don't want to the local brocante; and overseeing the restoration of the items they planned to keep. Simonetta sets herself up a week-long schedule to tackle each quadrant and take inventory, and drill down from there. It's an approach she learned from Nonno who, before he retired, had worked as an engineer designing medical robotics: anything was possible to do if one only broke it into small enough pieces.

Passively, she notes how many items are made of wood and need the careful hands of a carpenter, but she'll pass that road when she comes to it.

DAY 2

The rain lifts but the heat settles in, and today the tower attic is sweltering as Simonetta drags the furniture items she can carry to the doorway, to prepare for transporting them down the spiral staircase. That is certainly not a project she can manage alone.

Despite the discomfort of the heat and the soreness of moving around heavy armchairs and tables, Simonetta enjoys the work. Like the manuscripts she restored in her former career, she sees potential in each item of furniture and can envision its purpose elsewhere in the chateau. She pictures Lotte's bright summer bouquets perched atop a freshly painted end table. She can almost smell the paint and lacquer and stain, the freshly washed fabric, the aromas of work and improvement.

That morning in the chapel, she thought about work and faith. Nonna valued work in and outside of the home, often citing Bible verses chiding idleness. This was passed on to Simonetta, who appreciated having something to do regardless of the promise of money in return. If Simonetta would not embrace the faith of her family in their absence, she could still embody their values, and in this way, she has come to appreciate that work is a holy pursuit.

By the end of the day, she is starving. Jason and Diego are on supper duty, and together they prepared a series of savory tarts and a fresh salad from the garden. Simonetta eats with abandon; the everyday manual labor pushes her body to new limits. Occasional weekend hikes in the Berkeley hills were the extent of her physical activities, save for the walks across campus or a stroll through the farmers markets. Moving and manipulating furniture all day in the heat makes Simonetta achy and exhausted. After three slices of tomato and radish tartes, she sinks into the bath in the volunteer's bathroom to recover and gear up for the next day. But the work is good for her—she falls asleep as soon as her head hits the pillow and sleeps without dreaming.

DAY 3

Taxidermy day is far less pleasant.

Simonetta remembers Nonno and Nonna taking her to a Swiss-themed "chalet" in Lake Tahoe once for Christmas. Inside, above a crackling hearth, a row of deer heads had gazed down on her. There was something she found sweet among the utter gruesomeness—the deers' soft eyes, well-preserved, and their strong, sturdy antlers. She felt their protection, and ever since then, Simonetta always felt a kinship with deer, appreciating and admiring and aspiring for their combined beauty and strength, seeking them out from a distance when she visited the Sierra Nevada mountains.

Deer occasionally wander the chateau grounds. Early in her stay, Simonetta had woken early and gone outside where dew still clung to the pale green grass. She walked to the chapel at the edge of the forest, and there, among the trees, was a young doe. Dark speckles dappled the doe's fur, and she stood sentinel while making eye contact with Simonetta. *How can eyes be both soft and alert?* Simonetta wondered. She felt, for a moment, that she existed in a void of timelessness—how many women had gone into the forest alone, felt the dew on their bare feet, formed alliances with the animals? That is the foundation of witchcraft, the magic and harmony of women and the natural world.

The taxidermy collection lacks the majesty of her Tahoe chalet. For one, there is no deer head among the selections. Much of it is composed of trophies from faraway places that have been unfortunately poorly stuffed. Claudel had mentioned that the trophies belonged to the Marquis de Najarac, who owned the chateau in the 1920s. The marquis, heir to a French family who made their wealth in Northern Africa, had scooped up the chateau for next to nothing in the aftermath of WWI and lived a bachelor's paradise until the outbreak of the second World War, where he was taken hostage by Italian fascists and eventually killed when the chateau was mortared during a final stand-off.

There are other Marquis de Najarac belongings scattered throughout the chateau, and, to his credit, he was nothing if not an eclectic and thorough collector. Some of the larger sets of china were Najarac acquisitions, as were the Moreno chandeliers hung in three of the chateau's larger rooms.

Simonetta triages the animals as quickly as possible, moving the smaller items by hand toward the door—she'll enlist Diego for his help transporting the items downstairs to take to the brocante. She writes down a list to share with Claudel, although she is certain Claudel will be glad to be rid of most of the taxidermy. A poorly preserved massive wildebeest's head doesn't quite fit the style of Desrosiers.

It makes her sad and angry that people like Najarac amassed collections of living beings, with little care for their dignity in death. But there are enough museums and collectors and other chateaus in France that Simonetta is optimistic they'll find a good home, and she gives each one well-wishes in the afterlife.

DAY 4

Simonetta rewards herself for processing the taxidermy collection by spending the next day investigating the quadrant she has saved for last: the corner of the turret crowded with instruments stacked like priceless, unwieldy matchsticks. Clipboard in hand, delight swells in her chest as she considers how to best sort through the treasures and jots down a quick plan of action. For months Simonetta has felt distant from music, but the cravings are starting to blossom again—music, playing and occasionally composing it, has always been the way she processed her own emotions, her one creative outlet that unlocked the small part of her brain not dominated by logic and overthinking. Simonetta knows playing her violin more would be good for her; music unearths feelings that she avoids unpacking, but the instruments excite and inspire and entice her, give her the pleasant itch in her fingers to pluck something, make something thrum beyond the constant, pervasive uneasiness that hums and rumbles in her chest.

Satisfied with her plan of action, she grabs a cloth and starts dusting off a harp with flaking gilding, an instrument she has always wanted to try but never had room for in her series of small dorm rooms and Bay Area studio apartments. She tests a string, detects that it's flat and in need of tuning. From behind the harp, she extracts several wind instruments that lay dormant in velvet-lined cases: two flutes, a gleaming brass trumpet, and an oboe.

After moving the winds to the center of the room, she moves further into the strings and is pleased to unearth a cello, although the bow is missing. There are two violins, one with a scuffed neck and the other with a chipped lower bout, but nothing irreparable. She inspects them both to determine if they are of any value or notable origins, but all she can discern is that they are of local crafting, bearing the oak-leaf logo of the Sainte-Madeleine luthier.

A few rarer items are in the pile, including a hurdy-gurdy with a crank in dire need of rosin, and even a small triangular balalaika that reminds her of one of her favorite books, *Doctor Zhivago*. She moves the smaller items near the door to take to the Grand Salon for more thorough cleaning and repair, but she'll need help transporting the larger items like the harp and a mahogany baby grand piano. How someone got those up here in the first place, up the tight winding staircase and through the narrow-arched door designed for medieval-sized men, she has no idea. The window, perhaps? But the slats are immovable; the window doesn't open. Another Desrosiers mystery to add to the growing collection. In the meantime, she disassembles the teetering stack of music books, removing duplicate titles to donate to the brocante. There are several violin books in the mix, many of which include classical compositions she has not practiced in many years. These she adds to the items to bring downstairs, several of which she'll claim for practice. Her fingers already test out notes, estimating spacing and placement, treating the spines of the books as if they are fretboards, heeding an internal summons to play.

Wiping her brow with the back of her hand, she stops and takes stock of her progress, denotes on her clipboard which instruments she found and what requires repair and tuning. As she scans the corner, now emptier and less precarious, her eyes stop on something she overlooked in her initial investigation, a tall item covered in a black sheet of fabric. The dust-caked fabric blends in with the stone wall behind it, but the corner of a wooden cabinet—a warm, rich color with a golden filigree— peeks out from a gape. Another armoire? The still-sore muscles in her biceps protest at the thought; it took Simonetta, Diego,

Jason and Graham to move three of the armoires she found two days prior, and there are four more to go.

She lifts the veil tentatively like one peeps at a specimen under a cloche. To Simonetta's relief and surprise, it is not an armoire she sees, but a doll sitting atop a tall cabinet: a hand-carved wooden girl, the features of her face—wide brown eyes and a small red mouth—brought to life with faded paint. A wig of coarse dark brown hair (*horse?* Simonetta wonders) is attached to the doll's head, a long braid resting on her right shoulder, draped over a simple dark green linen dress.

Judging by the faded wood, the disheveled wig, and the rough-spun dress bearing some tatters, the doll is *old*. She reaches for it but finds it attached to the cabinet and pulls off the dust-caked fabric to perceive its entirety. Motes catch the sunlight, illuminated specks that dance around her as she waves her hand to waft away the plume.

Wooden articulating arms, crooked as if primed to perform, hold a small violin laced with silk strings that snake down into the gilded cabinet. The doll's head is slightly cocked to the left, the wooden fingers of her right hand clasped around the neck of the instrument and her other hand wielding a tiny bow that rests lightly on the strings. Simonetta realizes with a start what she is: an automaton.

She has found other automata in the turret, including a small robotic bird in a rusting cage and a glittering jewelry box with a wind-up ballerina, but none of this size or intricacy. Eager to see if it still works or if she can sleuth out any additional details, Simonetta pulls the automaton out from the corner and inspects it for a lever or some sort of switch. She assumes that, in theory, pulling a lever turns the automaton on, and the doll plays a simple melody on her violin.

Simonetta is daunted by the automaton's simultaneous delicacy and durability. It has seen better days; the grime caked on the cabinet and the doll is several layers thicker than the muck she cleaned from the other oddities. How long has it been here? The wood at the base of the cabinet is bloated from the damp floor—Simonetta is confident that it can be repaired, perhaps a half inch sanded off and coated with a water-resistant sealer.

She circles the automaton, seeking the lever, button, pulley, but finds none. A door embedded in the back of cabinet bears a small, round golden lock; she pulls a bobby pin from her hair and sticks it in the lock, maneuvers it around in hopes it will acquiesce, but the lock opening is tight and the serrated edge of the pin gets wedged, and she removes it before the lock jams completely.

Perhaps she can pop it open. The lock itself is wiggly in its base, and she gauges that she could probably force the door open. From the toolbox she retrieves a small crowbar, thin enough for her to slip into the gap between the door and the rest of the cabinet—and when she thinks she has enough leverage, she pushes her weight against it, but the crowbar instead slides out of the gap and across the door, chipping the filigree and leaving a jagged scratch along the door.

"Shit!" Simonetta drops the crowbar like it burns her and rubs her fingers along the damage. Feeling foolish, she steps back and takes a deep breath, reining in the impatience and insatiable curiosity overtaking her better senses. The doll's expression emits a hint of mystery and cleverness, her lips painted to slightly curve up at the ends, her wide brown eyes ever observing. Simonetta, aware that she is personifying the automaton, senses that the doll wants to play, wants to show herself, wants to be alive. She has never seen anything like it.

Or perhaps she has. A memory blooms in her mind, unbidden. Nonno was an engineer and it was not uncommon to see him sitting at his desk near the window, sketching out mechanisms on graph paper. When she was tall enough to peer over his shoulder, she had once glimpsed a more unique concept mapped out amongst the grid: a small girl sat before a calliope, strings attached to her limbs and leading upward out of frame.

"Is that me, Nonno?" she had asked. He jumped, startled, then laughed and pulled her into his lap.

"Your face is always on my mind it seems, topolina," he said, calling her *little mouse*, since she had the tendency to sneak up on him. He held up the drawing beside her face. "What do you think? Should I design a pocket Simonetta I can take with me everywhere?"

It was a musical puppet, he had explained, like one would find at a circus. Now Simonetta understands it was an automaton. When she had asked him why he was drawing one, he had only said, "I was just thinking about my father."

A stomach-clenching feeling washes over her as she takes in the discovery, a double-sided coin of dread and overwhelming curiosity. Simonetta knows next to nothing about machinery, but it takes little to trigger her problem-solving mode. What will it take? What tools will she need? The researcher's curiosity, core to her identity, perks up at the challenge.

Ignoring the objectivity she had pledged to maintain while evaluating the oddities, Simonetta, feeling like an automaton herself with gears turning and strings plucking in her mind, puts her plan into motion.

Seven

Scaffolding: A temporary framework, often wooden, built beside a wall to support builders in building or repairing a structure.

IT CAN'T BE HELPED: Simonetta needs to ask Jeremy for assistance.

There is simply no way to get into the cabinet without proper tools, and if it's as old as she thinks it might be, she can't risk another splinter. The damage she caused already provokes a grimace whenever she looks at it—what if she had broken it more? Snapped off a limb or crushed the perfect small violin out of impatience? If she's going to make this her new mystery to solve, she must be methodical and leave emotion at the door, even as wishful thinking and deep longing to uncover the truth plagues her every step.

Simonetta tosses and turns the entire night before she plans to approach Jeremy. She runs through every possible scenario, most of which involve him slamming a door in her face—which door, she has no idea, since his workshop is a covered area outside, between the garden and the forest, and it lacks walls, let alone a door, so that enough space is reserved for the long logs of fallen timbre that end up there regularly. It's an invisible door in her mind's eye, conjured there by her anxiety that loves to lead her to the worst outcome of every scenario. She imagines him scolding her for damaging the automaton—what if it was an old family heirloom and he became furious with her for being rough with it?

Simonetta talks herself out of that one. If it is special, surely Claudel and Jeremy would have kept it somewhere more visible and not shoved away in the oddities attic.

The next morning, she awakens early and asks fellow early bird Graham for assistance. She finds him reading in the alcove of the Grand Salon, fingers curled around a cup of tea. She needs help moving the automaton to Jeremy's workspace and knows Graham's presence will cushion the awkwardness.

Graham agrees to help, and they find Lotte in the kitchen and approach her, too, for an additional set of hands. Simonetta dreads that at any moment they will call her on her ruse—the ruse of avoiding being alone with Jeremy for fear that he will simply list all the ways she is somehow incapable of taking on this project, or any project. She wonders if they can hear the thoughts tumbling and ruminating in her mind; to her, the thoughts are so loud, like the sound will somehow leak out of her ears and fill the air with the melody of her incessant worrying.

Simonetta knows—she *knows*—it's ridiculous, the anxiety she is stoking about Jeremy Duvain. On the cusp of her mid-thirties, her self-confidence is healthy enough to keep most criticism in perspective, but the major upheaval in her life has thrown her awareness and perspective off-kilter, and every comment from Jeremy has so far hit her right on target.

If anything, she reasons, he probably doesn't think about her nearly as much as she thinks about him. Isn't that always how it works? She doubts he plans out routes to avoid running into her (she is, after all, at *his* home) and she is positive he feels like he has nothing to apologize for. And maybe he doesn't. *She* is the interloper—wronged as she might have been on more than one occasion, an opinion she holds fiercely—and she is so wound up in a strange concoction of anger, confusion, and sheepishness that her adrenaline spikes and she carries the automaton down the spiral staircase with unexpected gumption.

The tall machine is unwieldy. By the time they bring it all the way to the hall near the Grand Salon, the three of them are sweating. The hall is warm and close already, even though the sun has been up for a mere hour. Simonetta anticipates a hot day.

Jeremy is in the salon when they enter. Simonetta is surprised to see him there, figuring him for a night owl given the AGA-at-Midnight incident. By her logic, in her attempts to avoid him, she used that information to deduce his schedule—he stayed up late, perhaps well into the small hours. This meant he was rarely at breakfast with the volunteers (and, Simonetta assumed, he probably avoided the lot of them as well) and likely came in for meals well after the crew had scattered to their projects every day. He attended dinner on occasion, mostly at Claudel's behest. The volunteer he worked with the most was Graham, whom he seemed to like best, having known each other for some time—together they were working on restoring paneling for some of the bedrooms on the second floor.

So it's perfect, really, that Graham is her unknowing accomplice. Simonetta knows that if she had explained her thought process to anyone else, it would sound utterly incoherent. Overthinking is Simonetta's oldest and most familiar companion, and she has no idea how *not* to do that, so instead she simply embraces it and uses it to navigate weird situations made weirder by her overthinking.

"Looks like you made a discovery," Jeremy says to Graham, nodding toward the automaton.

"Simonetta did, actually," Graham says. "In the oddities attic. Mind if we bring it to your shop?"

"Of course not." Jeremy says with a smile, affirming Simonetta's theory that Graham was the correct co-conspirator. The salon's massive doors are open to the gardens and the pleasant floral aroma wafts in. "But I need coffee first. Have you all eaten yet?"

When they shake their heads, they follow him to the kitchen.

"I just need help opening it," Simonetta explains as they walk down the hall, then adds, "So I can check out the mechanisms inside. I have some ideas on its repair." A lie, but no reason to give Jeremy a reason to doubt her. Simonetta is compelled to justify her interest. She leaves out the fact that she already tried to pry it open.

Simonetta helps set out breakfast while Graham fixes another cup of tea for the three of them. Jeremy prepares coffee with a pour-over and the rest of the hot water in the kettle Graham hands over, and she feels a slight pang of longing and nostalgia at the scent of it. Graham's tea is the stuff of magic, but Simonetta has always been a coffee drinker. She suddenly misses The Olive Branch, the cafe down the street from her grandparent's house where she regularly indulged on pistachio lattes and cannoli; she misses Nonno's burbling Moka pot brewing up espresso; she thinks of the coffee cart parked outside of the restoration lab at Cal. Until this very moment she has never reflected on how many memories she had associated with coffee, and she understands how true it is that scent unlocks memories in a way other senses don't.

As always, the memories and thoughts bring with them a wave of mixed emotions—but this time, they don't knock her overboard. Fortified with Graham's tea, now seeding its own memories in her senses, she rides the tossing whitecaps as Earl Gray settles her stomach.

She must have been staring, lost in thought, because Jeremy lifts his cup in her direction. "Did you want coffee? If you ever want some, it's in that cabinet." He points over her head to the robin's egg blue cabinetry hung over the tea and breakfast station.

Simonetta blinks, at first, then smiles with surprise and hopes it reads as genuine. "Thank you. I might take you up on that sometime." She pauses. "Any chance you have a Moka pot?"

"What, is my tea not good enough for you?" Graham teases. "Typical American."

"I'm convinced your tea has magical properties, Graham," Simonetta answers sincerely. "It's somehow both soothing and energizing all at once, and I have no idea how you balance the sweetness. It's the best tea I've ever had."

Graham clinks his cup against her in cheers.

The clock chimes eight by the time they finish their breakfast. The washing up goes quickly with four people involved, and they leave out some of the breakfast items for the other volunteers just now stirring awake.

"Where is everyone, anyway?" Lotte asks, hanging up her apron on the golden hook.

"Alba's awake and already heading to the brocante with Claudel," said Jeremy. "They'll be back in a few hours. I think everyone else is still sleeping."

Back in the salon, the sun shines brightly, revealing a sheen to the pale green wallpaper that remains undetected when the sky is overcast. It makes the room glint and sparkle, and Simonetta can picture the glamor this room must have once inspired in its heyday. The instruments from the Room of Oddities will find a good home here, on display.

Which reminds her of the task at hand. She gestures to the automaton, covered with a clean sheet for protection. Her hand trembles and she clenches her fist, open and close. "This is what we need to move to your workshop."

Jeremy inspects it, kneeling to find the best vantage point for lifting it and carrying it across the garden. "I haven't seen this in ages. It could use some care, that's for certain." He gently touches the splintering where Simonetta had tried to foist it open but doesn't comment. She realizes now that the rest of it is still so covered in grime that he would have little way of knowing that the breakage was her fault anyway and relaxes a bit.

So far so good; no slamming doors or rude comments. Simonetta helps Graham and Jeremy lift the automaton and takes her own place on the other side. Laden with machinery, they cross the garden.

Jeremy's workshop is more like a makeshift garage. A wooden, steepled awning had been built atop the remnants of a stone structure, likely the original wood shop. Its proximity to the forest makes it easy to source wood and bring back fallen trees or other discoveries. It lacks doors on either side, open to the elements. Right outside against the left wall is a neat stack of logs, cut down to the right shape and size for use on the terrace fire pit and the many hearths within the chateau.

It's as organized as a workspace can be, one in constant use. Shelves are heavy with jars of stains and lacquers, tools are hung and labeled on pegboards mounted to the walls. In-progress projects each have their own space, a few chairs, a bed frame, and even a pew Simonetta recognizes from the chapel, covered in cloth to keep them free of sawdust. It smells sublime, the sharp scents of cedar and spruce filling the air. Overall, it's a comfortable, practical, and organized workspace that delights Simonetta, tickles her senses that crave order.

They set the automaton down on a wooden platform with wheels, increasing the machine's height by nearly a foot and making it officially taller than Simonetta herself. A fissure of excitement runs through her and she can't wait to see the state of it. She guesses, hopes, its interior is in decent condition, protected as it has been by the immovable wood door with its shoddy lock, but she'll find a way to repair whatever she discovers inside, no matter how rusted or tangled.

Simonetta thanks Graham and Lotte profusely for their help as they say their goodbyes. Pleading silently with Graham—*don't go!*—the message doesn't get through, and she is left alone with Jeremy and her violin girl, her new companion.

"Hmm," he says simply, inspecting the cabinet. "Have you tried already to pick the lock?"

"I didn't have picks, but I tried with a bobby pin—something inside is jamming the lock."

He taps his chin. "There's no outward hinge, but we can probably pop it open carefully."

Already tried that, thinks Simonetta, but his attempt will probably be more successful: he evaluates his wall of tools, selecting crowbars of various sizes along with a hammer. A hammer would have helped, she agrees; she had the leverage but not the right impact. Simonetta watches as he fits the sharp end of each crowbar into the thin slat separating the door from the cabinet. The smallest one fits the easiest, without having to wedge it further and risk splintering more wood. Simonetta sheepishly acknowledges to herself that she should have never even tried without the proper tools.

Satisfied with his selection, Jeremy holds the crowbar steady within the slat and lifts his hammer to knock it in. "Ready?"

Simonetta nods, holding her breath.

With a deft *smack!*, Jeremy hammers in the crowbar just enough to wedge it under the small lock. With a satisfying snap and click, the door swings open.

Inside, like a labyrinthine cave system under a mountain, is a gleaming mass of machinery—gold wire strung through copper gears in an intricate mechanism. It was remarkable, the detail and intricacy.

She exhales. Most of it is in good shape. There's a knot of wires that will need to be unraveled and some parts that don't seem to connect to the right pieces, but those seem like fixable problems. Above all she's relieved that nothing from her anxiety visions transpired. Jeremy's being perfectly pleasant, and she has yet to do anything to change that.

Giddy over her new project, she crouches down to peer further into the cabinet. On the back of the cabinet door is a golden plate depicting a rose and serif lettering encircled in an oval—presumably, the maker of the automaton. Simonetta touches the grooves in the design before she takes in what it says.

The maker's mark reads: *ALTOBELLA*

Eight

Mullion: A vertical division of stone separating units of a window.

———————— ⚬ ⚬ ⚬ ————————

IT TAKES SIMONETTA a full minute to process the sight, that this discovery is out of the ordinary and her brain should react accordingly. She's seen her name in print so many times over the course of her life that it's as familiar to her as her own face, something she takes for granted.

But there, encircled in an oval of gold, is *Altobella* in all capital, flourished letters.

She reaches out to touch it, runs her fingers through the grooves in disbelief. "Am I reading this correctly?"

Jeremy leans in over her shoulder, bringing with him a waft of wood oil and cedar. "Altobella, correct?" He glances back and forth from the maker's mark to Simonetta's shocked face, furrowing his brows in confusion.

Realization dawns and Simonetta balks. "Wait... you *knew*?"

"Huh?"

"There's an object here in France, a place I am *not* from and have never been, with my last name. What are the odds? Why didn't you *say* anything?"

"I thought that's why you were interested in it."

"Why didn't you tell me there was something with an Altobella maker's mark when I first arrived? You know my last name!"

Jeremy shrugs, a gesture that makes fury rise in Simonetta's throat. "I forgot about it, like everyone else has. I've only seen this thing once—when we had to scoot it around as we added the subfloor. But I've never opened the cabinet. I just know the name from a similar maker's mark on the bottom." He tilts the machine slightly on the wheeled platform, revealing a sliver of another, smaller golden plate.

"You could have mentioned it!" Simonetta says, cringing as she hears her voice rising several octaves. Overwhelmed, she forces herself to find ground: *focus on your feet touching the floor, focus on your own breath.* "I don't even know what to do with this information." *Maybe that's why I can't stop thinking about it.* "I attempted to open it on my own first." Admitting her transgression offers some peace, as does the deep breathing and the wiggling of her toes in her shoes.

Now that the cabinet door is open, she sees that the damage she caused is an easy fix—just some sanding to smooth off the roughness. The layers of grime absorbed the scratching. It gives her some relief to know that she didn't break it irrevocably. Now that it bears her name—*why does it say Altobella?* her mind is still asking—she is fiercely protective over it like one takes in a stray animal found matted and hungry.

He crosses his arms and inspects the cabinet. "If you were struggling to open it, why didn't you just ask me to help you first?" He gestures around. "I have the tools for these types of projects."

Speechless, Simonetta sputters in frustration.

"Because you've made it quite clear that you don't think very highly of me," Simonetta says, swallowing an outburst. It wells up anyway and sticks in her throat, turning the back of her tongue sour. "I didn't want to add to my repertoire of mistakes."

Jeremy blinks. "What are you talking about?"

"What are *you* talking about?" Simonetta says. "You've been… *nitpicking* me since the day I arrived!"

Jeremy raises his eyebrows in surprise and Simonetta wants to deflate like a balloon and fly out of the room, propelled by the air filling her chest. But he waits patiently and she is cornered.

She avoids eye contact and continues staring into the automaton cabinet, pleading with it to spontaneously combust so that she has an excuse to flee. "The very first comment you made to me was about my nose," says Simonetta, pushing the hurt and defensiveness out of her voice, although it cowers nearby.

He snorts with laughter and says, "You have a beautiful nose."

That is not the response she expects. It stops her short, dislodges some of the thickness in her throat. She tucks the comment away for later analysis. Still, she's compelled to make her case. Her pride depends on it. Sheepishly, she continues. "It was a weird thing to say to a stranger. And then you yelled at me about the AGA."

"That was my fault," he acknowledges. "I shouldn't have left that task to you so late."

"You didn't *say* any of that. You just embarrassed me in front of everyone as if I was supposed to know how everything in the chateau worked despite having been here for a handful of hours!"

"For that, I am sorry," Jeremy says. Simonetta detects a hint of amusement in his voice, but she is so used to reading his expression as aloof or critical that she suddenly realizes she doesn't know what to think.

Jeremy waits patiently for her to continue, and when she doesn't, he prompts, "Was that it? A compliment, and a miscommunication?"

Simonetta feels foolish continuing the line of questioning. Half-heartedly, she drudges up another past conflict. "You're allergic to tomatoes."

"I am," says Jeremy, now genuinely laughing. "Am I to apologize for that, too?"

"No!" Simonetta says. "Alba and I had made dinner that one night, and we put tomato on everything. You seemed—mad. I didn't know, otherwise we would have made something else."

"How could you have known?" Jeremy answers with a laugh, making no effort any longer to hide his amusement. "Claudel and I should have added it to the food allergies list in the kitchen." He scrubs his face with his hand in an attempt to be serious. "I have yet to hear about the time I insulted you."

Simonetta pauses again, wanting nothing more than to end the conversation and jump into the moat and disappear into the ether. "When Hanako and I went to the grocery store, you yelled at us about the stick shift."

"I don't think I did," he counters, and maybe he's right—*did* he yell, or was she just surprised? "Would you have preferred I let you crash?" he says, raising an eyebrow. It disappears beneath the fringe of dark curls. "It wasn't your driving I was concerned about—it's a quirk of the car. I just wanted you to be aware of it. I much prefer you to come back in one piece."

Simonetta is speechless. She runs a hand through her hair, where it catches on her bobby pin. She yanks it out in a less than graceful gesture and the bobby pin flies out, landing among the sawdust. Her hair tumbles down from the bun and she feels unspooled, unraveled.

"Well, now that you're making me say this all aloud, it sounds ridiculous!" She tosses her hands up in the air, a gesture that reminds her of Nonna. "Am I supposed to just take your lack of communication as some sort of display of begrudging respect? Like, 'when a boy is mean to you, it means he likes you' nonsense? Jeremy, that's so *juvenile*."

"Simonetta," Jeremy says calmly. It's the first time she's heard him say her name, and it stops her short. There's an underlying current of respect in the way he says it, and the anger seeps out of her bit by bit. "Listen. I am truly sorry that I gave you the wrong impression. I'm not the most—" he waves his hand, reaching for the right word, "—*talkative* person. I like doing things on my own, being by myself. Lots of people come and go through the work-stay program, and I try not to get too attached to anyone." He puts a hand on his heart in a genuine display of penance. "I apologize for not being more forthright with you."

So much has changed in a mere minute that Simonetta simply blinks as if it will process her thoughts more quickly. "For weeks I've been avoiding you! You should see the way I've mapped out your schedule so I didn't run into you."

"I'm flattered you've thought so much about me," he says. His impish grin is back and he extends a hand. "Mon ami?"

Friends? Are they? All Simonetta knows about Jeremy is that he's allergic to tomatoes, seems incapable of washing sawdust out of his hair, doesn't like to socialize, and thinks she has a beautiful nose.

She supposes she could be friends with someone who holds that opinion. Had she really read more into every interaction they had for no reason? Had she truly plotted out another person's schedule for the sole purpose of avoiding minor conflict? Yes, of course she did. She always does. She *doesn't* usually spill the contents of her mind to someone else—Jeremy would be well within his rights to call out her irrationality.

But he doesn't. He offers her friendship.

"Oui," she agrees, and clasps her hand with his. His palm is warm and dry, and he gives her hand a light squeeze before releasing it.

"Where is your accent from?" she blurts suddenly, unleashing a dormant curiosity.

Jeremy laughs again, and it seems a lighter sound to Simonetta now, less cruel, now that she has a bit more insight. "My mother is Irish. She lives in Ireland, near Galway. I visit her once a year. Claudel is my aunt on my father's side."

Simonetta silently surveys Jeremy's features, the dark hair, dark eyes fringed by long curled eyelashes, the dark growth of a two-day beard. They exchange a long, awkward look at each other for a long, awkward moment before turning back to the automaton.

"I don't even know where to start," Simonetta admits. "Of all of the discoveries, this is the last thing I expected." *That's a lie*, she thinks, and waits for him to call her on it. She has been forcing this very moment since she committed to going to France.

Jeremy crosses his arms and holds a finger to his chin. "Do you think there's any relation?"

Simonetta shrugs. "I honestly have no idea. As an Italian surname, it's not the most common, but it's not unheard of, either. I don't know much about Altobellas beyond my grandfather's generation."

"There used to be an Altobella Factory in Villaggio Primavera," Jeremy muses. "Not far beyond the border—a few hours away from here. But I think they make farm equipment." He pauses to think. "Where are your grandparents from?"

Simonetta's stomach clenches. "There's a factory? Nearby?" She pauses to think. "I don't know much. My mother's parents raised me—they're both gone now. My Nonna, she was a Cavalieri and I think her family was from a place called Cassinasco. In Italy, women don't take their husband's name when they marry, so she was always Emilia Cavalieri." Simonetta pauses. "But I have no idea about the Altobella side. I never have, really." Simonetta chews on her lip in thought. "Nonno was always mum about it. Some big family secret, I guess."

"And your parents?" Jeremy asks.

"Don't know my father, or that extended lineage." Simonetta reaches out to fix a loose wiry hair that has sprung loose from the automaton's head. "My mother died when I was six, from cancer."

Simonetta appreciates that his thoughtful expression is devoid of pity. Simonetta has never pitied herself—she remembers bits and pieces of her mother, has pictures and memories, and she has grown used to the void left in her absence, felt most keenly through her teen years. She wrote off her father long ago. But Nonna and Nonno had done everything for her, and it was an upbringing she cherished. Their absence leaves a much bigger void behind.

"How did you come to be here?" Jeremy asks, veering the subject in a new direction and into a path Simonetta avoids treading.

"What do you mean?" says Simonetta, frowning. "I applied through the website—"

"I guess I should rephrase it as, 'Why?'" he says. "What appeal does Desrosiers hold for you?"

It's the question Simonetta has asked herself many times before she made the move overseas, and many times since. "Nonna died last November," Simonetta explains. "I used to watch *Daily Life* with her and she loved it." What would Nonna think now, of Simonetta talking to Jeremy? She hopes she has earned a hand pat from the beyond. "She was my last living family member, the person I've been closest to my whole life. I realized that, although I had friends, I was alone in the world." Simonetta crosses her arms. "In a way, it awarded me a freedom I've never had. I could do anything—no one was keeping me where I was. I applied and hoped it would give me something to throw myself into."

"And is it helping?" Jeremy asks, cutting to the heart of it.

"I ask myself that every day," says Simonetta. "Yes. For the most part, it's all been enjoyable and eye-opening and a good challenge for me." She grins good-naturedly. "Except for you, being a thorn in my side."

Jeremy laughs. "I'll do my best to extract that from you." He holds her gaze for another weighted moment.

Simonetta clears her throat. "Do you suppose Claudel has books about automatons?"

"It's possible. The library is quite extensive. Viewers of her channel send her books all the time. You might even ask her to mention it during her next livestream."

That's a resource Simonetta hasn't considered. Claudel's livestreams have a dedicated following; every week, thousands of viewers tune in from around the world. Soon, she will interview the summer volunteers, something that Simonetta is slightly dreading. But it's an opportunity to ask Claudel's online community—full of passionate history buffs and experts—for their insight.

Jeremy walks around the automaton, surveying it. "It's odd, but don't you think the doll resembles Catelot?"

Simonetta blinks. "What's a Catelot?"

"Catelot—Catherine—Desrosiers was the daughter of the chateau's first family back in the 1300s. She was the only person from her family to survive the plague that took out most of Sainte-Madeleine, which was even smaller then. Quite a sad story, really. Anyway, her portrait is in the left wing, above the balustrade."

Simonetta knows the one: a young girl's pale moon face,

haloed by dark hair wound with ribbon. She wears a red dress with green sleeves befitting a daughter of her birth status. Behind her is the forest, with deer hiding among the trees—Catelot's silent protectors. There are many portraits in the chateau, most of them acquisitions whose subjects were unrelated to the chateau other than through relevant eras, to help put the chateau in the context of history in a way visitors could understand. One notable portrait in the entry hall depicts Marguerite de Sainte-Madeleine, a noble woman and the Desrosiers chatelaine in the 1700s. But it hasn't occurred to Simonetta that other portraits in the building portrayed other former residents, especially the very first.

"That's remarkable," she says. "That would make this automaton closely linked to Desrosiers, like it was *made* here and didn't just *end up* here."

"Claudel may know or can point you in the right direction. The lore is that Catelot's guardian—a servant who survived the plague and took ownership of the young girl—painted the portrait. I'm sure there's a story there, if you did deep enough." He leans forward, hands on knees, to inspect the doll more intently. "I only brought it up because there's an odd similarity: the doll has a birthmark painted on her right cheek, which is also depicted in Catelot's portrait."

Simonetta leans beside him to inspect the discovery. He's right—what she had mistaken for a circle of blush was, in fact, a slightly irregular blotch of red near the doll's ear.

"Is the doll supposed to be Catelot, then?" she wonders. "There's no way this machine could be that old, the mechanisms are far too anachronistic. And the violin—those didn't even exist in the 1300s. That was centuries later."

"Yes, but the doll itself is made of a different material, I think." Jeremy pulls back the doll's sleeve, then points to its arm and the violin. "Ah, look—I'm willing to be someone added the joints in much later. See where the wood changes slightly where the elbow crooks?"

Shocked, Simonetta asks, "Do you think the doll is from the 1300s? Can wood survive that long? Is that a stupid question?"

Simonetta knows how long well-preserved paper and other materials can last, but wooden artifacts are slightly outside of her repertoire.

"No, it's not stupid. Plenty of ancient and medieval wood structures and artifacts have stood the test of time, especially if care was taken to treat the wood. There seems to be some sort of lacquer applied, probably a pine tar." He shrugs. "It would take someone with more technology than me to properly date it, but it's certainly possible. The chateau has many relics from its inception—we're quite lucky to have what we have. It could be that someone had the doll adapted to the automaton. If you look, they cut out some of the doll's back to fit in the gear boxes—ouch! It's sharp, don't touch the gears, we'll have to file those down slightly—and then built the cabinet to accommodate all of the engineering," he says. "That's old as well, as is the technology. You'll have to research it to date it. My knowledge only goes so far."

Simonetta had mostly overlooked the automaton's cabinet in favor of its more fascinating top, but when she takes another look, she appreciates the artistry—the ornately carved panels (one slightly splintered, thanks to her), the routed edges. The automaton is rather large and Simonetta has a sudden, wild urge to hide inside the lower cabinet, to shut herself off from the world and be alone with the girl and her violin.

"Will it be safe if we keep it in here?" Simonetta asks. "I'm not sure it will fit in my room, and, as you said—" she gestures around her "—you have all the tools."

"It's no problem," Jeremy says. "On one condition: you have to share your findings with me." He starts riffling through a drawer and pulls out a roll of linen to cover the doll. "I'm invested now, you see. I hadn't thought much of this automaton in the years we've had it, truthfully, but I'm curious."

"Deal," Simonetta says, feeling like she is easily getting the better end of the bargain.

Simonetta stands under the portrait of Catelot. Now that she's looking at it, really studying it, she sees the resemblance between the young girl in the painting and the delicate doll. Jeremy is right; a small port wine stain marks Catelot's left ear, in the same spot the doll has a small blush dot.

The late afternoon sunlight from the stained-glass window reaches out to illuminate Catelot's face, as if the sun serves as a spotlight on the painting so that Simonetta can see it in its full detail.

She sits on the balustrade, smooth and gleaming from Jeremy's work, appreciates that she may no longer have to avoid this area of the chateau. Despite the sunlight, it's pleasantly cool in the entry hall. The stone walls fend off the heat, and Simonetta enjoys the respite from the humidity.

The portrait is peculiar, although she has little frame of reference for 14th-century art that would have been contemporary to Catelot's artist. There is something Botticelli-esque in the lines of Catelot's face, but unlike the Italian portraits Simonetta is more familiar with, featuring the subject looking away, Catelot gazes straight toward the viewer. Her face is oval, with the plump cheeks fitting of a young noble daughter. Her dark hair is braided away from her pale face, but the long end of the braid drapes over her shoulder, rests atop her dark green kirtle like a tree branch leaning over her shoulder. It seems a casual detail, almost modern to Simonetta—formal portraits often depicted their noble subjects in their finery, liberties taken to improve their appearance. The casual braid, tied off with a white ribbon that looks to be a strip of linen, seems so unique, such a thoughtful detail, that she is sure there is significance to it.

Catelot is painted standing before the tree line of the forest. Simonetta recognizes that same tree line, to the north of the chateau, not far beyond the ancient wing. It occurs to Simonetta that the chateau's initial construction as a fortress likely required clearing the forest to source the timber and the stones, and that its modern tree line is a 600-year-old relic of the past. The thought astounds her; the Catelot doll was likely made from wood sourced in that very forest. Jeremy told her that oak and sometimes walnut were the woods of choice in the 14th century. The trees in the forest are ancient and it raises the goosebumps on Simonetta's arms to think of herself traversing the same forest Catelot may have once explored. Did Catelot love the forest? Is that why her painter depicted her where she did?

The door opens, letting in a hint of heat that dissipates quickly, the humidity finding no purchase in the chilly hall.

"I was actually just thinking of coming to find you," says Simonetta to Hanako and Jason, who have just entered the hall. They wave and meet her on the balustrade. "Do you mind if I ask you two some questions about this painting?"

"It's different, I'll give you that," says Jason.

Simonetta relays the discovery of the automaton to them both, explains Jeremy's theory about the Catelot doll. Hanako gasps at the reveal of the Altobella name, a detail Simonetta glosses over quickly, as she is still deducing her own feelings toward the discovery.

"Simonetta! That's serendipitous, don't you think?"

"Is it?" Simonetta shrugs casually, although her stomach clenches again, as it has every time she thinks about it. "There may not be any relation. As of now, it's just a peculiar coincidence." She nods toward the portrait. "But I am curious about the doll and the portrait. It does seem like they both depict Catherine Desrosiers. But there are details in this painting I don't understand." She points to the braid, to the forest behind.

Jason peers in. "What's interesting to me is the composition. It's very direct. This style of portraiture wasn't really in fashion for another century."

"And the colors are slightly muted... how do you think the painter sourced their dye?" speculates Hanako.

Hanako and Jason muse amongst themselves, discussing art theory far above Simonetta's own knowledge. She mentally catalogs some of their initial analysis, adding it to the file systems forming in her brain. A warmth blooms in her chest and she knows why. The ley line pulses in her palm. A North Star guides her way.

Nine

SYMONNE
1347

LONG BEFORE THE CHATEAU was the jewel of Sainte-Madeleine, before the town around it even existed and had a name, it was a humble stone fortress nestled in the wild foothills of the ancient Southern Alps. What the fortress lacked in beauty it made up for in practicality—the heavy stones, sourced from the local forest, were painstakingly stacked with just the precise pattern to keep the walls strong and upright without the use of mortar, the rooflines slightly pitched to foster snow runoff in the winter. The fortress kept out enemies: beasts from the forest and mountains, armies from the north and west. Its remote location promised to keep its inhabitants, the many servants lured to the fortress with promise of work and stability and access to an abundance of resources, safe in their own private hamlet.

But even the strongest of stone cannot keep out a plague. The Black Death swept across the globe on its several-hundred-year-long tour, reaching its skeletal, pock-marked fingers into populous cities and trade routes. In winter of 1347, Marseilles was at the heart of the blight. The bustling city was brought to its knees in months, a bluster of pustules and choking. A terrible aroma rose over the cobblestone streets, the already stinking scents of city life now mingled with the rot of bloated bodies floating in the Mediterranean bay.

Had Roland Desrosiers not gone to Marseilles on business, he might have abstained from bringing the plague home to his family and his brand-new estate. The fortress was nearly finished; the western tower stood proud and sentinel, and the fortress' central hall needed just one more section completed. It was his pride and joy, this construction, an estate to call his own. For a humble son of a sailor, Roland's rise to riches was the result of sheer tenacity and a knack for timing opportunities.

The sickness was no matter, he thought. He'd recover on the journey home, try what the healers called "quarantine"—he was leaving the city anyway and would isolate on the road. It was what the shrewd merchants in Venice did: isolate themselves from those ailing on the ships carrying their goods and wealth. Enough isolation and prayer and fasting, and one would simply abstain from perishing, God will it.

He was two hours dead by the time he returned home to the half-finished fortress. By then, his wagon driver Joss was also feeling poorly, and Roland's young and lovely wife, Cateline, threw herself upon Roland's festering body, to her own detriment.

It didn't take long for the Black Death to sweep through the fortress. The staffing there was still minimal but servants, the stewards and the seamstresses and the grooms and the cooks lured there with promise of shelter and food, quickly succumbed; others fled to their families in the nearby village. Cateline brought her daughter, three-year-old Catherine, to her chamber to ride it out or meet their maker together. Catherine squirmed and cried in her mother's arms, until they no longer moved to soothe her.

It took three days for the laundress Symonne to find the girl. That's all the time it took for the plague to bring the newly blossoming Desrosiers to its knees. Down the stable boys had gone, followed shortly by Catherine's nurse, Marcella, whom Symonne had found collapsed in the hall en route to the kitchens.

Symonne had done her best to keep Marcella comfortable, knowing that it was already fruitless to keep her distance. A deep existentialist fear had pushed Symonne into action—her own days were numbered, and she might as well perish in pursuit of service. Her own mother was a healer, and Symonne had seen from a young age the great lengths her mother went to keep her patients comfortable, no matter the personal cost. Symonne had employed all she had learned, patting Marcella's forehead with damp linen, dribbling ale into her swollen throat, placing poultices over the huge lumps on the side of it to eke out the puss, but the fever persisted.

The resignation that she, too, was likely next up on the list of severed mortality left Symonne feeling hollow and fatigued, but two days after Marcella perished, Symonne awoke in the stables feeling surprisingly rested. The grounds were quiet, save for the birds rustling in the trees along the forest border. The sounds of the Desrosiers fortress were now ghostly echoes—no horses neighed, no axes met log, no cauldrons bubbled with food, no spinning wheels whirred and tugged at unrefined fiber. Even the kegs of ale had already gone rancid, as if catalyzed by the death that permeated everything in and around the chateau. The sharp, yeasty scent caught Symonne's nose as she passed through the kitchens, across the bailey, and went out to the stream to bathe.

The water rippled and gurgled over stones, and she stepped into the cool depths. She disrobed while submerged and attempted to scrub the remnants of sickness from her woolen dress, but the bloodstains persisted. Instead, she let the dress float lazily to the shore and stretched out naked on her back.

The trees formed strange patterns above her. She had never existed in such quiet. The home of her upbringing was filled with children; there was never a moment where she had a room or a bed or a trencher to herself. Leaving home was a sweet relief, and she had spent nearly a decade as a seamstress in the village before Roland Desrosiers swept through it one day, promising room and purpose for those who wished to serve at his new fortress. Newly ennobled, Desrosiers still had to recruit a staff on his own. Symonne had been at Desrosiers for mere months before the plague struck.

She felt keenly both the absence of external senses and the amplification of her own internal existence—the beating of her heart, the water sloshing against her ears, the goosebumps forming on her torso and breasts breaking the surface of the water. She was very aware of her own mortality and scanned her body for any signs of sickness, but felt, if anything, healthier than she had in many years. The lack of pressing work and the chance to bathe and breathe with leisure reinvigorated her.

A splash and a subsequent twig snapping brought her abruptly out of her daydream. Symonne sat up, sputtering, and looked around the forest. She saw nothing, no creature nor human lurking nearby, but circles rippled on the surface of the stream next to her, as if a stone had been tossed in.

In the distance, she heard a child crying.

Donning her heavy, sopping, blood-stained dress, Symonne followed the sound.

She traced the cries back through the forest, across the grounds, into the fortress, up the stairs. The stench of death and decay met her nose, but the crying persisted and so did she, taking a deep breath and rounding the corner—

Cateline Desrosiers, three days dead, lay curled on her side, arms cradling nothing. It was a pose Symonne had learned about from her mother, who often assisted in childbirths—a woman could safely sleep on her side, curled around her child, even when the babe was freshly born, without fear of crushing them. There was a secret sense that mothers held that prevented them from sleeping too deeply and rolling over on their child. This is the pose in which Cateline perished, this protective stance in which she cradled her young Catherine, and the only solace it gave Symonne in this vignette of loss was that it worked.

Little Catherine, disheveled and stinking of death, stood hale and whole beside her mother, screaming.

Ten

Portcullis: A sliding wooden door embedded in a gateway, lowered to protect a castle or enclosed village.

SIMONETTA

SIMONETTA EARNS HERSELF a half-day off and heads to the library in sleepy, ancient Sainte-Madeleine. She borrows the sputtering, clunky Renault, promising to fill it up with fuel and pick up bread from the boulangerie before dinner, and drives through rolling hills dotted with wildflowers.

After several days of letting her mind percolate about the automaton, Simonetta sprung into research mode. It reminds her fondly of her time in graduate school—once again, having a purpose, a goal, clarified everything around her. She is determined to understand the automaton's history, to bring it back to life, to make it pristine and perfect. She wants to know about Catelot and the violin and the cabinet and the machinery, all of it. The story of the automaton is found within its many layers, and Simonetta secretly resolves not to leave France until she has answers. Realistically, she has until late August.

A few preliminary Google searches turned up short. Thousands of Altobellas exist in the world, and no digital archives she has access to had records about an inventor named Altobella located in or around Provence. She is sure the maker's mark is a family name, since that's how names and marks traditionally worked, although it was certainly possible the maker had chosen the name for a multitude of reasons she would never know. Jeremy had mentioned an Altobella Factory several hours away, which piqued Simonetta's research senses and personal interest. Geographical proximity made sense, although all she could find about the factory's minimal online presence was that it had sold farming equipment since the 1920s.

As for her own Altobella link, any connection between herself and the automaton, that's tenuous as well. Simonetta is begrudgingly aware of what motivates her intense interest in this project—the smallest of sparks of possibility that she could potentially be connected to other Altobellas outside of her close family circle. At first, the discovery seemed utterly coincidental, comical almost (truly, what are the odds?) but she tries instead to think of it as serendipitous, to use the word Hanako had exclaimed.

Simonetta revels in the time alone. Although she's often solo in her tasks, there is always someone around at the chateau; there is never a moment when someone else in the building isn't awake, working, socializing, existing. It brings her comfort, the constant community and camaraderie that surrounds her, but on occasion she longs for a second alone to just be.

As she reaches the tiny medieval town, she becomes suspended in time—she thinks of her home in the Bay, the technology and the glossy cars and the graffiti and the tall buildings, all a stark contrast from this hamlet with its small stone buildings winding labyrinthine around the hilltop. She parks the Renault in a flat area just outside of the town. Everything seems small, somehow—the mini European cars, the humble homes and shops—against the gorgeous expansive environment surrounding it all. Simonetta appreciates how the town simply exists on the hill, how the stone structures are embedded in the side of the mountain like rows of uneven teeth. There is no competition between the human life that has found a home here and the ancient landscape that predates it. The inhabitants have let nature run wild, vines and foliage climbing up the facades and the longest tendrils spilling over roofs and windows. Wildflowers and weeds poke up through the cracks in the cobblestone. Mushrooms have bloomed along the town's main street, the soil lush from the recent warm rain.

She takes a deep breath and the fresh air filters through her senses. Even with the din of the townsfolk socializing, shopping, and working, it's so quiet. In this moment it gives her a sense of tranquility, but Simonetta can't decide if she misses life in a city. Living in a place like this holds a certain appeal—life here is slow, thoughtful, intentional, harmonious. Not without its challenges, but the pace allows a person the chance to process and do one thing at a time.

Is that the balm for a soul in turmoil like hers? Or would the quiet just bring all of it bubbling to the surface? Maybe she needs the hustle of city life to keep the demons at bay.

She focuses on the trek into town instead of the uncertain future that lingers in her mind always. From her pocket she retrieves a small hand-drawn map from Claudel, who sketched out the town and marked some notable locations for Simonetta: including the brocante, owned by Claudel's friends Paul and Malcolm (both history buffs), and the reason for Simonetta's visit today, a library that also serves as the local branch of the historical society.

En route to the library toward the north end of town, Simonetta passes the boulangerie, from which the pleasant and comforting aromas of yeast and sugar emanate. Her stomach growls; she had opted for coffee this morning which left her jittery, a decision made worse by the pain au chocolat she consumed with it. Eggs and toast would have been the smarter choice instead of caffeine and sugar, but the sensation of being hungry, jittery, and a bit anxious reminds her of her early twenties researcher's diet.

This is the mentality she conjures as she arrives at the bibliotheque. Like every spot in town, the library is, for lack of a better word, quaint, which doesn't instill confidence in Simonetta. On a normal day, being in a small, ancient library in a small, ancient town would have checked every box on Simonetta's Happy List, but today, the library's size works against her—how will she ever find what she needs here?

She pushes open the wooden door and steps into the lobby. The library is one wide, cavernous space with a domed ceiling. A skylight in the center of the dome brings in a soft beam of sunlight. Books of all shapes, sizes, and topics are stacked in precariously tall piles. More are packed tightly onto shelves bowing from the weight. Simonetta spots a microfiche machine in the back corner—that could be useful, actually—and a row of computers with CRT monitors that are a couple of decades old.

At the circulation desk sits a middle-aged woman with cropped gray hair, riffling through a box of papers. If Simonetta had been asked to describe a "French librarian," this woman would be it.

She swallows and opens her mouth to ask the simple phrases she rehearsed with Claudel: "Bonjou—"

"Americaine?" says the woman, her head snapping up.

Simonetta flushes. "Er—oui. How did you know?"

"Most locals don't lurk in the lobby, or say hello," the librarian answers in accented, but otherwise perfectly pleasant, English. Her face, however, expresses her annoyance at having to use it. "Can I help you?"

Simonetta retrieves her journal from her purse and opens it to the page she dog-eared the night before. "I'm looking for any resources you have about art local to this region."

The librarian beckons Simonetta over and leads her into the library, past several rows of tall, teetering shelves. Simonetta tries to learn the lay of the land, but the librarian—shorter than Simonetta by several inches, but somehow faster in step—weaves her expertly through the maze. She stops abruptly in front of an arched shelf onto which a faded piece of paper reads "L'art de France." Books of various shapes and sizes line the shelves, and Simonetta can make out regional names on the spines. Most of the books are, predictably, written in French, but a few are in English. She selects some, the shelf wobbling as she disturbs the disorganization, and the librarian leads her to a table and leaves her to her research.

She flips through the books, looking for any art that may loosely resemble the Catelot painting. After an hour of closely studying each page in a book about art in Provence, Simonetta closes it in a huff.

Discouraged, she takes the books back to the shelf and begins to reshelve them where she selected them when the librarian hurries over.

"*Non*, I do it," she says, waving Simonetta away.

Simonetta instead sits at an old computer logged into a French search database and opens her notebook to her research plans.

Perhaps art is the wrong starting point—she doesn't have to start with Catelot just because it's a piece of the puzzle that intrigues her. She goes back to the basics and starts by researching automatons, which seems like an obvious, if broad, first search.

She gleans quickly that the history of automata is extensive, with roots in ancient times. Upon learning about the complexity of ancient Greek machinery, the prospect of Catelot dating to the 1300s doesn't seem quite so outlandish, although the machinery within absolutely post-dates the doll. The cabinet is trickier. The discrepancy of design and material between the doll, the violin, the mechanisms, and the cabinet itself just seems too great for it to lack significance. Catelot is beautifully made, but the wood doll lacks the glossy texture and deft hand that forms the cabinet. Simonetta is compelled to follow her gut, a necessary component in her personal creed.

She drills down her search further to musical automata. It's clear that musical machinery has long been an interest of humans. She uncovers several fascinating gems of history in an issue of Mechanism and Machine Theory, which references "singing birds" from ancient Greece and water-powered "clocks" from ancient China that told the time through the ringing of bells. While these are interesting to her, her automaton is from a later era, so the next article she finds is far more promising: Jacques de Vaucanson, a Frenchman who lived in the 1700s, was a famous inventor and artist who designed several notable musical automatons. The era, the location, and the types of automatons de Vaucanson made, like an intricately designed flute player, all align with her own discovery, Simonetta notes.

De Vaucanson was even from Grenoble, which was not too far away from Sainte-Madeleine. Was that a thread worth pursuing?

It gives her much on which to percolate. What would be helpful is if she could uncover some schematics. Lacking an engineer's experience to make her own, she started a crude color-coded system that she hopes will keep her experimentation organized.

Satisfied with what she's found so far, she attempts to input "Altobella automaton" into the search engine in various combinations, employing every variation of the terms and all the search approaches she learned in library school, but nothing relevant shows up beyond social media profiles of other Altobellas from around the world.

She clicks through a dozen of them before giving up in frustration. What she's trying to figure out is threefold:

How does the automaton work?

When was it made?

Who made it?

She also wants to know the elusive why? but maybe that's an impossible question. Similarly, the question that truly won't leave her alone is: *why was I the one to find it again?*

SYMONNE

In her quest to take care of Catherine, Symonne found that there were, in fact, plenty of signs of life throughout the forest and grounds. What she had interpreted as hallowed silence in the aftermath of the plague seemed to be nature taking a deep breath of revelry in the absence of humans.

Symonne wrapped the thin and shivering child in the long, ornate cloth she found in the Lady Cateline's dowry trunk, strapped her to her back, and set off in search of sustenance. Little Catherine gulped down the goat's milk, practically inhaled the stale bread Symonne found tucked away in the kitchens, eagerly consumed the dried salted slices of onion and fish.

The girl looked up at Symonne with wide, dark eyes, said a calm "thank you," and settled into Symonne's chest to sleep.

For days, Catherine remained glued to Symonne. Symonne remembered fondly the way her own little siblings clung to her in the absence of their mother, and she enjoyed being needed. She did her best to placate the young girl, who, unlike her rambunctious little siblings, was quiet and observant. At first Symonne feared that the girl had been afflicted with the sickness, for she made almost no noise for the first day after her initial screaming that had summoned Symonne. Then Symonne grew worried that the girl was traumatized by witnessing her mother's death. But several days into their new rhythm together, when Symonne presented the girl with a small round oat biscuit to break her fast, the girl said, "Catelot."

"What?" Symonne was caught off guard by the small voice.

"My name," said the girl. "They call me Catelot."

The mention of her parents made Symonne's heart ache. She wanted to take the girl into her arms and comfort her, but abstained; she was still earning her trust. Instead, she asked, "Can I call you Catelot?"

Catelot nodded and nibbled her biscuit, looking up at Symonne with those luminous eyes. The girl's small red birthmark reminded Symonne of a drop of paint, and she wondered what plants she would have to source to recreate the color as dye. Catelot was a beautiful child, Symonne thought, and certainly the majority of that came from her mother. Young Cateline, with her long, silky dark hair and olive skin was the very image of a noble lady, even if she had been relegated to a rural life in an unfinished fortress.

"You can call me Symonne, if you'd like?" Symonne offered.

Catelot cocked her head to the side as if weighing this monumental decision. "Mama?"

Was she asking for her mother? Or asking for permission to call Symonne mama?

Once Catelot finished eating, she held out her arms. Perplexed by the speed at which Catelot had accepted her as her new guardian, Symonne obeyed and lifted the girl into her own. Small arms closed around her neck and Symonne sighed with pleasure at the embrace. She carried Catelot around the fortress during her daily sweep of errands. It had been years since she had embraced a child, and it made her feel whole.

SIMONETTA

The forest grounds near the chateau teem with life and the stirrings of deep spring awaken within Simonetta. She follows Jeremy down a trodden trail, across a rickety platform called a "moon bridge." When the river is still, the arched bridge curving over the water is reflected in the surface, forming a perfect O. And when one can view it from the ideal angle, the moon bridge encircles an enchanting view combining glimpses of the forest and river and sky, appearing like a portal into a mystical realm. Jeremy holds out a hand to Simonetta to aid in her crossing, pointing out the rotting planks that could give way with too much pressure, and the residual warmth in her palm takes its time to dissipate.

"Another project for this summer," Jeremy says, pointing to the crumbling slats in the bridge once they have both safely crossed.

In her effort to learn more about Catelot and evaluate the automaton from the top down, Simonetta holds fast to her starting theory: that the doll was made from materials in the local forest. Upon musing this aloud, Jeremy had offered to take her on a tour to show her what he assumed was native to the region and what was added later. Like rings in an individual tree, he explained, the order of trees in the forest hearkens to the history of the entire region.

Simonetta wasn't sure how much interest the forest held for her—she liked natural landscapes well enough, having spent her formative years in the fog-choked, grassy parks of the Bay Area—and accepted the invitation with lukewarm reception and mild curiosity. But now that she was immersed in it, she couldn't soak it in fast enough. It was still early in the day (Jeremy whisked her off before she could even have tea, to her chagrin) and the soft rays of sun set the dew-drenched trees alight on their branches. Pine needles sparkle, their points dripping dew like thousands of tiny paint brushes. Springing up from the soil are meaty mushrooms and verdant ferns unfurling at the first touch of light. The air is fresh and clear, and Simonetta takes hearty deep breaths that reach into her soul.

Jeremy, meanwhile, babbles about types of wood.

"Most of the these here are oak," he explains, glancing upward at the towering trees. "The varieties of oak trees here are mostly native to the region. We have different types of pine trees, too—" he points to the conifers with their dripping dew needles "—and throughout the country you'll find lots of plane trees. Their wide leaves provide lots of shade. You can thank Napoleon for that."

"Really? Why?"

"He had them planted strategically to provide shade for his troops, and sometimes to indicate an intersection or crossroads. Pretty clever, really. I doubt he could have anticipated that he would have an irrevocable impact on France's ecosystem." He places a hand reverently on a trunk, a gesture Simonetta finds endearing. "There's so much history and context even in the wilderness. It's rare for any place on this planet to remain truly wild and untouched by human impact."

She is beginning to recognize the topics that bring aloof, abrasive Jeremy to life. The automaton project is among these, and so is the forest, both of which make sense to her, given his role at the chateau and his career as a carpenter. But his passion for certain topics transcends his career and familial obligations— being a craftsman is his life's purpose. It's what drives him. Like herself, Jeremy enjoys having a project and a purpose. It gives them a conduit for their thoughts.

They traverse the forest for an hour, forgetting their original reason for being there, instead distracted by the delights and surprises of the wilderness. Simonetta can't remember the last time she explored for the sake of exploring, and it awakens something primal within her. She remembers that existing can be simple, that life takes its course without care for intent or impact. Roots breaking a large boulder in half remind her that sheer tenacity is a long game. Moss and fungi dappling the rotted trunk of a fallen tree demonstrate that growth exists in a state of chaos. There is nothing perfect about nature, and yet it is the ultimate system of pattern.

Jeremy eventually suggests they head back to the chateau for breakfast, his inquiry breaking the spell. She follows him back, accepts his hand again across the rickety bridge, and crosses back into the threshold of reality.

SYMONNE

If Symonne was Catelot's guardian angel, then someone else was Symonne's.

From that eerie day where she had lay in the river and a dropped pebble had alerted her to Catelot's cry, Symonne had a strange sensation of being watched but very little tangible evidence, other than occasional goosebumps on her arms and mysterious gifts that arose from time to time.

Was it just the mental scattered that accompanied motherhood that caused her to forget that she had already bundled those herbs? No, she certainly didn't remember weaving them into an herbal wreath. And what about the bread, warm and soft in the oven? She didn't even recall kneading the dough, which was Catelot's favorite part of the bread-making process. She checked under Catelot's fingernails for traces of flour but found only dirt from the little girl's passion for digging up loamy soil along the riverbanks where Symonne took them to bathe.

Symonne was sure it wasn't Bertrand, the former stable hand who had also emerged unscathed from the sickness. Bertrand, gray hair thinning on his wrinkly head, stalked around the grounds, nose in the air, self-appointing himself the new Desrosiers chamberlain; devout and curmudgeonly, Bertrand never hesitated to espouse his staunch beliefs that those who survived the plague were among God's Chosen People.

Bertrand and Symonne tolerated one another, as her survival also meant that God had chosen to spare her and who was he to argue with God? But there was little love shared, and she preferred to keep her distance. No, she was positive it wasn't Bertrand leaving her small gifts. Nor did she think it was Old Marthe, one of Cateline Desrosiers's personal attendants who had been absent during the plague on family matters and returned to find her mistress buried and the fortress empty. Old Marthe seemed pleased with the turn of events, no longer living a life of servitude, and was more than happy to let Symonne serve as Catelot's caretaker.

"I've done enough taking care of others," Old Marthe told Symonne one cold evening. Together they sat in front of the grand hearth in the fortress's largest chamber, where it had walls but little else. Catelot was asleep and sprawled across Symonne's lap. "God has given me a chance to be free."

Symonne wasn't sure if she agreed with Bertrand and Old Marthe's perspective on the whole affair, and although Symonne had maintained ambivalence toward the Desrosiers as a servant in their home, she couldn't erase from her mind the sight of dead and rotting Cateline, still donning a beautiful dressing robe, arms outstretched to cradle her daughter. Symonne had done her best to give Cateline a decent burial. What good was wealth and power when you went alone into a dirt grave, wrapped in expensive and exotic linen, and your daughter is found starving and screaming beside your corpse? She had no love for those who abused their station, but Symonne felt strongly that she had maintained the upper hand as a survivor and now Catelot's adopted mother. She knew now that people like Cateline were also just humans—mortal, fallible. Very little separated them, at the end of the day, beyond the vast division of life and death.

She tried to talk to Catelot often about her mother—she felt she owed it to Lady Cateline. The young girl listened with an air of duty, as if she too understood that she owed something to the woman who bore her and clearly loved her, enough to embrace her as they trudged toward death together. But a spark existed in the girl that seemed uniquely her own, and it was Symonne she clung to at night when a night terror struck; it was Symonne to whom she brought flowers and feathers and ferns she found in the forest; it was Symonne she loved to accompany to make bread or spin wool. There was very little resemblance between the dark-haired, dark-eyed little girl and her fair, golden-haired guardian, but their mannerisms and tastes aligned.

So when Old Marthe spoke of God and fate at the expense of Desrosiers, Symonne simply nodded. To her, there was something far more ancient and primal that drew her and Catelot together as mother and daughter, roles they both embraced. She loved Catelot as strongly as if she had come from her own body, and when the girl slept on her and the rhythms of their breath found a common consistency, the boundaries between their mortal forms blurred, and their needy hearts found each other in the ether.

SIMONETTA

"Tell me about your mother."

Simonetta is still getting used to the casual way Jeremy asks big questions. Almost always he is in a state of focus—as is she, beside him during the breaks in her day, when she comes to the workshop to look through books or peruse archives on her laptop in search of automaton details, making notes in her commonplace—when out comes an inquiry about her life or upbringing or identity.

At the thought of her mother, she frowns. "She died when I was six. My memories of her are mostly sensory." There is a scent that she associates with her mom: a clean, fresh scent, matched by the feeling of cool fabric against her cheek. She associates Berkeley and the bay with her mom, the chilly, foggy mornings and the eucalyptus trees.

"Do you miss her?" Another biting question comes as

he planes a long strip of birch, retrieved from a felled tree in the forest that he tagged during their morning excursion. He is making new paneling for the Chambre de Chat, and his blueprints are scattered across the worktable like debris on the forest floor.

Simonetta nods and swallows hard. "Always, but not in the same way I miss my grandparents." She struggles to share what she wants to admit. *I miss the feeling of being safe, the all-encompassing safety that only comes with being with your mother. I miss her body and the way it felt being pressed against it.* "I think often about who she was and who she'd be. She died so young. I'm older now than she was when she died." She lifts her head from the schematics she is studying and sighs. "I struggled when I turned twenty-seven, knowing I had lived longer than my mother had. It felt unfair."

"You said she didn't suffer long?"

"That's what Nonna said, but maybe she only told me that to make me feel better." Simonetta chews on her thumbnail. "Or herself. My mom only knew she was sick for a couple of months. I only remember going to the hospital once to see her before she died. I suppose it's a good thing she wasn't in agony for a long time, but it happened so quickly. I don't know. Is that a good thing?"

"How do you think she'd feel about your life so far?"

Simonetta laughs. "I've only had one cup of tea today and you're asking me questions that unearth my most complicated thoughts." She sobers. "I have no idea. I can only guess. I know she loved to travel, like me. And I know she loved history, like me. How she'd feel about me leaving my job to move to France—I like to think she'd understand. I hope she'd think I was an interesting daughter to have." She straightens then looks at him. "Alright, your turn."

"For what?" He crouches down to inspect the planed wood at eye level.

"Interrogation. How do you feel about *your* mom?"

"I like her more when I see her less," he answers, clipped.

"Jeremy!"

"What? I'm being honest." Satisfied, he straightens and brushes his hands together. "I love my mom, but she hovers. I prefer having some space."

"That I can agree with," says Simonetta. "I've always liked behind alone."

"I know. I could tell."

"What do you mean you could 'tell'? You say things as if they are obvious."

"I just could. I knew you were like me."

"Oh?" Simonetta raises her eyebrows at this, incredulous. "And what is that like?"

He gestures to her own workspace, where her notes are in messy piles mirroring his own. "You like the quiet. You like working on something. You like learning for the sake of learning. You need time and space to focus." He makes eye contact with her at last. "Am I wrong?"

She feigns a show of annoyance and tosses up her hands. "You've just got me all figured out."

"*That* I would never claim. The way you think baffles me."

"What the hell? I thought you said you were going to stop being rude to me."

"I'm not being rude." He begins whittling the bark off the next plank. "I'm being honest."

She turns back to her open notebook and picks up a pen, eager to escape this battle of wits that she knows she is losing. "Did it ever occur to you that you could maybe be less honest sometimes?"

"What's the point in that?"

"I don't know, maybe people's feelings?"

"Oh please." Jeremy snorts. "You appreciate honesty more than you admit. But *you* don't like being honest because you think you're going to hurt other people's feelings."

"Well in that case, I'll be honest with you and say that your hair is full of sawdust and looks disgusting." She smiles to ease the insult, but she knows he is well aware that the comment was made in jest. "I haven't had enough caffeine for this conversation. You're too much for me, Jeremy Duvain."

He stops whittling. "I hope you don't truly feel that way."

She opens her mouth to make another sardonic comment, then stops short at the serious look on his face. "Of course not. You just have a way of asking me things no one has ever asked. You make me think of things I don't like to think about."

"Fine. What do you *like* to think about?"

This question is easy for her to answer honestly. "Usually, history. Music. Books. Gardens. Hot caffeinated beverages. My grandparents. Being in new places. People I care about. Church bells." There are things she omits: food, wine, sex, medieval manuscripts. No reason to be too honest with her new companion.

"Church bells?" His genuine surprise pleases her.

"I used to tell my grandparents I wanted to live somewhere where I'd hear church bells ring every day. I've only heard church bells while traveling. Once I stayed in a small town in Switzerland and bells rang throughout the day, right in the middle of it all. As an American it just feels pleasantly Old World to me."

Jeremy snorts. "Americans are weird."

Simonetta laughs. "I don't disagree."

That evening, as Simonetta sets the table with Lotte for supper—tonight they are having a pie made with local beef and herbs from the garden, with a buttery crust crafted by Hanako— she hears a loud ringing that startles her.

"What on earth is that?" says Lotte.

Claudel emerges onto the patio, clapping her hands. "Jeremy got the chapel's bell unstuck! He said it just needed some oil and someone to wrest it back into order."

He chimes the bell eight times, signaling the eight o'clock suppertime, and the ringing reverberates in Simonetta's heart long into the night after.

Eleven

Coat of Arms: A heraldic design depicting the symbols that represent a noble house or faction.

SIMONETTA LEARNS THAT, for all its beauty, Chateau Desrosiers has no shortage of quirks.

For one, the floor is uneven in nearly every room. She discovers the center dip in the library one night at one a.m., tiptoeing quietly across the room to scour the bookshelves for texts about art history. She's tracing a train of thought about the Catelot painting, supported by some of the historical information that Claudel reminded her of during supper—that Catelot ended up in an abbey when she was an adult, as there is no record of the Desrosiers family line extending beyond the first official owners.

The Abbey of Sainte-Madeleine has some historical archives that Simonetta intends to visit and review soon, but in the meantime, she's looking for any books about the abbey that may set her on the right path—details about the painter of the Catelot portrait, or even the person who carved the doll? She finds a few choice volumes that each reference abbeys throughout Provence, tucks them under her arm, and scurries back across the large room—but halfway across, she steps into a dip in the flooring and it catches her so off guard that she stumbles and the books go flying, landing in a loud clatter.

Heart thundering, she crouches to collect the splayed books, but a creaking of the floor in the corner makes her jump and expletives spill involuntarily from her mouth.

"Simonetta?" inquires a familiar voice.

"Jeremy?" She squints and sees the outline of him sitting in a green armchair on the other side of a bookshelf. A lantern is lit on the small table beside him—one of the marble tables she rescued from the oddities tower, she notices, and it being in use now gives her a strange sort of pleasure.

"Are you okay?" He brings the lantern to her and it's as if they are transported to another era, using the light of a lantern to illuminate the room. The vignette is silly and she bites back an awkward giggle, adrenaline still spiked from her tumble.

"Yes, I just tripped." She gulps in a breath to steady her heartbeat. "I'm sorry if I disturbed you."

"Ah, you found the dip in the room. That's gotten me more than once." He adds the final fallen book to her stack and they both stand. "What were you doing?"

"Research," she says. "Trying to follow some leads about Catelot based on the discussion at supper." She realizes she's holding a hefty stack of books; although the volunteers are encouraged to use the library, Simonetta's sure there is a limit to that offer. "I realize I took too many—I was just taking them to my room to scan some pages."

Jeremy laughs. "It's fine, the library is a shared resource." He clears his throat. "I was actually doing the same thing."

"Research? What are you researching?"

"The automaton."

Her first inclination is to ask, "Why?" but that seems rude; he's been a part of the project from the beginning. Still, it ignites a small selfish spark of possessiveness that she snuffs out.

He saves her from following up and beckons her over to the table. "I asked Claudel if I could get out some of the older documents and relics from the chateau. When she bought it, there was quite a lot of stuff stashed away in closets and the towers—much of it was nothing, but there are some interesting documents tucked away that I thought you might be interested in checking out."

On the marble table is a stack of four very old letters. Simonetta's professional prowess kicks in and a spark of joy she once got from her work in the restoration lab ignites. She delicately picks one up, evaluates the paper type and handwriting. "Eighteenth century?"

"Letters that Marguerite de Sainte-Madeleine wrote," says Jeremy, "but never sent."

"The former marchioness of Desrosiers?" Simonetta asks, goosebumps prickling her arms. "How do you know they're hers?"

Jeremy points to the dark blue wax seal on each envelope; in the dim light, Simonetta discerns the outline of the chateau and some Latin writing encircling it. "This is Marguerite's crest—it's the same one above the entrance."

"Did you know about these?" Simonetta asks.

Jeremy shook his head. "I don't think Claudel even knew they were in there. They were stuck in some old early 1900s records about the chateau's accounting—interesting enough to keep, as even mundane ledgers are a part of Desrosiers' history, but Marguerite's letters are a more substantial find and may have some other details about the chateau."

"What makes you think these have to do with the automaton?"

Jeremy shrugs. "Nothing yet, but we've estimated that, based on the design and mechanisms, the automaton is likely eighteenth century, right?"

Simonetta takes out her leather journal, scribbled with notes and diagrams. "I've found information about quite a few automatons from the eighteenth century. They were all the rage here in France before the Revolution, apparently." Simonetta purses her lips in thought. "What made you think that the automaton is from the 1700s?"

Jeremy frowns. "It's just a guess. Or a hunch, I suppose. Marguerite de Sainte-Madeleine was known to be a lover of music. She had an extensive collection of instruments, many sourced from around the world. You can see some of that in her portraits: she's always holding an instrument. She was a collector of lots of things, including some of the grandfather clocks. So

I just thought that if anyone would have commissioned the automaton, it would have been her."

Simonetta considers this. "Not a bad guess. It makes sense to me that the automaton is a special commissioned piece, mostly because of Catelot. The doll is unique to Desrosiers. And we know Marguerite had an affinity for violins." Simonetta pauses; the theory feels thin and wobbly. "There's a lot of assumption in between those two things, but it's a start." She glances at the stack of letters. "I'm dying from curiosity, but it feels intrusive to open the letters."

"Why? They've been sitting untouched for three hundred years."

"I don't know. It seems disrespectful. Maybe she didn't send them for a reason?"

"Well, at present, you live in her house." He points up and circles his finger, indicating the room they're both standing in, one of the additions made under Marguerite's direction. "We've taken down walls in the chateau, added bathrooms, put up wallpaper. We've already intruded quite a bit on her legacy." He picks up the letters gingerly. "Personally, I think it's a privilege to be remembered. How many souls have passed through Earth that people will never know? Taking an interest in someone's life, even when they are long gone, brings them back to life again."

A shiver ripples up Simonetta's spine. *It's a privilege to be remembered.* She has thought this many times in her life, knowing that, eventually, the world will forget about her mom and Nonna and Nonno, and herself. It's a fear that has made her want to seek out a community even when her normal instincts urge her to find solace in solitude.

Marguerite had no children, that they knew about. Simonetta thinks of herself: mid-thirties, no family, a career in flux. It's not a reflection of pity so much as her attempt to justify opening Marguerite's letters.

Would Simonetta mind if someone in three hundred years read her journal? She can't imagine she would.

"Fine—we can read them for the sake of Desrosiers," she says. "I'm sure Claudel would appreciate any information we uncover."

"And for your sake," Jeremy insists. "For the automaton. You deserve information, too."

Simonetta blinks. "Do I? The automaton isn't even mine. We're just operating on a theory. But I have one stipulation: we have to be careful with the letters. As a conservator, I would like to take the lead on opening and preserving the letters themselves. We can put them on display for visitors."

"Deal." Jeremy holds out his hand and Simonetta shakes it in agreement. But his smile is cheeky when he says, "I look forward to seeing you in your element."

She slips back into her element with ease, like sliding on Claudel's decadent silk robes, like lowering into the river when the water is warm from the sunlight, like sinking her teeth into a smooth lemon tart.

A Saturday in late May marks one month since Simonetta arrived in France. Claudel, thrilled by Jeremy's discovery, wholeheartedly endorsed their plan to open Marguerite's letters. Claudel requested (well, told, essentially demanded) that Simonetta could facilitate a whole series on *Daily Life at Desrosiers* around the automaton project.

At first, the suggestion sent Simonetta mentally running for the hills; she very much desires not to be the center of attention on *Daily Life*. So far, beyond her initial volunteer interview that made its debut several weeks ago, she has managed to blend in with the others and abstain from being singled out in front of the camera. But once insecurity and panic ebb into reason, Simonetta realizes the feature is to her advantage. Claudel's channel has more than 100,000 subscribers, and the rapt viewership was composed of history buffs, many of whom would have suggestions or leads for Simonetta. So she reluctantly agrees, for the sake of the automaton.

She now finds herself surrounded by cameras. The volunteers set up a filming area in the formal dining room, and although the room is large and airy with huge arched windows that show a view of the mountains beyond, it's warm today in late afternoon. The room is filled with most of the volunteers, plus Claudel and Jeremy.

Hanako took up the mantle as director of the series and she flits around Simonetta now, rearranging the decor on the fireplace mantle for the dozenth time.

"Is all of this really necessary?" asks Simonetta, annoyance and nerves welling in her chest. "Claudel's videos are usually pretty slice-of-life. I don't think anyone watching expects us to have this so staged."

"Why not make your backdrop beautiful if we can?" Hanako protests. Lotte has joined her, bringing with her some green foliage in a navy vase. Simonetta reluctantly agrees that the foliage looks gorgeous above the marble mantle, and contrasts in a lovely way against the cream-colored plaster walls. Simonetta does love this sumptuous room and its understated elegance. Although her favorite parts of Desrosiers are its oldest spaces, those stone chambers and towers tend to be the smallest, and in this spacious dining hall, she can breathe.

Claudel chose the room for its size and lighting, but also so that Simonetta could make use of the huge wood table in the middle of it. She has her supplies orderly knolled: the stack of four letters, a magnifying glass, a pocket knife, and some cloths for wiping her hands.

Simonetta is, despite the cameras, excited. All day she's fended off waves of homesickness for her lab back at Berkeley, wonders (not for the first time) if they'd re-hire her. She loves touching history, protecting it, sharing it with others. It has always been her place of joy.

And being back "at work" feels good. She strategically planned out her "on camera" outfit, opting for one of the few nice outfits she'd packed just in case. Dressed in a starched button-up, with the sleeves rolled up so she has the full use of her hands and wrists, and her favorite khaki slacks, she's a conservator again, her professional self. She made sure to wear her signature lipstick and used every bobby pin she packed to keep her hair wrangled in a bun. For extra luck, she wore Nonna's pearl stud earrings and when she needs a jolt of confidence, she pinches her earlobe and remembers all the times Emilia gave her love and support—the day she spoke at her high school graduation, the day she defended her master's thesis, the day she interviewed for her first role at the restoration lab. Her nonna was always there to empower her.

Simonetta knows today isn't anything major, but for her it seems big somehow. She conjures New Simonetta, Venus with red lipstick, and introduces her to Previous Simone, Assistant Director of Book Conservation at UC Berkeley. Who will the two versions be when they meet?

When the room is ready, Simonetta takes her place behind the table. Jeremy gives her a thumbs-up and Claudel starts recording. Although she knows the video will be edited, Simonetta prepared and practiced her talking points for hours the night before.

"A few days ago, Jeremy made a fascinating discovery while looking through some of the chateau's old documents." Simonetta holds up the folder. "Most of these are old ledgers from the early 1900s, which we can show you in another video. But tucked among these were four unopened letters written by Marguerite de Sainte-Madeleine, whom long-time viewers will remember as the marchioness who lived at, and owned, Desrosiers in the mid-1700s. Marguerite is to thank for many of the additions made to Desrosiers, expanding it from a medieval fortress to the grand estate it became several decades before the French Revolution." Simonetta pauses, remembers Nonna telling her to speak slowly when she practiced her thesis defense. "Marguerite was a well-documented lover of music, a collector of instruments. We've recently uncovered quite a few instruments that may have been procured by her."

When she drafted the notes for this video, she and Jeremy discussed whether or not to share the automaton as part of this initial presentation. Simonetta decided against it; Marguerite's letters are already a compelling find that viewers will enjoy, and she is not yet ready to share the automaton despite Claudel's plans. She omits mention of it as she continues explaining the letters.

"At first, I wanted to keep the letters sealed," Simonetta continues. "It felt like an invasion of privacy to open them. But Jeremy rightfully pointed out that we live in Marguerite's home, and that her letters may give us insight into who she was, and we can continue to protect and share her legacy. Being remembered is a gift that not everyone receives."

Opening spiel complete, Simonetta launches into her standard talk about restoration. "If you watched my first interview with Claudel, you may remember that, prior to coming to Desrosiers, I worked as a book conservator in Berkeley, California. My department received historical documents from around the world, and my team and I would repair and restore them to the best of our ability so that museums, libraries, and institutions could study and share them with others. It's very rewarding work." Simonetta swallows the lump in her throat. She means every word. "I'm honored that Claudel entrusts me to open these priceless letters with you. You may notice that I'm not wearing gloves." She holds up her bare hands. "Contrary to popular belief, wearing gloves can sometimes prevent a restorer from carefully manipulating documents. We only wear them when old paper or materials are truly too brittle to be touched directly. Otherwise, it's best to use clean hands."

Delicately, she holds up one of the letters and turns it toward the camera so the wax seal is clearly visible. "I wanted to show you the seal. This is how most letters were sealed for centuries. The wax seal serves multiple purposes—it binds the folded corners of the paper together, it is easy to tell when a letter has been tampered with, and the seal bears the mark of the sender." She beckons Claudel to zoom in on the seal, where she points out the details. "This is how we know these were Marguerite's letters. We're lucky that we have one of Marguerite's stamps in our collection of Desrosiers artifacts. Her seal shows an outline of Desrosiers, and around the perimeter is Marguerite's motto that is now part of the Desrosiers crest: 'harmonia per lucem et per umbram'—'harmony, by the light and by the shadow.'" As part of her rehearsal, Simonetta had practiced the Latin using an online pronunciation guide and hopes she says it correctly.

"This Latin can be found engraved around the fountain in the courtyard, an addition to the chateau commissioned by Marguerite."

Simonetta then points to the paper. "Paper in the 1700s was made from a multitude of resources, typically fiber. You can see how rich the texture is." She indicates to Claudel to zoom in again to show the lines and patterns in the paper. Claudel gives a wordless nod in confirmation. "Without knowing exactly where Marguerite sourced her paper from, and without having the extensive tools from my lab, we can assume it's a combination of pressed flax and linen rags. Rags for paper were sorted into levels of quality, and given Marguerite's wealth and station, this paper was likely made using higher quality rags. The fibers would then be soaked in water and pressed. We take paper for granted now, but historically, documents like books and letters were expensive to make and possess. The quality of the paper is likely how the letters survived until today. When we put them on display here at Desrosiers, we'll be using some special light-filtering glass to protect them long-term.

"Because of the age of the letters, the wax is already starting to separate from the paper. I want to keep the wax stamps in-tact. Although Marguerite had lady's maids and servants to assist with letter-writing, she was a learned woman, and it's not impossible to think of her own hands melting the wax and pressing her seal into the paper." Simonetta pauses again and clears her throat, suddenly reverent about the intimacy of writing letters. "I'm using an extremely sharp razor blade to sever the attachment of the wax to the paper, to prevent the paper from disintegrating or tearing and to preserve the wax seal itself."

She's done this hundreds of times, expertly wielded a sharp object to open an old book or document. Preservation often entails some amount of nominal damage at the start, but a clear plan and the right materials ensure that the damage is temporary, just one step in the road to restoration. But Simonetta is at the whim of the supplies she has available to her, and she cuts short a line of thinking that threatens to stop her momentum, that maybe she should leave the letters closed—but she barely touches the razor to the paper when the letter falls open.

Delicately, she spreads open the folded paper to reveal the writing inside. But it's not rows of sentences written in elegant penmanship. Simonetta takes in the straight lines, the symbols and marks and numbers that adorn the page.

It's a musical composition.

"What is it?" Jeremy prompts. Remembering that she's being filmed and that the shock has rendered her speechless for several long moments, Simonetta holds up the opened paper to face the camera so the others can see what she sees.

"The letter is a composition." She turns it back to herself and scans it, grateful for her ability to parse the notes. "It's a violin sonata, but not one I recognize at first glance. In Marguerite's time, the format of a violin sonata was still relatively new." In the bottom corner is a small, flourished *M*. "It's signed with her initial, so we can assume it's a Marguerite original." She looks up, awed, to see similar expressions reflecting back at her. Claudel has her hand to her mouth.

Simonetta opens the other envelopes with careful urgency and, yes, each one is a composition—all different, all denoted with that swooping *M*.

"Are these pieces you could play, Simonetta?" Claudel asks, loudly enough for the microphones to pick up the question.

Simonetta thinks on this for a moment, glancing over the music, then nods. "Yes, although I'd have to practice them quite a bit. They're not complex at all but they are—layered. They're all in minor key, too, which is interesting. I've never really seen anything like these."

Eager to wrap up the recording so she can process this turn of events, Simonetta ends her presentation with a promise to perform the compositions in a future video. Once Claudel turns off the camera, the volunteers gather around the table to inspect the discoveries, although the same selfish possessiveness rears and she's compelled to scoop up the music and keep it for herself. It's not hers to claim, but like the automaton, the music calls to her, like Marguerite is reaching through time to give Simonetta a message.

Not letters, but music. Marguerite wrote songs for someone but never sent them. Who were they for?

Twelve

MARGUERITE DE SAINTE-MADELEINE
1718

E MINOR—that was Marguerite's favorite note. She liked the minor notes best; in her mind, they manifested in shades of dark blue, deep red, burnt umber.

It was the contrast she yearned for in all things, how the darkness elevated the light. And the depth, too, like the way shadows grew starker at the height of the day.

Marguerite rose with the dawn along with the servants, intent to capture every morsel of daylight. She watched from her bed as Elise prepared her breakfast on a gilded tray, appreciated her lady's maid and her features: the dark hair tightly coiffed, glinting ebony in the faint sunlight, the skin pale as the milk she poured into a glass for Marguerite, the navy dress with its fitted bodice. The contrast Marguerite yearned for was embodied in Elise.

Even the maid's name, in Marguerite's mind's eye, where every word and sound took on a hue, was awash in Marguerite's preferred tones. To her, Elise evoked blue—a deep blue, like the ocean, with a touch of cream, like the foam of white caps.

Elise reminded Marguerite of Catelot—the painting that hung above the staircase in the entrance of her ancestral home. As her tutor once explained it, Catelot was the daughter of the chateau's first owners, when the building that is now her home was just a fortress and a farm and not the grand estate it became two and a half centuries later under the purview of Marguerite's father. It was a peculiar painting, featuring the young Catelot outlined by the dark forest behind her, and her dark brown hair casually braided and draped over one shoulder. The dark hair and the dark eyes remind Marguerite of Elise, the way the girl's delicate fingers clasped the twigs in her small hands—Elise, too, had delicate fingers. In fact, Marguerite found everything about Elise to be delicate, lovely, and perfectly contrasted.

For years, it was easy for Marguerite to get away with her secret. No one questioned why the marquis's young daughter rarely left the estate—why should she, when she resided in the massive Chateau Desrosiers, restored to its former splendor and then some? In her father's absence—which was frequent, as the Marquis de Sainte-Madeleine preferred the Mediterranean coast to the mountainous terrain where his estate was located—the servants mostly left Marguerite to her own devices, assuming (not incorrectly) that she was simply a girl who preferred indoor activities like reading and musical composition to the outdoors. For the bulk of her adolescence and teen years, Marguerite remained safely and comfortably within the confines of Desrosiers without judgment. Ultimately, very few noticed that Marguerite's preference for remaining inside the sturdy fortress walls of Desrosiers was more than a simple preference, but an innate and powerful need that she could not explain to anyone—least of all, herself.

But Philippe noticed.

He noticed everything, and it irked Marguerite that on top of being handsome, tall, and quick-witted, he was also observant. As a girl who prided herself on being observant, she knew this was not a trait that many truly shared, and she found it unfair that Philippe, brimming with plenty of complimentary traits, should possess the one that she found uniquely hers. Why couldn't he be handsome but aloof, like her friend Isabelle's older brother

Louis, who would rather play ball on the expansive Desrosiers lawn when visiting instead of doing sums with the tutor?

No, Marguerite had the misfortune of having a brother who was, on paper at least, perfect, with his biggest flaw being that he was a year younger than Marguerite and not the eldest born. But the discrepancy in birthing order did nothing to prevent his cockiness and cruelty, nor did the attention and praise lavished on him by their father.

It was to Marguerite's detriment that keen-eyed Philippe was all too perceptive to the habits and personal rituals to which she clung, depended on, to keep the roar in her mind and body at bay. For as long as she could remember, Marguerite had fought an internal voice that made her behavior manifest in strange ways. At night, before sleeping, she had to touch the corner of every shelf and window in her chamber. If she didn't, her body felt restless and unsatisfied, and a keening sound played on loop in her mind until she acquiesced to the strange compulsion. A similar effect occurred while reading: if she didn't run a fingertip along every deckled page, starting at the top and going all the way to the bottom before turning it, the internal storm raged until the urge was satisfied. Marguerite had no idea why she needed to do these things, just that she had always needed to do them for as long as she could remember, and that surety affirmed her suspicion that this sort of behavior was unnatural and uncommon. Her astute observations of others had all but confirmed that, for she had spent hours and hours watching servants and visitors and her family navigate about their days and perceived no uncanny repetitive actions or external displays of restlessness that needed to be resolved in such a fashion.

The same sensation of mental chaos arose every time she attempted to take a step outside. She was sure that she had gone outside when she was little—her nurses would have given her infant- and toddler-self little say in the matter—but when she was old enough to be given a choice, a series of distressing, fitful episodes that she weathered alone had led to the realization that it was simply easier, calmer, and safer to remain indoors.

If Philippe witnessed her torment, or felt any sympathy

toward it at all, he didn't factor that into his desire to comment on her oddness.

"Why do you do that to the pages?" he asked, when he was six and she newly seven. She had been in her room, sitting in her window, her favorite spot in entire world, and, observant as she was, had not noticed him watching her from her bedroom door.

A flush crept into cheeks and a sweat broke across her brow. Instinctively, she deflected. "Do what to the pages?"

"Touch them like that," he said, grabbing her book from her hands. He let the book fall open and proceeded to emulate her actions with exaggerated gestures, sticking his tongue out as he did so. "You do it every time you turn the page."

"I do not!"

"You do! I *watched* you."

"Give me back my book," she snapped, attempting to snatch the book from his hands, but he flung his arm back at the last moment and the book fell to the floor, pages splayed. The creased pages and crooked spine made an unpleasant fissure ripple up her own. "Get out of my room!"

"You're so strange," Philippe spat. "Everything you do is strange!"

Her strangeness became his fodder. A few years later, when her habits and need to stay inside were firmly established, he found pleasure in taunting her and attempting to fruitlessly lure her outside. He took her favorite dolls and hid them in the garden; she watched him from her window, saw him shoving them in the dirt and rose bushes. Occasionally, a servant would find them and return them to her, puzzled, and she had to make excuses.

Rarely, her brother displayed glimpses of care that made her soften toward him. On a rainy day in spring, he had snatched her book from her lap as she napped, then forced her to chase after him through the chilly halls. He stopped at the threshold of the front entrance, backlit by the bleak sunlight streaming across the courtyard.

"Don't you want your book?" he asked, holding it behind him. "You can take it back whenever you want. You just have to—" he took a step backward, onto the ground outside the door, "—come outside."

Inside her head was a clash of sensations, anxiety creeping up into her throat, invisible hands pressing against her chest. But she tried to suppress it the best she could. "I don't even like that book," she sniffed, then crossed her arms. The gesture helped to ground her somewhat and she wanted to squeeze herself tighter in comfort but knew that would just give Philippe something else to taunt her about.

For a moment, something sincere and curious flickered on his face, and the mischievous glint in his eyes turned genuine. "Why don't you just come outside?"

"Because it's raining!" She gestured emphatically to the weather and had never been more thankful for the rain for giving her a valid reason to mask the real one.

"But you never go outside, even when it's sunny. Why not?"

She shrugged and hoped it was a casual, convincing shrug. "I just like being inside." A rare thoughtful moment passed between them, and she became uncomfortable at his peculiar, evaluating gaze. Bitterness bubbled up before she could stop it. "Why must you taunt me so much?"

The accusation broke the moment, and the curious furrow in his brow relaxed into his typical scheming expression. Still maintaining eye contact, he rotated and threw her book across the courtyard, where it landed on the edge of the fountain, splashing into a puddle.

Unable to contain her emotion any longer, Marguerite turned away from him and ran back to her room as the tears erupted and, for hours, didn't stop.

The next morning, she heard a faint knock on her door. She opened it to find her book returned to her, the pages bloated and stuck together.

"You're looking pale, sister," Philippe said, chewing his bread in the way she hated, all gnashing and squelching noises. When he turned to her, away from the passive gaze of the servants, he opened his mouth to chew openly, awaiting her disgusted expression. Even now, in adulthood, his immaturity flared.

Marguerite rolled her eyes instead, avoiding the bait. "I see your travels haven't improved your manners. What would Papa say?"

Philippe's sardonic expression flickered briefly at the mention of their father, and Marguerite was sure she landed a good shot, but the expression dissipated quickly and cockiness returned. "He wouldn't care, because he's secured a new deal." He tore off another piece of bread, baring his teeth. "He'll be back in a few days."

Marguerite stiffened. She hated it when Papa was home at the chateau. He preferred the rest of Provence to Sainte-Madeleine and Marguerite preferred it when he was gone, even more so when he brought Philippe with him; during these times she had the chateau to herself, could explore it and find privacy at her leisure. She had everything she needed—books, sewing, the atrium where she cultivated her plants, and the collection of musical instruments she was amassing. Above everything, Marguerite loved music. It was the only thing that quieted the chaos in her mind. Studying musical theory gave her mind something to cling to, her thoughts something to be absorbed in. And she loved to play it, too, to feel the vibrations and notes permeate her blood and breath. She was especially fond of the harpsichord her father had acquired for her, among the many string and wind instruments that now had a home in the Grand Salon, and she had most recently requested a violin.

Papa indeed brought with him a violin, new gowns, books, and a slew of new servants. His wealth had grown immensely thanks to his savvy deal-making and the smug enjoyment of his own success won out slightly over his impatience to return to Nice.

Marguerite steeled herself for his visit. A month prior she had just turned nineteen, and she knew her days of solitude and peace were numbered. He would have some tasks and requirements for her now, she was sure of it; she had earned a few extra years of freedom purely by luck. Marguerite was adept at maneuvering and coming up with legitimate alternatives and excuses that both complied with his requests and prioritized her own interests. Her father loved her, and ultimately, she loved him—he indulged her interests, encouraged her desire to learn, took a passive approach to her upbringing unlike the heavy-handed controlling nature that most noble fathers took with their daughters, viewing them as fodder for marriage. He appreciated her passion for music and did his best to send her instruments during his travels. She wasn't sure her father understood her, and she didn't understand him, nor his passion for business and investing. In that, Philippe was his chosen partner. But Marguerite took after Papa in shrewdness, even if hers manifested as a coping mechanism to keep prying strangers from analyzing her behaviors and disrupting her impeccably cultivated daily life.

She wasn't concerned that he would make her go to Nice; she was, after all, not her father's prized son. What use was a daughter, even a clever one, when a son was available? But there were other things he could ask of her that would require her to leave her carefully constructed routine.

She met him for supper in the dining hall. When her father purchased the chateau at age twenty-one, it was little more than a crumbling fortress, but at the time he was little more than a treasurer, a role he inherited from his father. Twenty years later, being ennobled with a sterling reputation throughout Provence had earned Nicholas de Sainte-Madeleine a grand estate and legacy built atop the almost ruins of Desrosiers. It didn't matter that Desrosiers had been sporadically occupied and maintained over the last two hundred years, or that it was a humble estate tucked away in a region that was hard to get to and often forgotten; a noble manor was a noble manor and it served Nicholas fine.

Marguerite, having grown up knowing nothing but beautifully furnished rooms and the decadent dining hall, preferred the areas her father had not improved, the medieval towers and stone walls that Nicholas had intentionally chosen to preserve. It looked good for him that the home where his family lived was ancient, because it gave him historical claim to his very non-noble lineage. But Marguerite loved these areas of the chateau because they were beautiful and old and quiet. She loved the history embedded in the stone that protected her. Desrosiers was her sanctuary, her refuge. She was grateful to her father for expanding it and giving her a home where she could be content inside its walls, never needing anything beyond it. Sometimes late at night she shuddered at the thought of growing up in a small cottage with family members all about; how could she have ever convinced them of her behaviors, her rituals? She would have been sent long ago to a nunnery, or a dangerous place where women deemed insane were kept in solitude.

It was with these heavy thoughts on her mind that she proceeded solemnly to her place at the table, awaiting the inevitable. She greeted Papa with a kiss on the cheek. He looked older than he did when she last saw him, his dark red hair streaked with gray at the temples, but he sat with impeccable posture and the glint in his blue eyes remained sharp as ever. Among the few features she shared with her father was the rich auburn hair and almond-shaped eyes. Philippe was darker in coloring, taking after their late mother, as handsome as she was striking.

At supper, Papa boasted proudly of his new servants—recruitment of qualified staff had long been a challenge for Papa, given Desrosiers' remoteness. Sainte-Madeleine was hardly a pinnacle of culture or prosperity like Nice or Marseilles. Small settlements encircled the main village, but travel in the mountainous region was often arduous and they'd had to make do with the employees they could lure from the village. But he had made the rounds in Nice and presented a compelling offer, bringing back a slew of those who would work at Desrosiers with the promise of their own cottages and parcels of land.

Among the new servants was Marguerite's new lady's maid, a young dark-haired woman named Elise. The thought of a new maid made her nervous; she was used to Old Eugénie, who had been her maid since she was ten. Nine years ago, Old Eugénie was already, well, old, and she paid little attention to Marguerite's peculiar habits.

"Marguerite, you must plan a ball," her father said as they worked their way through the final course.

Marguerite picked at her food, already full; across from her sat Philippe, inhaling each course as if he were a starving peasant. He was always hungry.

She groaned inwardly at the request but supposed it could be worse. At least he had not told her she must go anywhere.

"Yes, Papa," she said. "Whom would you like me to invite?" She knew the ball had a purpose—all balls had an intrinsic purpose, which was to display one's wealth and resources, but networking was typically Papa's goal when it came to hosting. It had been years since Desrosiers had hosted a ball; Marguerite and Philippe were children then and had been relegated to their rooms which had suited Marguerite just fine. She enjoyed listening to the music that emanated from the Grand Salon as she sat in her favorite window doing needlepoint by candlelight. Philippe, however, had been insatiably curious and kept sneaking downstairs to watch the festivities. Since then, the Grand Salon had been re-paneled, an exquisite new marble mantle built around the hearth. It was a room in sore need of people to occupy it.

"I will provide you with a list," he said. "Among whom will be potential suitors. Your new lady's maid has been instructed on how to prepare you accordingly."

Marguerite went white, any remaining color left in her already pallid coloring draining away. "Suitors?"

"For marriage," said Philippe, smiling wickedly. The cruel glint in his eyes sparkled.

Panic welled in her chest, started bubbling up her throat. She felt the sour taste of bile prick the back of her jaw. "But Papa, I am only just nineteen," she pled. "Surely marriage can wait a year." Or ten. Or forever.

It was the word Marguerite had dreaded throughout her entire adolescence. Marriage meant a life with a stranger, being forced to leave her home, being forced to bear children, being forced out of the safe and comfortable confines of the chateau. There was no way she could, on a daily basis, machinate enough excuses and justifications to maintain her mental stability. The mere thought at leaving the chateau made her want to die, to simply perish, and she begged her heart to stop beating, her lungs to stop breathing, to make it easy on her—but the blood coursed through her veins regardless, and if Papa noticed her terror he made no comment on it, and she somehow waded through the final moments of supper in a haze.

When they parted for the night, she ran straight to her room, chest heaving, the poorly suppressed emotions spilling out through tears and short, quick breaths she couldn't regulate. She clutched at her chest, the panic overwhelming her—

"Mistress?" A soft voice cut through the darkness and Marguerite spun around to find a small woman standing in her bedchamber. Slender, with dark hair carefully styled away from her face, the woman was bedecked in the simple linen dress and pinafore that befitted her role as a lady's maid. Her new lady's maid.

Marguerite slid to the floor, head in her hands, thinking quickly. "I'm sorry, I have taken ill. I have been feeling ill since supper."

"I will fetch a doctor—"

"No!" Marguerite shouted and stretched out her hand. "No, no need. I have a poor disposition and sometimes feel ill. It will pass. Please leave me be."

Her maid looked uneasy at the request, and even in the midst of her spiral, Marguerite couldn't blame her. It was her maid's job to ensure her mistress's well-being, and as a new staff member, leaving her mistress to her own infirmity would not go over well if others found out.

Several tense moments passed as Marguerite spiraled and the maid watched with uncertainty. But then the maid crouched before Marguerite like one does before a wounded animal and held out a hand in comfort. "My mother sometimes gets sick like you do. She can't catch her breath and she says her mind gets loud and her stomach turns. Is that how you feel?"

Marguerite, mouth agape, looked at the young woman, whom she guessed was around her age if not slightly older. There was a courage to how directly the maid addressed her and shared this insight. Marguerite bit off a harsh word of reprimand—how dare you address me so directly?—because what the maid said cut through. She had never before heard anyone else express something like that. Was it possible she wasn't truly mad? That others experienced the mental roar, the pressure on their chests, the chaos and turbulence that rocked her body and sent her mind scattered?

The woman's face lacked judgment and pity and instead held an expression of compassion and earnestness. It was the expression Marguerite cherished in her heart for the rest of her days, and on that night, it was what gave her the courage to nod in response to the maid's dangerous question and clasp her outstretched hand in gratitude.

Thirteen

Buttery: A cellar or storage space in which provisions, like food and drink, are stored for visitors.

SUMMER SETTLES IN LIKE a dragon exhaling over the land. The humidity hovers above and around everything; in the mornings, it mingles with the cool, dewy air and casts a shroud of dense fog over the forest floor. The forest is alight with greenery, moss and ferns and emerald pine needles. Roses erupt on their deep green bushes; tomatoes and courgettes grow shiny and plump on their vines, the squash tendrils unfurling every which way.

Simonetta, too, feels the stirring of summer, a thread of wildness that threatens to unspool. There is a weight within her, a longing, an awareness of her body that she hasn't felt in some time. She is drawn to the outside, with a strange desire to run, to move, to touch, to come alive and enjoy all that being alive has to offer. At dinner she drinks an extra glass of wine; in the morning, eats an extra biscuit; she scrubs and cleans the chateau with excess vigor. At night she collapses into bed, sore and exhausted and sometimes slightly drunk, and awakens sweating and tangled in sheets. She is learning to function on the whims of her body.

She strives to be very present, rooted in whatever the day requires. Plenty occupies her mind; her thoughts return constantly to the automaton. But she needs to find ways to address the physical restlessness. Despite her darndest attempts to wear herself out, there's a thread inside of her in need of pulling, a string in need of plucking.

It's not just the vibrant summer that has blossomed around her and awakened her soul. Simonetta knows a source of her own sudden blooming—Jeremy. Now that she no longer avoids him, their paths cross constantly and she wonders how many of the "accidental" meetings are subconscious or intentional by one or the other. Now she understands a bit more how he communicates. His thoughtfully chosen words make conversation easy; she takes him at his word, no longer interpreting intent based on tone or the situations she makes up in her head. It's easier for her, too—she replies when necessary, but much of her time around him is spent in silence during the few hours they have enough spare time to research and share findings about the automaton. Having no clear answers yet means that she still revels in the possibility of discovery. No proof otherwise means there is still a chance that the connections she seeks exist.

Simonetta wants something magical in her life, something to give her purpose beyond the mundane. She can't bear the thought of returning empty-handed to Berkeley at the end of the summer, a place where she no longer has her closest family, a job, a home. It's too late now to change course. She has already leaped desperately into the unknown, and Simonetta hopes the Altobella automaton is built strong enough to catch her.

SYMONNE

When Catelot turned ten, Old Marthe died, and that's when Symonne finally met the witches of Santa Maddalena.

It was June and summer had encompassed the fortress. Heavy storm clouds hovered overhead, releasing sheets of rain periodically to soften the land into which Symonne dug Old Marthe's grave. Catelot wanted to help—Symonne's first inclination was to prevent the young girl from doing so, worried that dressing and preparing Old Marthe for burial would unearth the trauma of her mother's death. But over the years, Catelot had witnessed the death of many of their animals, the neutral cycles of nature of which death was an expected element, and accepted it with a stoic curiosity.

Catelot was careful and observant as she helped Symonne wrap Old Marthe in the simple linens they could spare, lowered her carefully into the grave, and helped fill it with the moist soil.

When they were done, Symonne asked, "Would you like to pray?"

Catelot shrugged. "If you think we should."

Symonne frowned. "It's important that we ask God to protect her soul, no?"

"Wouldn't God already know her soul?"

"Yes, but we have to ask Him to guide her to heaven," Symonne explained, although her own belief in the words revealed a trickle of ambivalence.

Symonne grappled with how hard to push on this. Lacking the resources and knowledge to foster ongoing Catholic traditions, Symonne had done her best over the years to guide Catelot in faith. But with no dedicated chamberlain—aside from Bertrand, whose fervor for God had reached a fever pitch in the aftermath of the plague—she had to make do with what she could remember from her own upbringing. And although her mother met the expectations of being a devout and modest widow, the learnings Symonne had absorbed were mostly about the natural world—how to live among it, how to make use of it for healing, how to bring a babe into the world or help a suffering old soul depart it. Symonne's mother attributed her knowledge to God but there was an unspoken sentiment in everything she taught, that life is a thread that one spools with their own hands.

Beyond prayer, Symonne had little to teach or offer Catelot by way of Catholicism. The closest church was miles away over the mountains, and Symonne feared that leaving their blessed commune would disrupt the peaceful cocoon they had fostered for themselves. On holidays, Symonne and Catelot and Bertrand and Old Marthe and the few families who lived on the outskirts of the land gathered and prayed together. But daily, Symonne and Catelot found their faith through the labor required to sustain their lives—baking bread, cultivating the gardens, weaving textiles, cleaning the fortress, building and repairing furniture. And their life offered leisure. In the last few years, Symonne had become fascinated by painting, with young Catelot as her muse. Together they traversed the grounds and collected materials that they ground into pigments, then mixed with egg yolks to make them vibrant. Most of her first paintings depicted the landscape around the fortress, the mist-shrouded mountains and the dense forest and the fields of grass. But Symonne found that Catelot was her favorite subject, and she made special canvases by stretching out dried animal skins across smooth planks of wood that Catelot offered to plane for her.

They had lived for seven years in quiet bliss, Symonne and Catelot and their makeshift community of people who felt keenly that they had been blessed by God to enjoy lives of liberty. But Symonne knew they existed like this on borrowed time, that the seclusion of the fortress was the main reason they had yet to be discovered, and she felt a tradeoff of eternal damnation for the sake of her quiet years with Catelot was well worth the risk.

But when she awoke one morning to find Catelot feverish and trembling beside her, she knew she had strayed too far.

She ran out into the bailey only to find Bertrand, whittling. He stood up and made the sign of the cross when Symonne relayed the news, then ushered her out toward the river.

"God is punishing the girl," he said. "Do not let yourself be caught up in her sin. Let Him do what he thinks is best."

"God did not save her from the plague simply to let her die at ten years old!" Symonne screamed, then immediately regretted it—Bertrand's expression changed from stoic to suspicious. He squinted his eyes and she wanted to be anywhere else but in the line of judgment.

"You, a laundress, presume to know God's will?" he asked, a dangerous edge to his quiet voice.

Symonne chose her words carefully. "Of course not. Bertrand, we've known each other for many years. Like you, I believe that we were given a second chance. But so was Catherine. She was spared, like we were. I believe He has a bigger purpose for her."

He sat down again and returned to whittling. "There is nothing you can do. It is not for us to intervene in His plans. If she makes it through the night, then you'll know what He intended."

Symonne knew she was on her own, that the others would take Bertrand's side. But there was absolutely no way she would stand by and watch Catelot suffer, no matter what God or Bertrand or anyone else said.

She wracked her brain trying to remember how her own mother would treat them for sickness. She started with broth, stewing the carcass of a quail until the liquid was golden, oily and congealed. Catelot choked drinking it, and Symonne inspected her closely for boils like she had with Marcella and the others who had died years prior during the plague. But there was nothing marring Catelot's skin other than the fever inflaming it, and after the girl got some broth down the trembling ebbed and she slept fitfully for several hours.

When Catelot awoke, she was groggy and her voice cracked when she tried to speak. Symonne wrapped her in linen and brought her to the river to bathe. At first, Catelot shrieked and cried at the cold water, but when it eased the fever, she relaxed against Symonne. She slept again on the banks of the river, naked and shaded by the trees overhead. Symonne kept watch and gathered nettles to turn into a tincture. Then she wept.

Symonne awoke to darkness and the sound of the river lapping against the banks. She glanced beside her to find the blanket on which Catelot had been sleeping, empty.

"Catelot?" she said, panic rising. "Catherine!"

A light broke through the darkness of the forest. Standing among the trees was a hooded woman, holding a tallow candle that glowed golden among the black. She placed a finger to her lips, then crooked the same finger to beckon Symonne.

Symonne scrambled to her feet and followed the woman and candlelight to a clearing, where two other women, all with dark hair long and loose around their shoulders, knelt on the ground. The hooded woman joined them, and the three formed an L-shape. In the center of their vignette was Catelot, still naked, stretched out on dark fabric and surrounded by twigs and leaves bound into strange shapes. At first, Symonne thought wildly that Catelot was dead and that she had stumbled upon a dark ritual, but Catelot's chest rose and fell evenly. The hooded woman beckoned again to Symonne and pointed to a space near her, where Symonne kneeling would complete an even square surrounding Catelot. Too stunned to speak, Symonne obeyed and was handed another candle, which the hooded woman lit with her own.

Then, the women began to speak in low, syncopated voices; Symonne could only understand bits and pieces of the Latin. Although she knew she was witnessing witchcraft and should be shrieking and whisking Catelot away from this wicked magic, the chanting was rhythmic and hymnal. A warmth spread in her chest, and the sensation of invisible hands creeping up from the forest floor and finding the pressure points in her back and chest doused her with calm. This was healing magic, she understood— the women were trying to heal Catelot and cast out her sickness. She recognized it because it was like what her mother used to do, sans Latin and bound twigs.

She focused on the words they spoke and was able to understand more than she had at first. She heard words like roots and soil and moon. She gleaned that they were asking for the energy in the forest that makes the flora and fauna within it grow and flourish to be shared with young Catelot.

They began to sway and Symonne joined them, murmuring along with the parts she understood. She closed her eyes and got lost in the rhythm of the chanting, pushing intent into every word she spoke. They swayed and chanted for what felt like hours, but afterward Symonne was sure it had only lasted several minutes. When the chanting stopped, her eyes flew open and she saw Catelot sitting up, pulling the fabric around her shoulders to hide her nakedness although a sheen of sweat had broken out over her skin—and even in the lowlight, Symonne saw that Catelot was healthy, the sallowness in her cheeks replaced with the plumpness of youth.

The girl took a deep breath and asked for water, and one of the younger women, whom Symonne guessed was around her own age, nearing thirty judging by the bright eyes but a streak of gray at the crown of her hairline, handed over a shallow bowl. Catelot drank heartily and smiled with gratitude. The other one—younger, not much older than Catelot, perhaps still a teenager—brought out bread and Symonne recognized the scent and the shape of it, and she knew that she had found her guardian angels.

Once a month Symonne and Catelot gathered in the forest with the witches.

They knew little about each other, beyond names—Augusta was the matriarch, followed by Alessa, her daughter, and Alisabeta, her granddaughter. The four women, with Catelot in tow, said very little to each other, but somehow found a common language. Symonne learned that the women lived in the mountains in a place they called Santa Maddalena, and from the strange dialect that seemed partially Latin and something else entirely, she learned much from them about the ways of nature.

They showed Symonne and Catelot how to double-weave thick fabrics that remained warmer during the cold winters, and how to dye them using the abundance of flora found in the foothills. Symonne and Catelot's once-neutral palette of linen became an array of vibrant, lovingly made dresses that lasted for seasons requiring little repair. The witches brought them wool sheared from the sheep they tended to, and sometimes bone from the horned goats that roamed in the mountains. They showed them how to make new types of bread, how to bring a fermented yeast paste back to life, how to boil rounds of dough with herbs for something hearty and savory. They guided Catelot and Symonne through the foothills to find medicinal plants—how to brew or milk or distill them. The witches brought them the stuff of a prosperous life—dyes and seeds and herbs and propagated flora. And they never asked for anything in return, although Symonne always offered, beyond the chance to share their magic.

Above all, the witches taught Catelot and Symonne how to move in silence, how to perform magic infused with love, how to remain shrouded in darkness and away from eyes of judgment.

When Catelot turned thirteen and she bled for the first time, Symonne brought her to the forest to celebrate.

The women brought with them gifts. Symonne had expected the ferocity with which she loved Catelot to wane over the years—not because she loved Catelot any less with age, but because she thought maturity would make it easier for her to not be consumed with love and pride and worry over her ward. Symonne was convinced she would never swoon over teenage Catelot the way she did with the dimple-handed toddler she had initially adopted, but that couldn't be less true. She watched with pride as the witches applied oil to Catelot's beautiful skin, olive like her birth mother's, and braid her long gleaming hair into an intricate plait. Although Symonne rarely prayed anymore, she sent a thank you to Cateline Desrosiers beyond the grave for the gift of raising her daughter.

Catelot took the ritual in stride, exchanging bemused glances with Symonne when the beautifying became too invasive, but she gave a warm smile and sincere gratitude to the women who had kept her safe and healthy and nourished and educated and loved over the past decade. And when they were done adorning Catelot, she stood gleaming with oil, dressed in black, vibrant beads glinting at her throat and wrists. Symonne was moved by pride over the young woman before her. Despite everything, despite how small their lives were and had to be, Catelot was remarkable: beautiful not just outwardly, but internally, too: patient and kind and resourceful. She was content to be Symonne's companion although Symonne wanted so much more for her—Catelot was destined for more. She was a noble daughter and deserved a better life. When she was old enough, Symonne vowed, they would leave Desrosiers together, find Catelot a husband so she could have a family of her own, reclaim her noble birth, or embark on whatever future she wanted. And Symonne would be there to support her every step of the way.

Augusta gave Catelot a parcel wrapped in linen. Catelot unwrapped it to reveal a long, thin knife with a white-bone handle.

"For your woodworking," said Augusta. Catelot beamed; she loved woodworking and whittling like Symonne loved painting. "And for your protection."

When Catelot showed it to Symonne, the smooth iron caught the light of the fire. An astute gift, Symonne thought—lovely and practical, like Catelot herself. Symonne couldn't help but think that every girl's ascension into womanhood should be celebrated with a knife. But she prayed once more and, for surety, sent a second iteration into the fire for the flames to speak into the universe—that Catelot's blade would only ever be used for making something beautiful.

SIMONETTA

The work-stay program isn't all work. Aside from the humble stipend they all receive in exchange for their labor, Claudel does her best to provide them their own memorable experience at Desrosiers. Every Friday evening, she gives a historical talk, sharing riveting stories about the chateau and Sainte-Madeleine. Simonetta has never met such a lively, evocative storyteller. Had she not been a chatelaine, Claudel would have been an excellent radio host or stage performer, Simonetta thinks. Claudel Morin knows how to tell stories about the past that make them come alive for everyone who listened—it's in the cadence of her voice, the intonations, the gestures, the pacing.

Simonetta absorbs Claudel's stories like a sponge. After the discovery of Marguerite's compositions, Claudel told them more of the marchioness's story: her family, starting with how Marguerite's father, Nicholas Cavalier de Sainte-Madeleine, and the Cavalier descendants, owned the chateau for more than one hundred years, surviving even the French Revolution. Marguerite was a peculiar woman—she never married, but inherited wealth and the estate upon the death of her brother and father during the Provencal plague of 1720. Like the chateau's first daughter, Catelot Desrosiers, Marguerite was one of few survivors in her family and remained as the chateau's owner and keeper until her death at age eighty-two—"a remarkable age, really, for the time," said the spritely seventy-something Claudel, who looks and acts like she will live forever.

Serendipity, Simonetta thinks. Plague had struck the chateau twice, felling many of its inhabitants, and yet two strong daughters survived and thrived despite the odds. What were the odds, that two notable inhabitants had somehow made it through such traumatic events?

Simonetta wonders if she's seeking connections that aren't there; three hundred years separate Catelot and Marguerite, and they were both of noble birth, so it's not that surprising that they both were able to cloister themselves and survive, right? But it niggles at Simonetta anyway, that both the Desrosiers and the Sainte-Madeleine families had been so ravaged by pestilence and yet, two had survived. Simonetta has a certain kinship as the "strong daughter" left behind. She wonders if Catelot and Marguerite felt what she did—the freedom, the guilt.

Among many improvements and changes to the chateau—most of the right wing's expansion was Marguerite's doing, including the addition of large frescoes and sumptuous pale green wallpaper in the Grand Salon—Marguerite de Sainte-Madeleine had also established the tradition of the Midsummer fête, hosted in early summer every year. It was a lavish, lively celebration that brought locals to the chateau grounds for three days of camping and feasting. Over the years, the tradition had been upheld, although now it's less about impressing the peasantry and more about celebrating the local community. Claudel, like the other chateau owners throughout France, see their roles as stewards, not gatekeepers upholding the virtues of servitude. The chateaus are historical buildings, part of France's past in all its horror and beauty. The Midsummer fête brought people to the grounds and buildings, which were opened to encourage exploration and education.

When Claudel took over as chatelaine two decades ago, she had added her own piece to the fête: a request (more of a requirement, really) to dress in historical garb. She maintains several massive oak wardrobes stuffed to the brim with historical clothing and costumes, representing all the eras through which the chateau had existed. She even has a priceless replica Fortuny gown carefully tucked among the historical outfits, a collection composed of Renaissance-era brocades, kirtles and corsets, puffy-sleeved Regency gowns, chemises and bloomers and vests and waistcoats and ties. Every summer, work-stay staff made new items to add to the collection, and an array of styles and sizes is represented, to everyone's delight.

A week before the fête, Claudel had encouraged everyone to pick out their ensembles. During breaks in their projects, the volunteers went to the attic to sort through the garments. Simonetta had gone up in shifts, once with Jason and Diego—Jason opted for a very romantic yet understated Arts-and-Crafts era look, complete with dark brown trousers and a loose-fitting artist smock that he was sure Hanako would enjoy, whereas Diego took the opposite approach, pulling out fitted, vibrantly colored garments that fused together numerous eras: a yellow Regency vest, brown braes, shining olive boots from WWI. It was a chaotic look that worked perfectly on him.

The decision-making torments Simonetta, so instead of deciding, she commits to three different outfits, a choice made easy by the sheer abundance of options. Day 1's attire included a deep green medieval-inspired (emphasis on "inspired") dress, with short sleeves and a gold trim sewn around the edges. The wide neckline was vaguely 1400s in origin, although it was designed to be worn over an underdress, but Simonetta plans to wear it on its own with red lipstick and sandals, so historical accuracy wasn't necessarily the goal. It's a dress she felt good in; it was fitted in the torso but light on her skin, made of a dyed linen that moved comfortably around her body. She could easily traverse the forest or the garden in such a dress.

The same cannot be said for her second choice—an Italian

Renaissance gown, deep red, with a stiff, square neckline formed by the rich red brocade. The bust fit snuggly atop a white blouse with billowing sleeves. She found a pearled rosary to don atop the rest and planned to wind another string of costume pearls through her braided hair. The gown was lovingly made, the inside lining composed piecemeal with scrap fabric, the stitches impeccably neat. She has never worn anything like it; all trips to the San Francisco Renaissance Faire had included cheaply made corsets worn over jeans. She's committed now to each look, an excuse to wear something she'd not normally have a chance to wear, and she plans to revel in it every second.

The last dress is by far the best. Simonetta had sheepishly asked Claudel for the blessing to wear the Fortuny replica, which was, in its own right, still an expensive garment—"Dresses are meant to be worn, fine china is meant to be used… wear the dress!" It's the most exquisite thing she's ever worn. Beaded and pleated in the signature Fortuny style of the 1920s, the dress is a shade of dark gold that shifts slightly in the light. It has loose cap sleeves and a low back, and a strip of patterned fabric around the torso served as a belt. The first time Simonetta tried it on, emotion was thick in her throat—it felt perfect, and she felt beautiful.

Being beautiful has never really mattered that much to her. In the way looks mattered to everyone—a boon to some, a bane to others—Simonetta cares and is aware of her own appearance but had come to the realization in her early thirties that it didn't really matter; she couldn't change the foundation of how she looked, not in any permanent way that meant anything, and instead focused on the things in life she could control. She prides herself on being relatively put together every day—but beauty is somewhat of an elusive thought to her. But now, as something inside of her awakens, self-aware and hungry, Simonetta has a foreign urge to feel it. She wants the power the nymph possesses. It's more that she wants to be worthy of the place she lives in, even if the arrangement is temporary. Desrosiers makes her want to elevate herself in every way.

But time spent donning gowns will have to wait for several

days, for the chateau needs its annual deep-clean in preparation for the fête. Everyone jumps into help; although cleaning is an integral part of daily chateau life, there were some areas that didn't see as much attention, like under the AGA (Simonetta avoids that task) or above the bookshelves in the library.

Simonetta had made decent enough progress in the oddities attic that Claudel agreed that some of the visitors could briefly peek in, only if they were accompanied by a volunteer, for the winding staircase still needed repair and too many people at once would dangerously stress-test the structure. To make the space a bit more hospitable, Simonetta organizes the remaining items in the quadrants, arranges them in a more guest-friendly display, and gives everything a thorough wipe-down.

She's knee-deep in the unpleasant taxidermy quadrant, trying to unweave spiderwebs from an antelope's stiff and furry ear, when she receives an unexpected visitor.

"I haven't seen this floor in years," Jeremy says. He brings with him a waft of oak and stain. "You've done a lot in here in a short time."

Simonetta stands and wipes her brow, leaving a grimy smudge across her forehead. "I'm glad you see progress. Sometimes it's hard for me to tell if anything's actually getting better, or if I'm just shuffling things around." She wrinkles her nose and gestures to the taxidermy. "So what's this all about?"

"I think that belonged to the previous owner, the Marquis de Najarac," he says. "It's rather unpleasant."

Simonetta waves a hand at the sawdust covering Jeremy's jeans. "Which project? Stairs or pew?"

"Stairs in the right wing. Needed to finish those before guests arrive since it will take a couple of days for the stain to fully dry." He inspects the mechanisms in the quadrant Simonetta had neatly grouped along the wall opposite the door, so people could see it as they came up the stairs—the largest grandfather clock remains where she found it, for it's far too unwieldy to move on her own, but she had arranged the two cuckoo clocks on either side, opening the tiny doors to reveal the inner workings. The gramophone sits before the armoire, beside an old transistor radio. Simonetta had polished the items to the best of her ability. "Did Claudel give you a tour of her immense costume collection?" Jeremy asks.

Simonetta laughs. "She did. I think Lotte is there now. I couldn't decide what I wanted, so I settled on three ensembles. What about you? Do you even attend the fête, or is it no longer a novelty for you?"

"Oh no, I quite enjoy it," he says. "Having visitors here helps me see the chateau with a new perspective. I also feel like it's hard for me to see progress when I'm so close to the project." He sighs. "Sometimes it just seems like all that's ahead of us is an endless to-do list for the restoration. The chateau will likely pass to me in what I hope will be the far distant future." Jeremy smiles. "It's heartening when others only see the beauty and not the work."

"I hope I've adequately conveyed how special I think this place is," Simonetta says earnestly. "Even the creepy bits, like the taxidermy. It's all been very rewarding, being a part of it."

"You've certainly given me much to think about," Jeremy says.

Another one of Jeremy's strange, cryptic things dropped during conversation has Simonetta wishing that a cipher slide was among the many odd objects she had uncovered. She decides against prodding him for meaning and reins herself in from interpreting or clarifying.

He clears his throat. "I came up here to let you know that supper is ready soon."

"Already?" She glances outside the window to see the lowering sun, the nymph far below the tower backlit swathed in gold. "I lost hours up here. Who's on supper duty tonight?"

"Claudel and me," he says. "We thought we'd give you all a break after how busy you've been this week."

Jeremy leaves Simonetta to the last of her tasks and she heads to supper soon after, stopping quickly in the servant's wing to wash up and change her clothes.

"Simonaaa!" Diego exclaims, first in line for food. "Pasta night!"

His own plate is heavy with pasta and vegetables, and he ladles an herbaceous green sauced over everything—pesto, Simonetta presumes, from both the color and the scent. Everything smells heavenly and she's famished. The spread reminds her of Sunday dinners at Nonna's, a tradition Simonetta had diligently upheld long after she had moved out.

She gets in line behind Diego and fills a plate with food, then follows him out to the terrace. Fairy lights strung under the awning glow golden in the dusk, and with a long match, Claudel lights the pillar candles on the table. Simonetta gushes about the beautiful display, to which Claudel says, "It's a taste of what's to come for the midsummer fête!"

Simonetta sips the glass of white wine offered to her, feeling tired and introspective. The food is delicious, but halfway through a bite, she turns rigid as a cold sweat passes through her. Something in the food conjures up an old memory of Nonno and Nonna in the garden, plucking basil. Nonno had shown Simonetta how to propagate basil by cutting off leaves above a branching node. That summer, she had had a row of sprouting herbs in glass jars lining her windowsill.

The memory is lovely, as is her present atmosphere, but her anxiety has a way of showing up in waves that freeze her to stone, and it will take hours to thaw. This wave crashes down upon her as she tries her best to weather the storm—she stares into her wine glass, feeling the familiar stomach-clenching, nervous-sweating combination, the manifestation of the ever-present panic that rears its ugly head just when she thinks she is coping better, her heart reminding her of everything she's lost just when she is starting to revel in what she's gained.

MARGUERITE

As a reward for sending off invitations to Papa's extensive list of invitees and to keep the returning lamentations in her head at bay, Marguerite became obsessed with her new violin.

She had always loved strings the most of all the instruments she tried, and when she played the violin, the music it produced spoke directly to her heart. Papa had brought with it a book of instructions, with diagrams on how to hold it, how to manage the bow, and several strands of cat gut strings that she was sure cost a fortune. But mostly she figured it out by ear and it quickly became an extension of her body. She loved its range, loved the callouses on her fingers that formed as she practiced and perfected her vibrato. She loved how it required poise and good posture but was mobile enough for the player to dance a jig if they wanted to. And sometimes she felt compelled to, when she composed a jaunty, lively tune—the connection of bow on string stirred her muscles, moved her body like a tide.

Although she had always enjoyed composing and playing, the violin made it easy for her to let loose her creativity, and every night she pored over the paper Papa had brought from Nice. And she had another muse besides the source of music.

Having a new lady's maid did indeed disrupt Marguerite's daily life, but in the best of ways. Marguerite had assumed that it would be easier to have a less astute servant so that she could be left to her own devices, but she hadn't expected that having a maid who understood her would make life so much easier.

After Elise found her on the edge of hysterics in her room upon Papa's news about marriage and offered her a hand, the two had an unspoken understanding. It had never even crossed Marguerite's mind to tell someone how she felt or what she experienced; she had no vocabulary for how she thought or why she did the things that she did. To have someone who understood and accepted her was beyond her comprehension. Elise recognized early on that Marguerite didn't leave the chateau, and rather than pry or judge, she simply served as Marguerite's liaison to the rest of the household. She spoke louder than necessary about the non-existent walks she and Marguerite took to ensure others heard and knew their mistress had indeed explored the grounds, that she went into the village market, that she attended church.

It even worked on Philippe. Marguerite was in the Grand Salon, sat in front of the fire with her papers scattered about.

She had skipped supper to finish her current composition. Elise brought her a tray.

"Mistress, you haven't eaten anything since we ventured out today," said Elise, presenting the tray of fruit and cakes.

Philippe, en route to the library, stopped in his tracks. "You ventured out today?"

Marguerite, in on the ruse, tampered down her enthusiasm and bit into a strawberry, plucked fresh from the garden. The sweetness danced across her taste buds. Cooly, she said, "Yes, we walked through the garden. I was noting which flowers to use as the palette for the ball. Was I supposed to ask for your permission?"

For once, Philippe had no retort. "Of course not. I was just surprised." He frowned and glanced at Elise, who simply blinked back at him. Marguerite thought the woman's expression was a masterclass in acting; she held a pleasant, unchallenging gaze that gave Philippe absolutely no reason to suspect that it was she who had started the lie in the first place. He nodded curtly then continued on his way.

Marguerite looked at Elise, suppressing an elation she had never felt. She never thought she'd ever get Philippe off her back; he was relentless in his need to wheedle her, undermine her. Elise met her eyes and winked, smiling slyly like a sleek cat, and Marguerite's heart filled with air.

Marguerite came into her room one evening to find Elise studying the violin, head cocked to the side, dark eyes squinting and evaluating the instrument.

"Elise?"

Elise started and turned, her expression guilty, and she dipped her head. "I'm so sorry, mistress. What can I do for you?"

Marguerite waved away her apology. "You have nothing to apologize for. Do you have a question about the violin?"

"I have many questions!" said Elise, her face aglow. "I've watched you play it dozens of times. What does it feel like?"

"Which part?"

"All of it—does it hurt when you press your fingers on the strings? How do you keep your wrist straight? How firmly do you have to hold the bow?"

Marguerite laughed. "It doesn't hurt because I have callouses already from the instruments I play." An idea sparked. "Do you want to learn how to play the violin? I could teach you."

Conflict cycled on Elise's face, but then she nodded. "Only when it won't interfere with what you need, of course."

Marguerite suppressed another laugh, knowing full well her days allowed for plenty of leisure time. It's why she spent so much time playing her instruments and composing. Teaching Elise would be no issue, and Marguerite took pleasure in the idea of being a teacher. It gave her something new to look forward to, a tendril of joy that pierced through the dread Marguerite felt about the upcoming ball in a fortnight.

Invitations had been sent and Marguerite anticipated each day like one awaits a painful procedure, playing over the possibilities in her head, preparing her mind and body for the inevitable. Whether she wanted it to or not, her life would change monumentally soon.

If Papa found her a suitable husband, she'd have no say in the matter, no recourse. She would have to accept her future. But the thought of Elise being with her soothed her somewhat. Elise had become her source of comfort and reassurance. It frightened Marguerite sometimes when she thought of how well Elise knew her—would her secrets be wielded against her someday?

SIMONETTA

Simonetta is glad when the guests arrive, for the activity gives her less time to think. The local village pours onto the chateau grounds, and former volunteers have flown in from all over for the festivities. Every room in the chateau is booked; the rest of the visitors set up tents across the grounds.

The chateau is abuzz and Simonetta delights in it. The party begins early on Friday morning, just after sunrise. The villagers filtered in first, arriving on foot, bike, and car, bearing offerings: loaves of bread, cheese from their farms, books and teacups and miscellanea. Many were already costumed; Simonetta notices that 1920s-era garb seems to be the trend this year, marking the impending change in decade.

Most of the fête is unscheduled, attendees left to roam and socialize as they see fit. Long banquet tables are set up on the terrace for evening meals, although Graham told Simonetta that a few years prior, revelers had set up impromptu picnics throughout the entire grounds, even so far as the moon gate in the forest.

"Every year is different," says Graham, adjusting his cravat. It's early afternoon and Simonetta is running on adrenaline. She and Alba had agreed to wear their costumes later in the day, after they could help with setup and ensure that everyone was getting settled in. Then she had run into Claudel in the hallway, who urged her to go put on her ensemble, but before she could do so, had been pulled into Graham's room to help him tie the back of his vest.

Graham, very British despite his summer Francophile escapades, is in head-to-toe Edwardian, donning a crisp, cream-colored suit, a black tie, and a pair of small round-rimmed glasses. He is unfazed by the heat—Simonetta, meanwhile, sweats through her blouse—and looks dashing, the suit's neutral tone setting his dusky skin alight. She continues to find Graham altogether charming, drawn toward his easy demeanor and friendliness.

"What do you usually do during the fête?" Simonetta asks, running her fingernail through the velvet fabric covering the armchair. She catches her haggard reflection in the corner of Graham's mirror, where he stands primping, and grimaces.

Graham removes his glasses, bends the metal frame slightly, then replaces them on the bridge of his nose. He grins at her in the mirror, a wicked smile she has never seen before. "Meet up with friends."

She resists the urge to pry, but the wheels in her mind whir; what did that mean? She imagines a bacchanal and grows envious. It occurs to her that, as comfortable as she is with Graham, there is so much she doesn't know about him still despite their daily conversations and collaborations. She has always felt that everyone could easily read everything about her, could easily understand her life story and what she was about; she assumes everyone else's mysteries eclipse her own. In this case, she's certainly right.

"You're an enigma, Mr. Okafor," she says simply, suddenly resolute to seek out her own mischief.

Hours later, Simonetta has the tart taste of cider on her tongue, the scent of rose in the back of her throat, and the delicate touch of smoke dancing across her lips. She passes the cigarette back to Alba and allows a pleasant, foggy dizziness to take over her mind, an intermingling of alcohol and tobacco that gives her both a jolt and a sedative. She savors the feeling of being slightly off-kilter; it's far different from the part of her always reaching, clinging, to something rooted, her constant need for control and stability. It's only when Simonetta makes a conscious effort to indulge that she truly enjoys it.

The heady night around her makes full use of her senses. Surrounded by the stone wall heavy with rose bushes, Simonetta sits around the fire pit with Alba and several villagers—knotted-knuckled Nicholas and his daughter Marie, who own the boulangerie; Paul and Malcolm, proprietors of the brocante; Amelia, a retired photographer who has come from Quebec to her ancestral town. Everyone has several decades on Simonetta, but she's always liked being around people older than her, found it easier company than kids her own age. It comforts her to know that there are still elders who knew the way of the world, who could guide her in some way. She had always placed a certain amount of trust into those who were older. So when Amelia came to the campfire with a pack of clove cigarettes and two bottles of Normandy cider, Simonetta followed her lead without questioning it.

Alba had prompted Simonetta to tell the others about the automaton, and the cider had loosened any residual reservations. Simonetta, aware that she is slightly drunk and probably babbling, explains her true predicament.

"There may not even be any relation," she admits to a captive Paul beside her, who understands just enough English to communicate, although they both slip in and out of French. The cider makes it easy to jump straight into her biggest fear, the crux of it all—that the automaton didn't mean anything other than being a curious relic. "Il y a beaucoup Altobellas." *There are many Altobellas.* Simonetta accepts the bottle from Paul—they had claimed one for themselves and were passing it back and forth—and takes a swig to clear the doubt from her throat.

"But there *might* be!" Paul says, his French thicker than it might have been sans cider, and he falls into his native tongue. Simonetta is just sober enough to follow. "I will look for you, a la brocante. Pour certains livres, ou autre automatons. Nous avons d'autres machines qui arrivent parfois." he says, offering to find books or other machines that sometimes arrived at the charity shop.

Paul's wiry gray hair is long and unkempt; he's dressed as an absurdly colorful Huguenot in a high-necked ruffled brocade shirt, billowing shorts, and red stockings. The heat ebbed and a cool breeze has settled in, much to Simonetta's relief. She had quickly showered earlier and put on her deep green medieval gown, the border material on the hems dotted with small golden fleur-de-lises. Normally the garment was layered, with a solid color shift worn underneath the short-sleeved patterned overdress, but Simonetta had omitted that addition in favor of comfort and modernity. The linen dress had kept her cool during the warm afternoon but now, despite the fire, she's grown slightly chilly. She glances toward Paul, who is now dozing in his chair. The burning log in the fire crackles and Simonetta suddenly wonders where Jeremy is.

She hasn't seen him since early in the morning, when he

was putting away some of his prized tools to ensure that no wandering visitors would meddle. A day prior, he and Simonetta had brought the automaton inside the chateau for safe keeping, tucking it away in the entry storage closet. Simonetta hadn't wanted to seem paranoid or selfish about hiding the automaton while dozens of people were roaming the grounds and was relieved when Jeremy had suggested it first.

Thinking about the automaton makes goosebumps erupt across her arms and back. Excusing herself to grab a sweater from her room, Simonetta leaves her campfire mates, engrossed in their own deep conversations, to check on the automaton.

To her surprise, the foyer is dark. She can hear people mingling in the upstairs rooms, and raucous laughter emanates from the Grand Salon. Simonetta suddenly craves solitude. She moves quickly to avoid being seen; she cracks open the closet and pulls aside the cloth covering the automaton. Lacking a light source, she struggles to see it clearly, but she can make out the shapes—Catelot's delicate face, her small violin, the outline of the cabinet. It calms her to see it. Satisfied, she replaces the cloth, closes the door, and slips back out into the night.

She wanders toward the chapel, past a few tents erected near the garden. The voices of the visitors fill the night air like fireflies, bits of brightness and revelry. Simonetta makes up her mind to head into the forest when she spots Jeremy in his workshop.

He's alone, poring over a book lit by a small camping lantern. Simonetta stops briefly to take in the vignette: a potent golden glow of the lantern illuminating Jeremy's face, his features partially shadowed by his dark curls. He wears a dark tunic over his normal trousers. Beyond him, the forest looms. It's like a painting by a Dutch master, the play of light and shape and shadow. He looks timeless to her in that moment, and her heart thrums.

She continues toward him and, at the sound of her feet on the soft grass, he finally looks up.

Simonetta feels suddenly bold. Wearing her costume makes her feel timeless, too, or out of time. She could be anywhere, in any era, existing only in the liminal void of night, illuminated only by candle, nourished only by the provisions of the forest; the light of the lantern and the aroma of the woods and the taste of residual smoke and the distant din of revelry fill nearly all of her senses, save for one.

"Simonetta," Jeremy says. Not a greeting, really, or an acknowledgment. He holds her gaze. "I can understand how Botticelli was so enchanted."

Before she can recover from the momentary absence of breath, he beckons her over. "I found a book about medieval toys. Most of them are wooden, as you might expect. But look—" he points to a doll, comparable in size and appearance as Catelot. "1397. A bit later, but it seems entirely plausible that Catelot was originally just a doll—maybe even belonging to the actual Catelot."

"I can't believe it's so old," Simonetta says, startled by the sudden shift to research. Jeremy had a way of matter-of-factly dropping a flirtatious bomb in her lap, only to switch gears a moment later, leaving her reeling. "But we know for certain the rest of it was built much later. I doubt any Altobella connection would be any earlier than the 1700s, given the maker mark. Paul from the brocante said he'd look in their archives as well. If he's still awake, I can ask him more." Emboldened again, Simonetta asks, "Do you want to come with me? We're at the fire pit in the garden."

Jeremy shakes his head. "How about I just walk you back over there? It's dark, and I don't want you to twist your ankle in a gopher hole."

Chivalrously, he holds out his arm for her accompaniment. She loops hers through his and the sensory array is complete— the last puzzle piece, touch, slides into place. His arm around hers sends a fissure of pleasure up her spine, and she has a sudden urge to pull him to the cool grass and pour cider into his mouth and clamber over him as she does so. She thinks of Graham and hopes he's fully indulging himself in ways she can only hope to. Should she even try to wrest Jeremy to the ground in an attempt at drunken seduction, she suspects Jeremy would not find it endearing. It doesn't stop her from thinking about it anyway.

She snickers despite herself. Jeremy glances over, eyebrows raised.

"Sorry," she says, clearing the laughter from her throat. "Too much cider. Don't judge me."

"On the contrary," he says. "I'm glad to see you're joining in. I figured you'd be holed up in the library or in the attic."

"Am I that boring to you?"

"Did I say that? Didn't you just find *me* reading during the fête?"

He has her there. "Now I just feel guilty—you're doing research for my project while I'm conversing in terrible French."

Jeremy shrugs, a gesture that pulls her arm closer against his side. "I'm enjoying it."

"The research, or my terrible French?"

They arrive back at the fire. More had come to join—Simonetta spots Aurelia, along with some new people she doesn't recognize.

Jeremy extracts his arm from hers and squeezes her hand before releasing it. "Have fun. Don't do anything I wouldn't do."

Simonetta watches him leave, the fire illuminating his back until he eventually fades back to the shadow. His silhouette burns in her mind, the dark blue of his tunic the same midnight hue as the dark summer sky, the gold dotted hem catching the embers of light. Her arm, recently warm from where he had cradled it in his, is cold once again.

Later that night, as she drifts to sleep, Simonetta realizes that the symbol dotting the hem of Jeremy's tunic was a fleur-de-lis.

Simonetta hasn't been hung over in years. The last time she experienced such a pounding headache and a sour stomach was also the last time she had been in Europe, four years prior, when Alex had forced her to explore La Real in Barcelona and they had stayed up until dawn. Both times, Simonetta is grateful for fresh European bread to mop up the mistakes.

The morning is hot already, and campers and visitors are

up already making breakfast. Simonetta comes to the kitchen to find Alba and Aurelia also nursing post-cider headaches. She introduces her suffering comrades to the "hair of the dog," and makes them all very strong Bloody Marys packed with pickles.

After bread and breakfast cocktails, Simonetta is feeling considerably better, although the harsh sun has her rethinking her chosen outfit. She instead opts out of the blouse and wears just the Renaissance-era overdress, with its two brocade straps that tie at the top of her shoulders. She winds pearls into her hair, still smokey from the campfire and cigarettes. Red lipstick again, and she is ready for more revelry.

Lotte finds her in the garden and invites her to an impromptu flower crown workshop. Lotte had cropped her hair a week prior and wears a thin red scarf around her neck—a look from the French Revolution, where the pixie cut and accompanying scarf composed a look fondly and gruesomely known as "the Guillotine," with the red scarf signifying a severed head. On doe-eyed Lotte, the look was very effective.

Simonetta follows her to the edge of the forest, where a table that is covered in freshly cut flowers, ferns, and sprigs of herbs, along with scissors and spools of thin wire. Lotte, filming the workshop like a Sophia Coppola film with a heavy emphasis on aesthetics, demonstrates to Simonetta and two visitors—Bayara and Carly from England, fans of Claudel's YouTube channel—how to twist the wire so that it firmly holds the stems without pinching it too tightly. Simonetta chooses a combination of peonies, baby's breath, rosemary, and thyme for her flower crown.

Upon seeing Simonetta's selections, Bayara hums the melody "Scarborough Faire." Carly and Simonetta join in, singing:

Are you going to Scarborough Fair?
Parsley, sage, rosemary, and thyme
Remember me to one who lives there
She once was a true love of mine

At first the song warms Simonetta, until a tendril of cold passes through—still thawing from the bout of anxiety that started the other day during supper, the block of ice in her chest releases a rivulet of chilliness and she shivers despite the heat. She knows Nonna would say that a ghost had passed through her, and Simonetta senses that's true—perhaps it was even Nonna herself. She is surrounded everywhere by ghosts, even the ghosts of her former self, a version that was happy and untouched by loss—a version that never even existed, but taunts her with who she could have been, in another life.

MARGUERITE

"Start with it on your head, like I showed you."

Elise pursed her lips. "Do I have to?"

"It's the best way to ensure it's in the right placement. This is how I learned."

"But you were alone." Elise bristled and Marguerite grinned; typically composed Elise looked moments away from stomping her feet.

"Fine," Elise said, relenting. She placed the violin atop her head and gave Marguerite a look of disdain. Slowly, she brought the violin to the top of her right shoulder, and finally, to its place of rest below her chin.

"See? It's exactly where it needs to be." Marguerite smoothed her dress and sat up straight in her chair. "Shall we? From the beginning. Slowly."

Elise also adjusted her posture and brought the bow to the violin. She barely touched the bow to the strings when Marguerite interrupted—

"—drop your wrist," she said.

Elise huffed. "Marguerite! At least let me start." She lowered the violin in protest.

At the sound of her name on Elise's tongue, Marguerite grew warm. Elise was careful to maintain proper titles in the presence of company but took it upon herself to call Marguerite her given name in private. It made Marguerite's heart swell and her limbs tingle, her name spoken in Elise's husky timbre. The word spoken hearkened to that which wasn't, the other words they had yet to say, the ones that spill out in the things they do in one another's presence.

When Elise straightened once again and put the violin on her head without protest, Marguerite cherished the action for the declaration she knew it was.

Fourteen

Moat: A dug trench encircling a castle estate, often filled with water.

ON THE FINAL DAY of the fête, rain is imminent and the air is heavy and expectant. Simonetta, too, teeters on the edge despite the mostly blissful days. She awakens early and slips into the Fortuny replica she's been saving, its gold pleats rippling over her body. She repurposes the pearls from the day prior and wears them as designed, a long strand that drapes over her torso. Although she wants desperately to enjoy the day, her stomach is in knots, and no amount of deep methodical breathing seems to alleviate the anxiety that lurks nearby.

After days of revelry, the fête would conclude today with a final afternoon of activities before everyone bids one another farewell. Diego and Graham set up a small platform in the forest clearing, and all day, attendees would attend a performance or workshop. Simonetta knows Jason and Hanako plan to lead a plein air painting class, taking participants step by step through painting the river and the moon bridge, and thinks through her schedule to see if she can make time to attend.

A knock sounds at her door as she finishes applying lipstick. She opens it to find Jeremy, dressed brilliantly in a gold coat over a white shirt and black jodhpurs. A pearl brooch is pinned to his collar, visible below his trimmed beard. He had pulled his hair back into a ponytail at the nape of his neck, and rogue curls spring loose from their binding. He looks resplendent and Simonetta's stomach clenches.

"Looks like we match today!" says Simonetta brightly, inflicting her voice with more pep than she feels.

"Convenient, that," says Jeremy. He avoids her eyes, and Simonetta blinks—has he been intentionally matching her these past few days? She thinks of his fleur-de-lis tunic, the red vest she saw him wear briefly yesterday, and now his gold-and-pearl ensemble.

It now seems very obvious to her and she is speechless. The effort he must have gone to—who did he conspire with to learn her outfits? It must have been Claudel.

Simonetta doesn't know how to process this or understand the weight it holds. Was it just for fun, him matching her outfits? Maybe hers had given him ideas. Or did it mean much more— was it his way of conveying how he felt?

She wants to grab her notebook and write down everything he has ever said to her and analyze the data. *You have a beautiful nose. I can understand how Botticelli was so enchanted. You've given me a lot to think about.* Did they all add up to anything?

"I have a favor to ask," Jeremy says, sheepish in a way Simonetta has never seen him before, and for a moment it's nice that the tables have turned and he is tentative around *her*. Then she feels immediately guilty for thinking that way, knowing all too well what it's like to be on the other side.

"Of course," she says earnestly. "What can I do? Do I need to change my clothes?"

"No, you look—" he says, swallowing hard, then stops. "What you're wearing is perfect. It's not a chateau project. I was wondering if you'd play a violin accompaniment to the song I'm going to sing for the last performance today. In the clearing. Before the guests depart."

He holds up a small booklet: *Irish Ballads for the Fiddle*.

She clears her throat of the bubbles of emotion that build up there. "I'd be honored. I'll need to run through it a few times first, but I should have plenty of time." She accepts the booklet, glad to have a reason to look away from his face, although she wants to read what's written there, too.

A page is dog-eared. "'The Parting Glass,'" she reads. "Is that the one?"

"Yes," says Jeremy. "A favorite of my mother's. A somewhat sad song, I've always thought, but I thought it'd be a good send-off for the visitors."

"I didn't know you sang," Simonetta replies, smiling up at him. "I can play quite a few accompaniments, if you enjoy a duet."

"I knew you would," he says, sheepishness removed upon her acceptance of his request. "I'm sure you have other plans today, but I will be there late afternoon. We'll be the last show before departure."

When he leaves, Simonetta applies rosin to her bow and gives her violin a quick wipe-down. On the uneven music stand she pilfered from the Room of Oddities, she props up the music booklet in front of Marguerite's compositions that she's been practicing. Simonetta plays through the melody slowly first to get acquainted with each note. It's a simple tune, and the violin music follows the melody of the singer in a pattern that repeats itself. She runs through it again at a quicker tempo, and again a few more times, adding some subtle flourishes before it feels natural and familiar enough in her hands.

A couple of hours later, she continues to hum the tune in her head. It is stuck to her now and she plays it on repeat, the melody that rises and falls during each verse. She had looked up the lyrics on her laptop, seeking context beyond the music, and agrees with Jeremy's thoughts on the song: it was bittersweet. The melody is lovely but somber, and the lyrics meant for anyone setting off on a journey that no one could follow. Simonetta wonders what Jeremy's singing sounds like, imagines a rich, low tenor. Her heart skips a beat as she thinks of his voice, ready for it to resonate in her chest.

She spends the hours in between helping where she can before the Nomura's painting workshop and her performance with Jeremy. Lotte and Diego are on lunch duty, and the kitchen has been turned upside down in their attempt to make galettes.

Claudel's painstaking attempts to teach them to clean as they go have fallen on deaf ears, and Simonetta, despite her opulent ensemble, grabs an apron and jumps into help, if only to prevent Claudel from seeing the kitchen in such a state of chaos.

The three of them manage to produce two dozen galettes composed of various produce sourced from the garden, and Simonetta tasks Lotte and Diego with dishes while she sets the terrace table and carries out the plates. Many visitors had opted to continue camping, but as it's the last day of the fête, a large group has joined the volunteers for a "formal" lunch gathering. Simonetta makes use of Claudel's summer china, mismatched plates adorned with patterns of fruit and flora. The visitors and villagers she had met—including Paul, Malcolm, Marie, and Nicholas from the bonfire night—gather around the table. Simonetta spots Graham, at the side of a beautiful woman who had driven in from Belgium.

Claudel went all out for her final costume, wearing an eighteenth-century gown plucked straight from Marie Antoinette's wardrobe, pale pink with white and gold embroidery. Her gray hair is impeccably curled in an elaborate bouffant, and she even dotted her cheek with a black mouche. Once everyone is seated at the long table—made longer by the tables Simonetta and Jason had gotten out of storage a week prior—Claudel raises her glass of champagne and leads a toast.

"Those who once lived here imagined our era the far distant future," she says. "But these celebrations keep us connected to the past. The estates are meant to be lived in and loved, and celebrating the summer with you every year makes all of the work—" she gestures to the volunteers, where Simonetta sits with the others "—worth it. Thank you for keeping Desrosiers' heart beating. À votre santé!"

The table echoes the toast with gusto, in various languages—*Salud! Proost! Here here!*—and clinks glasses. Jeremy, who had slinked in as Claudel was making her toast, catches Simonetta's eye from down the table and holds her gaze as they each sip from their cups. She remembers what Nonna used to say: those who didn't make and keep eye contact during a toast would suffer bad luck (and bad sex, Nonna told her once she had turned eighteen) for seven years. Nonna, a logical Catholic woman, was not immune to bouts of superstition and had hung in the kitchen a horn-shaped charm to ward off the *malocchio*, the evil eye. Simonetta takes the toast tradition to heart, wanting to avoid all ill that could befall her. Jeremy's gaze remains unbroken even as they set down their glasses, and his heady stare puts even the curse-repellent cornicello to shame.

MARGUERITE

Feeling like a decorated poodle with her powdered hair and the red ballgown that doubled the width of her hips, Marguerite made the rounds in the Grand Salon, greeting the guests who had traveled far to praise Papa and his grand estate and meet his daughter. But despite all the work and money Papa had invested in Desrosiers, the reality was that it was still remote and attending the ball required a summertime trek through the rain-drenched roads that only the most dedicated deigned to venture.

She was surprised to find herself enjoying the evening, helped by the fact that only a few of Papa's invited suitors had managed to attend. His primary pick in attendance was Jean-Louis de La Perrine, an investor who was older than her father by at least a decade. But when he never asked Marguerite to dance and spent most of the ball imbibing and complaining about how much colder it was in Sainte-Madeleine than in the Caribbean, from where he had recently returned, Papa sneered and shook his head at Marguerite, who pretended to be upset by this decision.

It went on like that for most of the ball—the handful of Papa's hand-picked suitors quickly falling out of his favor for some faux pas or another. Marguerite was tentatively elated, glad to not have to force small talk and charm with these men but waited for the other shoe to drop—if there was no husband here, Papa very well could whisk her off to Nice or elsewhere on his travels.

Her one solace was that she would be able to take Elise

with her. She looked through the crowd to find her maid and spotted Elise at the edge of the salon, hovering near the door in case Marguerite needed her, and took comfort in her presence. Marguerite surveyed the ballroom, admitting that it was nice to see it full. She wished Papa had chosen a more palatable wallpaper; the orange toile with the hunting motif did little favors for this expansive space, and it clashed with the grand marble mantle surrounding the fireplace. Marguerite thought a pale green would better suit the room with its windows facing the garden; that shade would complement the lush scene outside. And perhaps the molding would be better in gold rather than white, as the room was where most of their festivities were hosted, and it should impress with its glamour.

Still, she enjoyed the activity. Marguerite cherished her time in the quiet, but it was pleasant to have Desrosiers alive with activity. Perhaps if she made more of an effort to bring people to Desrosiers, to host and entertain, Papa would expect less of her venturing outside of it. If important guests visited regularly, someone had to be there to receive them.

If she would never step foot into the world, she would bring the world to Desrosiers.

SIMONETTA

A swell of nerves erupts in her stomach as she reapplies rosin to her violin bow and lipstick to her lips and sets out toward the clearing. It's not so much the performance, or the song; the song itself is quite straightforward, and she enjoys fiddle tunes for their memorable simplicity. The performance space, too, is casual: the "stage" is a small wooden platform propped up on cinderblocks several inches off the ground, and the attendees sit on blankets spread out over the forest floor. The morning dew had saturated the forest and the earthy scent envelops Simonetta as she passes through the threshold of trees, the natural line demarcating the chateau territory and the wilderness. In her golden, draped gown, Simonetta feels like Artemis wielding a different bow.

Most of the visitors, more than a hundred in total, have come to the clearing for the final performance; afterward, they will make their way home, scatter back across France and beyond. There's a bittersweet note to the gorgeous afternoon, the shared acceptance that the communal experience has come to an end for another year. Jeremy is there already, talking with Claudel and Paul. He has removed his coat, leaving his white shirt tucked into his trousers, although his hair remains tied back. Nonna would have said he looked "dashing"; Simonetta thinks he looks like a very handsome pirate on the cover of a romance novel.

Jeremy excuses himself from the conversation and meets Simonetta. "Thank you for doing this with me."

"My pleasure," says Simonetta. "I'll follow your lead."

Jeremy holds out an arm chivalrously toward the stage and she takes her place while he addresses the audience.

"Claudel said everything best during her toast at lunch, but I just want to thank you all again for coming," he says. "Your presence here reminds me of our purpose, restoring and protecting all of this." He gestures to the forest and the chateau beyond the trees. "I appreciate you renewing my fervor for it. I wanted to leave you with an old Irish song, and I'm accompanied by the lovely Simonetta, whom many of you had the fortune to meet."

Simonetta is struck by his eloquence, the confidence with which he speaks to the crowd. He so frequently avoids speaking to a group, but he does so effortlessly. A smattering of applause followed by an expectant hush heralds the start of their performance.

Simonetta holds up her bow and waits for Jeremy's signal. He looks at her and smiles, then nods his head.

She plays the opening note, the sweetness of it reverberating among the trees. Jeremy joins in right on cue, and the passion in his tenor almost trips her up and makes her misplay the melody.

"Of all the money that e'er I had

I spent it in good company…"

His voice marries her music in harmony, in the truest sense of the word. The richness of his singing—imperfect and rugged, but more beautiful because of it, like a sailor singing a shanty on a doomed sinking ship. It resonates in her blood, the vibrations of the strings and of his voice and the weight the words hold. It's a song about leaving, about being left, and she gets lost in it, plays with abandon, the vibrato of her fingers emulating her fluttering heart.

She holds her breath until the last line rings out through the trees. "Goodnight, and joy be with you all."

The applause and whistling at the end are sincere. Simonetta smiles with gratitude but her heart is heavy, as if the music is a stone in her chest. She imagines it there like a sailor's knot, thick and intricate and strong to withstand an impending storm. There's a sound in her ears, a subtle roaring, an internal screaming, a chaotic bluster inside her heart. She builds a dam around it, places sandbags at the base of the scaffolds, to keep the turmoil at bay.

It gets worse as the day carries on.

Simonetta recognizes the feeling—the numbness, the panic, the shortness of breath, the long drop into the abyss of her heart and mind and soul. She has drowned like this before; anxiety and depression and dread like this had reared up at her a month after Nonna had died. Simonetta had just started to feel a glimpse of future normalcy, a subtle taste of a time when she wouldn't be wracked by guilt and loss, when the time had come to bury her grandmother. Nonna had already been cremated, her entire being encapsulated by a beautiful marble box that Simonetta picked up at the cemetery to place in the grave. It haunted Simonetta, the size of it—how could that be Emilia Cavalieri in there? Such a formidable woman, warm and loving and quick-witted, now just a box of ashes. It was a death Simonetta kept trying to pick apart in her head, in a way she hadn't before with the others she had lost. It made her too aware of her own mortality, the knowledge that, she, too, would be that someday. It transcended logic, for Simonetta knew, obviously, that everyone died. But it felt so lonely, the realization—what if she died tomorrow? Who would find her? Who would mourn her?

The burial and the feelings it brought up had sent her spiraling. Simonetta had spent weeks in a haze, awake during the nights sweating and trying to catch her breath, a specter floating through the days. She had stopped eating until the hunger pangs got too painful and she missed the sensation of sinking her teeth into something. It was a long journey out of the muck, and it was a long while before Simonetta felt like her true self again. Even months later, her sanity and stability felt tenuous, and she anticipates it now—the brink, the cliff.

The familiarity of the awful sensation stalking her today helps somewhat. The first time she had gone off the deep end, it was so unlike any level of anxiety or depression she had ever experienced before that it terrified her. Was she losing her mind? Was something in her fundamentally, irrevocably broken? In the worst moments, Simonetta felt like it had become her permanent state, a version of herself fossilized like a nautilus in her bed. It was another layer to mourn, and she fell deeper, covered herself in soil, hid from the light, until one day, something in her had enough strength to germinate and seek the sun.

The rest of the day passes in a haze, and Simonetta goes through the motions of being a normal person. Inside, though, her heart is in torment, mirrored by storm clouds rolling in overhead. Soon enough, the clouds break and rain begins to fall just as the last of the visitors leave.

The cool rain hits the warm ground and rebounds, forming a thick layer of humid mist that envelops the chateau. It's as if the grounds are fending off interlopers now that the visitors have departed; the lands fold in on themselves and Simonetta collapses into herself. As the cars peel away in the courtyard, she stands under the awning of the ancient tower, the gargoyles looming above her. She feels the cracks forming, the water rushing in, the scaffolding rotting and giving way.

She runs into the forest, the wolves at her heels.

Fifteen

Drawbridge: A bridge that can be raised or lowered over a moat to permit or deny entry.

THE MIST PUSHES HER into the forest and she runs with abandon. Wet soil seeps into her shoes and she welcomes the cool dampness that surrounds her. The trees could save her—she could build a wall with trees, she could build a moat, she could build a ship. There is nothing she couldn't build from them and she forces herself to envision herself doing just that. *Ground yourself. Breathe. Envision something that comforts you.* She tries all the tips she knows now by heart; she closes her eyes and the mist brushes her fingers like lace. Simonetta imagines herself suspended upon a cloud, far above the ocean—she envisions herself as moss leeching moisture along the wing of a gargoyle, binding herself to the stone guardian—

But the metaphors for the storm inside are becoming mixed, and she loses track.

She tries to envision herself sawing a stump of a fallen tree, its natural death a means to her own savior; but she splits it open to find it infested with maggots. She shifts strategies and climbs atop a cloud, but when it reaches the treetops, it dissipates and she falls to the forest floor. Once more she tries—she envisions the saw in her hand and changes it to a sword in her mind's eye, a weapon with which to fend off the huge, snarling gray wolf, the representation of her own fear.

A twig snaps and her eyes fly open, erasing the fallen tree and the clouds and the moss and the wolves. She is empty handed, no saw nor sword, just air and ferns she clings to. A figure appears in the mist, and she recognizes the shape of him before the rest of him becomes clear.

"Simonetta?" Jeremy asks. She thinks of him singing and craves that low rumbling voice in her ear, and again wants to pull him down to the ground, clawing up the soil and moss and covering them both in it, hiding forever together until they bloom from the rot as mushrooms. "I went to the tower to find you, but I looked out the window and I saw you go into the forest."

She turns to him and makes no effort to hide her anguish.

"Jeremy," she says, voice cracking on the third syllable. "I'm drowning."

He closes the space between them and they move in syncopation, his arms opening for her as hers close around him, his lips finding hers in the mist—is the salt on her tongue from him, or from her?—his hands finding purchase in her hair. She closes her eyes and conjures a vision of him on a beautifully built raft he makes just for her. Then it becomes a ship, and he is on the bow above the figurehead who looks like the nymph.

What she imagines doesn't matter, it doesn't matter how elusive and tenuous the fantasy is, because when the waves finally crash in, Simonetta finds that Jeremy is real. Simonetta tosses an anchor over the side of her heart and dives in.

A thunderclap makes a rabbit dash across the clearing, and over Jeremy's shoulder, she watches it disappear into the dense tree line from which they emerge. Rain falls with tenacity and Jeremy takes her hand and leads her to the chapel awning, the back of the structure partially exposed to the elements. He yanks aside several loosely nailed planks and pulls her inside the sacred space, where it is quiet, cool, and dry.

His touch is relentless and Simonetta wants to match his

fervor. He quickly disrobes and drops his sopping jacket and shirt hastily on a pew, then focuses his energy on her instead, reaching around her to find the zipper in the back of the dress. She lets him lead the dance, wordlessly moves with him as he multitasks—kisses, touches, pulls her dress down until it pools around her feet. The rest he pushes and tugs off her until she stands naked, slightly damp and shivering. She resists the urge to cover herself while being perceived in the pale light of the storm. But she remains defiant with her hands at her sides, and when he lays down on the few remaining dry clothes he spreads out on the ground, his strong arms awaiting her, his hands snaking up and down her body, she evokes the nymph, sure and strong and sensual, and pours over him in baptism.

MARGUERITE

As the navy night slid slowly into dawn and the last of the guests retired to their rooms, Marguerite went to her father, head bowed in faux defeat. She hoped the display of humility would mask her internal glee.

"I'm sorry, Papa," she said. "I know the night wasn't what you expected. Perhaps I could plan another ball soon when the roads are easier to travel."

He yawned and nodded at this. "That is a good idea. When I return to Nice with Philippe, I will send you a new list." He looked at her approvingly. "You did well tonight, Marguerite."

She had bought herself the gift of more time. She met Elise in the library and together they proceeded to Marguerite's room. The relief was palpable and Marguerite was giddy from her success and her realization: It was time for her to take charge of her life.

It excited her to think of all she could plan at Desrosiers. Why hadn't she thought of it sooner? Marguerite had assumed that her afflictions meant that she wanted to be alone—but what she wanted was for people to not be suspicious or control her days, and she had thought for many years that it was easier to be around fewer people. But what if she simply lived her truth in the daylight? What if she made Desrosiers such a desirable location that no one questioned why she never left?

She slumped into the chair at her vanity, and Elise began the process of preparing her for bed. Marguerite was ready to sleep like the dead after a successful night.

Elise's fingers in her hair were soft, lacking the tension they usually held to wrangle Marguerite's hair into intricate hairstyles. Marguerite closed her eyes at the gentle touch. She couldn't remember a time where she was touched out of affection and not duty beyond the occasional embrace from her father.

She was so grateful for Elise. It was her maid who had given her confidence and surety lately. She had never known anyone like her. Was it a risk to tell her so? Marguerite existed in the space between fatigue and elation, and it made her feel slightly drunk, and slightly impulsive, like nothing could hurt her. She turned to express herself to Elise, mouth open—

"You were very beautiful tonight, mistress," said Elise quietly. Her voice, typically sure and confident, broke the silence like one dips a toe into water to test the temperature.

It sent a ripple of goosebumps down Marguerite's arms and torso, and a potent warmth bloomed in her stomach. She reached for Elise's hands and the maid acquiesced. Marguerite pulled herself to her full height, a few inches taller than Elise's head, and took in the woman's dark, glossy hair, the luminous dark eyes that looked up at her filled with both questions and answers.

And then Marguerite leaped into the unknown. She pulled Elise toward her—or did Elise pull Marguerite toward her?— and when their lips met it was with mutual fervor.

"Do you trust me?"

Yes. No. I don't trust anyone. I trust you more than anyone on this entire planet. Instead, Marguerite nodded, wringing hands betraying her tightly held composure.

"We don't have to go any further than the garden," said Elise, extracting one of Marguerite's hands from its clenched knot and squeezing it. "I promise."

It had been Marguerite's idea to venture outside the walls. Despite her good fortune—Papa's failed pursuit of her future husband, her blossoming love affair with Elise, Papa and Philippe gone for an indeterminate amount of time—Marguerite knew that it wouldn't last forever.

The thought of leaving the chateau, even to step outside its walls into the grounds that belonged to her, filled her with nauseating dread that made her hands cold and her head swim. But accepting the grounds as extensions of the chateau, as places that were safe and stable for her, would extend her circle of freedom. It was a necessary step in her attempt to maintain control over her life, to dictate her days. She was already planning a series of parties, events that would keep Papa off her back and give her something to do, a way to meet people and be a part of the world. And in the summer, guests would revel in the gardens.

She had confided this all in Elise, who agreed. "We can start practicing. Your lands are gorgeous, you know."

Marguerite *didn't* know, and despite the torment and the *what ifs?*, she found herself somewhat curious.

But when it came time to take the first step, she froze. Together they stood in the Grand Salon, its large doors opening into the garden. The breeze was balmy and pleasant, carrying the scent of flowers and herbs. She took a deep breath and the aroma reached into her chest, soothing her nerves.

Elise stepped first, then held out a hand.

Like she had the first night she met Elise and had shown her who she was, Marguerite accepted it, entwining her fingers with Elise's. It bolstered her and gave her strength. And she took the first step.

The panic she was pushing away started to bubble, but continuous deep breaths kept it in place, and she focused on putting one foot in front of the other. Wordlessly, Elise took her across the patio and to the edge of the garden. Marguerite looked out over the land that she had seen thousands of times through glass, and agreed—it was beautiful, the garden impeccably designed and maintained. Flowers of different kinds and colors grew on neatly trimmed bushes, vibrant berries and herbs interspersed throughout. Beyond the garden was the stone wall marking the perimeter of the chateau, and beyond that was the river.

With a surety she didn't feel, Marguerite declared, "I want to go to the river."

"Are you sure? We don't have to do all of this at once, you know. I'll do this with you as many times as you need."

"I want to."

Together they crossed the neat, cultivated garden, went through the gap in the stone fence, and into the wild.

Marguerite preferred this view of the grounds; this was what she couldn't see from afar. The wildflowers, the ferns, the trees in the forest, all of it spilling over onto each other. The light was muted here, the oak trees blocking out much of the sunlight but letting through a few choice tendrils. She felt cocooned here in the lush woods.

They stopped at the bank of the river, the water rushing with tenacity from the snow melt that kept the river and the moat full. The current made the tampered anxiety in Marguerite's chest threaten to rise again. Elise let go of her hand and Marguerite nearly lurched for her, but she watched instead as Elise went to the river, unlaced her dress and stepped out of it, and went into the river in only her chemise. She lay on her back and Marguerite took in the sight of Elise's body to which the wet chemise clung, her heart in her throat.

"Come in with me," said Elise. "You'll like it."

Marguerite wordlessly obeyed. Elise was a nymph, a siren, and Marguerite a hapless sailor caught in her orbit. Elise watched with amusement as Marguerite, lacking the deft hands of her maid to undo her dress, struggled to get it loose, a task made harder by her trembling fingers. Eventually she succeeded and followed Elise into the water, feet slipping on the mossy stones. She tumbled in without grace, drenching her hair, but she felt the ground under her feet and relaxed. She didn't know how to swim, but the river wasn't deep; if she stood at her full height, she would still have at least two feet above the surface.

When she was immersed Elise embraced her and they found each other in the river. Marguerite felt delicate and vulnerable, but the pleasure Elise coaxed out of her came easily, her skin sensitive and touch-starved, every caress amplified by the chill in the water. Overwhelmed by Elise, by the river, by the sheer magnitude of being outside, Marguerite wanted to die, wanted to stop existing—because she knew that life was a two-sided coin, a contrast of light and dark, because if there was this much pleasure to be found, this much love and goodness, the inevitable fall would be devastating.

SIMONETTA

In her mind she builds a fortress.

Simonetta's inner turmoil has quieted, but just. The receding tumult hums and hovers still, more of a vibration than a noise, but it is on its way out and Simonetta does her best to push it along.

When Jeremy's voice finally did reach her ears, after his lips met her neck and her shoulders and her collarbone, new visions appeared in her mind: pillars, scaffolding, frames. She realized that what she needs to erect in her mind's eye is a castle, and it unfolds easily now in her imagination—the trees, the chapel, and Jeremy serve as the foundation and the walls.

She lay on her side, draped partially over his chest that rises and falls with a steady, calm breath. Simonetta takes the opportunity to stare at him, deconstruct his features and then reassemble them: the dark eyes that express so much, the strong nose, the black beard that hides pale skin underneath. He is beautiful to her, exquisite and perfect.

"So, is this always how you end the fête?" Simonetta asks. "Luring unsuspecting volunteers into a tryst?"

Jeremy grins then purses his lips, guilty. Simonetta pushes herself up on her wrists to better look at him, but he avoids returning the eye contact.

"Jeremy!" She smacks him playfully on the shoulder. "Who else?"

He remains tight-lipped, but realization dawns.

"Graham!" she exclaims, and Jeremy releases a nervous laugh.

He nods and, to her immense surprise, even blushes. "It was years ago," he says.

"And did you also deconsecrate the chapel with him?"

Jeremy pulls her back to his chest, and she acquiesces. "Of course not. Only the best for you, my golden girl."

The affectionate words slide over Simonetta like a warm blanket. He strokes her hair and she enjoys the mingling sounds of his heartbeat and the rain still pattering on the roof.

Feeling bold, she finally speaks. "I was jealous of Graham, the other day. He made the fête sound so fun, the way it was designed to be: something wild, indulgent." She pauses, then continues. "I wanted to kiss you the other night, when I found you reading in your workshop."

"I wanted you to," Jeremy admits. "But I wanted it to be real, not induced by cider."

"It is real," she says.

"Why were you in the forest?" The question is curious, lacking judgment or worry or pity, and Simonetta appreciates the tone. She hates when people treat her episodes with pity or overwrought concern.

"When you found me in the clearing, I meant what I said—I was drowning. It happens to me sometimes, waves of—sadness, doubt, guilt, misery. I can't explain it. It comes over me and I can't control it. I go rigid and my mind just becomes awash in chaos. When you touched me, it's like you broke through it."

"How do you feel now?"

Simonetta considers the question. The word that keeps coming to her mind is tenuous. Better, yes, but weary from the physical and mental cost of the panic attack. She feels—warm. Exhausted. Giddy. Relieved. Slightly manic. Comforted.

"A sense of clarity," she says. "Something to ground me." She shifts to look at his face. "How do you feel now?"

He answers by tilting her onto her back, kissing a trail down her sternum, and his hands spell out a sentiment without words.

Simonetta tiptoes around like she has a wicked secret, although there is no reason to feel so. Eventually, she and Jeremy had snuck back to the chateau—an easy feat, since most of the volunteers had taken long naps after the visitors departed. Simonetta was glad that Claudel would not see the state of the drenched Fortuny replica; aside from some soil along the hemline, it's mostly unscathed. Simonetta steams it in the shower and hangs it on the back of her door to dry.

She opens her journal and tries to write, but words evade her. There's too much to process from the day. She writes down snippets:

The Parting Glass, Jeremy's voice
The waves came, then the wolves: tried to build boats, wield swords, didn't work. Started to drown for real...
Jeremy—the ship arrived, with the nymph on the bow
Well, I was the nymph, for a little while

She falls asleep on top of her covers, fatigue bone deep. When she awakens in the morning, the sky outside is a half-hearted gray-blue, as if it can't make up its mind. She dresses in work clothes, sad that she can no longer frolic around the chateau grounds in beautiful dresses. It's back to work today, which means a return to processing the Room of Oddities, repairing the automaton, and working alongside Lotte and Hanako to repaint the baseboards in the Chambre de Botanique.

Jeremy's in the kitchen with the others at breakfast when Simonetta enters, squeezing excess moisture from her wet hair. She sits across him at the table and cuts herself a large piece of lemon cake, leftover from the fête, and pours a shot from the

Moka pot on the table.

He winks at her in greeting and she melts. Simonetta is sure, at this point, that her feelings for him are matched—but she had a passing wonder the night prior if their moment had been simply that, something fleeting that he would choose to move on from. Those thoughts dissipate as soon as she joins him and sips on the espresso he made for her.

"How are you feeling today?" Jeremy asks casually, pouring milk into his tea and then into hers.

"Good," Simonetta replies, attempting to match his nonchalance. "Why?"

"I thought you'd feel sinful after our escapades."

"Oh, you mean fucking in a chapel—"

"Simonetta!" Jeremy cuts her off with mock indignation. "Such American vulgarity." But his dark eyes glint with mischief.

Steam rises from her cup, and through it, his gaze turns hot.

"I'm glad you don't feel like you must atone for anything," he says seriously, and Simonetta realizes that he is no longer joking.

She sets down her cup and meets him in the eye. "Of course not. I would have thought that was clear. Or shall I express myself in another way?"

The mischief returns to his eyes and he holds her gaze in his.

"Come to my room tonight, ten pm," he says. "Don't be late for church."

Simonetta gets stuck halfway through *Marguerite #3*—again.

She has labeled the uncovered compositions *Marguerite #1* through *#4* as she works her way through memorizing each one. Through her exploration via play and practice, Simonetta wonders if Marguerite intended the compositions to go together, four parts of the same piece. Without knowing which one was intended to come first, she can only guess based off of the design and flow of each piece. And there's a strong possibility that parts are missing.

#3 is Simonetta's favorite but also the most difficult, although

overall, there's a simplicity to the music, a folksiness not unlike the book of Irish folk songs Jeremy gave her. And each composition is short, just one page, with a notation at the end of each to repeat the song from the beginning. There's something deep and dark and turbulent about this particular piece, a franticness that ebbs into something warm, and it resonates with her. It's why she thinks this one being *#3* in the order makes sense—musical compositions, like literature, often follow a narrative structure. And in this four-part sonata, *#3* was the falling action post-climax, the beginning of the end.

The part tripping her up requires quick strokes on the D and G strings that shift into a bittersweet E flat, a note held for a moment longer than Simonetta would expect.

She takes a deep breath and shakes out her shoulders, releases the tension in her neck and shoulders. Practicing a new piece for hours on end has made her stiff. She walks to her window and peers out into the night.

The church bell rings, signaling half past nine. Simonetta smiles. She knows it's Jeremy, summoning her, reminding her of their appointment. As if she could forget; she's thought of little else all day, feasting on the giddy, succulent warmth of new love and desire. She wants to capture this feeling of infatuation in a bottle, stopper it to keep it fresh and sparkling.

Regardless, it's a good time for a break. She needs to look at something other than sheet music for a bit, wants to touch something other than an instrument. She envisions a naked Jeremy backlit by the moon, his skin warm under her fingers, and supposes that will have to do.

Still, she turns over *#3* in her mind on repeat, and as she ascends the tower toward his room where he awaits her, her footsteps mirror the staccato halfway through *#3*. Simonetta pauses and her heartbeat finds the rhythm.

A heartbeat—*that's* what that part is emulating. And Simonetta suddenly understands the purpose of the composition, and its meaning, the deep heartache and passion and the bittersweet trail-off.

It's a love song.

Sixteen

Chemin de ronde: Also called an "allure." A walkway protected by battlements, used by patrolling guards or watchmen.

SIMONETTA PULLS A PIECE of paper from a gilded bowl. It reads: *Pinocchio.*

An easy one. She holds up a finger—one word. Her audience, composed of the volunteers and a few new guests staying overnight at the chateau, nods in understanding. Graham sits forward and rubs his hands eagerly in preparation.

The obvious action is for her to point to her own nose and slowly draw her finger out, mimicking Pinocchio's long nose indicating the puppet's lies. But Simonetta feels a rush of competition; she's neck-and-neck with normally meek Lotte, who has come alive during this game of charades in a way no one has ever seen her. She licks her lips and pushes her auburn hair away from her face impatiently, not daring to blink in case she misses Simonetta's gestures.

Simonetta decides against being purposefully obtuse about her knowledge of the famed Italian tale, one Nonna loved, for it originated in Florence, where Nonna's own mother was born. But she doesn't want to make it too easy, either, so holds up each of her arms and raises the right one first, lifting her right foot at the same time. She does the same with her left, mimicking the show of a puppet attached to strings. She repeats the motion a few times and then stops, holding out two fingers and moving them together and apart like scissors. With her pretend scissors, she holds up her right arm and cuts the invisible string attached to her hand and foot.

Lotte stands, practically vibrating with the answer. "Pinocchio! Pinocchio!"

Simonetta tosses up her hands in resignation; she was just getting started. Heart racing from the rush of competition and subsequent loss of the round, she sits beside Jeremy, chewing on her cuticle in annoyance.

The action gives her a sense of déjà vu. Sometimes she catches herself emulating Nonna at random moments, in the small memories that live in her muscles. She thinks of all the tiny life lessons she picked up from Emilia Cavalieri over the years, the way Nonna would open a bobby pin with her bottom row of teeth and slide it behind her ear to keep the coarse wavy strands tucked away. How she would choose a slightly different route home from work sometimes "just to keep things interesting."

And of course, the sting and annoyance that comes with losing friendly contests. Those were the only times Simonetta ever saw her even-keeled grandmother knocked off-kilter— on the rare occasions Emilia lost a game of chess against her husband, she would be so riled from defeat that she wouldn't speak to Nonno for a whole day. It was one of many small traits Simonetta had inherited from her, a strange temper that flared within her sparked by an entirely non-consequential loss.

Jeremy gently pushes her hand away from her mouth and gives it a squeeze, running a calloused thumb over her aggravated cuticles. Claudel calls out his name from the roster.

"We can do this," he says with a conspiratorial wink. He maintains her eye contact as he steps to the Persian rug spread out in the smaller, cozier Winter Salon as a makeshift stage, and pulls a piece of paper out of the hat held out by Claudel. His sly grin suggests that this will be an easy one for Simonetta. He rolls up the paper slowly and Simonetta fixates on his hands, his long fingers, the short-trimmed nails with faint traces of stain and sawdust, the palm she knows is warm from the times he has placed it against her body.

He holds up two fingers—two words. Simonetta leans forward intently, still thinking dreamily about Jeremy's hands. Under her breath she hums *#3*; the core melody has wormed itself into her head and she can't stop ruminating on it.

With a pointed finger, Jeremy draws a triangle in the air.

But her concentration falters—*#3*, and the strings of Pinocchio, lead her to thoughts of the violin, and then to the automaton—and then she has a sudden realization.

Lotte calls out from across the couch: "*Doctor Zhivago!*"

Jeremy groans in frustration and nods reluctantly at the correct answer.

"Simonetta! That one was just for you! I thought only you would understand that I was playing Lara's balalaika."

"I'm sorry," she says as he returns to his seat, waving her hand impatiently even as she apologizes half-heartedly. "But I was thinking about the automaton. I have a thought."

Jeremy stands and tugs her off the couch. "Good game, Lotte," he says to the triumphant victor as he pulls Simonetta out of the salon and toward the workshop.

MARGUERITE

Four months later, when Papa and Philippe returned, Marguerite's luck started to run out.

Papa, bitter about an opportunity that had fallen through in the Americas, stomped around Desrosiers, yelling at servants, snapping at Marguerite, and even Philippe couldn't escape Papa's criticism.

"When I return, Marguerite, you'll meet me in Marseilles," promised Papa, unaware of the anguish that gripped her, the cold sweat that broke out over her entire body. Philippe saw it and looked smug. "You can't put off finding a husband any longer. And you—" he pointed at Philippe, whose grin slid off of his face now that he was under Papa's critical gaze, "—must also find a wife. You'll both do what I say. I give you both everything and I have nothing to show for it!"

It was to everyone's benefit that Papa and Philippe's stay at Desrosiers this time was a brief one; they had returned only to prepare for a longer voyage that Papa hoped would help him recoup some of his losses. Marguerite bid Papa and Philippe adieu, hoping their trip would become an extended stay. She swallowed the panic until they departed and, in the comfort of her room and in Elise's presence, she broke down.

"They won't be back for almost a year," said Elise, stroking her back as Marguerite sobbed on the floor. "And we can practice before then. By the time he calls for you in Marseilles, it won't be so bad, leaving the chateau."

Marguerite prayed Elise was right. Papa and Philippe were going to the Middle East, to Lebanon, and then would sail on a ship back to Marseilles. Papa had made a hefty new investment in silks and intended to see that his investment was sound; plus, it would be good for Philippe to see more of the world. Papa's preferred location of trade was the Levant, places where silks and spices were abundant, and his debacle in the Americas had affirmed his choice of business. It was why he liked being in Nice or Marseilles more than Sainte-Madeleine, for the Mediterranean cities made it easy for him to hop aboard a ship and travel to the places where his investments originated. Many assumed Papa possessed an adventurous soul, to travel so far with some regularity—most merchants of Papa's level paid others to do that for them. But Marguerite knew it was because Papa was shrewd and untrusting and would only believe something was a good idea if he saw it for himself.

It would be a long trip, but it wouldn't last forever. And if Papa's investment paid off the way he hoped, Marguerite's dowry would be even more impressive, which meant the likelihood of finding a husband that met Papa's standards would increase exponentially.

She would enjoy her freedom while she had it. She had planned a winter fête for artists and musicians, sending out invitations throughout the country using a list she pilfered from

Papa's documents. He was pleased by her attempt to socialize.

"A patron of the arts you're becoming," he said in a rare calm moment where the optimism of his upcoming trip overruled his annoyance at his recently failed one. He offered to take her invitations to the port. He made additional suggestions, mentioning artists and tradespeople he had met on his own travels, people from in and outside of France, and she added them to the list.

SIMONETTA

Practice pays off, because when Simonetta runs through *#3* in front of Jeremy, she does so without stumbling. She follows it up with *#4*—by now she knows each piece by heart.

When she's done, Jeremy, the sole audience member, claps and she bows in jest. "So what do you think?" she asks. "Could a small robotic girl made in the 1700s play these compositions?"

Jeremy nods thoughtfully. "It seems possible. I think it would lack the flourish that you add to it, but mechanically? Definitely."

"It just makes sense to me," Simonetta says emphatically. "They're short, they're simple, and, as far as we know, one-hundred-percent original. Marguerite was a musician and she commissioned the automaton, so why wouldn't she have made the music for it?"

He nodded in agreement. "So what next?"

Simonetta pulls out her journal. "So far, we're pretty sure that the automaton was commissioned by Marguerite de Sainte-Madeleine, by an Altobella. And now I'm pretty sure that the four unsent compositions by Marguerite were written for the automaton." She frowns. "That's all we know with any certainty. We don't know much about the doll, who Altobella was, or how the automaton actually works." Simonetta flips through the pages of her commonplace, avoiding Jeremy's eyes. The earlier excitement has deflated, leaving her discouraged.

After a moment, he wades into uncertain waters. "What's

wrong?"

"That just doesn't seem like very much, does it? We don't really know the most important details."

"What makes those the 'most important' details?"

"They're the cornerstones of the whole endeavor—how it works and who made it."

Jeremy shrugs. "Only if you feel like those are the most important. We knew going into this that we may not have every question answered. Besides, what's the rush?"

Simonetta doesn't know how to express her internal urgency. She wants to figure this out before she leaves France, and her visa is only good through end of August. It's almost July, and she still has so far to go in unraveling the automaton's core mysteries. What if she doesn't figure it out in time?

Later that night, Simonetta checks her email to find her inbox nearly full. She hasn't checked it for some weeks; in Berkeley, she was practically glued to her laptop, but she has little reason to be on computers these days besides research. It's been nice, fully immersed in the real world. She hasn't been online watching new episodes of *Daily Life* where she has finally revealed the automaton project; she has no desire to view the filmed version of herself or analyze the hope she knows she'll hear in her voice. She hasn't kept up with social media or even the news. Simonetta exists in the bubble of Desrosiers, and it has started to become a cocoon. She hopes she'll emerge better and brighter after being ensconced in it, but she can't help but feel like she's in the stage of metamorphosis where the caterpillar becomes a writhing mass of goo before taking on its new form. She's formless, willing herself to grow a spine and stronger scaffolding to support herself.

To her surprise, most of the emails are from *Daily Life* viewers sending her suggestions and insight about the automaton. One admonishes her for opening Marguerite's letters; refusing to dwell on what can't be undone, she archives it and sends it out of sight. Claudel warned all the volunteers that rude emails and messages were an unfortunate byproduct of being minor internet celebrities, but Simonetta, despite her many neuroses, cares little for what some random person she's never met thinks of her.

The vast majority, though, are helpful and supportive. Charles, a museum director from New York, sent her some documentation about medieval dolls, including an assortment of pictures and commentary. Among the scans are marionettes from the 1400s.

Charles's email reads:

"Hi Simonetta—I'm a specialist in medieval toys at the Museum of Children's History in upstate New York. Thank you for sharing your automaton with us. I've attached some documents about wooden toys from the 13- and 1400s that I hope will be helpful to you.

You mentioned briefly your theory that the upper part of the automaton, Catelot's doll, predates the rest of the automaton. Based on the close-ups you showed, that's an accurate guess.

Wooden toys in the 1300s ranged the gamut of crudeness and intricacy. Yours seems somewhere in the middle, with the doll's features well-crafted but lacking perfection. My professional guess is that the wig, articulating joints, and the painted features were added when the automaton was made—it is highly unlikely that any hair added to the doll when it was made would have survived the 400-year gap between the doll's creation and the creation of the automaton, let alone the additional 300 years to present day. As an organic material, without proper maintenance, hair—animal or human—has a finite shelf life.

I encourage you to have a new wig made for your doll if you intend to keep Catelot in open air, as her current wig is still intact mostly because she has been undisturbed for so long."

Simonetta jots down Charles' suggestions and comments in her commonplace, grateful that he took the time to share this with her. She's keeping a list in her book of all the people she owes thanks to when she finishes the restoration.

There are more emails with resources and ideas, contacts for specialists at different universities and museums. As Simonetta shifts through each one, her earlier discouragement ebbs.

This isn't just her project anymore, she sternly tells herself. The automaton doesn't belong solely to her—dozens, if not hundreds, of people are now invested in it. Including Jeremy, whose attempts at reassurance earlier she brushed off.

When will she get out of her own head? Why is it so easy for her to get fixated on the negative, when around her is clear evidence of progress? Simonetta swallows the unpleasant taste of selfishness, pledges to maintain a better perspective, and goes to find Jeremy to share her new notes.

"I've never felt about anyone else the way I feel about you," Jeremy says one night on the terrace.

They are both still sweating, from work and the humidity. After supper (rice and vegetables from the garden—the volunteers are working through a surplus of zucchini) along with Graham and Diego, they moved the largest clock in the oddities attic into his workshop for some repair. The automaton consumes her thoughts, but she has a job to do still, and she's eager to finish the project to clear out the room in the tower. Like she does every time she has an ambitious goal, she manifests how she'll feel when it's done, when she's on the other side of it. The sense of lightness, the pleasure of accomplishment: all that awaits her after substantial labor.

Simonetta smiles coyly; she appreciates the casual way they learn about each other. She appreciates how Jeremy doesn't ask the intrusive questions men often do when they find out she has dated women and often prefers their company and companionship. She appreciates that he doesn't mince words, but sometimes his no-nonsense honesty catches her off guard.

She knows he doesn't need declarations in return but wants to say something in response. She decides on, "Likewise," and it's true—she hasn't felt about anyone else the way she feels about Jeremy. The last person she loved was Alex, someone she still loves for the memories and the experiences and the friendship but has long stopped feeling anything romantic.

A new lover was not on Simonetta's summer plans, but truthfully, she had set off to France with very few expectations beyond a clear goal to tug on the ley lines, so she considers it a bonus. A mystery to solve and a new lover to boot? What good fortune.

She knows Jeremy is more than a lover, but The Future still seems so cloudy and abstract that she can't seem to grasp what more means. A boyfriend? Calling Jeremy her 'boyfriend' as a 34-year-old woman sounds so juvenile that she almost laughs aloud. Partner? Companion? Husband? Father to her future children? Does Simonetta even want children? Would Jeremy run away screaming if she even brought up the very notion after they've slept together just a handful of times?

And yet Jeremy is the one saying deep things early in their relationship, and the way he's glancing at her out of the corner of his eye as they smoke the last of the clove cigarettes left over from the fête gives her another rare glimpse into Jeremy's sheepishness when it comes to her: that he is wondering if she'll run away screaming.

But neither of them run or scream, and Simonetta stops short her ruminating with a firm mental reprimand. She thinks back to their excursion in the forest, thinks of their intimacy before it included sex. She thinks of the roots splitting through rocks, thinks of moss and mushrooms, reminds herself to just be. Whatever they have right now—care, certainly, maybe hints of love, but also respect, infatuation, curiosity—doesn't need to exist in a perfect box in a perfect label.

And anyway, she'll have some time to muse: She's leaving tomorrow to visit the local abbey in the outskirts of Sainte-Madeleine, the very one where Catherine Desrosiers supposedly lived out the rest of her life. Simonetta has booked a room in the abbey's former dormitory, now converted into rooms where pilgrims can stay overnight. Claudel explained that there is a trail passing over the mountains from Saint Madeleine over into the border of Italy, to Villaggio Primavera, and devout Catholics who revere Sainte-Madeleine make an annual pilgrimage over the trail. When the abbey was founded a century after the saint was canonized, the Roman empire was in its final days, and there was not yet a border separating France from Italy. Simonetta is learning how much this region of France overlaps with Italy's history, territory that has been contested and challenged and blended over the course of a thousand years.

When she feels borderline sinful making her own pilgrimage up the steps to Jeremy's room the night before her excursion to the abbey, she banishes the hovering angels back to their realm.

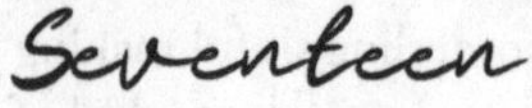

Seventeen

Chancel: The space surrounding a church's altar.

PAST THE MAIN winding route through the mountainous village of Sainte-Madeleine is the abbey honoring its namesake. Like Desrosiers, the Cistercian abbey itself is an amalgamation of architecture reflecting the history of the region; ancient Roman ruins meld with medieval walls and ornate Renaissance-era wooden pillars and arches round out the structure. As if the modern era needs to make itself known in the historic town, a crane is perched overhead. Claudel told Simonetta the abbey's garter house is undergoing renovation when the ceiling threatened to collapse during an especially heavy snowfall last year. The long, white-washed structure remains simple, but framed paintings decorate the outside perimeter, magnified versions of the frescoes inside the abbey, which, although it remains a practicing monastery, also functions now as a museum.

Although she is not a pilgrim, Simonetta is here with a mission: to view the original documents that supposedly prove that Catelot Desrosiers spent the second half of her life here. She's hoping that there is more to find in the abbey's archives, giddy at the chance to access such old documents; her fingers are itching to touch more historical manuscripts. Marguerite's compositions have been a special treat, but it has been years since she had a chance to touch and read manuscripts older than five hundred years.

With the promise of discovery ahead of her, Simonetta parks the Renault in the gravel lot and follows the signs into the alternate entrance. The domed entrance has ropes denoting where a queue should line, but she is the only one there, and she proceeds to the front to the wood desk. After several minutes of waiting, she hesitantly taps the small bell, and a very old nun emerges, her face wrinkled like unshelled nutmeg ensconced in a crisp white habit.

"Bonjour," says Simonetta. "I rented a room for the night here, for research. I'd like to check in."

The nun nods but says little in response; Simonetta hopes she hasn't disturbed her in the middle of a task. She strains her ears to listen for other activity, but in this part of the abbey, all is quiet. The nun waves Simonetta forward. "ID and reservation, s'il vous plait."

Simonetta retrieves her passport and the printed reservation and presents them to the nun, feeling like a girl again in Catholic school, squirming with guilt and amusement and the desire to both affirm that she is, in fact, a good girl, but also that she derides the archaic expectations of gender. Does the nun know the thoughts that have passed through her mind recently, the activity she was up to the night before?

When she opens Simonetta's passport, a strange expression passes across the nun's face in the form of a furrowed brow and pursed lips.

"Altobella?" the sister repeats tentatively.

"Oui." Simonetta confirms and shifts the weight of her bag on her shoulder, heavy from the books she brought with her to study.

Upon confirmation, the sister's expression turns suddenly fierce, like a specter emerging from a body they inhabit. The change is so sudden and unexpected, so much verve emerging from the old nun who just moments ago had ambled down the hall, that Simonetta flinches—and then the nun steps out from behind the desk, bares her teeth, spits at Simonetta's feet, and storms off down the hallway.

Stunned, Simonetta's heart thunders in her chest. *What the—? * She is frozen to the spot, but her muscles scream at her to move, to run, to do anything. She wonders wildly if she has just been cursed, for the ferocity in the sister's anger was tinged with ill-wishes. Can one be cursed in a holy place? The lobby remains empty and Simonetta's open passport sits on the desk.

What the actual fuck? Simonetta is awash in shame and confusion, replaying the moment. She must have done something horribly offensive, but no play-by-play of the situation reveals her unforgivable discretion. Some cultural faux pas, maybe, but what? Surely the nun didn't actually read her mind?

Perhaps it was simply the existence of her American passport. She can't blame Europeans for feeling that way, but that doesn't seem right, for the anger arose when Simonetta confirmed her name.

She knows she has no choice now but to leave, but a live wire of defiance surges within her, and she at least wants to apologize or get some answer before departing.

Simonetta peeks hesitantly around the corner, down the stone-walled hallway, and tip-toes quietly lest she stir up additional ire. She can hear the sister moving about in the next chamber; even her movements are filled with anger. Simonetta decides it's best to keep her distance.

She clears her throat and muddles through an apology in French, hoping her attempt at speaking the language isn't what caused this situation. No, she's pretty sure that wouldn't have been the problem, right? "Je veux juste dire que je suis désolé pour ce que j'ai fait." *I just want to say I'm sorry for what I did.* She switches to English, just in case. "I'm leaving now but please put my registration fee toward donations. Au revoir."

As she turns to leave, the sister's footsteps echo in the chamber and just as Simonetta is about to round the corner, she hears, "Tommaso?"

Simonetta stops and turns, frowning. Did the sister confuse her for someone else? She is, after all, elderly—maybe there was no catalyst to this whole situation. Maybe the nun is suffering from dementia; Simonetta knows that can sometimes lead to angry, violent outbursts. Simonetta's shock turns to concern: Is there anyone else here to care for her? "Non, je m'appelle Simonetta."

The sister waves her hand impatiently as if that is obvious. "Non—êtes-vous lié à Tommaso Altobella?" *Are you related to Tommaso Altobella?*

The name pricks a small spark in the annals of Simonetta's mind—Tommaso, is that familiar? She has read so many Italian and French names lately that she can't trust her memory. She can't recall a Tommaso she knows and shakes her head again.

Then the nun says, "Paolo?"

At her grandfather's name, Simonetta's blood turns cold.

"Oui, mon grandpere," Simonetta confirms in a rush before remembering with a sting that this woman has just spat at her upon seeing her surname. If this is a test, she just failed it.

But at the confirmation, the sister's furious face softens just slightly. "Paolo was a good boy, but Tommaso—" she spits again and Simonetta wishes she'd stop doing that, mostly because it's gross and seems a borderline sacrilege, but she is not sure of the etiquette on telling a sister what she can and can't do in the place of worship to which she has dedicated her life. "How two brothers can be so different, I will never know."

Brothers? Dormant memories emerge. Simonetta knows Nonno had siblings, but he never, ever wanted to talk about them and eventually she learned not to ask.

She knows only that his sister's name was Rosa, knows Nonna sent Rosa a Christmas card every year in secret without telling Nonno. But Tommaso? If Simonetta's heard that name before in relation to her own family, it would have been few and far between, probably a slip-up from Nonna.

Is she even positive the sister is talking about the right person? Sainte-Madeleine's proximity to the Italian border, and the abbey as the pilgrim's destination, makes it likely that those who live here know many Italians.

"Did Tommaso have a sister named Rosa?" Simonetta asks.

The sister nods and a gasp escapes before Simonetta can

contain it. Simonetta is overwhelmed—still offended by the spit, stunned by this woman knowing her family.

Her knees buckle despite her attempts at composure and tears spring to her eyes as she seeks stability from the stone wall beside her. "I'm so sorry. I had no idea. There is so much Paolo didn't tell me." She takes a shaky deep breath. "And I'm sorry for whatever Tommaso did to you."

"Stop apologizing," says the sister, waving her hand again. "It is not me who can grant you forgiveness." She points to Christ in a faded fresco above her. "Your family has much to atone for."

PAOLO ALTOBELLA
1943

War came to Europe in the form of machines. Trains, planes, mortars, guns. The best of human invention was now wielded against its makers.

Paolo, with his engineering mind and deft fingers that itched to tinker, thought this a tragedy. But the war had started when he was only eight, so no one really listened to him.

His older brother Tommaso, on the other hand, had a mind for strategy. He couldn't get bogged down in the minutiae where Paolo found solace—Tommaso had eyes only for the Bigger Picture. So even though it was Paolo, and not the eldest Altobella *fratello*, who matched their patriarch in scientific prowess, Tommaso secured his spot as their mother's favorite solely through his passion for *spazio vitale*.

Young Paolo was sure that his father, the late Paolo Sr., would be dismayed to know that, in the months after his untimely death in a factory explosion, his wife and children had openly embraced the National Fascist Party rather than remain on the fringes of it, as Paolo Sr. preferred.

Paolo wasn't sure anyone was more devoted to Benito Mussolini than his mother, Maria Benedetto. Although she was devoutly Catholic and bore an amulet of Santa Maddalena around her neck, little else about Maria fit the mold of a model Fascist woman—she had inherited Altobella Instruments from her husband and had led the business through a booming couple of years despite the country's struggling economy. She had only three children—Tommaso, Paolo Jr., and Rosa—all of whom she'd bore well into her late thirties and beyond. Now in the latter half of her forties, she was hardly the picture of youth as portrayed in the *giovinezza*.

Paolo heard the speeches, listened to the talks at the Primavera city hall, and none of it made any sense. Mama was bold, stern, smart, hard-working and—to anyone besides Tommaso, upon whom she doted—reluctantly maternal at best. But Mussolini insisted that women should take pride in being mothers and abstain from employment.

Instead, he thought of his mother as the "she-wolf of Rome," the mythical lupine that his *paesani* revered as the founder of Italy and its blood-drenched history. When he looked at his mother, that was what he saw—the gray streaks in her hair, the fierce glint in her dark eyes, the thin lips that pulled back over her pointed incisors. Tommaso looked like her, tall and slender and sharp. Paolo felt soft in comparison, and in his softest moments he longed for his soft-spoken father. But all he had for camaraderie was his toddler sister, Rosa, and at three years old, she wasn't much for solidarity.

Now seventeen, Tommaso was nearly of age and was about to be given ownership of Altobella Instruments—in name only. Mama would still have full control of the daily operations, of which there were many. Papa had died three years earlier, months before Rosa was born, and in that time, Mama had not only restored the factory that was beginning to fall to disrepair, but secured contracts across the region for the farm machinery she and Papa had designed that increased collection of grain. The demand was so great that Altobella Instruments could hardly keep up, and so Mama had expanded into another factory. Tommaso would eventually oversee that one.

Altobella Instruments did not always have multiple factories or farm equipment. For more than a century and a half, its main output was clockwork and, on occasion, automata. Paolo strongly believed that his father was Marco Altobella reincarnated—the original Altobella who had set their family legacy in motion, whose eighteenth-century portrait remained in Papa's office. Papa even resembled Marco with his mop of curly dark brown hair and aquiline, slightly crooked nose. Marco was sought after by wealthy patrons from across Europe to design custom clocks and automata at the heyday of the art form. And like Marco, Paolo Sr. was an artist, an inventor in the truest sense of the word. He loved to tinker with the historical machines hand-crafted by his ancestor, and young Paolo loved to watch him work, to be witness to the turning of mental gears. It was with reluctance that Paolo Sr. turned his attention to practical inventions needed in the turbulence of wartime Italy, during Mussolini's rise to power that he treated with equal reluctance, for Mussolini cared little for art for art's sake, saw artists without a Nationalist bent as a threat rather than embrace them as the glory of Italy. When Paolo Sr. designed farm equipment alongside his wife whose view on engineering was shrewd and scientific, the glint young Paolo so loved and longed to see was nowhere to be found.

Sometimes Paolo would sneak into his father's old office, which had emerged unscathed during the factory explosion. Often Paolo wondered why Papa couldn't simply have been in that room instead of fixing some other machine in the building. Maybe then he would have survived, and Paolo wouldn't have to face the she-wolf alone. Mama and Tommaso were cut from the same cloth, and to Paolo that cloth felt scratchy and stiff. In Papa's office, he sat among the vestiges of Altobella Instruments—a few automatons remained, several hundred years of history left behind in the name of the Future that Maria Benedetto and Tommaso Altobella and Benito Mussolini aspired for: one in which Italy re-emerged as a global power, the wolf at the world's borders.

It shouldn't have mattered anyway, because by 1943 when Paolo was twelve, Mussolini was on a downward spiral. But Maria and Tommaso held firm to the Fascist legacy promised by the dictator, insisted that the news was wrong, that it was all propaganda designed to undermine Mussolini's efforts. Still, Paolo caught glimpses of the protests in Primavera, watched the factory employees go on strike, read the graffiti sprawled across the village's oldest buildings, Morte Mussolini! dripping red down the stone. It was all ugly: the speeches on the radio, the fights breaking out in the streets, the stolen glances with the neighbor kids he once played with.

But when he could, Paolo gingerly fingered the original Altobella inventions—a little drummer boy bedecked in green velvet Christmas robes, a small girl that plucked at harp strings when the angel wings at her back were pinched together—and envisioned a more harmonious legacy.

"Mining?" Paolo asked in anguish. "But I don't know how to mine."

Tommaso shoved the last piece of bread into his mouth and brushed the crumbs hastily off his shirt. "You'll learn. You'll be given tools."

"But what about school?" Paolo was learning math theorems at school and it was just getting good. Leaving now would put off his progress.

"You don't need to be in a classroom to learn, Pao-Pao." Tommaso waved his hands at Paolo's protestations, the one gesture and trait he had inherited from their father. "In fact, it would be good for you to be out in the world. It's time for you to become a strong man."

Paolo thought this sounded terrible. He didn't want to be strong; he wanted to be smart. He wanted to study math and build machines that did beautiful and amazing things. "Where are we going mining?"

"Across the border," said Tommaso. He pulled out a crude, hand-drawn map that depicted their commune, Primavera, with a line weaving through the summit to a place called Santa Maddalena. "Across the mountains. Where we are going is on the other side."

"In France?" Paolo frowned. He had listened to enough of the radio to know that France was dangerous. It was dangerous to cross any borders right now, and even though France and Italy had agreed on a truce, any alliances were tenuous. "Why there?"

Tommaso was growing impatient. "Don't ask so many questions. We're going there because there is metal to mine and our factories need it. Mama wants us to go because she knows she can trust us." He swiped the crumbs off the table and onto the floor. "We leave tomorrow. Go get ready."

It wasn't the first time Paolo had suspected his brother of lying. That was another one of Paolo's skills: a keen sense for when something was somehow amiss. Tommaso and Mama often chided him for overthinking, but Paolo knew no other way of thinking. He was of the mind that most people weren't thinking enough about the right things. When he packed up his backpack with his meager belongings, said goodbye to Rosa (who shrieked and cried) and Mama (who, in a rare and uncharacteristic display of affection, cupped his face and gave him a kiss on each cheek), and set out on foot with Tommaso to France, Paolo knew he wasn't going mining.

The three-day journey from Primavera to Santa Maddalena didn't seem that bad to Paolo, at first—until they reached the base of the Southern Alps, and Paolo realized that three days of walking would instead be three days of moderate mountain climbing. Reluctantly athletic at best, Paolo spent the first day in utter agony, counting down the time to their destination one minute at a time.

He let himself daydream about math to distract himself from the pain in his boots. The first kilometer of the trek was fine, almost enjoyable. It was hot in Primavera Valley but as they made their ascent up the mountain trail, the air cooled just slightly. He took in the flora of the mountain, typically only seen from a distance, and made a scientific study out of it, keeping mental observations in the open notebook that was his mind.

He knew better than to share these thoughts with Tommaso, who was uncharacteristically stoic. Oftentimes, Tommaso was the outgoing one, spouting his thoughts and opinions and beliefs. Tommaso and Mama would have passionate conversations in the small kitchen, talking animatedly and occasionally angrily when Mama would scold Tommaso for growing too bold. Paolo and Rosa would listen in from the next room, and even though she was but a toddler, Rosa would exchange a look with Paolo that suggested that she, too, was already questioning her place in this family.

Eventually, though, as the day wore on, the scenery started to blend together and the pain in his feet became too hard to ignore. In late afternoon, they stopped briefly to eat. Mama had packed them just enough food to get them to their destination. They ate small fish pies, the dough crumbly from insufficient flour, the filling scant. When the pies were consumed Tommaso stood up and indicated for Paolo to follow, to his utter dismay.

The trail led over the lowest peak in this point of the Alps, although to Paolo, they might as well have been cresting the summit. Every muscle in his short legs screamed.

"Can't we please stop?" he eventually begged as the sun slid low in the sky. He flopped down on the ground, ignoring the sharp pebbles that pressed into his knees and elbows.

Tommaso turned to him and a strange combination of emotions cycled on his face: a flare of annoyance that had him pinching the bridge of his nose, softened momentarily by sympathy and a relaxed jaw. But then Tommaso's expression turned hard.

"Paolo, I need you to understand that from here on out, you must listen to everything I say and not question it."

"But—"

Tommaso reached out a hand and slapped Paolo hard across the face.

His brother had never hit him before, not even in jest. No matter how much Tommaso yelled and teased and taunted him, he had never laid a finger on him in violence, not like the other siblings in Primavera who were constantly squabbling and shoving and pulling one another's hair. Paolo was so stunned that it took several moments before he even felt the sting from the hit.

Tommaso crouched down in front of him. "From here on out, you do exactly what I tell you to do. What we are going to do is extremely dangerous. Our lives depend on your obedience." Tommaso took a deep breath and gave Paolo a look that he would remember even years later. "Do you understand?"

Paolo didn't understand, he didn't understand any of it—where they were going and why, why Tommaso had struck him, why his brother had a look of thunder in his eyes that he had never seen before. But he swallowed the torrent of whys that threatened to spill out and instead said simply, "I understand."

With the lingering feeling of his brother's hand striking his cheek, Paolo kept his mouth shut despite his exhaustion, hunger, and homesickness. By the time they set out their bedrolls and lay down on the sharp, rocky ground, Paolo was too tired to care about discomfort and fell instantly into a deep sleep.

Awaking the next morning felt like pure torture. Tommaso roused him roughly, handed him another hand pie, and they set off again in silence. The trek was more arduous today, and Tommaso said little to Paolo beyond a half-hearted assurance that the trek down the mountain tomorrow would be easier. They were tackling the hardest part today, said Tommaso.

Paolo tried to get lost in his mind, a strategy that usually worked when he was in uncomfortable situations, but the physical discomfort was too much. All he could think about was how much his feet hurt—the balls of his feet pulsed with pain, blisters formed along the sides and in the tenderest spots, the bones and the skin and everything lower than his knees simply ached. He would have given anything for Tommaso to carry him but the memory of Tommaso striking him was just enough to get him to keep his mouth shut even in his agony.

He couldn't even appreciate the vista. Paolo was seeing the familiar mountains whose foothills he lived in from an entirely new perspective. And the valley below was so scenic in late spring, Primavera living up to its name. A rainbow of wildflowers poured down the base of the mountains, spilling into the valley, awash with green. But Paolo could only see the danger that lay sleeping in Europe's hamlets like Primavera. The mountains cast a long shadow on either side of the border, both sides holding tension like a stretched rubber band—who would let go first and fling the other side into crisis?

Among Paolo's many unasked questions was: *how were they to cross safely into France—weren't the borders being patrolled?*

Tommaso pre-emptively answered this one toward the end of the second day. Paolo was sure they were well into France by now, but Tommaso was the one with the map, and he had no way to be certain. One more night awaited before they would make their descent and Paolo had never longed for sleep more.

They set up camp for the night in a rocky alcove. The rocks offered some concealment, so Paolo made a fire and Tommaso pulled out the last of their provisions.

"Do you know what 'armistice' is?" Tommaso asked, breaking the silence.

Paolo shrugged. "Heard them talking about it on the radio."

"It means France and Italy aren't fighting right now," said Tommaso, although Paolo suspected this was a simplified definition for his benefit. "It's why we're able to cross the border right now without soldiers patrolling the trail." He bit into a strip of dried and salted aubergine and chewed thoughtfully. "But we're technically breaking it."

"Breaking what?"

"The armistice."

Paolo grew frustrated by Tommaso's withholding. "You told me we were going mining for the factory."

Tommaso snorted. "You didn't actually believe that."

No, I didn't, so why did you lie? "So what are we actually doing here?"

Tommaso evaded this. "Did you know all of this—" he

gestured around them, "—used to belong to Italy?"

"Most of Europe did," said Paolo, "During the Roman empire. If that's what you mean."

"Sort of, but you're on the right track. Where we are now used to be part of Italy. Italy is a great country with a long history. We're descended from the Romans. We're powerful."

Paolo wasn't sure he agreed. He saw how hungry many of his neighbors were, noted that some people they knew had gone missing in the past couple of years. He heard the radio broadcasts where Mussolini spoke emphatically about Italy and its future, saw Mama and Tommaso listening reverently to it and nodding along, but where was the evidence? No one around them was happy or fulfilled. A sense of quiet terror permeated daily life. At twelve, Paolo knew he didn't fully understand the ways of the world, but he knew enough that he disagreed with the life view that Mama and Tommaso held, and if they were devotees of Mussolini, that was almost enough to make him not.

"So what are we doing in France, then?"

"We'll be staying at a *castello*," said Tommaso.

Paolo didn't expect *that*. "What?"

"We're going to a place called Chateau Desrosiers in Santa Maddalena," Tommaso explained. "There are other men from Italy there already, and they're in touch with others throughout France who support our cause. The castello is our base of operations."

Our cause. "What are we doing at the castello?"

"We're going to claim it," said Tommaso succinctly. "We're taking Santa Maddalena back for Italy."

SIMONETTA

Simonetta sits in the church. She has spent more time in holy places in the last three months than she has in the last ten years.

She had begged the nun, Sister Agatha, to tell her more. At first the sister was reluctant, but upon hearing the condensed version of Simonetta's move to France and the discovery of the automaton, she became slightly less withholding.

"How did you know my grandfather and his brother?" Simonetta had asked. Sister Agatha had taken her to the courtyard to talk, and they sat on a bench under the shade of old, twisted yew trees that felt out of place in the Catholic setting, a blip of primeval paganism.

"They were part of the occupation," said Sister Agatha. "They came from Italy in droves—the boys. Even after Armistice, they had a mission to reclaim the region for Italy. Fools, all of them."

Simonetta had tried to fill in the gaps without discouraging Agatha from sharing more. "During the second World War?"

Agatha nodded and paused, thinking. "This was in 1943. Those stupid boys thought Mussolini would triumph even when he was already ousted by his own country."

Oh god, Simonetta thought. Mussolini. Her family were Fascists. It's not the first time she's wondered about that, but her nonni never spoke of it and Nonna's family had left Italy not long after the war began, when Emilia was a small child. Nothing they ever talked about implied they had any love or support for Mussolini, but it would have been easy to sever any link there in shame after Mussolini fell.

"Tommaso killed my brother," said Agatha after a long silent moment in which Simonetta was in her own head stewing. But that reveal made Simonetta shout in anguish.

"Oh, Sister Agatha—I am so sorry. I truly had no idea!"

Agatha waved away Simonetta's emotion. "Jean-Luc knew the risks. All of the Resistance fighters did. But they thought they would die fighting the Nazis, not young Italian boys too big for their britches. Tommaso and the others, they had no idea what they were doing. But my brother died for it."

Agatha, despite her spryness, grew tired during their conversation. But Simonetta got the gist: Tommaso and Paolo were part of a group of Mussolini youth who had occupied Sainte-Madeleine, by way of Chateau Desrosiers, to reclaim the territory for Italy. They trusted Desrosiers' then-owner, the Marquis de Najarac, who had formed alliances with every faction—the French resistance, the Nazis, and the Fascists—and betrayed each one. And when he sold the Fascists to the Resistance, he was killed in the final standoff, a battle on the grounds of Desrosiers.

The chapel damaged from mortar—that was her family's doing. Saint Madeleine's broken stained glass, the chipped stone—her grandfather and his brother were there. They had nearly destroyed Desrosiers, the place she was now helping to restore, and for what? Simonetta ran the numbers: Paolo would have been twelve then, Tommaso seventeen according to Agatha. Why would they have done this? Had they been compelled? Agatha's own brother was also just seventeen when he died during the final siege, and she only a few years old, with this story told to her by her surviving brother, Gabriel.

Guilt roils in Simonetta's stomach. She has actively participated in anti-fascist politics her entire life; it was a byproduct of growing up in a place like Berkeley where protests were constant, where progressivism dominated even in the shadow of the libertarianism cast by Silicon Valley and encroaching gentrification. She had worked at the anarchist bookstore during college, volunteered regularly with Alex at the centers for queer youth, joined countless marches in support of Palestine and abortion and causes that endorsed freedom of speech and expression. Simonetta knew new and dangerous forms of fascism were alive and well in the modern era, but the Italian-born Fascism of the first half of the twentieth century had seemed to her (naively, in retrospect) a severed branch of the Axis powers, rightly burned and buried when the war ended.

Ghostly boot steps waft across the courtyard and she envisions a young Paolo Altobella, and an older boy beside him, among them. No wonder Agatha spoke of "atonement."

But where can Simonetta work toward that? It's not here, in this church, despite its beauty and the traditions with which she is familiar. Simonetta understands the comfort that faith offers. If she could hand someone else all of her suffering, would she? Could she relinquish control to soothe her soul? What was the cost of internal peace—a lack of skepticism? That had always

been her problem—she saw through its attempts to placate, always poking holes in anything that felt too easy.

"She *spit* at you?" Hanako is aghast.

It's past midnight. Simonetta arrived back at the chateau close to ten, when the sun had finally made its descent and the stars were bright in the sky. But Simonetta hadn't stopped, like she usually did, to look up and appreciate the cosmos and the small space she takes up in it. Instead, she hastily parked the sputtering Renault and ran to the kitchen to get something strong to drink, and that's where she found Jeremy at the table with Lotte and Hanako, rolling dough into buns to proof overnight. Jeremy had taken one look at her expression and poured her a dram of whisky.

"I was mortified," says Simonetta, wanting to hide her face with her hands at the mere memory. "I thought I committed some egregious crime against the French. I guess that's true, in a way—my family did some truly horrible things during World War Two."

Lotte shrugged. "In your defense, most of the world was doing something pretty horrible during World War Two."

"*Your* ancestors were local leaders of the Dutch resistance, Lotte," counters Hanako.

"That's why I said 'most.'"

Jeremy wordlessly pours another shot and Simonetta sips on it thoughtfully. "I just don't know what to do with this information."

"You don't have to do anything with it," says Jeremy. "It's just information. It's history. You can't change it."

Simonetta winces. "It's not history to Sister Agatha. Her brother died during the siege when she was just a baby. Her brother died *here*! She holds a grudge, and I don't blame her. She says I need to atone. She has every reason to hate my—" she pauses on the word *great uncle*, it suggests familiarity—"relative." She laughs bitterly. "When she first spit at me, I thought she was cursing me. My Nonna used to say spitting was evil magic.

Maybe we *are* cursed." It's a thought Simonetta can't get out of her head—maybe there *is* something sinister plaguing her family line. She thinks of her mother dying so young. She thinks of her own anxiety.

"Maybe you're already atoning," says Lotte.

The warmth of the whisky is starting to settle in, spreading through Simonetta's chest, loosening the tightness that she carries there. Tension has had her shoulders tucked into her neck. "What do you mean?"

"You're here, aren't you?" Lotte nods to the room around them, hands covered in flour. "Repairing the place your family tried to destroy."

Simonetta winces again, the harsh words cutting through. *Tried to destroy.* But Lotte is right—she is here, repairing it. "I guess. I didn't know I was coming here to do that. I feel like atonement should be intentional. How do I undo the fact that my relatives were Fascists?"

Jeremy taps his chin. "You said that Sister Agatha spoke highly of Paolo."

Simonetta nods. "He was twelve when he was here. She said he sent her letters when she was older, apologizing. He spent most of his time here away from the others."

"It sounds like he was already trying to do right," says Jeremy. "He was so young. How much can you expect a kid to do?"

She groans and puts her head in her hands. "I need to process this."

"Did you find out anything about Catelot?" asks Jeremy.

"A little bit," she says, but thinks instead of the information Sister Agatha unceremoniously dumped on her lap. Simonetta riffles through her satchel and pulls out some photocopied papers. She's frustrated that she didn't get to enjoy the old, original documents more, or celebrate what she's learned; it all seems silly in comparison.

"They do have record of a Catherine Desrosiers arriving at the abbey in 1360, with a death year of 1382. And there was mention of another woman—a guardian, according to the historical society's analysis made about a decade ago. That woman also died there, under Catherine's care. Their notes are on display in the exhibit," Simonetta explains. "In the records of Catherine, there are some details about her character: *she was an astute healer, woodworker, and artist*, skills she attributed to her 'guardian.' She had painted several frescoes at the abbey that are now lost to time."

"It's interesting that they documented those things," says Lotte.

"Scribes in abbeys tended to document a lot about life there," says Simonetta, grateful for the change in subject. "It's called 'ad perpetuam rei memoriam'—like a perpetual record of something. Archives in monasteries are a big reason why we know as much as we do about medieval times. We're lucky that Catherine ended up there, because her history is connected to both the chateau and the abbey."

"That helps, right?" says Hanako. "With your project?"

"How so?" A headache creeps up the back of Simonetta's skull. She's glad she decided to come back to the chateau instead of staying overnight at the abbey. She wants to sleep in her own bed—or the bed she's come to know so well.

"That confirms the legend that Catherine's guardian painted the portrait," inserts Jeremy. "And maybe made the doll, if it wasn't by Catelot herself. So you have confirmation of how old that part of the automaton is."

"Yes, I guess you're right." She is so unsettled by Sister Agatha that those discoveries were overshadowed. Simonetta sits up. "At least we have that part of the automaton figured out."

"You don't look pleased—this is a major breakthrough!" He brushes flour off his own hands and finds hers under the table, giving one a squeeze in support.

Simonetta knows that's true: It's a big piece of the puzzle, a priceless insight into history that has a compelling story all on its own. But she can't stop thinking of young Italian boys crawling over the Desrosiers grounds like a swarm of spiders, devouring everything in their path, seeding the soil with a perennial rot that would still germinate long after it had been rooted out.

PAOLO

The air at the peak was biting and Paolo settled deep into his bedroll. Beside him, Tommaso was already asleep. Even in sleep Tommaso's face still looked pinched with worry. Paolo tried to figure out what it meant to "take Santa Maddalena back for Italy." Could places be taken? He knew from history they could be conquered—Rome's legacy, conquering Europe and beyond. But Rome had fallen. There was no ceding of territory that didn't result in violence. Were they soldiers now?

But Paolo didn't know what to think, had no context, and so the threads of thoughts in his head continued to get more and more tangled. With nothing tangible or specific to grasp, everything felt knotted, like crossed wires in the Altobella automatons. He longed for a project, something that required concentration, something that would be a conduit for his internal turmoil.

Stomach churning, he forced himself into a restless sleep and awoke to darkness, shaken by a frigid wind that pierced his bedroll. He glanced over to see Tommaso still asleep.

Despite the exertion from the trek, Paolo suddenly felt wide awake. He sat up in his bedroll and surveyed the mountain around him. It was very dark, the fire long extinguished. The moon above was a small sliver, emitting just enough pale light for Paolo to see the silhouette of a wolf.

He froze, his stomach dropping. The wolf stood a mere ten feet away, at the edge of their rocky alcove. He thought about waking Tommaso but reasoned that it would be better to remain still, moving only to clap a hand over his mouth to stifle the sound of his breathing.

But the wolf came no closer. It simply stood facing the moon. Paolo braced himself for a howl, but it didn't come. But another rustling sound did—and coming into view was a second silhouette, that of a rabbit, with its long ears limned by the moon.

Paolo opened his mouth to cry out a warning to the ignorant rabbit—*No! Turn around!*—but the creature, unlucky with a poor sense of timing, had emerged right into the path of the wolf. As if sensing Paolo's presence, the wolf turned its head toward him and in the darkness, Paolo saw the glint of the wolf's eyes, the flash of his teeth, before the wolf lunged after the rabbit in one swift, graceful moment. And Paolo, unable to move for fear he would be next, shut his eyes to avoid the gruesome scene masked by night, but even hours later he couldn't erase from his ears the sounds of the devouring.

Paolo and Tommaso made their descent to Chateau Desrosiers at midday, an easier trek due in part to Paolo's blisters beginning to callous. Still, by the time they spilled into the valley, Paolo was sweating profusely.

He tried to coax some information from Tommaso as a village came into view.

"So this is France?" Paolo asked.

"Sort of," said Tommaso, also breathing heavily by now. That phrase seemed to be embedded in everything Tommaso said now—*sort of.* "For now. Really, it belongs to us."

"Us?"

"No, Paolo," Tommaso said, annoyed. "Italy. Everything we do is in service to our country. Don't forget that." He wiped his brow. "We'll be at Desrosiers soon. There is a person there, a Frenchman, with resources and connections. He believes in our cause."

Us. Our cause. Tommaso spoke of these things as if they belonged to him, and Paolo felt once again that there was some message he had missed.

Paolo tried to summon up some national pride. Would that make all of this easier? He supposed there were Italians he respected. Galileo Galilei. Leonardo da Vinci. His distant ancestor, Marco Altobella, inventor and artificer. He liked it when his countrymen were people of math and science. Those were things to be proud of, but they weren't about a place; Galileo's discoveries transformed all of humankind. What did that have to do with Italy?

Paolo thought of the wolf again, and then of the legend of Rome—it seemed his country was determined to bare its teeth instead of smile in welcome, to bite instead of savor, to force its prowess and might upon the world instead of embracing what made it truly special. Because Paolo thought Italy's best legacy was its long line of those who wanted more of the world, who made art and discoveries that changed the course of history. Not for the first time, he wished he was born during the Renaissance, envisioned walking down the streets in Florence, a city he had never visited. He would have rubbed shoulders with other mathematicians, discussed theorems and formulas.

Instead, he followed Tommaso reluctantly into France-Not-France, into the strange and sober Santa Maddalena, fearing the wolves at the door, heading straight into the belly of the beast.

Eighteen

Inner Ward: The open area in the center of a castle.

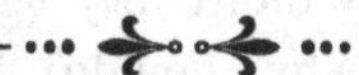

THE JULY SUN OVERHEAD lays bare all of Simonetta's inner questions and concerns: what to do about the secrets of her family legacy she inadvertently unearthed like one finds bones in the mud after a rainstorm? How to proceed with the automaton? Where to live after her visa runs out? What does the future look like with Jeremy?

Although they have no official discussion of it, both Simonetta and Jeremy decide to keep their relationship under wraps—not so much a secret, but just theirs. They're in the very precious but precarious early stage of a new relationship, and this one has the makings of being long-term.

Simonetta is no stranger to serious relationships. Once she decides she's in love, that's that. Love, to her, is like a light switch—once it was turned on, she would always remember the way the glow felt and what it revealed inside her. She's been a serial monogamist since she was seventeen—her first love was Danny, who she met the first day of college and remained with until graduation day, when they decided to join the Peace Corps and wanted to be on their own "without strings" (their words). Simultaneously crushed but relieved, Simonetta remained single for a whole three months after college until she met Alex her first semester in graduate school. At the time, Simonetta assumed that Alex was her future; they traveled together, lived together, talked about marriage. But when the time came for Alex to seek a post-doctoral fellowship six years later, and Simonetta was on an upward trajectory in the lab, a rift had formed that could not be undone. They tried long-distance for months until it simply fizzled, even when Alex eventually returned to Berkeley.

Part of Simonetta is stubborn, unchangeable; she has never wanted to be the one to give up *her* life, *her* career, for another. She had been raised to be independent, and she didn't mind being alone. So when it came time to fight for those who left, it wasn't a fight worth having—it was already lost.

Because in her low moments of self-pity, Simonetta felt that she had frequently been left behind by those she loved, through death or decisions. Why didn't they fight for her? She always understood the logic: why shouldn't Danny join the Peace Corps, and why shouldn't Alex go where she could potentially earn a tenured position? Those were admirable things, important things, things that transcended a young relationship in its potential impact on the course of a life. It never bothered her on a practical level. And obviously, her mother and Nonno and Nonna didn't choose to leave her and the mortal coil. In her heart, though, she still believes that the one who can leave holds all the power.

Now, the situation is very different, and *she* could be the one to leave. Jeremy had not yet asked her to stay, and Simonetta doesn't know what she'll say if he does. There are worse options than staying in the idyllic French countryside with a lover. She's more than halfway through her work-stay program and the looming thought of Next now hovers around her like a wasp she swats away.

Her excuse, for now, is the automaton. Simonetta is singularly focused on her current goal: to make the machine play again. She delegated the cabinet repair to Jeremy, a relatively straightforward task for him, and together they planned to restore Catelot. In the meantime, though, it's on Simonetta to keep moving the project forward.

She knows very little about machinery. Not for the first time, she wishes Nonno were here to give her guidance. He was an engineer, spent years working in automobile factories. Simonetta asked him many questions over the years, but mostly about what the equipment did, not how it was built. Jason is usually happy to answer her questions, but Simonetta doesn't want to constantly pull him away from his summer art endeavors with his wife.

She finishes her basic schematics, inspired by some she found online from historical records and recreations. She maintains a meticulous spreadsheet and research document on her laptop for tracking sources and materials. After several fruitful late-night Googling sessions, which she did from the comfort of Jeremy's settee in his tower room, she traces a new line of thought.

Like Jeremy had mentioned, there is a place called Strumenti d'Altobella—Altobella Instruments—not far beyond the nearby border severing France and Italy. According to the sparse website, they had been in operation since 1926 and made farm equipment. It was a small operation, it seemed, with minimal web presence. Simonetta ran the page through Google Translate for any other information, to little avail. If there's any relation to the automaton, a link is tenuous—save for its logo, a tiny A encircled by a stalk of wheat. There's something about it that tugs at Simonetta.

"Is it possible they didn't always make farm equipment?" she muses aloud. It's past midnight and Jeremy sits on his bed, a book propped open on his lap.

He shrugs. "It's possible. You said they've been in operation since 1926—that was before the war, so perhaps they had to change their business when the war started. That happened to a lot of businesses across the continent."

"I wonder if I should write them a letter," says Simonetta. "I don't feel comfortable enough in my Italian to call, and I could probably express myself better through writing."

"It's worth a shot. If anything, they could probably point you in the right direction. You said the web of Altobellas seemed relatively small." He sets down his book and gestures to her laptop. "How's everything going?"

Simonetta glances over the timeline tab in her spreadsheet,

seeks out any detail she can pick at. "Marguerite de Sainte-Madeleine never married, right? So she had no heirs. Who took over the chateau after her?"

"It was a rather unusual arrangement," Jeremy explains. "She had bequeathed some of her belongings to someone unrelated to her family—some noble person in Portugal, I think, not sure of the arrangement there. But her will was overturned and all of it passed instead to her nephew."

"Lucky nephew," says Simonetta.

"Is he? Sometimes I wonder." He stretches out on the bed and places his hands behind his head.

"Is this not what you want to do?" Simonetta asks, gesturing to the room around her. She takes in the beautiful scene, much of it made by his hand: the smooth wooden beams, the intricate paneling, the desk under the window.

"I don't know," he says after a thoughtful moment. "I've been very fortunate to find work, room and board, here with Claudel." He runs a hand through his hair. "I wasn't happy back in Ireland. Took a lot of odd jobs but couldn't ever find my footing. My favorite job was building sets for the National Theater in Cork, but when my contract ended there, Claudel invited me here and I've been here ever since." He pauses to think. "That was about six years ago."

"But restoring and maintaining the chateau isn't your long-term plan?" Simonetta asks this tentatively, for the thought makes her sad—once Claudel is gone, who will love this place the way she has? Simonetta hopes that someone out there will cherish and protect Desrosiers.

"It wasn't," Jeremy says, but the rest unspoken lingers in the air between them.

Simonetta cuts to the chase. "But? Has something changed?"

Jeremy slips off the bed and plops into a chair opposite Simonetta in the settee. He moves her laptop and notebook to the floor to free up her hands.

"Of course it's changed," he says, taking her hand. "You've turned my whole life upside down, Simonetta." He doesn't wait for a returned declaration and continues. "The thought of being here alone, having all of this fall to me, sounded miserable. It made me feel trapped—this was Claudel's dream, her vision and work, not mine. But the way you see it makes me want to believe in it, inspires me to work alongside you to make that vision real."

Simonetta gapes at him. "Do you remember when you yelled at me about the AGA?"

He laughs. "Have I not done enough yet to make up for that? I am truly sorry. That was an awful way to get acquainted with you."

"Well, I just meant that you'll have to have more patience with me as I learn how everything in this place works," she answers coyly, as if her heart isn't beating out of her chest at the words he had casually tossed in her direction like a hot bun straight from the oven. Her hands and face burn and she turns serious. "If you want me to stay, Jeremy, I want you to ask me. It's a big ask, and I want to know you mean it."

His face brightens, a burden removed; had he already been planning to ask? "Simonetta, will you—wait, what's your middle name?"

"Julia. What's yours?"

"William." He takes her other hand from the desk and holds both of hers between his. "Simonetta Julia Altobella—"

"Simonetta Julia *Cavalieri* Altobella—" she corrects indignantly. "Italian women don't take their husband's name so Nonna never—"

Jeremy interrupts her lecture. "Will you stay in France with me once your work-stay commitment is finished?"

PAOLO

Paolo would have sold his soul for a bath, but there was no time to rest, for he immediately was swept up in the fray of nearly fifty other young Italian men, from Primavera and surrounding villages, all unified on their quest for *spazio vitale*.

Paolo wasn't surprised to learn he was the youngest among the group. He still wasn't entirely sure why he was there, suspected that his mother wanted him out from underfoot and Tommaso thought it was time for Paolo to "become a man," whatever that meant.

The sky above Santa Maddalena was bright and sunny when they reached Chateau Desrosiers. Tommaso and Paolo followed the river to where it met the moat surrounding the chateau; through the iron-wrought gate, Paolo took in the sight of the imposing fortress that must have awed during its heyday. But now the facade was faded and weathered, the windows caked with hard water, the garden overgrown, the fountain water green with algae. But it was busy; dozens of young men filtered in and out. To Paolo it seemed like some sort of boy's camp, not a serious undertaking.

"Tommaso!"

A tall, lanky boy Paolo recognized from Primavera came bounding across the courtyard to them. Tommaso grinned as he clasped hands with his friend.

"Francisco," Tommaso said. "Good to see you."

"And you. Although I am surprised to see your company." Francisco raised his eyes and Tommaso shrugged, as if Paolo wasn't standing right there.

"Mama insisted. And he's smart, you know."

"Is that true, young Paolo?" Francisco said.

It was Paolo's turn to shrug. "*Boh*. I like math," he said.

This made Tommaso and Francisco laugh and Paolo felt that it wasn't in kindness.

"Come, you must meet Etienne," Francisco said, ushering them into the fortress. Paolo breathed in a sigh of relief in the cool foyer, took a blessed moment of respite while Francisco went to find their host.

Etienne Richelieu, the Marquis de Najarac and owner of Chateau Desrosiers, was unlike anyone Paolo had ever met. For one thing, he had the straightest, whitest teeth that gave him an uncanny air. The white teeth, paired with gleaming chestnut hair parted neatly to the side and an impeccable mustache sitting atop the remarkable mouth reminded Paolo of a marionette who bears one expression permanently painted on a wooden face.

The unreal quality to Etienne was amplified by his way of speaking, where he seemed to say much that equated to almost nothing. To Paolo's surprise, the Frenchman spoke fluent Italian—and Spanish, and English, and even a bit of Turkish and Arabic he picked up during his early years and subsequent extensive travels through the Middle Eastern and most of the African continent. He code-switched with ease, showing off his skills to the impressionable youth. Paolo guessed Etienne was in his fifties, tried to calculate his date of birth, but it was an estimate at best, as Etienne had a way of overloading the listener with details while obscuring important ones. And only those who were truly observant caught the inconsistencies.

"I thought you said you were born in Morocco," said Paolo, frowning, as Etienne gave Tommaso, Paolo, and two new additions from Cassinasco a tour of Desrosiers' trophy room, filled to the brim with stuffed animals Etienne claimed to have killed on his many hunts. Etienne was describing a riveting tale of felling a Barbary sheep with his father during his childhood in Tunisia.

"I was *born* in Morocco," Etienne said with confidence and a tone that suggested Paolo was being ridiculous. "My family moved around a lot so I also lived in Tunisia as a young child."

But several moments before Etienne had just specifically referenced Tunisia, not Morocco, as his place of birth, despite conflicting information he had said earlier when Paolo had first met him. Paolo opened his mouth to clarify but Tommaso shot him a look of warning, and he kept his mouth shut. Instead, he studied the Barbary sheep with its curved horns arching away from its face. The sheep, like the other creatures, was poorly preserved; one of its empty eyes was packed with some cloth.

Etienne shepherded them into the library next, a room Paolo took a liking to, for its deep green shelves were packed full of tomes. But they passed through this room quickly, to Paolo's dismay, as Etienne was already talking about the Grand Salon.

"Do you have books about mathematics or science?" Paolo asked before they crossed the threshold into the next room.

"You ask a lot of questions, don't you, young Paolo?" Etienne said, that broad smile plastered on his face. Paolo felt he had been involuntarily assigned a new name, Young Paolo. He missed being simply Paolo. "Yes, there are many books about science. Is there a specific topic that interests you?"

Tommaso looked murderous, but Paolo didn't understand why. Why not use the time here to read and learn? What else was Paolo supposed to do if no one would tell him anything?

Etienne backtracked and gestured to a section of books, and to Paolo's delight, he saw plenty of titles with words that interested him. But they were all in French, so Paolo realized he'd have to learn that as well. Everyone talked about Santa Maddalena as if it was in Italy, but to Paolo it was definitely, obviously France. The signs on the roads they passed as they trekked down to the chateau, the books filling the shelves, Etienne himself. If the Italian influence was supposed to creep its way in, it had yet to do so.

A week passed in a blur. Paolo met dozens of people whose names he couldn't keep track of. He and Tommaso slept outside near the garden, which Paolo preferred; so many unwashed young men filtering in and out of Desrosiers all day left an awful reek. He tried to follow Tommaso around, seeking something to do, but Tommaso told Paolo to find something to do help and instead left him for numerous secret "meetings." So much for learning the ways of manhood, Paolo thought, thinking that Tommaso, despite being on the verge of seventeen, still looked very boyish in comparison to the others, although very few there seemed older than twenty-five.

There were so many things Paolo didn't understand that he started writing them down. Left to his own devices, he found respite in the Desrosiers library. He uncovered a section of journals and claimed a mostly empty one for himself; the first ten pages or so were filled with some random notes in French, lists of instruments, and what he assumed were song titles: *The Day by the River, Under the Navy Night Sky, Slender Hands.* But the rest left plenty of room for his own thoughts.

Paolo Altobella didn't understand:

Why he was here and not back home in Italy (the real Italy).

Why Etienne treated everyone like he was hosting a grand party and not an occupation, giving tours and showing off his collections.

Why Tommaso seemed to be a different person among the other *soldatos*, as Paolo heard the other boys call each other.

Why everyone walked around so sullen and secretive.

Why green onions returned every year with such tenacity (a hardy cluster grew in Desrosiers' unkempt garden and it made Paolo think of the ones that grew near the buildings in downtown Primavera).

Why the other boys, including Tommaso, seemed to trust and revere Etienne.

Behind the never faltering enthusiasm and wide, toothy smiles, Paolo detected a glint of something off and it unsettled him. He saw the wheels always turning in Etienne's mind the way he used to see them whirring in his father's, but the reasons could not have been more different. Paolo's father was driven by curiosity; Etienne, by showmanship.

Paolo spent days wandering around the chateau. No one paid him much mind; there was lots of secrecy about—people meeting behind closed doors, talking in hushed voices, some venturing into the village. There was a sense of quiet chaos that dominated the chateau, every man for himself but aligned on one clear goal that Paolo simply existed on the periphery of. And so did Etienne.

Etienne spoke often of Mussolini, spoke most often in Italian. One day, Paolo went into the Grand Salon, a room that was once grand but now had peeling wallpaper and scuffed floors, to find Etienne and three soldatos standing around an intricate radio. Etienne was demonstrating to the boys how to use it and, despite himself, Paolo couldn't resist the curiosity to take a look.

"—and the frequency, measured in the vibration of sound waves," said Etienne with that confident smile. Paolo must have made a face because Etienne said, "Young Paolo, our resident scientist! What do you think?"

Paolo frowned, his brow creasing in thought. "I don't think that's correct. You're talking about resonance. Like harmonic resonance, where a sound wave meets an already oscillating object—" In his mind's eye he saw Tommaso's disapproving face and clamped his mouth shut. Instead, he asked, "Are we allowed to use the radio?"

"I'm afraid not, my friend. Radios are extremely difficult to come by. You have no idea the lengths I went to in search of one. It's only for use when we really need it, in case we need to communicate with the Motherland." Etienne winked as he said and it made Paolo's skin crawl.

Paolo added to his list of questions: *Why is Etienne helping us?*

Two weeks later, Paolo crept through the chateau deep into the night. He was hardly the only one awake; his fellow soldatos were often meeting or playing card games, and it was easy enough for him to poke around undetected.

It was quieter toward the medieval tower where Etienne lived, where a smattering of rooms occupied the upper floor. And the oldest and largest chamber in the whole estate was where Etienne slept. Paolo had begun tracking the Frenchman's schedule, noting a consistent inconsistency, and tonight he had earned himself a tenuous few hours to use the radio.

After Etienne's presentation, the radio had been moved out of sight and into an old room in the chateau's turret, and Paolo could not stop thinking about it. He had only used the Phonola radio Mama kept in the kitchen. The scrappy one Etienne procured, with knobs and a frequency gauge and a headset, held endless appeal.

It took him a few nights to get the hang of it, to find the right frequencies. Paolo figured out that certain adjustments to the radio opened up more frequencies. It was dangerous; it was one of the few things Etienne said that Paolo believed. Radio technology was hard to come by this far into the war, a powerful vessel for communication. Etienne had urged them not to use the radio when he wasn't present, claiming that the rig he had built was unstable and only those knowledgeable in that technology should try using it. The radio was a tool for "our cause," he had said.

But Paolo, with his engineering mind and hands, couldn't stay away. Four days into his experimentation, he struck gold: the right frequency at the right time. And Paolo heard his first broadcast.

Like the radio itself, the broadcast was scrappy—French people, young men from the sounds of it, took turns speaking, their voices breaking through the static. At first, Paolo understood very little of the spoken French, but he loved the way human voices sounded coming through the headset. He tried deciphering the French and, deep into the night, sat in the shadows of the window slats bisecting his vision, with the receiver to his ear and a French-Italian dictionary illuminated by the light of the moon.

After another week, he was getting the hang of it, the radio and the language and the schedule of Etienne's sleeping and the broadcasts. He longed for the moments where it was just him and the radio and the quiet attic. There was a satisfying cadence to French that Paolo appreciated, an effortless rhythm. There were similarities to his native Italian tongue, but Paolo felt that Italian had a bite to it in comparison. If Italian was a wolf, French was a sly fox moving languidly under fallen trees.

And that's how he came to hear the nightly coded exchanges with the French Resistance, holed up in the abbey in the village.

It took him a while to get used to listening and translating a live French broadcast but once some of the vocabulary became more familiar, he made the realization that they were sharing parables, myths, fairytales. It was almost like the pre-war radio programs he used to listen to, Italian children's hour programs. But the French usually told stories unique to their country, tales with names like *Bearskin, Princess Rossette*. Paolo, notebook and dictionary open on the table beside him, picked apart the stories and reassembled them. He searched through Etienne's library and found a few old collections of French fairytales. Sometimes, a couple of the stories repeated, which gave Paolo a chance to learn them better.

Then one night there was a new story, one that he recognized. The word Pinocchio came through the broadcast, clear and crisp. A story Paolo knew well, like many Italian youth. The tale of the wooden puppet and its maker, Geppetto. Paolo liked the story because he liked the idea of making something that would come to life. It reminded him of his ancestor Marco Altobella and his automata. To Paolo, magic and engineering could be wielded very much the same.

Excited to hear the familiar tale, Paolo wondered why they had ventured into non-French folklore. He listened as they relayed a concise version of the story—most of their versions were short, for the broadcasts themselves were brief, clandestine and secretive.

Then he heard Etienne's name, clear as day.

It was so jarring that it gave Paolo a start. The broadcasts were his escape; it had given him purpose to listen to people other than the boys around him talking of things Paolo didn't comprehend. Hearing Etienne's name brought him back to his body, his location, his purpose here that he wanted no part of.

Was it this Etienne they referred to? That could be anyone; was Etienne a common name in France? Paolo thought of the other Paolos he had met, the many Tommasos.

He strained to hear, as if listening harder would make the French words and meaning clearer.

"Le trompeur—," one of the speakers said. In his notes, Paolo had labeled this voice "Jean," using a name he had found in the book of French fairytales. He flipped quickly though the dictionary. *Le trompeur: Betrayer, trickster.* "—Est-ce Geppetto, le trompeur? Est-il vraiment un marionnettiste? Dans son château?" *Is he Geppetto, the betrayer? Is he really a puppeteer? In his castle?*

Paolo's blood went cold. The betrayer, in his castle.

The second speaker, whom Paolo called "Louis," gave a hearty laugh. "Avec ses nombreuses marionnettes!" *With his many puppets.*

Together, they said: "Tant de Pinocchio!" *So many Pinocchios.*

Paolo pieced together his notes, assembling the puzzle pieces, realizing that all this time, the stories were a code, and he had just cracked one.

Etienne: the betrayer, in his castle, with his puppets.

SIMONETTA

Will you stay in France with me?

It's an easy question, but Simonetta refuses to decide until she has done her due diligence picking apart every potential outcome and anticipating every obstacle. The answer is an easy one and she knows it; *yes* sits on her tongue like a sugar cube, but she abstains from swallowing the sweetness until she is sure the substance is there in equal measure. Despite Jeremy's proposal, Simonetta insists on sleeping in her room for the rests of the summer. It isn't because she doesn't adore Jeremy's room in the left tower and its comfortable goose feather bed, and the man she finds in it, but her stubbornness has reared up, and she heeds its call.

Simonetta knows she's still prone to more bouts of the waves, and it will take her some time to understand what it meant to coexist with those feelings alongside a new partner. Additionally, a permanent move overseas comes with logistical requirements that she needs to figure out. The easiest way to remain in France is to get married, to which Jeremy had agreed without blinking ("We have the chapel here so that's easy." "Jeremy! Claudel doesn't even know we're dating, we can't just *get married*.") He seems to interpret big romantic moments as simply logical developments, which Simonetta finds both endearing and frustrating. Another option is to apply for Italian citizenship, which she is entitled to through Nonno's birthplace. This option appeals to Simonetta, for it ties her to her family in a different way, like she's protecting their memory by maintaining the link to Italy. But maybe they didn't want her to maintain it; it had occurred to Simonetta that Nonno Paolo was likely deeply ashamed of his family's Fascist involvement, that Tommaso's actions were the reason why he had cut off contact. Would Nonno be proud or dismayed that Simonetta so desperately reached for this connection to Italy?

She just wants time to process. In a matter of months, her entire life has changed—she had lost Nonna, quit her job, sold her grandparent's house, moved oversees on a whim for a summer program with no back-up plan, then met a back-up plan and fell in love, and said back-up plan had then asked her to stay with him and run a massive estate that she still knew relatively—all things considered—very little about.

To fend from overthinking and inevitably spiraling into the anxiety abyss once again, Simonetta turns to tinkering. She claims a workspace in one of the stables near Jeremy's workshop, and it has a large wooden surface plenty big enough to spread out the inner workings of the automaton.

With Jeremy and Jason's help, she had carefully extracted Catelot and her gears from the cabinet. It was not an easy task; the tiny, gilded screws threatened to break, and several had fallen to the sawdust floor and had to be hunted for. Simonetta's knees are still covered in the dust and she sneezes every few minutes.

Despite her lack of engineering knowledge, Simonetta thinks the automaton's age works in her favor. As a woman of the twenty-first century, she's privy to informational access that someone in the 1700s simply did not, and could not, possess. That made the task somewhat easier, as it wouldn't be a matter of coding, one of many skills she had attempted to glean during graduate school that did not come naturally to her. Simonetta considers herself an analytical thinker, but not a mathematical one, the main difference there being in understanding the abstraction of things. She appreciates that which she can see, feel, touch, dissect, understand, and that is what informs her logic.

According to her findings, for most automatons, activation is a matter of pulling the right proverbial strings. Simonetta has one significant advantage—as a violinist herself, she understands how fingers on strings work in the overall scheme of the universe. On a zoomed-in level, the beautifully carved small violin in Catelot's dainty fingers, Simonetta identifies each finger as it relates to each string on the violin. This equates to five strings—one for each finger holding the violin, including the thumb under the fretboard—all of which stretch down the doll's body and wind into the cluster of gears. Using a small box of ribbons from Claudel's sewing stash, Simonetta creates a color-coded system to identify which string goes to which gear by tying a small strip of ribbon on the corresponding areas. The other hand is deceptively simple, for Catelot's bow arm has one string attached to it, but that string went to multiple gears to account for the doll's different potential bow placements on the violin.

Not for the first time, Simonetta is struck by the sheer intricacy of the machine. Several hours into her tinkering, she's filled her notebook with several pages of notes and musings, with one in particular plucking at her own data-driven heartstrings and forming the crux of her research:

What actually activates the automaton?

The last question is the main bump in the road. After several hours of pulling strings, pushing gears, jotting down notes, and updating her schematics, Simonetta is frustrated by the lack of an obvious answer. There's no switch or a lever that turns it on via electricity. A lever, or even a wind-up, would have made sense to her, but neither is found on the cabinet nor the doll itself. She assumed, then, that it was a matter of setting tension—pulling a particular spring, perhaps, so that another loosened and set the whole thing in motion. How that works, Simonetta has absolutely no idea. She'll have to reassemble Catelot in the cabinet to experiment.

Her color-coding has at least been worthwhile. Now that she's identified what did what, it was now mostly a matter of restoring that system. She hopes that by focusing on some of the repair tasks—there's a thick knot of thin wire lodged deep in the gears that needs unraveling—the answer to her Big Question will reveal itself. She looks into the metal for answers, for guidance: What is the catalyst?

"Saint Madeleine lives again!" Hanako exclaims, holding the paper sketch over the empty stained glass window frame in the chapel; the morning light backlights Hanako's drawing, and from down below, Simonetta can envision what it will eventually look like for the window to be filled once again with the silhouette of Saint Madeleine embedded among the colorful glass.

Simonetta keeps experiencing jolts of realization that she may stay in France longer than expected. On a whim the night prior, she submitted the first application for Italian citizenship, reasoning to herself that she is simply keeping logistics moving along while she made her final decision. Jeremy talks about the chateau as "theirs" so casually that Simonetta often forgets that she is part of the equation now. She's surprised by how quickly he has become so serious, and how little it bothers or frightens her. If anything, she appreciates how resolute he is when making a decision and it's new, for once, to not always be the main decision-maker in a relationship. That has typically been Simonetta's role, the long-term thinker and planner. What was life if one wasn't constantly thinking about the Big Picture? But now it's the smaller, granular, mundane minutiae that consume her thoughts, and she's finding that approach to be helpful when learning how to "live in the moment," which was supposedly a good thing, according to anxiety management forums on the internet.

In this moment, she can quite literally smell the roses. The heady scent from the garden wafts over to the chapel on a light summer breeze. The rains have let up for now and a heat wave has followed. The small chapel is warm and close inside and sweat pools uncomfortably under her breasts.

Simonetta claps in approval at Hanako's drawing and helps her descend the ladder.

"I'll get these sent off to the glass company," says Hanako. "Claudel is so excited to get this project taken care of. I wish I could be here later this year to witness the installation."

Simonetta swallows. "I could take pictures for you." It's the first implication she has made to anyone about the potential to stay, and she tests it out on her tongue to see if she means it.

Hanako opens her mouth in surprise. "Have you made arrangements to extend your stay? I'm sure Claudel will be so happy about that!"

"I hope you're right because I'm sort of, um, seeing Jeremy," says Simonetta in a rush. Why does this feel like some sort of massive confession? "He asked me to stay."

Hanako throws her arms around her and the sketch paper crinkles slightly against her back. "Simonetta! That's wonderful!"

"Really? You think so?"

"You're asking me if I think it's a wonderful thing that you met someone who asked you to stay in France with him and run his chateau?" Hanako laughs. "Yes, I do! What a great adventure! Claudel will be thrilled, although I'm surprised you haven't told her."

"I guess I just feel that—none of this could be mine," Simonetta waves a hand around, gesturing to the chapel and beyond. "I don't deserve it, especially with everything my relatives did to ruin it."

"But that's why these places still exist, why there's a whole movement now to restore them," says Hanako, turning thoughtful. "It's not about upholding some lifestyle from a bygone era. It's a communal space—it's actively being reclaimed with every new generation. Remember what the spitting sister said at the abbey? You're atoning. Stake your claim in it, too. You're a part of it now." She holds up her sketch where the young, robed saint holds out her hands in offering. "Look. Saint Madeleine gives you her blessing."

Nineteen

Inner Curtain: A high wall that surrounds an inner ward.

SIMONETTA FINDS CLAUDEL in her study, red varnished nails clacking a staccato on her laptop. The Moreno chandelier above the desk catches the light of early evening, and small colorful dots twinkle against the toile wallpaper. Claudel's room is a vibrant array of bright colors, pink and yellow and blue, with a large, sumptuous bed and satin bedspread. Photographs of volunteers and events from over the past two decades cover many of the walls, and although the beauty and strength of Desrosiers is evident in every corner of the estate, Simonetta thinks the many photos of Claudel's friends and fans from around the world are the chatelaine's real triumph.

"Bonjour, my dear," Claudel says when Simonetta knocks on the door frame. "Please, sit!"

Simonetta acquiesces and waits patiently until Claudel finishes typing and closes her laptop.

"How are you, darling?" Claudel asks. She pulls her blouse away from her collarbone. "Not wilting in the heat, I hope!"

"It's warmer than where I'm from, but I'm getting used to it," Simonetta answers, hoping she doesn't look as hot as she feels. Part of the warmth is from nerves. She takes a deep breath and cuts to the chase. "I was hoping I could talk to you about something."

Claudel smiles and waits for her to continue.

"I've started seeing Jeremy," Simonetta says in a rush. She avoids saying "dating"; the word makes her feel juvenile.

Claudel laughs, a pleasant sound. "Yes, dear, I know that."

"Oh."

"Jeremy told me a couple weeks ago," says Claudel. "Well, I suspected before that, but he confirmed."

A thought strikes Simonetta. "Did you help him coordinate his outfits with mine for the fête?"

Claudel's eyes twinkle. "I may have played a part in that. It was, however, entirely his idea. He expressed early after your arrival that he was interested in you. I am glad to know it's reciprocated."

"Well, I thought he hated me for a while there," Simonetta admits. "He was rather—blunt."

"Yes, he can be," Claudel says with mirth. "He's always been very stubborn."

"I've noticed. He also asked me to stay with him, after the work-stay program ends," Simonetta says, ripping off the Band-Aid. "I would never want to take advantage of you and your home. If I decide to stay, I will gladly find work and contribute to the household. I just wanted to make that clear."

"Simonetta, there are more than two dozen rooms in this chateau and I cannot live in them all," Claudel says. "Of course you can stay, especially now that you are Jeremy's partner. I have no desire for him to leave, as you can imagine." She clasps her hands. "And? Have you decided to stay?"

Has she? "I'm not sure. I think so. I didn't want to commit to doing so until I had spoken to you directly. It seemed very odd to just invite myself here for the foreseeable future."

"I know you've lost much," says Claudel. "Jeremy is a good man. I helped raise him, so I feel entitled to that opinion. I'll also admit that I find the thought of him having you as a partner a bit of a relief. I like to think I have many more years in me, but all I have will go to Jeremy when I am gone. I think that prospect will be more appealing to him with a woman like you alongside him."

Simonetta wants to ask—and what kind of woman is that? She knows what she hopes it means: someone who is strong, resourceful, capable.

"Is that something you want?" says Claudel. "Because if you two are together, what's his will be yours. Does this place hold enough for you?"

Simonetta thinks of the automaton and all that has yet to be uncovered in it. That was one item in one room and it has changed the course of her life—she thinks the chateau could hold several lifetimes of discoveries for her.

The very notion is both a dream fulfilled and terrifying beyond measure, like a Biblical angel with its many eyes: is it a gift or a horror? Simonetta can't help but feel like she is somehow committing to a forever path that she is not yet ready to tread. But the worst part is that there is no valid reason to say no. She doesn't understand the source of her fear—is it that she's making a permanent, lifelong decision, or is it that an opportunity like this seems exceedingly rare, unexpected, and completely beyond her own knowledge and capability?

The ocean of her heart stirs from a tiny quake; she represses the white caps that start to disturb the otherwise still surface. Inside her chest is a heavy iron lock without a key.

Early July shifts to late July, and Simonetta decides to change her tune.

Too many big, complex things weigh on her. Family atonement. Fixing the automaton. Deciding where she's going to live after August. Figuring out what to do with the last of her belongings in Berkeley. Each question sits perched on her shoulder like a Desrosiers gargoyle, heavy and watchful.

Simonetta longs for a sense of lightness. Instead, she thinks of things in binaries such as: Is she in love with Jeremy? Yes. Does she think that Alba was the best cook in the house? Yes. Does she want to dress up like a French Revolutionary with Lotte for the Bastille Day fête? Yes. White wine or red wine with dinner? Yes.

Instead of analyzing, she'll simply go with her gut. She tries to conjure the stirrings of wildness she had felt back in June during the midsummer fête. That was a Simonetta she enjoyed; someone with more confidence and fewer inhibitions, who balanced indulgence with diligence, who sought to dive into things with abandon. Her actual self, at present, seems disconnected from everything around her and she is too focused on everything internal.

She thinks of the automaton and envisions herself with strings on her fingers. What leads where; what did what? Jeremy's an easy one; when she thinks of him, the heartstring tugs. Nonna and Nonno are linked to multiple gears, like Catelot's bow; strings of joy and grief and respect that hum in equal measure. It's Simonetta's own identity that's tangled up in the wires.

Sharp and metallic, the mechanisms bite Simonetta like a cat weary of being brushed.

"Goddammit!" she exclaims, then regrets the sacrilege and the shouting. Luckily, no one is around to hear it. She brings her bleeding finger to her mouth and evaluates her progress, or lack thereof.

She is in the stable workshop again, untangling the knotted wire. Jeremy had brought her some tools to help, but she had shooed him away to let her work in peace, and he reluctantly gave her space, as long as she shares her findings with him later. People hovering and looking over her shoulder disrupts her concentration. It's of the utmost importance to her that she is the one to figure out how Catelot works, to bring her back to life.

From her research, she has gone down the rabbit hole of the types of automata and the generalities of how computational machines work, but the 20th-century math and theory make her head spin. She instead went back a few centuries where the automata design was much more closely aligned with Catelot. She's especially fascinated with a machine from the 1740s called "The Digesting Duck," in which a robotic duck designed by

Frenchman Jacques de Vaucanson could actually consume, digest, and excrete food. To aid in this, de Vaucanson had to come up with a chemical effect within the automaton that would essentially mirror the digestive process of a real duck.

All of de Vaucanson's designs make Simonetta feel like she is on the right track. The discovery of the duck led Simonetta to another genius de Vaucanson schema: a mechanical flute player. So far, this was the closest Simonetta could find to her own automaton. Even the size and shape of de Vaucanson's machine held similarities to Catelot: de Vaucanson's flute player was a doll-like figure that stood over five feet. The mechanisms were so thoughtfully designed that those standing in front of the flute player could feel the resemblance of a real breath via exerted puffs of air. The automaton's capabilities, to play the flute emblematic of how a human would actually play such a complex instrument, heartens Simonetta, makes her feel like some of her hunches aren't totally off base.

She looks over de Vaucanson's musical automata schematics, including another set she found online, made at a later time by another engineer that guessed at his design and intention for a tambourine robot. She has pages of notes about de Vaucanson, whose automata designs not only mirror Catelot's, but the era makes sense to her, too. His machines date to the mid-1700s, which was encouraging after her early research on complex musical automata had initially resulted in the famous Maillardet designs from the 19th century. But even Maillardet had gone uncredited for many years, until his very machine gave him proper attribution when it was finally repaired and activated and, by its own admission, wrote out, "Written by the automaton of Maillardet."

If only it were so easy for Simonetta—maybe Catelot will someday play notes like Morse code and Simonetta can glean more from that. Somehow she doubts it.

But according to Paul from the brocante to whom Simonetta is bonded through their fireside cider chat during the fête, the automaton is likely from the eighteenth century and a Marguerite commission, confirming her and Jeremy's long-standing theory.

"What makes you think that?" she asks, notebook in hand, when Paul stops by the chateau one day to bring Claudel some requested items.

"It's made from French oak, which was the material of choice in most of France until the early 1800s," Paul explains. "And look at the screws here—" he points to several of the screws inside the cabinet. "They're handmade, see? Slightly imperfect. Screws made with molds came later during the Industrial Revolution."

She trusts Paul's intuition and expertise, since he has seen and evaluated thousands of artifacts over the several decades his shop has existed. Even though his training was independently procured and hers academic, Paul is an astute conservator and she recognizes that skill in others. Even if he's wrong, having some timeframe gives her a way to narrow the scope of her research. Casting too wide a net does her no favors.

Were it not for the Altobella maker's mark, she would have gone as far as to think that de Vaucanson was the designer of her automaton. She had briefly wondered if it were perhaps a copycat, or even a collaboration; Marguerite was born in 1699 and died in 1781, and de Vaucanson's duck was made in the 1760s. All is possible, she assumes, but without any documentation, she has no way of knowing the intent or context.

So she forges on. Overall, the gears aren't *that* complicated and her color-coded system helps somewhat. Ultimately, like de Vaucanson's flute-player, it appears to Simonetta that Catelot is designed to emulate a human violinist. She has her hands in the right placements on the bow and on the neck of the violin. Within the mechanisms, Simonetta identifies the wires that connect to the four strings and verifies that they are intact. Another series of wires connects the doll's limbs to a complicated group of gears, all of which are oriented on a slight lean—to create some tension, Simonetta guesses, similar to the tendons and muscles in the arms of a musician.

She sees and draws everything correctly connecting to each piece. She delicately untangles a mass of wires and painstakingly traces each one back to its proper placement, a project that has taken her the better part of three evenings. Most of it is intact again, although the wire connecting to the D string has slipped slightly off its track, so she carefully pulls it taut again with tweezers.

The mechanisms are done: clean, reassembled, but there is no sign yet of the activation point. Simonetta sighs. It doesn't seem like it's a matter of the automaton's mechanisms being broken. This is the biggest difference between her automaton and the famous ones of de Vaucanson and Maillardet—there is no obvious lever, crank, button. But it can't be that complicated, right? Why would someone obscure the starting point?

She glances at the quote she wrote down among the schematics: *"Without the voice of le Maure and Vaucanson's duck, you would have nothing to remind you of the glory of France,"* Voltaire had written. The automata were a source of pride among the French, it seems, with numerous machines making appearances throughout the 1700 and 1800s. It was a trend among the nobility—who could commission the most intricate automaton and impress the others?

Simonetta straightens as a thread of thought and possibility begins to unfurl.

A commissioned machine—yes, by Marguerite de Sainte-Madeleine. She thinks of Marguerite's portrait in the balustrade, the moody, flame-haired marchioness surrounded by instruments, the violin in her hands cherished and cradled like an infant. The compositions in the letters… Songs for E. Songs written for someone else, unsent and unanswered duets.

Puzzle pieces slot into place. Simonetta quickly writes out every train of thought in her head so she won't forget. Like a detective exploring a case, she draws out a mind map with bubbles and lines connecting to one another.

Then, mind whirring like the internals of a clock, Simonetta sprints across the courtyard, notebook in hand. It's past dinnertime, as her stomach reminds her upon physical exertion, and the sun remains up but low in the sky, just beginning its evening descent past the horizon. The late summer glow makes the fountain glint and glitter, and the nymph winks at Simonetta in encouragement as she races past and flings open the wooden door in search of Jeremy.

MARGUERITE

It was so warm inside the Grand Salon that one would never guess a blizzard had enveloped the chateau. Alas, the visitors were trapped for the night, and the chateau was the fullest it had ever been in Marguerite's memory.

Luckily, the company was all of her choosing. This winter fête was significantly rowdier than the stiff ball where she had reluctantly entertained potential suitors. Marguerite's primary criteria for her fête was that everyone invited needed to have a talent or a skill of some sort, and that peculiar request had brought an eclectic crew from across western Europe to Chateau Desrosiers.

Among the guests was Arlene de Bacque, a porcelain painter from Limoges; she brought Marguerite a set of white bowls painted with deep green foliage. At present she sat at the harp, her long gray hair let loose from its bun, and she played alongside a trio of musicians from Grenoble who had claimed the other instruments. Their impromptu music-making filled the hall with revelry. Marguerite had sent most of the servants to their homes for the three days she had planned for the fête, keeping only a select few who were bribed to keep the fête activities a secret from Papa and Philippe—and who could keep the partygoers plied with plenty of wine and food. As such, everyone was feeling loose-tongued and creativity permeated the air. When given the chance, artists needed very little prompting to discuss their art. Musicians and painters and dancers mingled, sitting on the intricate rugs Papa had procured on his travels.

She had aided Elise in tracking down as many candles as they could muster, and the Grand Salon was alight with burning candelabras. Rather than send the attendees throughout the chateau for the night, everyone had decided to sleep in the salon. *Philippe would have a fit to see the salon like this,* Marguerite thought with a mischievous grin. But Philippe was far off in Lebanon, and she was determined to enjoy every minute of her freedom.

She glanced across the room to find Elise deep in conversation with a Portuguese man, a noble named Diego something-something—Marguerite, feeling warm and buzzed on wine and an empty stomach, couldn't remember what kind of noble Diego was, but ultimately didn't care. There were plenty of people in attendance who had no noble claim, and it was their talent to which Marguerite was drawn. She was at the periphery of a conversation between a young Italian inventor named Marco Altobella, who lived across the border in a small hamlet, and Jean-Louis, a gray-haired clockmaker from Normandy. Together they were in rapt discussion about musical instruments, Marco keeping up the pace with proficient French.

Marco held Marguerite's violin and pressed down on a string, where it bent under his finger. "See? It's just a matter of pressure."

Jean-Louis tapped his chin. "It's not unheard of. But it would have to be rather large, don't you think?"

Marco nodded. "That's part of the splendor, like with your clocks—making them big, grande!" Marco animatedly unfolded his arms to demonstrate the size. "Imagine, a mechanical musician—" he stopped, looked around, and then pointed to the musicians playing nearby. "—a whole host of machines, performing orchestras!"

Marguerite, who had been passively listening to Marco and Jean-Louis's discussion, now had her interest piqued. "I must know what you two are discussing. Machine musicians?"

"Automata," Jean-Louis clarified. Marguerite knew the term vaguely, recalling books she'd read about Ancient Greece, their obsession with invention and innovation. Papa had seen various machines on his travels; once in Sardinia, Papa witnessed a street performer dance alongside a marionette cat whose strings were pulled by an intricate pulley system tucked into their mobile stage; when wound, the unwinding set the cat into a jig.

As a musician herself, Marguerite was both curious and skeptical of a machine that could emulate the human experience. It could play notes, sure, but so much about music was intangible, brought to life by the musician's personality and style—no two people would ever perform the same piece of music the same way. Would a machine ever encapsulate that? It could never know the passion that playing the violin or the harpsichord or the lute inspired in Marguerite.

But life would be simple if she were made of gears and wires, brought to life with a pulley or a lever. There would be no labyrinthine thoughts around which to navigate; she would simply do what she was designed to do. She thought of herself and Elise as two automatons, playing their violins together side-by-side, each with painted faces like marionettes. Once again Marguerite was reminded of Catelot and the old wooden doll Papa kept locked away with the other original Desrosiers relics. If she put strings on the Catelot doll and gave her a violin, she would look like a miniature Elise.

Amused by the prospect, Marguerite listened as Marco Altobella continued conceptualizing his mechanical orchestra. That would be something to see, she thought: an attraction to lure visitors to Desrosiers. She wondered if Papa would find the idea worthwhile or ridiculous, then decided she didn't ultimately care what his opinion would be, knowing that she'd have to still procure her own way to fund such a project.

Hours later, when most of the partygoers had found a place to lay their heads and the raucous din had ebbed to hushed, wine-drenched discussions in front of the hearth, Marguerite took her leave to enjoy the aftermath of a successful fête. She stepped out of the salon and into the dark hallway leading toward the ancient tower. It was cool and quiet here, and Marguerite turned to see her beloved walking down the hall in nothing but her white shift, and her breath caught in her throat at the sight. The vignette made her feel suspended in time, Elise barefoot on the cold stone floor, her face half-shadowed by the slats in the window, one visible eye luminous in the moonlight. She moved in syncopation toward Elise as her lover approached, every nerve ending humming before their lips even touched, and when they finally did, a resonance formed deep in her chest, in her very soul, the notes undoing every secret thought woven up tightly in her heart, rewriting it with a song she knew she'd never be able to sing aloud.

Twenty

Pinnacle: An ornamental architectural element crowning a tower or spire.

THE VOLUNTEERS ARE GATHERED in the Grand Salon, enjoying the placid evening and socializing, when Simonetta bursts through the doors without a trace of grace. Jeremy is crouched beside the hearth, rag in hand, dusting the molding. Simonetta flushes with warmth at the sight. Lotte and Jason sit at the circular table under the large window playing Blackjack, and a balmy breeze drifts lazily through.

Everyone glances up at Simonetta's noisy entrance and she gives an awkward wave.

"Hi," says Jeremy. "Eventful afternoon?"

"I think so," says Simonetta, heart still pounding from the exertion. She holds up her notebook. "I'll fill you in if we go to your workshop."

"And leave the rest of us out?" says Graham, sitting on one couch parallel to where Diego is splayed out on another. On the coffee table between them are dozens of small metal items and tins of polish.

"That's rude, Simona," Diego says, egged on by Graham.

Simonetta puffs out her cheeks and exhales some air. "Fine. I'll formally present my theories. Are there any Biscoffs around? I'm starving."

Hanako waves Simonetta over to a table where small sketches are scattered around art supplies. A tray stocked with cheese, bread, fruit, and various brined vegetables calls to Simonetta. "We got peckish after dinner. Saved you some Camembert, your favorite."

Touched by the small detail Hanako remembered about her preferences, she glances around at the people she has come to know so much about in such a short period of time and realizes she's comfortable here now. It's a pleasant sensation, being in a room surrounded by people she cares about, who care about her. She takes a mental snapshot of the fleeting moment. Could she one day have her own wall of photographs like Claudel's?

Munching on an olive, she glances over Hanako's shoulder. Hanako has been sketching the nymph, and Simonetta is struck by how much of Hanako's voice comes through the art—the confidence in the lines, the fluidness and slight abstraction to Hanako's interpretation of the statue. It's emblematic of Hanako herself: technical prowess, skilled artistry, and self-assurance. Simonetta is inspired and impressed, and she gives Hanako's shoulder an affectionate squeeze. "Thank you."

Hanako pats her hand. "Thank Diego—it took a lot of willpower for him to not eat your cheese."

Diego gives an exaggerated bow from his seat on the couch.

"Thank you, Diego," says Simonetta earnestly. She is filled with emotion over Camembert and knows it's silly. She wants to tell everyone in the room how much she loves them, because she does. She is overwhelmed with gratitude for each person, especially Jeremy, and feels guilty that she shooed him away earlier. Sometimes her need for solitude overrides her better judgment. But she needs him now.

She clears her throat and stands by the mantle. Jeremy winks up at her. "My seminar is starting," she says facetiously. The volunteers turn toward her and give her their attention; Lotte holds up her phone and starts filming. Simonetta opens her mouth to ask her to stop, but has no good reason to, and she thinks *Daily Life* viewers would probably enjoy a peek into the process. At the very least, someone watching this video later may confirm her thought.

"Today I repaired the automaton's internal mechanisms," she explains. "Jason, I was able to untangle the wires and I think I put them back in the right spot. Thanks for your thoughts on that." She wants him to get proper credit for the insight he gave her, for she is sure the tricks he shared about oiling prevented her from causing damage. "But I'm still stuck on the main issue—how does the automaton turn *on*?

"So there are several ways automatons, historically, were—activated, for lack of a better word," Simonetta continues. "*Something* would begin their mechanisms. It wasn't as straightforward as a switch being flipped, like we'd assume, because most automata didn't have some sort of energy store." She runs a hand through her hair, trying to work through the theory. "I've narrowed it down to a few primary ways people did this prior to modern electricity: there was often some sort of control, like a button, a crank, or lever that would essentially get movement going by generating energy. Or an external power source, like water being poured onto or into something. But an external power source can be so many things, right? Like heat—if something gets hot enough, it could melt. So say you had wax binding something together, and you heat it, it would release its hold."

"What are you thinking for your machine?" prompts Graham.

"My guess?" Simonetta shrugs. "The latter. I've scoured the entire machine, and I can't find anything that would suggest the control is missing, you know? No holes or cranks or missing parts in the machinery."

Jeremy nods in agreement. "What would be the 'external power source'"?

"Well, that's where I've been stuck—but I have a theory." Simonetta chews on her lip. The idea that seemed so brilliant now seems implausible and doubt seeps in. "A theory to build upon my theories, I suppose is more accurate."

Hanako glances up and snorts at Simonetta evading the reveal. "So what are your theories?"

She borrows some of Hanako's self-assurance. "I've felt—*we've* felt—" she nods to Jeremy, "from the beginning that the automaton was made in stages at different times. The doll predates the machinery by a few hundred years, from what I can glean about the design and materials. Violins, like the one Catelot holds, weren't even around in Europe until the late 1600s, so we know that was added later, probably when the rest of the automaton was built. When Paul evaluated it, he surmised it's an eighteenth-century design. But here's what I realized today: the automaton was probably commissioned to be an accompaniment."

Her rapt listeners give her blank expressions. Finally, Lotte asks. "What does that matter?"

Excitement ripples up her spine. "Who do we know who lived here and had a passion for music and plenty of wealth?"

"Marguerite de Sainte-Madeleine?" Graham guesses. "The marchioness here from, what, seventeen-something?"

"Like I said, this is just a theory," says Simonetta, trying to turn down the smile that quirks at the edges of her mouth. "But Jeremy and I have long thought, and Paul all but confirmed, that Marguerite commissioned the automaton. We know she loved violin compositions, so much that the paintings of her favorite instruments feature the violin front and center. We know she composed pieces of music that she never sent, perhaps intended for an unrequited love. And I have suspected for a while now that the compositions were written for the automaton." She falters when she sees that the others don't seem to be following, and doubt seeps in; maybe this all doesn't make any sense.

"You said you thought you'd figure out how to make her work, though," Jeremy prods reassuringly.

Simonetta finds his eyes—dark, kind, encouraging—and pushes the self-doubt out of the way. "I think the 'external power source' is more music."

PAOLO

Paolo steeled himself and blurted out: "I don't think you

should trust him. Etienne, I mean."

He was outside in the forest with Tommaso, cutting wood. Rather, Tommaso was cutting wood, deftly swinging an axe into a stump of wood, the sound of the splicing metronomic. It was one of the first times they had been alone in weeks for longer than a quick meal.

Tommaso gave him the same look, the only look, he'd given him since they arrived—the lips pressed into a line, the hard eyes, an expression that usually meant be silent. The look seemed embedded on Tommaso's face now, second nature. But Tommaso looked around and, once he confirmed that they were well and truly alone, he replied in a low voice, "What makes you think that?"

Paolo was caught off guard and his carefully planned argument dissipated, but he tried to conjure back his main points.

"His name comes up on the radio," Paolo said, starting to feel sheepish. Maybe the weird niggling feeling in his gut was truly nothing. Maybe he was just bored. Or maybe he wanted to get a rise, a reaction, out of Tommaso beyond the expression that said, *Keep your mouth shut.*

But this made Tommaso pause. "What radio?"

"The one in the attic." He took a deep breath before his next admission. "Etienne had shown us the radio he got and then moved it, probably so we wouldn't touch it. I expressed interest in it and I don't think he liked it. But I've been listening to it every night."

"Why do you do that?"

Paolo wasn't sure how to answer. It had seemed logical to him to listen; he was curious how the radio worked, pleased he figured it out on his own. He liked parsing the puzzles communicated by the French. Instead, he said what he thought Tommaso would want to hear. "I wanted to be useful. I found the band that the locals use. They talk in code."

"How do you know that?" Tommaso asked, face intent. "That they talk in code?"

Paolo shrugged. "I thought it was weird that they kept talking about fairytales. Then I heard Etienne's name."

"You can understand their code?"

"I think so. Some of it, at least. I don't know French that well so I write down what they say and then use the dictionary to translate."

Tommaso kneeled before him. "I'm impressed, brother. Mama will be, too."

The sentiment made Paolo feel queasy when he should have felt pleased by his brother's praise. If Tommaso and Mama approved, that meant Paolo was helping in our cause that he had come to think of as their cause.

"What do the French say about Etienne?" Tommaso pressed.

Paolo hesitated. "They call him names. They call him 'le trompeur.'" The word got stuck on Paolo's tongue. "Trickster. Betrayer. Deceiver, I think."

A dark look flickered across Tommaso's face. "Why do they call him that?"

"Something about the Germans—that he talks to the Germans. And he broke a promise to them. The French, I mean. And they talk about us—they call us his Pinocchios, like marionettes. Last night they said, 'les fils fantoches.' 'Etienne's puppet boys.'" Paolo frowned. "Or 'sons.' I get that phrase confused."

Tommaso went white and the hard line of his lips returned. But he put a hand on Paolo's shoulder and with his other he wiped his sweaty forehead. "Thank you for telling me, Paolo. I need you to do me a favor that is incredibly important."

Paolo sat up straighter. It was the first time his brother had entrusted him with anything beyond silence and compliance. Tommaso came over to him and kneeled before him. Paolo thought his brother looked older, and tired. He wanted to give him a hug. It had been a long time since Paolo had gotten, or given, a hug.

"What do you want me to do?"

"Keep listening to the radio and document everything you hear. Can you do that for me?"

"What if Etienne catches me? What should I say?"

Tommaso thought on this. "Go at the same time every night.

I will tell Francisco what you're doing and we can help. Don't worry about Etienne."

Tommaso reached out his arms and pulled Paolo toward him, a quick, gruff embrace that made Paolo's throat thick with suppressed emotion. But Tommaso released him too soon and Paolo brushed the tears from his eyes before his brother noticed.

SIMONETTA

"Will it be enough?" Simonetta whispers, surveying the room and chewing on her fingernail.

Jeremy rotates the automaton. "This is the best spot in the room for acoustics. So if the choir stands there—" he points to the adjacent corner, "—the resonance of their voices will carry this way. And their voices will meet with the instrumentation coming from there." He points to the wall opposite from where they stand.

"And Claudel was okay with me bringing the other instruments down?"

"Are you kidding? You promised to clean them and get them properly tuned. She's ecstatic that someone is finally tackling that. Monsieur Aubert will make use of them, too, I'm sure."

Simonetta and Jeremy have taken over the grand salon to test Simonetta's theory—that music is the key to getting Catelot to play again, that she was designed to be an accompaniment. To back her gut feelings with science, she spent the last week delving into research on harmonic resonance, the science of vibration and sound and frequency. She found plenty of promising leads: most machinery was affected in some way, positive or negative, by sound. Many engineers had to account for harmonic resonance in their designs.

She tries to place Catelot and Marguerite together. In her mind, she envisions a scenario not unlike this one: the marchioness standing here in the Grand Salon, accompanied by the automaton. Was it the marquess's voice or another instrument that set Catelot to playing? Perhaps Marguerite also played the violin? The night prior, Simonetta had tried already, performing Marguerite's compositions beside Catelot to little avail, and the unsuccessful attempt fills her with uncertainty.

Her stomach somersaults as the summer choir workshop attendants begin to fill the room. Simonetta had approached Monsieur Aubert with her strange request: was there a choral piece powerful enough to generate a large amount of harmonic resonance?

Monsieur Aubert, Desrosiers' guest music instructor with his big bushy mustache that reminds her of Nonno, was thrilled to even be asked. During his following visit after Simonetta's request, he had brought with him a stack of music books—operas and symphonies. She had spent days listening and even playing some of the suggestions. They have a few options to try, some of which Simonetta recognizes from her own years of music study. Among the heavy hitters are composers like Sibelius, Mozart, Stravinsky. Not for the first time, the craving to compose has taken root in Simonetta. Perhaps that will be her backup plan if none of their selections fit the bill: compose something so powerful, so all-encompassing, that the automaton has no choice but to react and join in.

The one piece they're saving for last is from Aida, the opera by famed Italian composer Guiseppe Verdi. "Italiano!" Monsieur Aubert had exclaimed in his thick French accent. "You Italians love your big expressions." He had held his arms out wide.

Simonetta couldn't help but smile. It pleases her when the others group her in with Italians. Despite her heritage, despite all she's learned from her grandparents, she knows she is very much an outsider to the real Italy. But being in Europe, closer to Italy than to America, has helped her feel more like a true *paesana* and less like an impostor. And her citizenship application is pending.

And it felt right, enlisting Verdi to awaken an Altobella machine. That morning, while scouring her notes for the umpteenth time, Simonetta had a moment of panic that nearly unspooled her entire endeavor: what if "Altobella" wasn't a name at all, but simply a descriptor? After all, "alto" is a musical term, referring to a voice range in the middle and lower registers. An "altobella" roughly translated to a "beautiful middle."

She had shared this thought with Jeremy, who seemed unconvinced.

"I don't think it's just a word," he said. "It's a maker's mark."

"Sure, but that doesn't necessarily mean it's a name. A maker's mark could be so many words. It's just easy for us to assume it's a name since it's, well, my name."

"It was rare for makers to use something other than their names to claim their work," Jeremy pushed back. "If the automaton was commissioned by Marguerite de Sainte-Madeleine, then she would have had to find someone to make it. The best way for a maker to spread his reputation was through the quality of work and his name. It's not like they had YouTube."

Simonetta isn't totally swayed by this argument but doesn't have anything good enough to counter it. She knows that, in part, she's trying to poke holes in her own hopes and theories. She knows she's trying to prepare herself for any outcome. It's what she has always done—think through every possible route, every possible thread, so that she can mentally prepare herself for every possibility. It exhausts her, being like this, and she knows she's starting to spiral, but she can't seem to talk herself down with so much on the line.

She tries to focus on the task at hand. The Grand Salon will be full soon, with a ten-person choir and a dozen musicians, plus Monsieur Aubert and Jeremy and herself with Catelot. The music will certainly be loud. Simonetta wants to leave nothing to chance, although she supposes it's overkill to strive for such a robust performance. Surely if Marguerite intended for Catelot to be an accompaniment, it was with a handful of other performers, not an entire orchestra.

The musicians begin filtering in and Simonetta's stomach clenches with nerves. She has already given them all the spiel, an overview of the automaton and a version of her theory.

Monsieur Aubert comes in last and claps his hands in delight. "What a joy to use music in such a way!" he exclaims, taking Simonetta's hand in his and giving it a supportive pat. The gesture bolsters her somewhat; if Monsieur Aubert thinks there is potential, then she can muster up some confidence.

He addresses the group first. "Thank you all for joining us in this endeavor!" he says with his jolly, thick French accent. "We'll start with the Sibelius." He waves the choir into place and leads them through some warm-up vocalizations. Although the Grand Salon is the usual location for the music workshop, it's rare for all the singers to sing at once as a choir, and their gorgeous voices fill the room and weave into Simonetta's chest, alleviating some of the tension she carries in her shoulders. She wants to hear them sing in the chapel, where their voices would raise high into the painted ceiling, filter out through the open windows, echo and reverberate within the stone walls.

Then the musicians warm up, and Simonetta remembers the pleasant nervous stomach she used to feel at the beginning of concerts and recitals, the sounds of her fellow musicians getting ready. It has been many years since she played in a symphony, but she suddenly misses fiercely the feeling of being a part of one. There are few things more special than being a contributor to masterful performance.

"Are you ready?" Jeremy asks as the singers and musicians await further instruction.

"As I'll ever be," she answers honestly. She clears her throat and turns to the performers. "Like Monsieur Aubert said, thank you so much for helping us with our research. Truly, I have no idea if this theory has any legs, but it's the best one I've got, and I couldn't explore it without you. So, thank you." She nods to Monsieur Aubert, who has his conductor wand at the ready.

She takes her place behind Catelot—she left the back of the cabinet open to watch the internal engineering and track any indications that the abundance of music is enough to activate it.

The music begins. The Sibelius composition is powerful, arguably the most powerful of the ones they picked, so Simonetta is concerned that if it doesn't work, the others won't either. The performers give it their all, playing the winds and strings and drums with vigor, and the singers emit their voices from their cores.

Simonetta is moved by the gravitas and it stirs her—but not Catelot.

Nothing moves in the automaton. There is no indication that any of this powerful music is having any effect. A pit forms in Simonetta's stomach, and she feels stupid that she even considered any of this. They try each of their chosen pieces, concluding with the Aida. By now she knows the experiment is undoubtedly a failure and the music thrums in her chest, strumming every chord, the internal vibrato leaving her shaken.

She swallows the emotion in her throat as she bids farewell to the performers. The effort they gave her means so much, even though it didn't yield the results she'd hoped for. She is touched to the core by how many people came together to help her. No one displays any annoyance or disappointment at spending their time trying this, other than sympathy that her theory led to a dead end. On the contrary, the performers are chatty and energetic as they depart the Grand Salon, discussing the pieces they just performed together.

Simonetta tries to fixate on the good—people care about her. People listened to her idea, respected her enough to try. That should mean everything to her. But she is so desperate for a triumph that the nothingness is horrible. Bitter disappointment pricks the back of her throat and leaves a sour taste.

She looks at Catelot, her carved face stoic, and pleads with her to make her secrets known. *Why won't you play for me?* Simonetta begs. *What are you trying to hide?*

MARGUERITE

Papa and Philippe were indeed gone for longer than Marguerite expected.

And when the plague of 1720 swept through southern France, Marguerite found that it was easy to stay inside. No one questioned her desire for quarantine. No visitors were allowed in or out. In spring, the garden was full, the water was clean, and they had plenty to sustain them while they waited out the worst of it.

But a courier arrived, despite the odds, bearing letters in which fates were sealed.

Marguerite stood frozen in the gloomy foyer, bloated letter in her hand, Philippe's last words smudged and nearly illegible.

> *Sister,*
>
> *I have never been very kind to you and suppose, in my final hours, that I should make amends. The truth is that I have simply never understood you. I see in you the same wit and intellect I saw in myself. Most of the women I've met have little of your thirst for knowledge and talent for the arts. If I have a wish upon my deathbed, it's that you cast out the demons that live inside you and make some effort to see the world beyond Desrosiers.*
>
> *Papa is dead. He died yesterday, in agony, and I know I am next for the infection is already torment and I pray that God cuts short my anguish. A terrible sickness took over the ship and most of the crew has died. They plan to burn the ship soon; I have given all my belongings to one brave chaplain who will attempt to bring our last letters to shore. My last prayers are that this letter will reach you.*
>
> *There is a will in the library. It entrusts Desrosiers and all of Papa's assets to me as his heir. But I ask that you find a trustworthy forgery to change the document so that it reflects my son, Henri. He is but a year old, and with his grandmother in Marseilles. I married his mother before she died in childbirth. Please take in Henri as your charge and heir. I know you do not want to marry so Henri will allow you to live and claim Desrosiers and our family's wealth as your own.*
>
> *There is no love lost between us, Marguerite, but I bid you farewell and long life, with a fervent hope you will do right by Henri, even though I never did right by you.*
>
> *Your brother,*
> *Philippe*

She ran her finger down the edge of the pages, the letter and the accompanying details about where to find Henri, and the sensation of the paper's rough texture under her fingernails gave her thoughts something to home in on as she processed this news: Papa was dead. Philippe was dead. By the time she received the letter, dated late February, they would have been dead for nearly two months, bones rotting at the bottom of the Mediterranean. She hoped Philippe was right, that they burned the ship—to Marguerite, their corpses burned before drowning seemed a better grave than bloated flesh marred by plague. It truly was a miracle the letter arrived in her hands.

Her family was gone. Well, most of them, save for her infant nephew, Henri. She would honor that request without question, despite the torment Philippe caused her for most of her life. Henri deserved access to the wealth and resources that Marguerite now claimed, and to her chagrin, Philippe was right; Henri's existence gave her options.

She grappled with a series of emotions that overcame her. She mourned the loss of her father, and even of Philippe—or at least, the glimpses of Philippe that endeared him to her. She regretted their estrangement, to a point. She chose to remember him instead as the little boy he once was, with dimpled hands and cheeks, toddling around after her. Marguerite wished she would have taken up the mantle as his big sister with pride. She had a second chance with Henri, although she would need to act quickly to ensure his safe arrival during the plague.

But the dominant emotion that overtook her, that had her knees buckling in a way that Elise mistook for grief, was relief.

She was free.

Twenty-One

Ramparts: Walls or embankments surrounding a castle, designed for defense against intruders.

SIMONETTA WAKES EARLY to the sound of something shattering and a subsequent scream. She throws off the blankets in her own bed—last night she slept alone and reveled in the coolness without Jeremy's warm body heating the sheets—and runs down the hall to the kitchen where she finds a crying Lotte cradling a shard of porcelain and a bleeding finger.

"Claudel is going to be so upset!" Lotte cries. On the floor around her feet are the blue-and-white remnants of a Limoges cup. From a neatly broken triangle, Simonetta can see that the toile is the rare woodland pattern that Claudel treasures.

"It's a loss, but not irreplaceable," says Simonetta soothingly, rummaging through the first aid kit for bandages.

The broken cup is a harbinger. Bad luck makes the rounds throughout the chateau. While Hanako is installing a plexiglass prototype of the new Saint Madeleine stained glass, she slips on the ladder and narrowly misses falling into a pew on her descent. Still, she now sports a gnarly bruise on her knee and a sprained ankle. And while Diego is attempting to sheer Bartholomew, the naughty sheep escapes, traveling almost as far as the village. Diego takes the Renault to try to lure Bartholomew back, but the front tire goes flat and he winds up in a ditch. Jeremy and Jason have to rent a truck to pull him out, and the Renault's driver-side door has a new dent added to its already marred body.

It goes on like this for several days, a series of disruptions and dangers targeting each volunteer. Simonetta helps when she can, providing bandages or cups of tea or a soothing word of support, but she's unsettled by the chain of events and knows she's next on the list.

SYMONNE

When plague struck again, Catelot and Symonne were ready.

Symonne knew it was coming. Earlier that week, several of the plants were dead, despite it being the peak of summer and the conditions ideal for good growth. Then she had awoken one night to feel a strange chill sweep through the warm night, like a ghostly hand caressing her hair.

When word spread that the LaMotte family was sick with boils on their necks, panic followed. But Symonne and Catelot sprang into action. Under the cover of darkness, they stole away into the forest and met with their witches.

Together the women formulated their plan to cast preventative magic over Desrosiers and its grounds. According to Augusta, this is what the witches had done the last time the plague swept through the region. The preventative magic was based on three key tenets: maintaining isolation, fostering a healthy environment, and trusting that nature would protect them if they respected it in return.

The women quickly assembled their supplies and set up their sanctuary in the kitchens, where Symonne knew they would be safe—only Catelot and Symonne used the space, with Bertrand claiming the rest of the fortress. But she underestimated the chaos that ensued during times of crisis, the way it brings out the best in some and the worst in others.

The first day passed without incident. The women took turns being on watch, casting rituals, keeping the candles lit, slipping outside periodically to make offerings to the river (for cleanliness) and to the oldest thicket of trees (for strength). Symonne reveled in their safe space. Catelot, too, seemed to enjoy being tucked away with Symonne and the witches. She was whittling a new doll, thoughtfully and carefully forming the doll's face with the sharp edge of the beautiful blade bequeathed to her by Augusta two years prior.

But fear lurked in Symonne's heart. What if it wasn't enough? Old memories unwittingly sprang to the forefront; she remembered watching Marcella descend into death, remembered finding Lady Cateline several days gone, remembered finding Catelot beside her mother's body. Was Bertrand right, that God would protect those worthy of being saved? Symonne knew no one more worthy of life than Catelot, but when she prayed to God for the first time in many years, it felt strangely like a betrayal.

PAOLO

"Here are all of my notes," said Paolo, handing Tommaso the notebook in which he had documented nearly two weeks of broadcasts. It contained the times of the broadcasts and general summaries of each one, with some of Paolo's analysis. He had made new discoveries in the code, that the tales they chose to share were analogs for the countries and players in the war. When they told the story of Hansel and Gretel, for example, Paolo made an educated guess that they were actually talking about the Germans.

But Paolo had spent most of his analysis sharing the morals of the fairytales relayed in the broadcasts. He had come to enjoy Jean and Louis's voices, their humor, their camaraderie, and felt that the nights he caught their broadcast to be fortuitous. Their boyish banter is what he wished he could find among his fellow countrymen, but the occupiers of Desrosiers were intense and secretive. Paolo wanted Tommaso to see Jean and Louis's friendship and purpose like Paolo did: they were fighting for something good, the Resistance. They spoke openly about the Resistance and used the fairytales to posit themselves on the side of the heroes. What did that make Paolo? And Tommaso? What were they even doing, these boys from Primavera and Cassinasco and Cuneo, holed up in the crumbling chateau owned by a charlatan? In the most recent broadcast, Paolo had deciphered that Jean and Louis, and the rest of their cadre in the abbey, had procured goods: food and medicine, distributed to the children made orphans by the war, sharing residence with the Resistance. This wasn't an easy one to translate; the fairytale had something to do with ogres and children and witches, but Paolo got the gist. And it frustrated him. He wanted to do something. Sourcing food for orphans seemed like a worthy effort. Why weren't they doing things like that?

Paolo and Tommaso had been there for over a month, and Paolo had yet to witness some major shift in their part of the war, any substantial or meaningful change. He spent his days trudging around the chateau by day, exploring the gardens, studying French in the library, and his nights listening to the Resistance share the continent's wealth of fables and feeling increasingly like he was on the wrong side.

If any of this turmoil showed on Paolo's face, Tommaso made no mention of it. His brother clapped him on the shoulder. "Well done, Paolo, well done."

"I put some information about how often they spoke of Etienne," Paolo said, trying desperately to steer Tommaso down a particular path without being heavy-handed, for he knew Tommaso would reject the manipulation. "It sounds like he is planning something. His name came up when they talked about the Germans, too."

He expected Tommaso to react with surprise the way he had when Paolo had first told him about the broadcasts, but his brother waved a hand as if to brush away the impact of the comment. "There's much you don't know, Paolo, context you don't have. There is always another side. But know that you've played an important part in our cause."

Paolo's stomach sank at Tommaso's words. Why couldn't he see that this could be simple? In fairytales, there were heroes, villains, and monsters. The line between good and bad was clear. In the stories Jean and Louis shared, the good almost always prevailed—and anyone standing in the way of the heroes suffered an eternity of torment.

Paolo waited for a sign that Tommaso had had a change of heart. But if anything, Paolo's notes had Tommaso more serious and closed off than ever.

Paolo kept listening to the broadcasts, his safe haven, the voices of the jovial French boys. And that week, Paolo made his biggest breakthrough in translating the Resistance's code: Mussolini had fallen from power.

This knowledge was hard-won, for Jean and Louis were experts at weaving in major news into their storytelling. And besides, Paolo assumed, they would be getting their news elsewhere—the broadcasts were more to foster solidarity and hope than serve as a reputable news service. Still, it was how Paolo had gleaned updates over the past couple of months, learning of an increase in riots and rebellions throughout France and Italy. And the boys at the chateau came up not infrequently, always called the Pinocchios.

"Le grande Pinocchio," said Jean, voice crackling through static. *The big Pinocchio.* "La plus grosse marionnette—ses fils ont été coupés!" *The biggest puppet—his strings have been cut!*

Instead, Paolo changed tactics. He thought about Jean and Louis and the Resistance in the abbey, sharing stories and news. He thought about the fairytales and their characters, the woodsmen and the witches and the puppets and the puppeteers. Paolo knew that he had to speak to Tommaso directly, but the truth was that he feared his brother, feared being slapped again, feared the dark shadows on his brother's face, feared the flicker of fire in his brother's eyes. Paolo had tried to wrap his head around it, the fervor that drew Tommaso to this quest in Santa Maddalena.

Eager to take his mind off from how he would best approach his brother, Paolo crept across the chateau that night. He was several steps up the stairway when he heard screams coming from the room—the room with the radio.

The sounds made the blood rush to his head and he swayed. He tried to tell himself the howling and screaming came from tormented ghosts and not a living, breathing person. But when he continued to ascend, he knew the screams were real. He faltered halfway up—whatever he was about to see, he could never unsee.

And when he heard Tommaso's voice, he knew the choice had been made for him. He proceeded up the tower, steep step by steep step, and stopped outside of the door.

The screaming was cut short by a harsh whisper, Tommaso harshly saying, "We cannot stop now. They're already on their way."

Another voice answered, but Paolo couldn't make out the words. And then the screaming resumed, and Paolo took a deep breath and pushed open the heavy wooden door. The hinges shrieked in protest as if to warn him away—*no, don't look!*

But Paolo did look, and he saw his brother, Tommaso, covered in blood, his fist barreling into the chest of a man whose arms and legs were held aloft with rope keeping him suspended and unable to move. The man's face was bloody, too, all features obscured by crimson.

Francisco saw him first and shouted, "Tommaso! Your brother—"

Tommaso turned his furious face toward Paolo, a look Paolo would remember for the rest of his life. Fury had turned Tommaso's face white-hot and his hair was mussed, and Paolo thought he looked like a madman, a man possessed. What could possibly possess someone like this?

"Get out of here, Paolo!" Tommaso shouted, waving a hand covered in the mark of his actions.

"What—Tommaso, why are you…?" Paolo could hardly speak, overwhelmed and horrified.

The tortured man met Paolo's eyes and grinned with a mouth

full of blood; it dribbled down onto his already saturated shirt, and Paolo's stomach heaved.

"Do you see?" said the bloodied man in broken Italian. "What your brother did? This is what your people do! This is the world they want! Is this what you want?"

He turned back to Tommaso and spit in his face. Tommaso lifted his fist again and Paolo tore his eyes away—

—and then he was off running. He ran down the spiral tower stairs, nearly stumbling—he sprinted down the enfilade through each room he had come to love and hate—he fled into the gardens, trampling the green onions. He didn't want any of this—the violence, the control, the strong words, the dirty secrets and deals. He didn't want to be Tommaso's brother anymore, didn't want to be his mother's son, didn't want to live in a country that wanted the Fascist future they were going to such great lengths to fulfill. Paolo would have given anything to be anywhere else, anywhere that wasn't dangerous, but there was nowhere to go. Where on the entire planet was safe?

Paolo slowed to catch his breath, his mind reeling but grappling for a solution. He would go into the village, find the Resistance members he'd heard on the radio. Maybe he could exchange some of his knowledge with them for temporary shelter. Or he could simply hide in the abbey until the war was over. The one thing had gained in his time at Desrosiers was a new sense of resourcefulness; he knew enough French and the landscape to sustain himself by foraging. He would live in the forest, in the secret corners of the abbey, wherever he could if it meant he never had to go back to Chateau Desrosiers, never have to go back to Primavera.

Out of the corner of his eye, he watched a rabbit dash into the forest, and Paolo, escaping from the wolves, followed its path.

MARGUERITE

"Married?"

Marguerite had never liked the word, nor the sentiment, but the venom in which she spoke it aloud was laced with the bile that pricked the back of her throat.

Elise turned toward the window. "I knew you wouldn't understand."

"You knew I wouldn't understand you marrying a man you barely know, to move to a country you've never visited? You are right—I don't understand."

The look in Elise's eyes when she finally turned back toward her stopped her short. "It's a change in my station. Diego is part of a noble family! I never even dreamed that was ever a possibility for me. This changes everything."

"And that's what you want? To be part of a noble family?" Marguerite spat, more venom.

"It's easy for you to spit on that when you gleefully rejoiced at your own brother's death!" Elise retorted.

"Gleefully rejoiced?" Marguerite shouted. "Just because I didn't cry over his loss? Philippe tormented me—for years! So, yes, maybe I do have some relief that he is no longer around to make me feel horrible about myself." Marguerite felt the words thick in her throat. "Why are you treating me as if I am cruel? I never wished for any of this!"

"Didn't you?" Elise spat, accusingly.

"And so what if I did? I have no magical powers! Don't you think if I could change things simply by wishing that I would have changed other things about myself first?"

That was Marguerite's soul laid bare, the thought that had plagued her for weeks since learning of Papa and Philippe's death—had she wished for their demise, subconsciously or otherwise?

Since she met Elise, so much had gone in her favor: the suitors never materialized, Philippe and Papa spent most of their time elsewhere, and now she was given a chance to live to her fullest freedom, in charge of the chateau, wealth at her disposal, and no one could question her. Was her desire for this type of freedom so strong as to impact the cosmos?

If she could do this, what else could she do? Could she learn to accept going outside the confines of Desrosiers? Could she sway the minds of the nobles to openly accept her love for Elise?

The possibilities frightened her. But ultimately, Marguerite was not so delusional to think that her thoughts could have that much of a ripple effect. She was no stranger to how much thoughts could affect one's life, but she was sure that was unique to her own behavior. She surely didn't summon plagues or storms simply to avoid those who wanted to meddle and control her life. And if anything, whatever Marguerite had inadvertently manifested by sheer will had brought her consequences: Elise's declaration, that she was leaving to marry someone else, was the other side of the coin Marguerite had dreaded for months, years, since their blissful day in the river.

Marguerite, knowing this argument with Elise made everything precarious, reeled in every tendril of emotion exploding out of her. With a deep breath, Marguerite asked, "Is marrying Diego what you want?"

Elise continued to pace in Marguerite's room, shoulders rising and falling as if pelted by invisible raindrops "What I want is to not be a servant anymore. What I want is my freedom."

Marguerite opened her mouth to retort—*you're not a servant, you've never been that to me*—but the anger turned to sour guilt in her stomach. Of course Elise was still a servant; Marguerite had done nothing to change that. She hadn't seen an alternative, fearing any elevation or change in Elise's role would result in suspicion that would shine a harsh light on Marguerite. But she hadn't tried very hard, either, had she?

She wanted instead to offer Elise something to stay, but what could she offer beyond herself? What would compare to Elise having her own home, her own family, a lover she could be with outside—and not just outside, but openly? A new country to explore and embrace. A marriage endorsed and celebrated.

There was no path for them. It was fruitless, stupid to even entertain the notion. Marguerite was left with nothing to say, and in the bitter days leading to Elise's departure, the walls that she always depended on for strength started to close in on her.

SIMONETTA

Simonetta realized at a young age that there was something different about her brain, that not everyone picked apart everything they couldn't understand and filled in the gaps with their own theories and interpretations. In third grade, she asked her classmate, Jillian, about "the pang"—the pressure in her chest that she couldn't remember not feeling.

"What?" said Jillian, licking sour candy powder from her fingertips.

"You know, the feeling in your chest," said Simonetta, poking her sternum. "When it feels like someone's squeezing your heart. Do you feel it at night, too? Or just during the day?"

Jillian looked at her, lips blue, and blinked. "Simone, I have no idea what you're talking about. Maybe you should go to a doctor."

Interactions like that over the course of her life made Simonetta realize that her brain works differently and it wasn't always a good thing. She is constantly torn between trusting her own perception of things more than others, knowing that her anxiety makes her hyper-vigilant, but distrusting herself for the same reason. She perceives and overanalyzes, dissembles things and makes up stories to fill in the gaps. Simonetta has always seen silhouettes everywhere, has always defined life by the light and shadow and the liminal space in between.

Years later, the setting sun still sets off Simonetta's anxiety. On days where her mental stability is precarious, general contentedness is a snuffed candle as soon as the night comes. She had abated it through her teenage years and early adulthood by reading deep into the night, reading until she could no longer keep her eyes open, exhausting herself so she would fall into a deep sleep. And tonight, knowing that the chateau's curse lies in wait, she's employing the same tactic.

As the storm makes the chateau and the forest around it creak and wheeze, Simonetta tries to immerse herself in her book to fend off the nighttime demons. She remembers the Slavic folklore Nonna once told her about the domovoy—tiny fairy-like spirits that live in a home and serve as its protectors. In the illustrated tome Nonna had shown her, the domovoy were quite frightening, depicted as small troll-like entities that maintained a domain's safety. But she had liked their impish appearance, found the whole notion charming. Simonetta allows herself a superstitious indulgence—if any place is occupied by domovoy, it's a place like Desrosiers. She envisions them living in all of the silhouettes, surviving off the movement the shadows make.

She flips through an old copy of *Le Compte de Monte Cristo*, which features a chateau out at sea, wonders if any domovoy there aided Edmond on his escape. Beside her, Jeremy sleeps deeply, undisturbed by the howling outside. Some of the wind seeps through a minuscule gap in Jeremy's window; Simonetta feels a hint of the bluster on her arm and it forces goosebumps to the surface of her skin. She imagines a team of domovoy coming to her rescue, sealing shut the window with spit and old candle wax. The oak trees outside sway and lurch, casting chaotic shadows on the wall, a feast for the spirits.

She tries not to dwell on the storm, get caught in it. She uses her grounding exercises, focuses on the book, on the feeling of the cotton sheets against her skin, on the rise and fall of Jeremy's chest beside her. She tries not to think about the rotting tree near the chapel that will be cut down soon, its insides infested with the harmful fungi that ate away at the wood until it started to split.

"Will your workshop be safe?" she had asked Jeremy several hours earlier. Together they sat on the floor, poring over Simonetta's notes and Jeremy's sketch of the cabinet's interior, a nicer version of her own initial sketch. She had resisted the urge to stand at his window and watch the storm blow through, as if her attention would keep the worst of it at bay, force it to behave.

He snorted. "In the years I've been here, there have been countless major storms. Two winters ago, the snow was relentless. A summer rainstorm is nothing to worry about." He had lured her to bed and she welcomed the distraction, but afterward she lay awake with her mind churning.

The scent of ozone is thick in the air and the humidity presses in on her. Eventually she tumbles into a restless sleep, still somehow conscious of how it engulfs her.

MARGUERITE

Outside the window, the land was a blur. The lashing rain and the fog and the darkness engulfed the chateau, and for the first time in her whole life, Marguerite felt entrapped by the walls surrounding her. Despite the gale outside, she felt like that is where she would be the safest. She was safest wherever she was with Elise, and Elise was no longer there with her.

The panic of loneliness rose up and coated her tongue with a sour taste. For once, loneliness overrode the panic of leaving the chateau. When Elise's carriage departed earlier, Marguerite's heart went with it, and now she knew she simply could not live without it. The heartbreak was so excruciating she felt the pressure manifest physically on her chest, but a numbness was beginning to seep its way upward through the cold stone under her bare feet. A recklessness followed; if there was nothing to lose by remaining inside, if safety and stability and comfort were no longer sureties, then what was there to risk by going outside?

The hall outside her chamber was quiet. She had sent the servants away, couldn't bear the thought of anyone else dressing or undressing her, touching her hair, being present in her space. Candles burned low on their wicks, and the shadows allowed her to pass as if she was a shade haunting the halls in which she once lived. Maybe she had truly died from heartbreak, and that is where this sudden manic lightness came from, an openness of possibility, that there was no longer anything that could hurt her because there is no pain greater than what she had already felt.

A rough patch of stone under the sole of her foot brought her back to her own mortality, and she faltered for a moment on the staircase. There was still time to turn back, to return to her room, to burrow in her bed until the storm passed and the nightmare of Elise's departure was no longer so overwhelming. But she was halfway down the stairs already, and she felt a pull to go outside, to be drenched in the storm. She brought to the forefront of her mind the day Elise brought her outside into the garden and to the wild beyond, the crushed moss and river stones under their bodies, the earthy, heady scent they unleashed. The memory of that scent filled her and she continued outside, down the stairs, into the front hall with its newly gleaming banisters. Then she was pushing open the door and the rain poured in as she stepped into the muddy courtyard, before she took off running.

Marguerite flew through the garden gate and spilled into the wild beyond. Although it was mid-afternoon, the sky was dark with the storm, the land shrouded.

The river spilled out over its banks, turning the ground muddy and soft. Marguerite stepped into a marshy puddle and the ground gave way, and she slid into the muck, grasping for purchase but finding none, until she tumbled into the waters.

She was pulled into the current immediately, yanked to its deepest points. Panic set her limbs to flailing but she remembered Elise's calm words—*if you find yourself in deep water, save your energy and your breath*. The smallest bit of Marguerite's mind still open to logic heeded this warning and she forced herself instead to reach the surface. But she didn't know how to swim, and the rocks underfoot were slippery and jagged, and her limbs grew heavy.

This is what she had always feared—being out of her depth, out of her element, alone, overtaken by the greater world. But maybe everything she had ever done was leading to this—maybe she wasn't supposed to live without Elise. As despair enveloped her, a sense of peace and acceptance pushed its way in. Papa and Philippe dead, Elise gone, the region still reeling from the plague. What was left to live for? Who would mourn her?

But then the river heaved her out onto the banks, like strong invisible arms pulling her out, or some angry river nymph ejecting Marguerite from her territory. She poured onto the riverbed and crawled out of the water, enveloped in the mist, the taste of blood in her throat. She coughed until she was sure her ribs were bruised; everything hurt, every muscle aflame, her head spinning with the oxygen quickly returning. When she looked around, she saw the garden gates in the far distance, and with a jolt realized she was the farthest she had ever been from home.

SYMONNE

Halfway through the second day of their self-imposed cocooning is when they heard the screaming and shouting, an angry voice emanating from the rooms above. Symonne strained to hear; across the room, Catelot met her eyes with concern and worry. Symonne started to tell Augusta that they would be safer outside, when heavy footfall sounded on the staircase and pounded down the hall, headed for the kitchen.

A loud *bang!* made them all jump and their sanctuary was torn asunder—standing in the doorway looking like the vengeance of God himself was Bertrand. With horror, Symonne saw the scene through his eyes: the hooded women in black, the patterns on the floor, the wreaths and the bouquets, the candles and the bones. It looked like what it was, witchcraft in every sense of the word, and it wouldn't matter to him that they were casting protective magic over the fortress, that the smoke they were creating would keep the plague out, that their devilish women's magic also included protection over him.

"I knew it," he said. "I knew there was something foul in you, that you brought this upon us." He thrust an accusatory finger toward both Catelot and Symonne, who clutched each other. At the others he simply sneered and then spat. When he turned on a heel and left, Symonne knew he would return and bring with him the consequences of witchcraft.

"We have to go," said Symonne, shoving apples and clothing

into a satchel.

"Mama, where can we go? People in the village are sick and dying. This is our home!"

"We'll go to the mountains with Augusta for now. Get your things."

But by the time they were ready, it was too late. Night was at its peak and the sky was as inky black as it had ever been. For the first time ever, Symonne cursed the darkness—it had always been her refuge, her cloak, but she wanted to be in the full light of the sun. Instead, rain came down in aggressive sheets, turning the grounds muddy, dousing torches. It was in the darkness that she fought off the band of mercenaries who had come at Bertrand's command.

He had been gone for several hours and returned to the fortress with a small army—it wasn't really an army, but a dozen armed men against Catelot and Symonne felt like one. The soldiers surrounded them, high on their horses.

"I'm Catherine Desrosiers!" Catelot said in a desperate attempt to fend them off. "This is my family's fortress. It is mine by right!"

"Where is your father?" one of the mercenaries demanded.

"He's—away!"

"He's dead," said Bertrand. "He's been dead for ten years. Roland Desrosiers had no heirs."

Catelot sent Bertrand daggers with her eyes. "I am his heir! This fortress belongs to me. It is he who is trespassing!"

"Your stake in this fortress died when your father did, girl! And you should have, too." He sneered again. "You are a girl, unmarried. It is only because your father was not cruel to me that I spare you. The only prospect you have is to be sent to the nunnery."

Two mercenaries grabbed her and Symonne lunged for her, but another pulled her by the hair and she shrieked and fell into the muck, and when she was prone, he backhanded her.

Symonne spun and fell face-forward, stunned by the strength of the assault. But Catelot's scream injected her with adrenaline and she twisted upward, pulling herself to her feet using every remaining ounce of energy. Trudging through the storm was like trying to run in waist-deep water, like trying to throw a punch in a dream. Bertrand urged his horse toward her and he opened his mouth to speak, likely to condemn her to death and make accusations that she would never be able to undermine.

Desperate, she shot out a hand and pulled him by the boot. The action startled him and his horse, and he slid off unwillingly, plopping into the mud beside her. He reached for his horse but found its leg instead, and in reaction, the horse brought his leg up and then back, the hoof colliding with Bertrand's skull.

Even through the chaos of the storm, the screaming, the shouting, Symonne heard the tell-tale crack of death. Bertrand lay in the mud, dead.

She would have to deal with that later—Catelot was screaming and trying to claw her way out of the mercenary's grip. "Mama! Mama!"

"Please don't take her!" Symonne begged, clambering to her feet. "He was wrong, everything he said was wrong. I don't know what he promised you and look, he's dead—"

The mercenary holding Catelot in his grip narrowed his eyes. "So Roland Desrosiers is alive?"

"Yes!" The lie burst forth with no effort and Symonne prayed to God that he believed it.

"And you can prove it?"

"Yes, and you won't want to have taken his daughter!" Symonne threatened. "If he returns and finds her gone—"

Another mercenary interrupted. "Then he'll pay a hefty ransom, won't he? He can find her at the abbey."

"Then take me, too! I'll go with her as her chaperone—"

She lunged for Catelot, and their hands outstretched to one another almost touched—

"Bertrand said you're a witch—do you know what they do to witches?" the mercenary sneered. "Make one more move and we'll have you killed for your sorcery."

"She's my daughter!"

"You challenge her legitimacy?"

"No, I adopted her—" Symonne tried desperately to connect

the dots of her own story amid pelting rain and overwhelming terror.

"Why would you adopt her if her father is still alive?" he asked astutely.

Oh God, no, what do I say? "Because he's away a lot, I didn't mean truly adopted her…"

"Did you bewitch her?"

"No—!"

But then something hard collided with her head, and everything went black.

PAOLO

When night fell, Paolo walked the perimeter of Desrosiers and looked in the darkness for the rabbit.

The woods were silent. Paolo felt the tension in his chest. Maybe he was wrong. Paolo was scared—he didn't even want to be here. He didn't want to be home, either; where even was his home now? He didn't think of where Mama and Rosa were as home anymore, although he wondered about his little sister. He missed Papa's office, the room in the factory where he would find a quiet place to just be. When Paolo thought of home, that's what he thought of.

Paolo couldn't get the sight out of his mind, Tommaso's face white and manic. In that moment Tommaso was the wolf, devouring the rabbit, evoking their Mama, ever-stoic, speaking fierce and dangerous words.

Then he thought of Tommaso's face when he realized Paolo was in the room, the flicker of guilt and shame. Was it possible that a kernel of doubt lay within Tommaso? It's what Paolo thought the broadcast notes would do: make Tommaso realize that they didn't have do to this. That Etienne was a liar and not to be trusted. That their mission was a foolish and fruitless one. Instead, Paolo had fed Tommaso the very information he needed to torture.

Lost in turmoil, his boot caught the underside of a root and he went sprawling across the forest floor, head nearly colliding with the trunk of a tree. Scraped but unharmed, heart thudding, he pulled himself and sat atop the tree and put his head into his hands.

He didn't want to be here. He was alone, confused, horrified. Paolo felt betrayal deep in his bones. What kind of mother asks this of her children? What kind of brother, not even an adult yet, has that level of fury in him? What did Tommaso see in Mama, in Mussolini, that made him so dedicated to this cause that it drove him to extreme violence?

But Tommaso was his brother. And he, too, was alone in this strange country, and surrounding them on all sides was war, and they were on the losing side. There was still time to change course before Tommaso would be ruined forever. Did Paolo owe it to him to try?

He lifted his head and a shaft of moonlight penetrated the canopy of trees. Sitting quietly before him, several feet away, watching him intently, was the rabbit.

They looked at each other for several moments, boy nor rabbit moving. Paolo strained his ears to listen for a wolf, but no tell-tale twigs snapping alerted either of them to an incoming predator.

The rabbit moved first, its nose wriggling at some scent Paolo couldn't detect, and it bounded further into the forest. It seemed a lucky night for the rabbit. And Paolo knew what he must do.

He stood up and rubbed feeling into his lower back, which had gone numb from sitting on the trunk for so long. Paolo traced his way back through the forest, back down the river, following the moat, its rippled surface glinting with moonlight, and the outline of Desrosiers came into view—and the sky lit up with explosions.

BOOM! Boom, boom!

Explosions and gunfire erupted around the chateau and Paolo ran into the fray. Where to go? He saw dozens of people about, all silhouetted, their features masked. Who was who? He beelined for the courtyard, passing the chapel, where he heard a mortar fire, then glass shattering and stone falling and someone screaming. It pained him to think of the stained glass breaking, the angels in their alcoves quaking. But he couldn't go there; there were too many people. Paolo stayed his course and ran toward the fountain, which was better lit—and there he saw some people he recognized.

"Francisco!" he gasped, sprinting toward his brother's friend, who held a rifle Paolo had never seen before. "What's happened?"

"The Marquis betrayed us to the French," Francisco said, riffling through his pockets for bullets. "And the French to the Germans."

Gunfire, and another mortar. The ground rumbled. Screaming and shouting, French and Italian hatred exchanged in a volley. "Francisco, where is Tommaso?"

"Still in the tower," he said. "With Etienne, unless he's killed him already." Paolo couldn't clarify if Francisco meant Tommaso had killed Etienne, or vice versa, because a bullet whizzed between them and found purchase in the dirt. "*Minchia!* Paolo, you must go—go into the forest and hide—go to the abbey, they'll take you in—"

But Paolo was already dashing toward the chateau. Most of the battle raged outside, and boys passed him as he ran inside, and a waft of smoke told him why: the chateau was on fire.

Sleeve held over his nose, stomach roiling in fear, he followed the path he knew well by now, the stone stairs spiraling into the tower, the pilgrimage he had made every night for weeks. He braced himself for more sounds of torture, and he did indeed hear the sounds of a struggle, shouting and grunting and something scraping against stone. At the top of the steps, the air not yet filled with smoke, Paolo hesitated—what would he see this time?

Once again, his brother's voice decided for him. "Why, Etienne?" he heard Tommaso shout. "We trusted you!"

Fueled by adrenaline, Paolo heaved open the door; something on the other side had been placed there to block it. The table with the radio. The radio, Paolo's lifeline, clattered to the floor, tubes shattering.

Tommaso had Etienne in a chokehold against the wall beside the turret's shattered window. Outside, booms! and bullets lit up the night.

"You stupid boy!" Etienne choked out. Tommaso turned at the sound of the door scraping open, which gave Etienne the chance to backhand him. Tommaso stumbled and collapsed, and Etienne punched through the glass and clambered outside onto the crenellations.

"Leave him, Tommaso! *We have to go!* The building is on fire. We're surrounded—"

But Tommaso lunged after Etienne, shirtsleeve tearing on a jagged piece of glass. Paolo watched in horror as his brother climbed out after le trompeur; a stone broke off the tower under Tommaso's feet and he stumbled again, and Paolo's stomach clenched—but Tommaso pulled himself up and grabbed the back of Etienne's shirt, gaining precarious purchase. A mortar fired nearby; the thundering reverberated in Paolo's ears, and the ground lurched and Etienne broke free of Tommaso's grip, tumbling backwards off the crenellations, and plummeting to the ground below.

Tommaso froze, wild-eyed. Paolo reached through the window for his brother's arm, shaking it with vigor to snap his brother out of shock.

"Tommaso, we *must* go," Paolo said—but two men burst into the turret, guns raised.

SIMONETTA

As if on cue, Simonetta awakens with a jolt a moment before the storm escalates. Outside she watches a bolt of lightning lance through the air, so rich in hue it fills the sky with a flash of amethyst. It strikes the rotted tree at the edge of the forest and a black mark ripples down its trunk before the wood splits, its charred, dead trunk now careening toward the workshop. Smoke fills the air, despite the rain, and an orange ring of fire around the base of the fallen tree alights the darkness. She watches with horror as the flames begin their ascent toward the workshop, the burnt tree now serving as a convenient bridge to where more kindle awaits.

Including the automaton.

"Jeremy, the workshop is on fire!" she says, pushing at his shoulder. She doesn't wait for his response; she flings open the door and nearly tumbles down the spiral staircase in the dark, ignoring the loud thudding of her footsteps that will wake the whole wing of the chateau. She jumps to the base of the stairs, flies down the hallway, distantly hears Jeremy's sleep-ridden voice calling after her: "Simonetta, wait—!"

Logic and reason are overruled as she dodges into the storm. The rain may help keep the fire at bay, but the wind works against her now, slowing her movement but encouraging the flames to eat whatever they find. There's enough fire that the light reveals how much of the workshop is now engulfed in it. Through the northern side, she sees the automaton cabinet, partially covered under a cloth and tucked underneath the bench, mere feet from the fire. How could they have left it out here? She should have kept it in her room, never let it out of her sight. Catelot, at least, is stored safely in the chateau, and the stable workshop is far enough away from the main building that she is sure they can prevent the fire from spreading that far. She can't think about anything else beyond what's in front of her, doesn't weigh the risk before dashing into the fray.

She reaches the automaton and tugs it from under the bench, plans to drag it out. Whatever damage it takes from the rain will be easier to repair than fire damage, and a surge of adrenaline boosts her strength. It comes dislodged from its storage place with a loud scraping sound.

But she's wrenched backward by strong arms that envelop her waist. Her outstretched fingers reach helplessly for the cabinet when a burning roof beam of the workshop comes crashing down. Embers, smoke, and fire fill her senses and she shuts her eyes against the heat. Why isn't the rain helping? There's not enough of it to compete with the dry timber and the roaring wind.

"It's too dangerous!" Jeremy yells into her ear, pulling her away from the inferno. Everyone in the chateau is awake now; Graham, Jason, and Claudel all grip large fire extinguishers and begin dousing the flames.

Lotte, hair and robe wet and muddy, cups the phone she speaks into, "Les pompiers are on their way! Fifteen minutes."

A buzzing sound and sensation overwhelm Simonetta's mind. She watches, heart in her stomach, as the trapped automaton cabinet, now lodged under a burning beam, begins to wither away under the flames.

Twenty-Two

Dead-ground: The space close to the wall of a fortress from which defenders are unable to fight.

IN THE LIGHT OF DAY, the damage is evident. Much of Jeremy's workshop is ruined, but most of his tools survived unscathed. Once the fire department arrived, the fire was contained efficiently. The most important projects, like Catelot and the church pews, were luckily stored elsewhere. Some of the cabinet is salvageable, even; the maker's mark is still readable but warped from the heat. Overall, everyone agrees that the worst was avoided.

The sun rises, bright and cheerful, as if the atmosphere had simply needed a good cry and now felt better. Simonetta, on the other hand, is bleak as winter. The waves crash in and Simonetta sinks to the bottom of the sea.

She holes herself in her room. The guilt of her lack of productivity becomes another stone tethered to a rope that keeps her firmly lodged in the mire. But she can't see a way out; everything in her vision now is a deep, dark blue. It engulfs her and she wonders about the peace she could feel if she simply let it overtake her.

In a moment of desperation, Simonetta summons Alex to a video chat. She wants to connect with someone who knew her "before," before the automaton, before Nonna's death. It's morning in Berkeley when she calls and the familiar neat rows of bookshelves in Alex's office are another strange gut punch.

"Simone!" Alex says brightly. "It's so good to hear from you! How are y—oh no."

Simonetta knows her face must be a map of her inner self. She feels gaunt, pale, weak. She winces. "That bad?"

"Let's just say I've seen you look better," says Alex, corners of their mouth turning down in an expression of concern. "What's up? When I got your letter a few weeks ago, things seemed to be going well for you."

"I just—" Simonetta begins. The words get stuck but she tries again. "I—…"

There is a boulder lodged in her throat, sitting on her vocal cords. She thinks of how she mutes her violin during performances: by placing her index finger across the strings lightly to mute the sound, to prevent accidental plucking. She wishes the feeling in her throat were as delicate, but she can't lift the finger off. And the thought of the violin brings in another wave of memory of the automaton's destruction.

It all seems silly, to be so distraught at the damage to the cabinet and the mechanisms within. The one bright spot is that Catelot, with her violin and some of the attached wiring, remains hale and whole in her room—that truly would have been an irreplaceable loss. But Simonetta is wary and distrusting of her surroundings now. She's keenly aware of the chateau's age, and where the stone walls once gave her comfort and strength, all she sees now are its cracks. Maybe there is a frailness to places like this, she thinks. Maybe everything is, eventually, meant to crumble. How can she trust that these walls, too, won't come caving in?

"Do you need me to fly there and come get you?" Alex offers. "You know I will."

The very thought touches Simonetta but also makes her feel weak. She shakes her head. "No, it's just—you know how I get.

I was doing better. But then it just came crashing in and I'm just—" she stops to sigh and select her next word; drowning, sinking… "—stuck."

"Have you been journaling?"

"I was." Simonetta nods off to the side where her leather-bound journal sits on her nightstand. "But I didn't tell you in my letter. I met someone," she admits in a rush. She gives a wry smile. "He has dark curly hair."

Alex lets out a genuine laugh, and their own curls bounce from the gesture. "You are nothing if not consistent, Simone. Is he the source of your state right now?"

Simonetta shakes her head vigorously. "No. If anything, he's helped keep it at bay."

"Have you told him how this gets for you?" Alex suggests. Simonetta shrugs. She thinks of the afternoon in the chapel during the midsummer party, when he found her in the forest. *I'm drowning, Jeremy,* she had said. And he had pulled her into him to weather the storm. Is that what she needed again? Somehow it didn't seem enough right now.

"I don't want to drag him down into—" Simonetta waves her hand around in the air, gestures to herself. Why can't she finish a sentence right now? *The muck.*

"Maybe you should let him in," Alex offers. "You know the people who care about you won't turn away, right?"

Simonetta's walls are up the highest she has ever built them. She envisions them forming a half-moon dam to keep the water contained. Can she find a way to float in the mire? What good are walls when they can't keep out a fire? What good is a ship if it sinks?

Under the beast is a column of moss growing thick between the stone. The line of water pouring from the creature's mouth falls so cleanly that the verdant growth looks intentionally delineated from the rest of the facade, the part that gets the most sunlight. Simonetta understands things that choose to grow in the shadows.

At present, her watchful gargoyle is releasing an inconsistent drip above her head; rainwater is blocked in the creature's mouth, where moss and residue and leaves have congealed and blocked the gullet. Simonetta stands underneath with a large pole, pushing the debris out of the way.

The rain has returned again but this time remains a drizzle, a mirror of Simonetta's mood. A lingering malaise hovers overhead. She decides not to fight it. Sometimes the only way out is through.

She takes solace in the stone beings around her. Her gargoyle is her guardian angel, with its curved wings braced to fly to her side at any moment; the nymph is her muse, the glittering water sluicing off of her body offering conspiratorial winks in the late afternoon sun; the carved visage of Saint Madeleine is her confidant, the thoughtful listener to whom Simonetta can share her truest and darkest thoughts.

Simonetta knows she's holding the others—the warm, non-stone humans who reside within the chateau—at arm's length. She hears the creak of the eggshells they step on in her presence, wants to tell them it's not necessary but also appreciates the distance at the same time. Sometimes it's just too much work to be cared for: to explain things, to reciprocate appreciation, to ask for, and accept, help. The thought of it all makes Simonetta weary, so she allows herself time to retreat into herself a bit. The silence of the stone creatures is enough for her, for now.

She stabs at a particularly thick piece of debris in the monster's mouth and it comes loose, releasing a steady stream of rainwater. She stands under the battlements as it pours, as if she's behind a waterfall, that liminal space where the world is loud and quiet at the same time. She looks out at the garden through the stream, doesn't bother parsing the view through the blur.

A week passes and the late summer storms finally clear, bringing in a slow exhalation of warmth. The grounds dry but the garden flourishes. Simonetta resumes her projects, makes progress in the Room of Oddities, but can't bring herself to revisit the automaton. There's too much road to retread; her obsession was doused in the aftermath of the fire. Emails sit unopened as she avoids any mention of it. Jeremy tried—once, twice—to address it but she waved it away and he took the hint.

A knock on her door brings Simonetta out of her afternoon journaling session, a habit she promised both Alex and Jeremy she'd commit to. It's helping, the no-pressure way to get the thoughts, no matter how intrusive, out of her head.

She answers to find Lotte clasping a bursting bouquet of flowers.

"Simonetta! Here you go." Lotte foists the bouquet into her arms and Simonetta gingerly cradles the vibrant assortment of dahlias and peonies.

"Merci—these are gorgeous, but what's the occasion?"

Lotte shrugs. "I knew you liked these colors, and I have more I need to cut from the garden. Plus I ran out of table space."

"Wow, that many?"

"No, I just don't have my full table since Jeremy's been in there."

Simonetta frowns. "Jeremy's in your flower shop?"

"Just until he finishes rebuilding his workshop. He didn't want to lose momentum, he said, so he asked if he could work in my studio."

"Momentum? On what?"

"He's been restoring your machine since the fire," Lotte says. "He's almost done, in fact. Didn't you know?"

"Why didn't you tell me?"

Simonetta leans in the doorway and her shadow stretches long into the cavernous space. On the table is the scene Lotte had described: wherever there aren't vibrant bouquets or discarded leaves and trimmed stems are tools and crates from Jeremy's studio.

And on the table is the automaton cabinet, patches of new

wood still light and raw. A nest of melted wires extracted from within sits nearby, reminding Simonetta gruesomely of entrails.

"I didn't *not* tell you," Jeremy says calmly. "It's never something I would hide from you. I knew you'd come back to it when you were ready."

"But I told you I was done with it."

"Do you really feel done with it? If so, I'll put it back with the oddities and we'll never talk about it again."

Simonetta bristles. She feels like a child, annoyance welling up inside her chest. She acknowledges this is unreasonable and juvenile—he's not wrong. Seeing the automaton's cabinet again, almost whole instead of charred, kindles something good inside of her. It's far less distressing than the last glimpse she got of it, withering under flames, her family name gleaming in the inferno. Even the memory of it had haunted her dreams for days. But there's still something off and incomplete.

She chews on her words.

"Something is just off," she says, putting out the thought and hoping she can follow it to an eloquent untangling of what she's feeling and why.

"It's not finished—" Jeremy says, gesturing to a section where the wood is still burnt and uneven.

"No, it's not your workmanship or progress," she says quickly and emphatically. It's true—the repaired areas are smooth and thoughtfully patched. She's sure he's spent most of the week on it and the thought eats away at her with guilt. While she was spiraling and having an internal crisis, Jeremy simply went to work and did what he did best: using his own two hands to fix, improve, create.

Perhaps she should do the same.

She swallows and continues. "I guess I felt that it wasn't my place to change it. Just restore it. Protect it for what it is."

"It's been sitting in an attic for decades," he says. "You've given it a new life just by taking an interest in it. Why can't you be a part of its future?" He rubs his hands together and she smells the wood oils on his skin. "I'm sorry it got damaged, truly. But we both wanted to make it better in the first place. Don't you want to hear her sing again?"

"I was looking for answers that it probably doesn't have for me," Simonetta admits in a rush. There it is—the crux of it all. "I don't know what I wanted, exactly. It just felt so special, like it called to me. Like I was meant to find it, to bring it back to life. But maybe that's all there is to it. Maybe it's just a project."

"Do you really believe it? There are too many coincidences you've uncovered to make it that simple."

Simonetta folds her arms around herself. "I don't want to get my hopes up."

"So what if you did? What's the worst that could happen?" *I break my own heart again.* She doesn't say it aloud, but Jeremy knows. "What would you feel that you haven't already endured?"

"Well, ideally I'd like to *not* feel certain things again, if I can help it."

Jeremy laughs. "Wouldn't we all?" He comes around the table and unfolds her arms from around her torso and takes her hands in his. "Would you admit that I know you pretty well by now?"

Simonetta raises her eyebrows in amusement. "I'd say so, yes. Why?"

"I know you well enough to know you want to see this through."

She takes a deep breath and squeezes his hands in return before releasing them. "You're right. I do. I'm sorry I haven't been here working on it with you. You know me well enough to know how easy it is for me to get in my own way."

"Well, you're in luck—there's still plenty to do." He gestures to the wires and gears. "There's still a chance for you to finish it. Leave your mark on it."

"Alright," she says, and means it. She remembers a thought from earlier in the summer: *work is holy.* This is her atonement.

Twenty-Three

Voussoir: A tapered or wedge of stone used to fortify an arch.

IT'S FINISHED.

The cabinet is whole again, the new parts sanded and stained and varnished to match the older pieces. She and Jeremy painstakingly mixed and sampled stains until they found the right combination, and Jeremy made a large jar of it that he named "Catelot."

And screw by screw, with new color-coded elements, Simonetta recreated the internals, salvaging much of the metal scaffolding and exchanging the melted bits with shiny modern wiring.

The doll, too, has been cleaned and carefully updated. Paul from the brocante had advised on the adjustments and maintenance of the old wood, supplied some horsehair that Simonetta braided and placed upon the existing wig. Hanako helped Simonetta repaint some of Catelot's features and the doll looks bright-eyed and alert now, her light pink lips curved into a subtle smile.

It's on display in the Grand Salon and Simonetta studies it. Evening sunlight streams in and illuminates the whole machine, and Simonetta does feel proud to see it whole and assembled and restored.

She remembers the first time she held her violin, and the first thing her teacher showed her: *put the violin on your head, then touch it to your cheek, then slide it down to your shoulder.* Although she had felt silly following the instructions, Simonetta never forgot that trick to ensure the proper placement of the instrument. Gently, she lifts up the doll's arm holding the violin and taps the top of the wooden head, then brings it down slowly, tucking the violin under the chin. She puts the doll's hands into position, with the small bow resting across the strings, then plucks at Marguerite's favorite note—E minor rings out into the room. The note holds for an extra moment, like smoke lingering from an extinguished candle. To Simonetta, E minor has always been bittersweet and uncertain, the note a herald or a harbinger, its legacy dependent on whatever note follows.

A clicking sound makes Simonetta jump. Has she broken something? She puts her ear to the cabinet, hears a whirring sound. Her heart leaps in response. Gears shift, strings pull and creak like atrophied muscles being stretched and brought back to strength. At first the changes are all internal, muffled from the wooden cabinet, but then the changes unfurl upward like a flower blooming in a timelapse. The doll, always leaning slightly forward, begins to straighten. The small arms lock into place around the violin and bow with a satisfying click.

The tension pulls the doll's posture upright into position, and Catelot begins to play: *Songs for E, #1* through *#4*, Marguerite's sonata now imprinted on Simonetta, every note ringing out like a church bell.

The E string held all the tension, Jason explains after Simonetta ran throughout the chateau, gathering the volunteers to make sure that what she had witnessed actually happened.

"When the E string vibrates, it starts oscillating and uncoiling the tension bound in the latch," he says, pointing to a wire-wound gear Simonetta had replaced and reattached to the cabinet after the other one had melted in the fire. Now she can see it rotating, letting loose the weight holding back the pins that pluck the strings from below, following the melody of the four songs. Once the songs conclude, the latch strain needs to be re-established by slightly pulling the violin out from under Catelot's chin, placing it atop her head and sliding it down until it clicks into place again.

"So it *was* harmonic resonance, then?" she asks.

Jason shakes his head. "It still needed a lever, so to speak. That's how the doll's arm functions: when you lift it above her head, it coils the latch for the E string." He pauses to think through his explanation. "Did you replace the connecting wires, too, when you put in the new gear?" When she confirms, he smiles. "That was the likely the key to the repair. You may not have discovered that at all if it hadn't been damaged in the fire."

Simonetta is happy for the collective joy, but a piece is missing that she'll never understand—why is E minor, and the placement of the violin, the trigger? Upon Catelot's first performance, Simonetta tried plucking other notes to see what songs would play. But E minor is the catalyst for every song, the four in Catelot's rotation, the four compositions Marguerite wrote but never sent. All four songs begin and end with E minor, *Songs for E.* In her heart, Simonetta knows E is a person and not a note.

Before departing after the final music workshop, in which the Altobella automaton is discussed and celebrated at length, Monsieur Aubert helps Simonetta denote the compositions. As a thanks, she gifts him with special decorative copies of the originals that Hanako illustrated, drawing local flora onto the margins.

He is moved beyond measure. "Thank you for including me in your research," he says, his great mustache wriggling with poorly suppressed emotion. "It was an honor to help you play again."

Simonetta feels strongly that she has gotten more out of their collaboration, and even though she knows she'll see him the following spring for the next cohort of music classes—to which he has enthusiastically invited her to join as a guest teacher—she can't help herself from weeping in the courtyard when Monsieur Aubert leaves.

"It never gets easier watching people leave," says Claudel, patting her reassuringly on the shoulder and wiping her own eyes. "But it just means you have so many people to love."

Two envelopes arrive for Simonetta the next day: one containing the next steps on her Italian citizenship application—she has passed the initial screening—and the second bearing the letterhead of Strumenti d'Altobella, with the decorative encircled *A*.

The automaton sits in the Grand Salon on display, and the letter in her hand weighs heavily as she passes by it en route to the kitchen. Since Catelot came back to life, Simonetta, too, feels born anew: Venus with a violin. Inside her chest where a storm usually resides is a cloud, precarious and fragile. If someone touches her the rain will come out.

Jeremy is with Graham and Lotte at the long table when she arrives in the kitchen. He looks up as she enters and glances to her hands, where she holds the Altobella letter with shaking hands.

"You got a response," he says, a statement. "Have you read it yet?"

She shakes her head, her throat thick. "I wanted to share it with you."

He hands her a knife and she slices open the letter delicately. It's written in Italian, so she scans it once over first to give herself a chance to translate, then reads it slowly aloud:

> *"Dear Simonetta,*
>
> *My name is Adriana. I'm Rosa's daughter, so I think that makes us cousins! When I spoke your name to my mother, she smiled and said, 'Paolo's girl.' That is who you have always been to her and to us. I know your grandfather—my uncle— chose to keep his family away from the rest of us for many reasons, but in the few letters he sent to my mother over the years, he always spoke of your mother, and of you. The loss of your mother was very hard on him, but you were always his*

pride and joy."

Simonetta stops to regain her composure. Tears and words in her throat tumble out and blur the words on the page.

> *"France was a special place to Paolo. It's where he chose to stay after the war, where he felt safe and inspired, where he made a life, and where he met your grandmother. In a way, I am not surprised that you also found your way there. It seems you were destined to follow your Nonno's legacy.*
>
> *I am sorry for the loss of your grandmother. I never met her but I know Paolo adored her above all. You have known much loss in your life but those no longer with you loved you deeply, and in that way, they will always be with you.*
>
> *You asked about Altobella Instruments. The history of this company is complicated and although it remains as a company now that I oversee on behalf of my mother, it is far from what it used to be. I do have some documents and machines, including old automata by our mutual ancestor, that may be of interest to you. If you would like to visit, I know my mother would be overjoyed, although I must warn you that her memory is failing and she tires easily. I would very much like to meet 'Paolo's girl' and share with you what I can about our—your—family.*
>
> *You are, after all, an Altobella."*

PAOLO

Nothing would break Tommaso: not the beating he received in the chateau's turret at the hands of the French, not the walk of shame as he was taken in manacles from Desrosiers to the Sainte-Madeleine town square to be glared at by the villagers, not the month-long imprisonment in the abbey. Paolo's only saving grace was that Tommaso had insisted, even under torture, that Paolo had nothing to do with his efforts, with his cause.

And when questioned at gunpoint, Paolo answered the same.

He had taken a risk and had responded in French to the two French soldiers whose faces were shrouded in darkness. Outside the turret, the sounds of the battle ebbed.

"Ils fils de la radio?" Paolo had asked, tumbling and tripping over the language he had never had a chance to practice aloud. "Ils sont, er, OK?" *The boys from the radio—are they OK?*

These Resistance members were not expecting such a question. And when they were done with Tommaso and carried him unconscious out of Desrosiers, Paolo was shown slightly more care when he too was escorted out with his hands bound.

Paolo did indeed feel a deep, soul-burning shame when was on display with Tommaso in the cruel light of morning. He couldn't bear the ire-filled stares of the townspeople but knew he deserved every one of them. Were Jean and Louis among the glowering citizens? Paolo lamented the loss of the radio, the stories—he tried to tell himself the stories were never just stories, but codes, meant for someone who wasn't him. But they remained alight inside him anyway, the memories of the French fairytales and the voices of the boys who brought them to life.

Paolo had assumed the local resistance faction consisting of hundreds of people, but they numbered a mere dozen. Several had died during the stand-off at Desrosiers, and Paolo wondered how many soldatos were lost. Was Francisco among them? Did any flee, or were they all as steadfast as Tommaso? A handful were in holding at the abbey, in make-shift cells next to Tommaso, and they would soon be sent back to Italy for a tribunal.

Mussolini was with the Germans. Pinocchio with Hansel and Gretel, Paolo thought, but the metaphors no longer made sense, and he no longer wanted to mar the stories that gave him comfort with code that served a purpose.

The Resistance in the abbey was composed of not just boys, but girls, too, and Paolo was curious about the dynamic. Most of his life had been spent around boys and young men, with Mama and Rosa the only exceptions. Paolo endeared himself to a young woman named Amelia with short blonde hair by asking after Jean and Louis, whose whereabouts she didn't know.

"Members of our cause come and go," she explained. "We have different assignments that sometimes require us to travel. By the way, you were wrong about one of their names—you made a good guess. Jean goes by Jean-Luc, though, and Louis is actually Muriel." Paolo accepted this information but, in his head, the voices on the radio would always be Jean and Louis.

"He taught himself French," Amelia argued to Emeric, one of the fighters who had brought Paolo and Tommaso to the abbey to await consequences for their occupation. "He's the same age as *my* brother," she said, softer. "What was he supposed to do? Where is he supposed to go?"

Emeric sneered at Paolo, who was not-so-subtly listening by the door where Amelia and Emeric were keeping watch over the prisoners, and simply said, "Then he's your problem."

After earning her trust by way of being an annoying barnacle who wouldn't stop offering to help, Amelia let Paolo out of his imprisonment in exchange for his labor—cleaning, cooking, helping wherever extra hands were needed. He was thrilled to have something to do, at last. And she let him say goodbye to Tommaso before his brother was loaded onto a truck headed for the Italian border. The Fascists would be a good trade for the Resistance and the timing worked in their favor. Paolo recalled the journey to France several months prior, the trail that turned his feet to shreds.

Tommaso was stoic, even with his hands bound and the unknown hovering before him. But even beneath the scruffy beard and unkempt hair, Paolo saw glimpses of the person his brother used to be, the familiar angles of his face and some final vestiges of youth.

"Someday, Paolo, you will find something that you believe in so strongly that you will give your life for it." He reached out his hand and cupped Paolo on the cheek, his palm warm. "Goodbye, little brother."

Paolo thought he would feel adrift in Tommaso's absence, but he awoke with a sense of lightness, like a burden had been lifted. Guilt slinked in afterward and it made Paolo feel terrible, to be grateful for his brother's absence. But it was the first time he could think what he wanted to think, say what he wanted to say, do what he wanted to do.

The room he awoke in was empty, though. In the days he'd slept in the abbey outside of his initial cell, there was always someone around keeping watch, always someone sleeping off a grueling rotation of labor. Had he slept late? Had he slept so deeply in relief that even the squawking chickens couldn't rouse him?

No, the feeble dawn light that peeked through the abbey window suggested that it was dawn. He listened for the others, heard sounds of discussion and the moving of crates in the courtyard. Hackles raised, he crept to the door to observe—but it was just the cadre members packing up carts and a small green truck.

"Are you going somewhere?" This he said to Amelia, still rubbing sleep from his eyes.

"We're going to Marseilles," she said. "You should go home, Paolo. Take the pilgrim's path back to Primavera. No one will bother you. I will write papers for you."

Panic rose in his throat. "Can't I go with you?" Paolo said, tampering down the swell of anxiety. If they left without him, what would he do? "I would like to do something useful."

Amelia shoved her satchel in between the crook of two crates and sighed impatiently. She glanced at the sky as if looking for something, and he wondered what—planes? The time? Dragons? "Paolo, are you sure you don't want to go back to Italy? To your family?"

For once, Paolo didn't overthink the possibilities, the many routes ahead of him. The answer was clear in his heart and he felt a kernel of what Tommaso spoke of, a kindling of what it felt like to have conviction and a purpose.

"I want to go to Marseilles with you," he said. "I never want to go back to Italy."

SYMONNE

Symonne awoke to a bright morning, squinting at the sun through eyes nearly crusted shut from the mud.

She pushed herself to her feet, body cold and aching. Her head throbbed from where she had been struck. The sun was high in the sky—already midday. Wherever Catelot had been taken, she was long gone. Had the mercenary taken her to the abbey, like he said he would? Bertrand lay dead nearby and Symonne spared him no passing thought, no final prayer as she made her way to the village on the muddy trail ransacked by the previous night's struggle.

She weighed her options. Sickness was sweeping through Sainte-Madeleine; outside of the carefully curated confines of the fortress, she was at risk, and so was Catelot. Who knows what she would find in the village, in the abbey? Putrid deceased bodies, pestilence lurking everywhere, the village brought to its knees once again? But Catelot would be protected with her and by her, and the risk was worth taking.

Symonne went to the abbey first. A still silence lay over it like a wool blanket, and Symonne feared the worst. Holding her breath, she knocked on the door.

An elderly sister answered, her linen dress blood-stained, but the stains were faint and not recent. "Do you have any signs of sickness? This is a safe house for healthy people."

Symonne stopped herself from clearing her throat, lest it suggest she was ailing. "I'm looking for Catherine Desrosiers. Has a young woman arrived recently?"

The sister frowned. "I will inquire." She returned a few minutes later. "There is no one here by that name."

Fear roiled in her stomach; where would she be? Catelot was worth more alive, if the mercenary had believed her story. Or maybe he had left her somewhere. Or maybe she was sick. Or maybe she was with the witches. Hope tasted bitter as Symonne spent another day trudging through the mountains, looking for Augusta. But the witches found her first, awoke her where she was sleeping fitfully in the shadow of an oak tree.

Augusta shook her head at Symonne's pleading. "We've had no sign of her since they took her."

Despite Augusta's protestations, urging Symonne to remain with them indefinitely, Symonne insisted on returning to Desrosiers. The fortress was nearly empty again, like the last plague, but where that one had somehow given her new life, this one had Symonne wandering through the halls like a ghost.

Adrift, purposeless, Symonne knew no path without Catelot. She could return to the abbey and devote her life to God, but Symonne didn't feel much of a kinship with the Heavenly Father. What Symonne knew best was caring for her daughter and all that went with it. She could find work again as a laundress, or a weaver, if there was anyone left who would hire her.

Grief thick and heavy in her throat, in her chest, Symonne found solace in the kitchen and the remnants of magic she had created with her daughter and the witches. She sat in the middle of the floor, surrounded by sketches and symbols they'd scratched into the floor. A pile of refuse was beside her, hastily formed— Symonne envisioned Bertrand stomping around, ripping the threads twined around twigs, stomping on the herbs, tearing down their wooden signs adorned with runes.

Something caught her eye in the pile, beneath the twigs and twine: a small wooden hand. Symonne pushed aside the broken spells to find Catelot's carved doll, and her knife.

The discovery shook her to the core, as if it were Catelot herself found in the refuse, and the hot tears she wept were laced with anger. She thought of Lady Cateline on her deathbed, body curved around young Catelot in protection and devotion. Symonne wasn't dying but wished she would, so she emulated Catelot's birth mother in the same tradition: she stretched out on the floor and placed the doll beside her and curled around it like a crescent moon, orbiting her star.

After hours on the floor, Symonne lost feeling in her limbs. She forced herself to a sitting position and rubbed sensation back into her body.

What use was she on the floor? She thought of what her mother would do finding her there: she'd caress her head then say, *"Get up, love. There is work to be done."* The one truth Symonne knew of life was that there was always work to do, always someone who needed aid. She had to keep looking for Catelot. Until she knew for certain what had happened to her daughter, she'd never stop trying, never stop looking. And she'd do so by helping others, spread the protective magic she had learned. That was how she saw and understood witchcraft: a pool of love that could be savored or shared. There was nothing Bertrand had said that she would ever believe, but perhaps she had survived one plague and maybe two for a purpose: to be Catelot's mother. But the purpose didn't come from God, it came from the universe itself, had brought them together despite the odds, and it gave Symonne a strange sort of peace even amid her terror and grief.

She packed up as much as she could from the kitchen, food and tinctures she had made, cloths and poultices in clay bowls. Small vials of paint that she had mixed with Catelot found a home in her satchel; Symonne would never be apart from them.

Before departing Desrosiers in search of souls in need of protection and healing, Symonne set Catelot's doll on the kitchen table, flour and their fingerprints embedded in its rough wood, remnants of more than a decade of devotion.

Symonne had remembered a lesson Augusta had taught her years ago: how to use a simulacrum of a person to protect them. The doll would be the vessel for Symonne's protective magic over Catelot, wherever she was. With a small brush and her paints, Symonne adorned the doll with the features she knew so well: the wide, bright eyes, a wry mouth upturned in a smile, and with each loving brushstroke, Symonne brought Catelot back to life.

SIMONETTA

Simonetta stands in the doorway and surveys the empty room, then makes a note on her clipboard.

~~Clear out the Room of Oddities.~~

The feeling of long-awaited triumph doesn't come. Many times throughout the summer, she imagined how she would feel finishing this project. Clearing out this room and fixing the items within it had been her primary goal this summer, and it is done. It was hard work. She has new strength in her body from the effort.

But there is no sensation of achievement that washes over her. Among her many faults is a constant desire to set an ambitious goal solely for the feelings of relief and accomplishment that come with meeting it—she knows now that she is constantly seeking that feeling, that it is what has propelled her through most of her life so far.

Or maybe not anymore. In a way she is proud she's not spinning with joy. She can view this for what it was: a goal met, a job well done. She is pleased; the room has been emptied and cleaned and now the entire part of this tower can be inspected, repairs made. That makes her happy. The medieval tower is her favorite part of Desrosiers, besides the chapel, and she wants it to remain structurally sound for decades to come. She is honored to have played a part in its preservation.

And the items within have been put to good use. Most of the instruments are now on display in the Grand Salon, enjoying ample use from the visiting musicians. Claudel took two of the violins to the luthier, who was thrilled to have some of its older models returned to display in their shop. The taxidermy has, thankfully, been processed—she, Diego, and Jason took most of it to the brocante, and a few choice pieces were shipped to select *Daily Life* viewers. Only a few remained, some creatures local to the area, used as decor in some of the chateau's larger visiting rooms.

The clocks and the stone-topped side tables and apothecary cabinets and even the mechanical bird in its cage have all found homes throughout the chateau. Everything salvaged from the room has been given new life and purpose.

And so has she. Simonetta sees the ghost of her former self here, a lonely, lost figure roaming among the dust and forgotten artifacts. She had tried to be the New Simonetta then, Venus with red lipstick, emerging bloody from rebirth, but she is now just Current Simonetta—less lonely, less prone to the extremities of grief and anxiety, and seeking out her next step. It is still daunting to take another leap into the unknown, but that's all she's been doing for months and it's starting to adapt like second nature. She no longer fears the dark abyss of uncertainty, although there is a shadowy vignette that exists around the edges of the future still. Perhaps she is simply understanding that, with every passing day of life, there is no way of knowing. Days are filled with music and intrusive thoughts and glasses of wine and hands dirty from gardening and labor.

So she is pleased, yes, and satisfied, and for now that is enough. Simonetta looks out through the windows where she can see the crenellations much more clearly. She pretends to shoot an arrow through the slats, imagines it navigating through the chasm between the stone, lancing over the nymph, finding purchase in the grass. Then she closes the door and heads back to her room to finish packing.

Twenty-Four

Lintel: A horizontal beam or pillar of stone that bridges an opening.

SIMONETTA SIPS FROM the tiny coffee cup and looks out the window at the landscape rolling by—the green foothills she has come to know so well, although there are pockets of gold sprouting, hints of the autumn to come.

She will get to see the Alps in autumn. Months ago, she had assumed that she'd be back in Berkeley soon, figuring out her next move. Simonetta is relieved she's not heading home empty-handed. She understands now how much home is a concept, not a place.

"Would you like something to eat?" asks the uniformed woman pushing a trolly laden with snacks and beverages down the aisle. Simonetta gets a refill on her coffee and a Milka bar that melts on her fingers.

Appreciating her solitude still brings with it a sense of guilt. Just a few months ago, being alone had felt like a curse, when grief had threatened to eat her alive. But upon meeting Claudel and Aurelia and Jeremy and everyone at Desrosiers, the loneliness ebbed, and she is now overflowing with camaraderie.

Still, she craves isolation again. It's her default state, being alone. It's where she is most herself. All summer she has been honing the New Simonetta, but the old one peeks through sometimes, and she no longer suppresses that—it's all part of becoming the version she will be next.

She thinks of Nonna, gone now almost a year. She thinks of Nonno, who, although he has been gone for half of her life, still leaves such an imprint on her. The thought of learning more about him makes her stomach lurch. She is nervous to meet his relatives, doesn't know what she'll say or do, wishes she had more time to plan and think, but, knowing that Rosa is getting older, makes her feel that time is not on her side.

Outside, a green valley whips by in a verdant blur. She caught the train early; it travels between France and Italy twice per day. Most of the other people on it are commuters, heading to work, and she thinks fondly of her trips on BART to the Cal campus.

Leaving Jeremy back in France was not an easy decision. She winces when she thinks of his crestfallen face when she asked to go alone.

"You don't think you could use some support?" he had asked delicately. He knows he is thinking of the many times Simonetta has unraveled this summer, and the thought embarrasses her. She shouldn't feel shame at the emotions she's revealed to him—after all, he seems to have fallen in love with her despite the peaks and valleys she has exhibited—but she does anyway, feeling vulnerable and tired of being vulnerable. She misses the woman she used to be, someone more stoic.

Instead, she focuses on the coffee, hot and lightly sweetened with hazelnut—and looks out at the Italian landscape. This is where her family is from—they lived among these hills and trees and rivers and buildings. It's surreal to her still, that she is not in America and hasn't been in some time and realizes with a jolt that she's not sure when she'll return. There are logistical considerations that she needs to figure out. And she has items in storage that will need to be shipped over to her new home. She thinks of Chateau Desrosiers as her new home and it catches her off guard. It sounds so fanciful, living in a French castle, even if the daily reality of that is far less romantic.

When she steps off the train at Primavera station, Simonetta experiences the same fissure of excitement and nervousness that rippled through her upon her first visit to Desrosiers. It's the same sensation of anticipation, the nerves making her stomach clench. She tries to channel the anxiety into positive feelings, rather than linger in a sense of foreboding. She tells herself again that she has nothing to lose: if her new family resents her or simply dislikes her, she isn't losing anything she hasn't already been missing. Instead, she thinks of Jeremy, and Claudel, and Graham and Hanako and Jason and Alba and Diego and Lotte and Paul and Monsieur Aubert, and a fern unfurls in her heart, warm and true, blooming in the light.

Villaggio Primavera is smaller even than Sainte-Madeleine, and flatter, a humble hamlet spread out in the valley. The Alps loom overhead, casting a wide shadow over most of the village. The train depot is in the heart of the old commune. Simonetta booked a room at an inn down the street, and she'll walk to Altobella Instruments on the other side of the town.

Her heart is in her throat as she walks the steps of her grandfather's home. She can't help but wonder if this is a betrayal—he never spoke of Primavera, of his family, and although she now has more context about why, there are layers she'll never understand. She imagines calling him and revealing where she is, imagines his voice of disappointment and disapproval. Once when she was newly fifteen, she made the poor choice to go with a friend to San Francisco, making the risky trip in the back of a beaten-up Jetta with a driver who only had his learner's permit. She regretted the decision as soon as she made it, as the driver, a friend-of-a-friend-of-a-friend, wove the squealing car down I-80.

And it was no surprise when, hours later, Simonetta had been abandoned by her "friends" in Nihonmachi and left her wallet in the Jetta. Simonetta, tail between her legs, begged the karaoke shop owner to use the phone and she called Nonno for pickup. She's never forgotten the sound in his voice.

"Ah, topolina! How did you end up there? Your nonna

thinks you're at Katie's! I can't believe you lied to us." He sighed, resigned. "Stay put, I will come get you."

And he had, an hour later, and she sat sheepish and guilty in the passenger seat. "You're a good girl, Simonetta. You know we expect more of you."

"I know, Nonno," she had said, tears welling in her throat. "I'm sorry. I feel awful." And she did. She had never felt so awful. She was a good girl, she had always been a good girl. But she had lied, and for what? She had tried to be rebellious, and for what?

She felt his glances at her but avoided his eye contact. Eventually he reached over and patted her knee reassuringly. At his touch, the tears spilled out. "It will be okay, topolina. But don't tell your Nonna." He pointed to the glove compartment. "Pick out a CD. We have a ways to go until we get home."

As she checks in at Refugio Primavera, standing in queue behind a group of backpackers planning a trek over the alps, she hears it in her mind: the disappointed *Ah, topolina! How did you end up there?*

She's led to her room, small and comfortable with a single bed and a desk. The building is composed of wood and stone like a rustic cabin to cater to the abundance of hikers and outdoorsy folks who venture to this region. The air is fresh and cool as tendrils of fall start to permeate the atmosphere.

She considers a nap, but the nerves and curiosity would make sleep impossible. Simonetta freshens up and checks her satchel for the essentials and makes her way across town.

The industrial area of Primavera lacks the quaintness found throughout the rest of the town. The buildings here are practical and modern, many of them garages or workshops. Altobella Instruments is among the older establishments. It's a humble building, a small factory and office space tucked in the back of the commercial building. But the sight of the name Altobella encircled in an oval, brings tears to Simonetta's eyes. She's as reverent as she did the day she first arrived at Desrosiers—that strange, wonderful, complicated, stomach-clenching feeling taking over her body. A few people walk by and she waits for them to point and laugh and yell, "Stranger! Interloper! Impostor!" But of course, they pay her no mind, and why would they? *No one thinks about us as much as we assume they are.* Her internal turmoil is detectable only to her.

She steels herself and pushes open the front door; a bell rings to signal her arrival. Inside is an L-shaped desk, behind which is a wall with a window separating the office from the workshop beyond.

A woman crosses the workshop and Simonetta can immediately tell the family resemblance—the woman shares Nonno's rich dark hair, full lips, and, of course, the Altobella nose with which Simonetta is intimately familiar.

The woman pushes through the door and smiles in passive greeting. But she detects what Simonetta does, the family resemblance, and her face breaks into a wide smile. "Simonetta?"

Simonetta nods, unable to speak, but chokes out, "Si. Adriana?"

Adriana nods in confirmation and opens her arms for an embrace. "Sono così felice di incontrarti finalmente!" *So glad to finally meet you at last!* Simonetta embraces her and stifles the sob that threatens to spill out. Adriana holds her at arm's length and looks her over. "Vedo Paolo in te! Ma anche Emilia. Era molto bella!" *I see Paolo in you! But also Emilia. She was very beautiful!*

Simonetta takes in Adriana, her cousin, and feels simply overwhelmed. Adriana, in her mid-fifties, is a bit younger than Simonetta's mother Julia would be now and Simonetta wishes desperately that she could receive a maternal hug in this moment.

When Simonetta still can't speak, Adriana's brow furrows in misunderstanding. "I can switch to English if that's easier for you."

"I'm just—this is a lot for me," says Simonetta, shoving the words out. Her throat constricts with the effort. "When Nonna died I thought I lost the rest of my family."

"Oh, Simonetta! God brought you home. You are where you're supposed to be. Come, come—my mother can't wait to meet you."

Simonetta is not sure she can take meeting Rosa; just being in Adriana's welcoming orbit has her wishing she had brought Jeremy after all as a buffer between herself and the torrent of emotion washing over her. She barely hears Adriana's pleasant chatter as she leads her down the road to a small duplex.

"We're on the first floor," explains Adriana. "I'm glad you arrived when you did. Mama does best in the afternoon when it's still light outside. But I will translate for you—English is hard for her these days."

Without fanfare, Adriana opens the door to the flat. It's charming inside, with slatted windows bringing in afternoon light. A comfortable living room decorated with floral sofas and wooden tables is bookended by a kitchen and a bathroom. Against the wall, opposite the door, is a large grandfather clock that Simonetta assumes is an Altobella creation.

A TV on the wall plays an Italian talk show featuring some sort of game, and sitting in front of it in an armchair is Rosa.

"Mama!" says Adriana. "I brought you a special visitor, your grandniece." Adriana beckons Simonetta over. Simonetta drops her satchel onto the wooden dining table and follows Adriana.

She crouches in front of Rosa, Nonno's sister. Nonno's genetics continue to permeate the Altobellas, although Rosa's wispy gray hair has traces of blonde, like Simonetta's.

Simonetta wills herself to speak, to greet Rosa. "Salve," says Simonetta, the Italian feeling heavy and foreign on her tongue. "I'm Simonetta. I'm so glad to meet you." Her voice cracks.

Rosa smiles widely and leans forward at her grandniece. "Ah, Simonetta. Tuo nonno sarebbe arrabbiato se sapesse che sei qui!" Adriana hesitates before translating, but Simonetta gets the gist—*your grandfather would be mad to know you are here!* But Rosa says this with a smile and a wink, and Simonetta lets out a nervous laugh.

"I thought the same thing. But how could I not come meet you?"

When Adriana translates, Rosa cups Simonetta's face, turning it left and right in a loving inspection. Simonetta lets her face be studied, wants to know what Rosa thinks—does she approve?

She hopes she does, because Simonetta is the product of her nonni's loving upbringing, and she wants nothing more in this moment than to make them both proud. Unable to meet Rosa's eyes, she looks instead at the grandfather clock and sees from a distance the same gold oval bearing the Altobella maker's mark. It gives her strength to see it, the maker's mark that set her on this path.

Rosa follows her gaze. "Your grandfather used to love to hide in the lower compartment," translates Adriana as Rosa points to the largest clock. "You look so much like him. Paolo's girl."

Something within Simonetta cracks and shatters, the delicate egg she so closely guards, and it seeps into her body in a wave of love and warmth and comfort and overwhelming sadness. She'd had the very same urge when she had first found the automaton, a desire that seemed to run in the family, a shared passion for seeking out the world's hidden pockets and hiding.

Simonetta buries her face into Rosa's lap and weeps.

Twenty-Five

Finial: A decorative stone element adorning the tops of towers, merlons, towers, or balustrades.

SIMONETTA STEPS INTO the inn's lobby, inhales the pleasant scent of coffee and pastries still lingering from the morning buffet even though it is well into the evening. She nearly fell asleep on the taxi ride back across town, the adrenaline of the day finally wearing off and leaving behind a bone-deep weariness.

To her surprise, it is a pleasant feeling—the anxiety that was knotted in her chest this morning has loosened and made way for both grief and relief. She's keenly aware of her own mortality, the swift passage of time, the way history and present and future happen simultaneously, the main difference being perspective.

She and Rosa had conversed, with help from Adriana, for hours almost non-stop. Simonetta gleaned quickly that, for many years, Rosa had lived in the shadows of her brothers and mother. Simonetta had, not for the first time, said a prayer of thanks to her Nonna Emilia for being a warm, loving caretaker unlike the imposing Maria Benedetto, her great-grandmother, whose complicated legacy reached its tendrils even as far as her great-granddaughter's existence. It was clear by her conversation with Rosa that such a legacy had come with a steep cost.

Simonetta felt peace knowing that Rosa and Nonno had had some correspondence throughout their adulthood. It was strange for Simonetta to talk about her own mother with someone besides Nonno and Nonna, and although Nonno's heartbreak at losing his daughter had unearthed much of his earlier familiar trauma, Simonetta was proud that her tight-lipped grandfather had made his anguish known to someone. It was a side of him she never had the chance to see, but it humanized him to her to know that it did, in fact, exist.

Names and places and stories swirl in her mind, and she pledges to write down what she can in her journal before she undoubtedly crashes from exhaustion.

She has so many more questions, but her solace is that today's conversation was the first of many she'll have with Adriana and Rosa, for Adriana asked Simonetta to move in with them. At least, for a little while, so Simonetta can help care for Rosa while Adriana manages Altobella Instruments. In doing so, Simonetta can expedite her path to citizenship and stay in Europe for the foreseeable future.

This is where the ley line ends, where it has led her, for now.

Outside of the inn, evening settles in and the mountains are swathed in gold. Simonetta thinks of the golden hour light in Desrosiers' chapel, her sacred place. Even in her ancestral hometown, where the church bells ring with surety and the verdant mountains loom strong and sentinel, she finds herself longing for Desrosiers, and a sense of homesickness washes over her, a kernel of doubt at her commitment to live here in Primavera instead. It's brief but potent, and a different kind of homesickness than the painful and nebulous variety she had first felt upon leaving Berkeley.

She wants to call Jeremy and tell him everything she learned, how she's feeling, the monumental choice she has made. She wants to know everything that happened in her absence, despite it only being a single day since she was gone. She finds herself pleasantly desperate for details about Desrosiers, and the notion that she will remain hungry for the chateau for years to come fills her with a joy she could have never expected to feel after months of anguish.

Resolute to make coffee so she can write before sleeping,

Simonetta heads to her room, mind aflutter and rehearsing her call to Jeremy—and when she opens the door to her room and finds him waiting there for her already, the declarations spill out as she pours herself into his arms.

"Well, what do you think?" Simonetta asks Diego, although the answer is apparent on his face. He grimaces and sets down the cup.

"Needs more sugar," he replies, and Simonetta rolls her eyes at Jeremy as she claims the rest of Diego's espresso for herself.

Her gesture of annoyance is purely for show, as Simonetta is practically bursting with love sitting at a rickety table with Jeremy, Diego, Lotte, and Hanako in Primavera's ancient quarter.

Once she had extracted herself from Jeremy, reeling from the shock at seeing him in Italy when she had left him in France, he filled her in on the plan—her friends had debated at length on following her to Italy, then decided to risk her wrath anyway by showing their support.

Upon hearing this, Simonetta is appalled. "My wrath? Is that truly what you all think of me?" She tosses up her hands. "Why on earth would I be mad that you came to Italy for me?"

Jeremy takes her expressive hands in his, linking together their fingers. The gesture calms her, the feeling of his palms pressed against hers. "Because we knew it was important for you to go alone, to see this through by yourself. And I know that's what you wanted."

Simonetta acquiesces to this, unable to counter-argue. "I appreciate the respect. But you all coming here to be with me, coordinating your travel and everything—it means more than I can say." The thickness in her voice betrays her then, validating the earnestness in her words.

Jeremy smirks. "We had our own motivations, too. Hanako wants to go to the art museum while we're here. And Diego said he would try espresso at a real Italian cafe."

"He didn't!" All summer long Diego had refused coffee,

proclaiming it too bitter, instead preferring to indulge on anything sweet. It had become an ongoing joke, Simonetta and Hanako waxing over-dramatically about how enjoyable their coffee was whenever Diego was in ear-shot.

Jeremy nods. "It seems your bravery inspired others."

She avoids Jeremy's gaze, unable to tell him how vulnerable she had felt going to the factory, the way her hands had shook and her heart had thundered in her chest. She can't find the words to express that the fear of loss again could crush her completely, that she worries every day that she'll be pulled back into darkness, and that one day there will be nothing bright enough to extract her. The constant battles she fights against her own mind—Simonetta doesn't know how to stop it.

"I see the look on your face," Jeremy says, serious again.

"What look?"

"The one where you are choosing your words carefully to contest what I say."

"I just am trying to reconcile what it means to be brave," she says simply. "I learned today that my grandfather was twelve when he ran into Desrosiers looking for Tommaso during the siege at Desrosiers. Twelve! At twelve, I was most afraid of jumping off of the high dive at the swimming pool."

"Simonetta, you are the bravest person I have ever met. I knew that the day I met you."

Simonetta scoffs. "You did not know that. How could you have possibly known that?"

"Because I knew that you had uprooted your life to volunteer at Desrosiers, that you were seeking something and weren't afraid to go great lengths to find it. I knew you had lost much and didn't have much of a family. From your application I knew how hard you had worked in your career, where you had traveled—your passion for travel and knowledge is evident in everything you do. That's just what I learned about you on paper." Jeremy walks to the window. "And then we fixed the automaton. You ran into the burning workshop to try to save it. You have poured your soul into that project, knowing all the while it could amount to nothing beyond a curious coincidence." He turns and meets her gaze. "And you opened your heart to me when it would have been easier to continue forging your path alone."

Simonetta chews on the inside of her cheek, lost for words. She feels obligated to thank him, or return the sentiment, but speech evades her as her mind churns. After a moment, voice thick in her throat, she finds her voice. "You don't have to say those kinds of things to me. I'm not looking for compliments."

"I didn't offer any. Because the underlying theme here is that you are also incredibly stubborn and your overthinking is going to be the death of you. And probably me."

She smiles. "That's better." *I am still figuring out what it means to be a person without defining myself by my family, but I feel more connected to my own history than I ever have. So determining what I define as brave is still a work-in-progress.* "Is simply living life to the best of my ability bravery? Or is it privilege?"

Jeremy shrugs. "Neither? Does it have to be either?"

"I guess not." But still she wonders, *how do I live life if I can't quantify it?*

"Are you sure about this?"

Simonetta and Jeremy stand beside a train—another moment-out-of-time vignette that makes Simonetta feel like she is sending Jeremy off to war. Or maybe she is the soldier in this scenario, since it is he who is getting on the train—alone, without her, as she remains behind in Italy.

"No," she says, laughing. "I've been sure of very few things in the past year."

Jeremy swallows hard. "You always have a home at Desrosiers." *With me.*

"I know," says Simonetta. "You have made it my home. I promise I will come back to you."

He pulls her in close and buries his face in her shoulder, and she lets herself be gripped tightly, absorbs the sensation of his arms around her. And then he releases her and climbs aboard after Diego, and Simonetta tries not to look back at the departing train as she heads into Primavera.

Twenty-Six

Keep: (noun) A stronghold, or (verb) to hold something close.

SYMONNE
1373

IN THE YEAR LEADING UP to the end of her life, Symonne assumed the pain in her left breast was the manifestation of her heartache. It had never gone away, the grief, although eventually she learned to live with it—or at least, became numb to it. So when the pain, that sometimes stung and other times throbbed, began to do both at the same time and never relented, she wondered why she was so keenly aware of the heartache after so many years away from Catelot.

The pain strengthened and spread, and with each passing day, Symonne grew sicker and weaker. When she collapsed over her mortar and pestle for the third time, Mistress Jeannette loaded Symonne onto a wagon and dumped her unceremoniously on the steps of the Abbey of Sainte-Madeleine. It was in God's hands now, although Jeannette regretted the loss of a talented healer.

Symonne was unconscious for most of the journey, slipping in and out as she was eventually discovered and brought inside a long white hall, where she was prayed over and given last rites.

In a fleeting moment of lucidity, she felt lips press against her forehead, cool hands cupping her cheeks. In the haze of death, shadows forming in the perimeter of her vision, she saw the face she had seen in her dreams for years: a face now older, marked by life, but still pure and beautiful and haloed in a white veil, the hazel eyes bright and wide and luminous.

A quiet, familiar voice said, "It's alright, Mama. I'm here."

Symonne's mouth was gently opened and a liquid poured in—warm milk, infused with hemlock. Soothed by the touch and voice of her daughter, Symonne faded into the darkness, awash in memory.

"Mama," Catelot whined. "I don't want to sit on the rock. It's uncomfortable!"

"Fine," Symonne replied, tossing up her hands in surrender. "Where would you prefer to be?"

"Near the trees," said Catelot, pointing to the tree line. "I like the green."

Symonne smiled. "I like the green, too. It's my favorite."

Together they trudged toward the jagged line of the forest. A wide tree stump had been recently sawed and sanded by Bertrand, and Symonne pointed to it. "How about that?"

"Can't I stand?"

"Yes, but you can't wiggle so much." Symonne set the basket of painting supplies down and knelt in front of Catelot. "You can only wiggle when I do this—" she reached up and gently pinched the spot at the top of Catelot's rib cage, where she knew the girl was the most ticklish. At the sensation, Catelot arched and giggled and thrashed about until she had her fill of tickling, then gave Symonne a brief affectionate squeeze before clambering on the tree trunk.

Dutifully, Catelot stood relatively in place for the hour it took for Symonne to paint the foundation of the portrait. She tried to capture the lines and shapes of Catelot's face and body, and the contrast of light and darkness, the way the afternoon light glinted off of her ebony braid that Catelot preferred to have draped over one shoulder so she could run her fingers through the ends and toy with the twining keeping it plaited. Catelot's dark hazel eyes caught the light and turned pale green outlined in mahogany. Symonne crafted Catelot out of the same palette as the forest, hues of brown and green and gold, with undertones of navy and gray.

It was the palette of Symonne's memory. In the lonely years that came later, when the sound of young girlish giggles left ghostly echoes in the empty fortress, this was how Symonne remembered her daughter Catelot and how she thought of her now as death claimed her—not the young child she had found screaming and covered in sickness, but a free girl of the wild, who preferred sleeping among the trees instead of in the castle of her birthright, whose eyes held an ever-present gleam of curiosity, whose beautiful slender fingers had delicately and lovingly clasped the end of her braid and her mother's hands.

MARGUERITE
1722

> *Yours,*
> *Elise*

Marguerite swallowed hard and folded the letter, creasing it with her fingernail. The fire taunted her, its tongues lashing out in hunger seeking the taste of paper, and she almost fed it with the letter. Instead, she took a deep breath and pulled from her well of composure, counting, grounding herself: *focus on your feet touching the ground, focus on the pattern of your breath, count to four and then again*, she murmured like a mantra. And it helped suppress the welling of emotion sparked by Elise's unexpected letter.

It had been more than a year since Elise left, and the letter arrived to Marguerite's surprise. She left it unopened for days on her desk, until finally curiosity won out and she broke open the navy-blue seal bearing Elise's new name and legacy.

The letter was brief, revealing little, but Marguerite read between the lines. Elise confirmed her contentedness, her health. She said she was continuing her music studies and intended to teach her future children. Marguerite could easily envision Elise as a mother, lovingly tending to her babes. Marguerite surprised herself when she felt a spark of joy at the thought, although every thought of Elise would always be tinged with the dark blue of deep, irreparable heartache.

Elise inquired after Marguerite's health and happiness in a close-ended way that made Marguerite feel that it was best not to send a response. Marguerite had nothing to say beyond *I love you forever*. But she could no longer put words to how she felt and the sentiment would remain unrequited for the rest of her days. Instead, she put them into her music, her compositions, her festivities. She was in the middle of planning her next winter fête. Resolved to find some semblance of purpose, with wealth to spend and time to waste, she would bring the best of Europe's artists to Desrosiers.

A servant cleared his throat and Marguerite looked up from the fire, the flames still dancing in her vision. "Monsieur Altobella is here with your commission."

Simultaneous feelings of elation and dread plagued Marguerite as Altobella wheeled in his creation, months in the making.

Marco Altobella removed the sheet with a flourish. "Your new machine, my lady."

Before Marguerite stood a tall, gleaming automaton. In almost every way, it was a product of Desrosiers—the doll, the wood, the violin, even the intestinal strings made from animals harvested from the forest.

It was the manifestation of her dreams. Even though the doll wasn't Elise, Marguerite saw her in every part of the automaton— the long, elegant neck, the wide eyes, the dark horsehair wig, the slender fingers clasping the neck of the violin.

Emotion thick in her throat, she managed to choke out a compliment. "You did a remarkable job."

He reached out a hand in invitation. "It works as requested.

Please, give it a try."

The automaton, which, although tall, was not quite at eye level. She thought again of Elise, the top of her dark head meeting Marguerite's nose; an unintentional design feature, but now intrinsic to it.

She plucked the E string on the small violin, and the doll sprang into motion, playing the first of its four songs. The song was simple and sad, a thread pulled directly from Marguerite's heart, and as the doll played her recital, each piece built upon itself, weaving a layered tapestry.

Upon its conclusion, Marco looked at her with an eager expression. Marguerite straightened and compressed all emotion until it sat like a stone in her stomach. With collected composure, she gave Altobella a smile of approval.

"Thank you for your masterful work, Monsieur Altobella. I shall be sure to share your services with the court."

He placed a hand on his heart in gratitude. "*Grazie*, my lady."

She pulled the bell rope next to the mantle to summon the servants. "Please see Monsieur Altobella out and let Henri know I'm ready for him."

A few minutes later, her young nephew emerged, his still chubby hands knitting together in uncertainty. He looked so like his father that it sometimes brought up dormant triggers in Marguerite, and she was still training herself to release the fear.

Henri looked up at his aunt with wide, dark eyes. It seemed her heart was destined to be destroyed by wide, dark eyes.

She crouched before him. "Bonjour, Henri. Are you well?"

At eye-level, he softened a bit and gave a small grin, revealing a dimpled cheek. "Yes, auntie."

"Are you ready for your first lesson?"

He nodded eagerly. She stood and gestured toward the small music stand and stool, atop which sat a small violin designed for a child. Marguerite found her place on the sofa and smoothed her dress.

"Now," she said, placing her hands in her lap. She smiled at the young boy. "Let's begin with how to hold it properly. Start by placing it on your head."

❦

PAOLO
1959

Finally, it arrived. The stupid piece of paper he'd been waiting on for months, the one piece of paper holding him back.

Paolo took the envelope immediately to the foreman. Fingers trembling, he crossed the factory floor, climbed up the metal ladder, and emerged into the hallway that overlooked the activity below.

He took a deep breath before entering the foreman's office, knocked twice, then opened the door without waiting for admission. Sitting behind his desk, the foreman, Luc, glanced up through the smoke of his cigarette and rolled his eyes. "You again, Altobella?"

Paolo nodded and handed over the envelope. "The qualifications you said I needed, sir," he said, and cringed while doing so. The foreman's hands were stained with oil and Paolo didn't want his pristine diploma marred by the fingerprints. Perhaps he could get another copy.

Luc pulled out the document and glanced down between the paper and back up at Paolo. Paolo resisted the urge to lean over and read the words himself, but he knew what they said: *Paolo Altobella, Master of Science: Engineering*. After years of late-night study, he had earned the title that the foreman said was necessary for running the new factory opening soon.

Luc furrowed his brows, ashed his cigarette, then riffled through his desk drawer for another one. "What's this all about?" he said, waving a smoking hand at Paolo's diploma.

"The degree you said I needed, sir," said Paolo, his patience being pulled taut like a thread about to be severed. "To qualify for the position, with the new factory opening." Even after a decade in France, French did not come as fluidly to him as he wished, and his long-practiced pitch came out clumsy.

Luc snorted. "I already promised that position to Gervais."

"What?" A cold sweat broke out over his arms and shoulders,

an uncomfortable clammy feeling that made him squirm like he was a young boy again. "Months ago, I asked you what it would take to be selected to run the new factory. You told me I should get a master's degree, and so I did. What do you expect me to do now?"

"The position was never yours, Altobella," Luc said. "I just told you that to get you off my back. And to be honest, the position is beneath you. You're a talented engineer—you were even before you slaved away to get this." Another casual hand wave toward the evidence of Paolo's relentless work, and it made Paolo seethe even when cushioned by the compliment. "You're better than all this. Why not go back to Italy and find a position there?"

Incensed, Paolo nearly spit. "I will never go back there."

"America, then? Big automobile market there. They need engineers. You'd find something good there in no time, especially with your fancy new title." Luc cackled, then coughed. "Look, I'll make it easy for you. You're fired—for your own good. Go find a better purpose. Bonne chance."

Stunned, Paolo scooped up his diploma and stomped back down the ladder. Of all the outcomes he'd anticipated, most of which involved him and Luc discussing the responsibilities of his role overseeing the new factory, that was not one of them. He hadn't expected to lose his entire livelihood over his academic pursuits. All of the sleepless nights, endless study, the projects and the papers—was it all for nothing?

Truthfully, he had enjoyed it. It had been years since he'd had a tangible goal and the degree had given him direction. Luc was right—he needed a better purpose.

He was almost thirty and still schlepping around in low-level factories. France had been his home for a decade and a half, but Paolo was feeling an internal pull he hadn't experience before, something that told him it was time—time to move on, time to explore, time to be challenged.

He walked down the block, toward the docks of the Marseilles port that was once a hub of prosperity. The golden hour poured molten sunlight over the docks, and the view was majestic.

He looked out over the Mediterranean, wondered about the bones and ships in its depths. What would it take to retrieve some of them from beneath the waves? His mind went to its default state, engineering, and he mentally began designing a rig that would carefully extract a shipwreck from the depths. But if the wood had rotted, it would need to be delicately brought to the surface. What if the rig would scoop the wreckage—

"Do you ever think about all of the history down there?" a voice asked. He glanced over to see a young, dark-haired woman sitting on the dock, her bare feet hovering several feet above the ocean. There was an accent to her French that Paolo picked up immediately; she clipped her consonants in a way that marked her as a *paesana*, as did the lovely wide, mischievous dark eyes evaluating him through a fringe of dark lashes.

"I was just thinking about it," he answered in Italian. His own language felt strange on his tongue. She perked up.

"Did you know that Marseilles used to be part of Italy?" she answered in kind. "This used to be ours!" She gestured to the picturesque scene. It was idyllic, if you were a tourist. If you were an out-of-work engineer, it wasn't the best place for career development.

Ours. Paolo stiffened. He thought Marseilles was better off in France. Instead, he said, "I think it's best just as it is."

"You're probably right." She closed her eyes and took a deep breath. "I'm trying to absorb everything about it before I leave."

The girl was baiting him, but he accepted it anyway. "Where are you going?"

"America," she answered. "Some of our family left for America, before the war. They say they have houses with four bedrooms! My cousin Mia wants a taste. I want to finish college, and I said I'd go with her."

In his many tentative life plans, moving to America hadn't even crossed his mind, and yet there were two mentions of it in the past hour that now had him considering it for the first time. He had planned to remain in France indefinitely—he owed his life to it, felt a loyalty to it he had never felt about Italy, but what was for him here? He didn't even have a job. Paolo had read about the automobile companies in the newspapers, the prosperity people were finding in America. Would that be a better purpose? Or did it just seem like a compelling option because the beautiful young woman beside him had mentioned it?

"I'm Paolo," he said, leaning over and offering his hand.

The woman accepted his hand and shook it. "Emilia."

SIMONETTA
PRESENT DAY

"Cosa ne pensi?" *What do you think?*

Adriana taps her chin with her index finger, thinking. "Let's switch these two." She gestures to an automaton partially hidden behind the large grandfather clock.

"Good idea." Simonetta glances at her notes. "That makes more sense, anyway, since the clock is older by a few years."

The two women carefully rearrange around the two Altobella machines. Simonetta stands back to survey the scene.

The large room in Villaggio Primavera's library is filled with centuries of Altobella history. For the past several months, Simonetta brought out every automaton in Altobella Instruments, many of them worse for wear. Adriana worked on the mechanical restoration while Simonetta put together the placards for the exhibit, fact-checking and writing and rewriting and making phone calls. Together they got photos scanned and enlarged; Simonetta cherishes the glimpses she now has of Paolo as a young boy. She sent tons of footage to Claudel for the special video she's making for *Daily Life*.

Simonetta names the exhibit after Desrosiers: "Harmony, by light and by shadow." The exhibit chronicles Altobella Instruments' history first as designers of automata, then briefly of clocks, then farm machinery. Interspersed throughout are placards about the different eras in which Altobellas lived, including several that acknowledge the extent of their contributions to Mussolini's Italy. It was part of her ongoing atonement, to share the truth of history, to make a small dent in righting the many wrongs.

It has been a strange dichotomy, living in Italy—familiar and foreign. She rents a room in Adriana's home. The sounds of casual spoken Italian, the gurgling of a Moka pot, the aromas of fresh herbs cut before dinner—there are sensory reminders of her grandparents. She feels them both all around her, always. She knows Paolo would grapple with his feelings about her being in his ancestral home, but she hopes he would feel some relief that she knows the secrets that haunted him his entire life. And Simonetta feels like that is what she has learned love to be—a true acceptance of another's demons.

Catelot remains at Desrosiers, where Simonetta feels she belongs. Wherever the automaton is home is where she finds her own.

Epilogue

IT IS LATE WHEN Simonetta pulls up to the iron wrought gate at Chateau Desrosiers, but someone has lit the torches on either side and left it open for her. The sight is warm and welcoming. The driver lets her out in front of the nymph, whose sensual body is dappled with rain drops. From where Simonetta stands, the nymph is arched toward her, and Simonetta taps her fingers against her stone companion in greeting.

A year away hasn't dampened the thrill of excitement she feels at the sight of it all, the vines tumbling over the door frame, storm water dripping from the gargoyles. And Simonetta has returned to Desrosiers—this time to stay, to write the next chapter of her life, to compose the next song in her sonata. No one greets her as she steps into the foyer, but she hears voices coming from deeper within and she follows their trail.

Inside the Grand Salon is a small group of people—a few she recognizes, including Claudel and Graham and Monsieur Aubert, but mostly a gaggle of visitors watching an impromptu performance. Jeremy stands near the hearth, singing in that devastatingly rich tenor. Beside him, the Altobella automaton plays its haunting compositions with surety.

Simonetta watches from the doorway, sets down her violin

case, unclips it quietly and rosins the bow.

Jeremy sings a song about Desrosiers atop Marguerite's melody brought to life by Catelot and Simonetta's ancestors. Hundreds of years of pain and turmoil and loss weave together to form a tapestry.

It's almost a full harmony, but something is lacking, the last thread to make it vibrant—until Simonetta joins in.

Author's Notes

I began drafting this book during the early days of the COVID-19 pandemic. Like any history geek trying to process and cope with the threat of a deadly virus, I dove into research about plagues. Plagues are cyclical events and, historically, had varying levels of impact on the communities most affected by them. While I was obsessing over medieval plagues, I was also binge-watching a YouTube series called *The Chateau Diaries*, about a charming group of people restoring a chateau in France. These two sources of inspiration, plus my wanderlust that had to be tampered when the world was on lockdown, led to the development of this book. Once the automaton came into the picture, this story became far less about plagues, but that is one of the links that connects the different time periods explored in the narrative.

Chateau Desrosiers is a fictional chateau set in a fictional town; Saint Madeleine is not part of the real holy canon. (Simonetta's hometown, Berkeley, is indeed real though and also happens to be my own place of birth.) I've slightly exaggerated the effects of the plagues and the remoteness of the chateau in service to the story. In reality, while plagues were certainly deadly, some (like the Bubonic plague referenced during Symonne's timeline) had a lower mortality rate than expected. I hope these slight adjustments do not affect your enjoyment of this book.

The recurring trick of placing a violin atop one's head and lowering it until it is in the proper position was the first thing I learned when taking violin lessons several years ago. Although I sorely lack the musical talent that many characters in this book exhibit, I love the violin and always found the violin-placement-process a delightfully embarrassing, but necessary, part of the joy—of being out of one's element while learning something new.

Acknowledgments

I offer my deep gratitude to everyone who helped me bring this book to life. To my writing group, the Northern Nevada Author's Community (NNAC)—I am endlessly grateful for your support of my writing and my wild ambitions. Thank you for your invaluable insight on a pivotal part of this book, and for the constant encouragement. To Mary McMyne, whose expertise and editing transformed not only this book, but my entire writing process. I'm so thankful I got to work with you! To Grandma and Grandpa Ghione, I thought of you often while writing this book. I love all the moments I spent with you. To my daughter, Julietta, who was present for much of this book's writing and revisions during long breastfeeding sessions and contact naps. I love you, my "bublanina topalina princess muffina." Someday soon I will take you to "T-aly" (Italy). To my husband, Andrew, who listened to me babble about this book for a long time and ask him complicated, out-of-context questions about automatons and engineering. I love you, Peebz. To my mom, who has always been my constant champion (and the best personal assistant I could ever ask for)! You are my role model forever.

And to the many friends and fellow authors who have inspired and motivated me—thank you.

About the Author

A. N. WARREN is an award-winning writer known for her immersive fiction that blends themes of folklore and identity. She holds an M.A. in Literacy Studies and founded the Storytelling Collective, a global literary learning program serving 16,000+ independent creative storytellers worldwide. She is best known for her contributions to bestselling *Dungeons & Dragons* books including *Icewind Dale: Rime of the Frostmaiden*, *Heckna*, *Legendlore*, *RealmsBound*, and the *Uncaged* anthology series. When she's not teaching or writing, she enjoys planning her next adventure. She lives in Northern Nevada with her husband, daughter, and their cat.

FLEURON ❦ PRESS

STORIES WITH HEART ON EVERY PAGE

WWW.FLEURONPRESS.COM